P
Lola

Claudine Cullimore was born and raised in Waterford, Ireland. She has lived in France and Belgium, and now lives in Winchester with her husband and their daughter. *Lola Comes Home* is her first novel. She is working on her second.

Lola Comes Home

CLAUDINE CULLIMORE

PENGUIN BOOKS

PENGUIN BOOKS

Published by the Penguin Group
Penguin Books Ltd, 27 Wrights Lane, London w8 5tz, England
Penguin Putnam Inc., 375 Hudson Street, New York, New York 10014, USA
Penguin Books Australia Ltd, Ringwood, Victoria, Australia
Penguin Books Canada Ltd, 10 Alcorn Avenue, Toronto, Ontario, Canada m4v 3b2
Penguin Books India (P) Ltd, 11 Community Centre, Panchsheel Park,
New Delhi – 110 017, India
Penguin Books (NZ) Ltd, Cnr Rosedale and Airborne Roads,
Albany, Auckland, New Zealand
Penguin Books (South Africa) (Pty) Ltd, 5 Watkins Street, Denver Ext 4,
Johannesburg 2094, South Africa

Penguin Books Ltd, Registered Offices: Harmondsworth, Middlesex, England

First published 2001

1

Set in Monotype Garamond by Intype London Ltd
Printed in England by Clays Ltd, St Ives plc

For Michael and Alanna, and Mam and Dad

Acknowledgements

Thanks to Elizabeth Wright at Darley Anderson and Harrie Evans at Penguin for all their hard work. And thanks to all my friends and family for encouraging me every step of the way. It was a full-time job that I'm sure they thought would go on for ever! Special thanks to Michael, who never once suggested that I get a proper job, even on the 'three lines a day' days!

1. What My Father Would Say

Anytime

'Lola?' he will ask, and laugh. 'She's the eldest daughter. Gone with the fairies, that one. Doesn't know whether she's coming or going.' Another deep, rumbling laugh, an explosion from the heart, as he imagines me tiptoeing through a frosted fairyland, delicate fairy wings flapping madly, shouting for his attention: 'Daddy, Daddy, look at me . . . *Daddy*.' Just like I used to. But I don't do that any more. I'm too big now.

And with a soft nod he drifts off. He's floating back to the days when I sat proudly on the cross-bar of his high Nelly, the old bicycle with the sprawling frame. I had a red leather saddle, my very own throne, in those days. And him happily pedalling through the main street in Ballyhilleen. He was the only man in the whole wide world for me then. Him *and* Father Rourke, that is. I *loved* the priests.

'And there's Belle, too,' he will say, with that gentle smile. 'She's got a heart of gold, she has.' An honest sigh, before he reveals, 'But her bladder's too near her eyes for her own good . . . always has been. She's the youngest . . . I need to mind her.'

Solid fingers, dependable fingers, trace a hesitant pattern across a heavy folded leg as he sits quite still now. 'Perri, Perri, Perri.' It's a bewildered song. 'I can't fathom that one out at all. And that's the honest to God truth. Flies off the handle for no reason.' He shakes his head. 'She's the second youngest daughter.' His expression is troubled, and a little sad. 'I *just* don't know.

'Right. *Yes.*' The fire is back in his eyes. 'JP, *my son* and the eldest, too,' he announces proudly. Shoulders square and straight, head held high. 'The only other man in the family besides myself. He's bound for great things, you know.' The rough purr can't hide his pride. 'Mark my words, he's bound for great things.

'And, sure, I can't forget my wife, Elise.' *Elise.* The stubborn tilt of the chin, the hard glint in his eye, the determined line of his mouth dissolve into a pool of tenderness. It's unexpected and the honesty is shattering. 'She's *French*,' he whispers, with a boyish grin. 'She's too good for me,' he adds then, in a humble voice. But that's not true. No, that's not true at all.

Now, *that*'s what my father would say, if you asked him to tell you about us, his family.

And it would be a fair enough description.

But it's just the beginning.

2. The Flanagan Family

My name is Lola Flanagan. That's Lola *Estelle* Flanagan. I'm Irish – you might have guessed – but there's also a fair dose of French blood mixed in there, coursing proudly, as French blood would, through my veins. But that would be a lot more difficult to guess. In all honesty, I don't know how you'd be able to tell at all.

My mother is from Nantes, in the Loire valley, wine country. She has lived in Ireland for more than thirty years now. She's an honorary Irishwoman. And the only person in the country, who can say the Our Father in Irish with a French accent, and be taken seriously by the parish priest, Father Rourke. But she's still French. Her name is Elise. Elise Flanagan, née Rousseau.

The men in the village where I grew up, Ballyhilleen – a main street and lots of land – are *very* fond of my mother. They think Sergeant Flanagan, my tall father with the stately bearing, tripped over the five-leaf clover when he married her. My father thinks they're right, too.

Being French, she's considered exotic. Now, it doesn't take a lot to be considered exotic in Ballyhilleen. Being French is definitely enough.

Elise first laid foot, and a very dainty foot at that, in Ballyhilleen when she was seventeen. It was summertime. She'd come to teach French to the three children of a local farmer who had fancy ideas about having his children speak foreign languages. Elise had eyes of a watery grey that you could drown in and skin that glowed like the finest honey, at least that's what my father told me. He was a few years older and had never seen anything like her.

She spoke very little English. She survived by flinging delicate hands around and making funny shapes with her slender fingers.

She met my father and never left.

The man in the navy-coloured Garda uniform with the silver buttons and the rigid, peaked cap cast his spell. And he never knew how he did it. It was still, to this day, a mystery in Ballyhilleen. Like the statue of the Virgin Mary with the bleeding eyes.

My father was the sergeant in the town for many, many years, which has left him with a blinding devotion to justice and the everlasting hat of popularity. He's retired now, after serving thirty years as a garda, and five years before the law could dictate to him that he had to retire at the age of fifty-seven. I think that was his life's rebellion, resigning before he absolutely had to. That and marrying a Frenchwoman.

He spent most of his working days being courted by the people in the village. He often had *three* lunches in the same day. 'Come in for a bite, Seamus,' someone would bellow, and as he didn't like to refuse food when it was offered to him, in he would go.

These days he spends his time reading old western books he buys for 50p at the weekly market, weeding Elise's garden, which doesn't look anything like the Provence-style haven she had in mind, and fixing things, which could also be called doing irreparable damage to the family home.

The happiness of his children is very important to him. He would like to see to it that we're all happy and safe. He tries very hard. His devotion to Elise is as strong as ever.

It was hard growing up as the daughter of a local legend. I can remember a time when RTE, the national television station, planned a programme on foreigners who had made their home in Ireland. It was to be called *At Home Abroad*. My mother read about it in the Sunday newspaper and the house became a frenzy of activity as she looked for the good writing-paper and her ink pen to let them know that *she* existed down in Ballyhilleen.

I was too young to read the letter she penned to RTE but all her Gallic charm must have flowed through the nib because two weeks later an RTE film crew descended on our house. They brought with them a jungle of lights and wires, and big furry animals strapped on to sweeping brushes – microphones, they called them.

The three-man crew spent a day with Elise as she went about her daily business of feeding the neighbours' chickens, smiling forgivingly as they ran over her leather loafers, helping out in the local creamery with perfectly painted nails, reading stories to the dumbstruck children of first infants at the local primary school, and then rushing home to make enough blackcurrant jam for the whole village.

A busy day. A formidable woman. The RTE men were smitten. They couldn't tell that this wasn't anything like a *real* day in the life of Elise Flanagan, née Rousseau. This performance was for *them*. Normally Elise would wring the neck of the first chicken that laid a claw on her leather loafers.

Elise floated from room to room, with the RTE men shadowing her every move. The last cut was to be an introduction to Elise's husband, Sergeant Seamus Flanagan, and her four children, JP, Perri, Belle and me.

My father took down the plain suit he wore for all special occasions – weddings, funerals and other religious happenings. Over the years, my mother had tried to add a bit of chic to his wardrobe but she'd failed. My father thought cravats were for fairies. End of discussion. He waited patiently in the front room, known as the good room, sitting in the middle of the wiry jungle the RTE men had created.

JP, then aged seven, sat beside him wearing his Holy Communion outfit – cream-coloured knee-length shorts, white shirt and navy blazer.

Belle was with the neighbours because she was too young for all the bright lights. She was only a few months old. There were photos of her everywhere anyway.

Elise dressed Perri and me for our turn in front of the cameras. I was six and Perri was nearly four. We were wearing matching sailor dresses and hats. When she'd finished, Elise rushed back downstairs leaving a smell of roses behind her.

I was a big girl and Perri did what I told her then. 'Perri, we're going to change our clothes as a surprise for the RTE men.'

'OK, Lolly.'

'Wait here and don't move.'

'OK, Lolly.'

I knew where Elise kept all her fancy lacy things in the beautiful colours. She'd explained to me one day that they were to make my father happy. I asked her why and she told me that they made all men happy and I would understand one day, when I was a big girl. I was a big girl then and I *knew* they would make the RTE men happy too.

'Take your clothes off, Perri,' I instructed.

Perri battled her way out of the navy sailor dress and I helped her to take off her socks. I quickly slipped out of my dress and everything else underneath it.

'Now, Perri, you take these.' I handed her some frilly bits. She giggled and put her arms and legs wherever they would fit. She looked like a rag doll.

I was a little bit more experienced with the frilly things than Perri. I'd tried them *all* on before. I was wearing my favourite ones. A white bra with firm pointed cups and very frilly knickers that you could see all the way through. I was *lovely*.

Perri had black frills wrapped all around her. She was lovely, too.

Our tiny feet sank into the high-heeled shoes I'd chosen for us, lost between the straps. Mine were red and Perri's were black. Even then I knew that you could wear red with white but you had to wear black with black. One of Elise's lessons.

'C'mon, Perri, we'll go downstairs to say hello.'

'OK, Lolly.'

We were at the bottom of the stairs, standing, shivering. 'We're coming in,' I shouted, in my best grown-up voice.

'Yes, *chérie*, please do,' Elise called back.

I swung open the door and marched in boldly, pulling Perri behind me and tossing my head from side to side like a circus pony.

A silent moment slid by. My father glanced around him warily. JP's hand was covering his mouth but his eyes were perfect, surprised ovals. Then the men from the RTE threw back their heads and roared with laughter. I was feeling very pleased with myself.

The camera equipment sat idly on the carpet as they hugged their quivering stomachs and shook their heads. Bet they didn't see *that* in Dublin.

'Mummy, I made the men from RTE happy,' I squealed joyously.

'Yes' said my father sternly, 'but Father Rourke,

who's just arrived, is sitting behind you, and *he*'s not very happy.'

I turned to gaze at our parish priest, half hidden by the door. 'That's not true, Daddy. Father Rourke is smiling,' I said. And he *was* smiling, too.

Did I mention that I have a fierce fondness of priests?

Us four Flanagan kids are grown up now. I mean, older. We all speak fluent French. A real nineties Irish family, my father likes to say.

Jean-Pierre, known simply as JP, is twenty-nine and holds two privileged positions, those of first-born and only son. A lethal combination in any Irish household. He lives in London where he works for a renowned financial institution, a *renowned* financial institution, I'm telling you, with a reputation for forming the real movers and shakers of the financial markets. I only know it's a *renowned* financial institution because he told me it was. He also told me the bit about them forming the movers and shakers of the financial market. I would *never* be able to judge something like that for myself. I wouldn't know a financial market if the bus pulled up and dropped me off in the middle of it.

Hah! I haven't got what my father would call a *proper* education. I left secondary school at eighteen and that's where my education ended. My father tried to warn me that I'd need a proper education but I didn't listen. And it didn't help that Elise didn't care if I didn't get an education either. She just presumed that I'd marry into land. I don't know where she got that idea from, just because there happened to be a lot of it around Ballyhilleen. And me, at eighteen, I was determined to *live*. I thought a proper education might tie me down!

I'm me, Lola, twenty-eight. I live in Brussels and I'm a *nanny*. I change nappies for a living, imagine that. I hate admitting it but I think it might be because I never got myself a proper education. It's hard to believe that I was only going to come to Brussels for a year to kick-start the rest of my life. And here I am ten years later. *I want to go home.*

I have an unholy fascination with priests. Truth be known, I've had it since I was a child. That's when the mystery of the men dressed head to toe in black first began. Ireland is probably the worst place I could ever go. The country is *full* of them. My father always said that I learned best the hard way. It'll probably happen again.

My sisters, Perri and Belle, live in Ireland with a ferocious appetite for life, in their own very different ways.

Perri, that's short for the French *Perrine*, lives in thriving, hip Dublin, a safe one hundred and forty miles away from Ballyhilleen and the parents. Dublin wasn't like that when I first went to Brussels ten years ago or I'd never have left in the first place, you can be sure of that. These days, everyone I know is leaving Brussels to go live in Dublin, and not only the Irish. I sure as hell don't want to be the last one to go. I'd already been the last to do enough things. The ship might sink with me still on it, looking for a way off. And there was no way I was going to let that happen. In my head, where there was lots of empty storage space, I had definite plans to go back to Ireland very soon, to go back for good. Back to what I thought I knew.

Perri dreams. She dreams of a career in singing. In the crystal ball of her mind, she sees herself setting up a band, *her* band, all girls. Convent-educated deviants like herself probably. In the meantime, she pays the rent by giving English lessons to foreign students on language breaks in Ireland, at the Vocab-U-Lary School of English on Grafton Street, in the centre of Dublin.

Perri is a lesbian. She's twenty-five, she's out and she's proud, and she's the bane of my father's life. Thanks be to God that homosexuality isn't illegal in Ireland. I don't know how he would cope, him being a man of the law and all. Elise is *delighted* that Perri is a lesbian. She loves anything that might pluck her from dull ordinariness. I think it's OK too but I've only ever had to live with it from a distance. I try not to think about the nitty-gritty of it too much – you know, the *graphics*. JP thinks it's just a phase she's going through, to get back at some fella who must've dumped her.

Perri wears men's suits bought at the Oxfam shop in Ranelagh and tight T-shirts. She looks good, though. It's the French genes. She's got sleek hair and golden skin. The *cow*. I'm pale with fuzzy curls. Guess who takes after the Irish side of the family?

Not too long ago, Perri was fired for *extra-curricular activities* with one of her students, an eighteen-year-old Spanish girl called Bea. Bea was thirteen stone of pure sin, Perri told me. Perri likes her women *big*. But she got her job back when Elise paid the school director, the limp John Dooley, a visit. He was no match for her. Perri's on her best behaviour now. I don't think it can last. *Snigger*. I definitely don't think it can last.

At twenty-two, Belle is the youngest. She said she wanted her independence, so she moved to a Portakabin at the far end of the garden in Ballyhilleen. She was just about brave enough to go that far: close enough to home to get her washing done and far enough to claim to everyone that she'd moved out, left home altogether.

The Portakabin is painted in hues of purple and has words of peace and love splattered throughout. Belle's sensitive. She cries a lot. It's her emotions. She works in the local primary school, as a teacher's help with the small children. It's the kind of job that would drive the rest of us insane, even worse than my nanny job. She wants to help build a nation of happy little people. But they're allowed to cry. Crying is good. You can be happy *and* cry, Belle tells us. The daily realities of upturned potties, vicious brawls and mass hysteria at knee level slip way over her head.

Besides this noble cause, Belle has another celestial

purpose to her life, which we've all known about for years. Belle is waiting for Kevin Brady to ask her to marry him. She has been waiting for Kevin Brady since the day he saved her life when she was five.

At twenty-nine JP thinks he has died and landed in heaven, as God's number one mover and shaker behind the golden gates, of course. Unfortunately, God gave him good looks. He could have given them to me instead but He probably decided that, as I wasn't going to get myself a proper education – He could tell these things in advance – I wouldn't need looks either. They might be a hindrance in getting nowhere. Elise once told me that I looked *friendly*. JP has never known a humble day in his life.

JP's best friend in London, and everywhere else for that matter, is the thoroughbred Tom Hutherfield-Holmes. Tom comes from old English stock and I think JP might be slightly in awe, though he would never admit it. Tom has a proper Cambridge education. He came to Ballyhilleen once with JP and lasted less than six hours, though that had been JP's fault, before fleeing the one hundred and forty miles north back to Dublin. He *adored* Elise, though, absolutely *adored* her. And I think I might have started adoring him then, too, only it would take me a little while to figure it out.

We were all on the same rung on the ladder of life. The second last one from the bottom. JP was a few rungs higher but he was about to fall off. It would bring him running back to Ireland. And it would also bring Tom Hutherfield-Holmes, someone from JP's present whom I wanted in my future.

3. The Homecoming

Sunday, 8 March 1998

So there I was: ten years after arriving in Brussels for the *one* year only, as I'd adamantly insisted at the time with all the cockiness of an eighteen-year-old who knows exactly what she's doing, I decided to go back to Ireland. To be honest, by then I'd been thinking vaguely about going back for about nine years and three hundred and sixty-four days anyway. And, anyway, the cockiness and certitude had deserted me the moment I left my teenage years behind, just when I needed them most.

The strongest of these compulsions to go home usually appeared as visions of wisdom in the early hours of the morning, during sweltering blasts of melancholy brought on by lack of sleep or too much booze, or sometimes both, and not necessarily in that order.

Brussels wasn't really the kind of place you thought about staying unless you were one of the several thousand civil servants working for the European Union with a tax-free status that bound you with its welcome chains of velvet. Whereas Ireland was always someplace you thought about going back to. And now that there was no shortage of good jobs many of those who'd left were taking lemming-like leaps back across the waters to grab that job before Johnny next door with his six years' international experience in Düsseldorf and Taipei nabbed it. Well, they needn't worry about my international experience.

Even though I'd been toying with the notion of going back for years, it was still a big decision when the time came, simply because it was the decision that was going to change my life. The life of Lola Flanagan would suddenly take flight, something it hadn't done in the last ten years. I'd be going home to a country in full bloom, joining the most highly educated work-force in Europe. Yeah, the most highly educated workforce in Europe, that's what everyone said about Ireland these days. I felt a stab of pride. But then I remembered that I *didn't* have an education and, not for the first time, commiserated with myself that I hadn't listened to my father who had tried in vain to make me see the benefits of a few years well spent in university. Well, you don't see these things at eighteen. I hadn't married into land either, as Elise had optimistically counselled.

It was too late to do anything about the land but maybe I could still do something about my stunted education. Frankly, my lack of education bothered me. It bothered me all the more because everyone I met in Brussels seemed to have a good education, some of them were even over-educated in my opinion. They knew too much. I'd settle for less. And they all spoke about seven languages fluently, too. Back in Ballyhilleen, the Flanagan family had been considered linguistic geniuses because they spoke fluent French, thanks to Elise, of course. But here even the postmen were trilingual. It was time to go home. I was tired of feeling inadequate. And even if Ireland now boasted the best-educated workforce in Europe, my family certainly didn't, so I'd be in good company.

Perri certainly wasn't any more educated than myself but she could sing, which meant that she was somehow excused from having an education at all as soon as she opened her mouth and twitched her vocal cords. Belle hadn't a real education either.

'Of course, we'll be at the airport to meet you,' Elise insisted forcefully, the night before I was due to fly home. Every word was chopped and firm. 'All of us, we will be there,' she declared. '*Even* Coco.' Coco was Elise's pet Chihuahua, named after Coco Chanel, and the latest addition to the Flanagan family. Coco went everywhere with Elise, nose held high as she trotted along, showering disdain on all things human. Of course, my father *hated* the dog, though he would never admit it in front of Elise and risk her wrath. He was fond of saying that she was the next best thing to a rat, the dog that is, make no mistake. The only animals he relished were the ones served up warm on a plate with floury potatoes.

'Elise, there's no need to – ' I started to protest, but stopped abruptly knowing it was pointless to try to persuade Elise from doing something she had set her mind on. They *would* be there. Please let me get the bus, I wanted to beg. A family reunion at Dublin airport was nearly enough to make me drop the idea of going back to Ireland but the other option was to stay in Brussels. Our family gatherings never went smoothly. They were never just, well, just *normal*.

'Nonsense,' she replied sharply. 'I *want* to be there for your big return to Ireland. We *all* want to be there. *Voilà.*'

'Fine.' I sighed, with more than an air of resignation. 'See you tomorrow then.'

The taxi with me and all my belongings in it slid into one of the many underground tunnels that circle Brussels, disappearing under a low ceiling of concrete. At this time of day, it would take only twenty minutes to reach the airport at Zaventem. Only a few minutes earlier, the family I'd worked for as a nanny for several years had stood in a neat bundle at the top of the steps leading into their *maison de maître* and waved goodbye as I climbed into the taxi. The kids smiled hopefully, almost expectantly, thinking I might change my mind and jump out of the taxi shouting that it was all a mistake. I barely remembered to wave out of the back window, surprising even myself with the lack of emotion I felt to be leaving them behind. It was definitely time to go. The one overriding emotion I did feel was relief. A liberating relief that felt like a strong wind blowing freely through my hair, but probably only to make more tangles over time.

The taxi driver careered around the sharp bends of the tunnel, one hand lightly controlling the steering wheel as if he was simply following the car's lead, the other hand dipping into a plastic bowl of roughly sliced chorizo, the smell of which wasn't quite masked by the lemon-shaped, lemon-coloured car-freshener mysteriously shaped like a banana and dangling from the rear-view mirror.

The subject of education still on my mind, I decided to interrogate the taxi driver. 'How many languages do you speak?' I didn't ask the question deliberately to make myself feel bad – but that's how it ended up.

He stopped chewing and swallowed reluctantly. He thought about the answer for a moment. 'Spanish and Polish because my father's from Seville and my mother and her family come from a small town near Warsaw,' he explained, and I nodded as if it were the most natural thing in the world. 'And French, of course.' He slid another slice of meat into his mouth and sucked it noisily.

I sank back into the scuffed leather seat, relieved that he spoke only one more than I. I'd be leaving Brussels on a high note. It would have been torturous to discover that he spoke several languages and sat on more qualifications than I did – which wouldn't be difficult.

'And Flemish, too,' he continued unexpectedly, and my spirits plummeted. 'I went to a Flemish-speaking school. And Italian. That was my third language at school and I married an Italian – and her family,' he muttered. 'How many's that?' he wanted to know, eyeing me in the mirror.

I held up a hand, five fingers rigidly upright. He might be able to speak five languages but he obviously couldn't count too well, I consoled myself. But the thought did little to raise my bruised spirits.

'And I'm taking Russian as part of a business course I'm doing. Russia, now that's where the next boom will be,' he predicted solemnly.

Well, I wasn't too sure about that but wouldn't be able to put forward a valid argument – my late-night confidantes in the vodka bar downtown weren't exactly a reliable or sober source; they probably knew less then I did. So I said nothing and instead stared at him intently, cursing his metamorphosis. When I'd climbed into the car he'd been just another taxi driver. And in the space of ten minutes, he'd turned into a multilingual, aspiring business leader, ready to chase the next big boom. I was furious with him and every little thing about him began to annoy me. The tubby hands, the stray tufts of stubble that his razor had bypassed that morning, the loose way he held the steering-wheel between his hands. Everything.

We'd already resurfaced into the daylight and soon the Nato building sped by on my right, television vans parked haphazardly outside, creating a shimmering patchwork of antennae and satellite dishes. It came as no surprise to me that I didn't know what was going on inside and I promised myself vehemently to make more of an effort to keep up with current affairs once I was back in Ireland. Yet another thing to catch up on. All these things would be easier back home.

The buildings of Zaventem airport were a welcome sight. Over the years the airport had come to mean the first step in the journey home. I usually made the trip back three times a year – always for Christmas and then whenever there were cheap flights going. I and all the other Irish nannies, who were just as eager to get a cheap deal home, would rush to the airport and descend on the check-in desk.

Last Christmas had seen an especially good start to the journey. The plane we were due to fly home on was stuck in Heathrow due to fog and at check-in we were told there would be a long delay, maybe two hours. With a kind of numb acceptance that we were marooned in the airport for a few hours, I wordlessly shepherded the other nannies on the flight, who were huddled around me looking for guidance, towards the upstairs bar in the departure area. I'd been playing the part of the wise nanny for the last five years, the one who knew the paediatricians' home numbers off by heart, the one who knew how to prise the chocolate biscuits out of the video machine while balancing a gurgling infant on one hip and a guilty toddler on the other, and the one who knew where the husbands really were when they had a 'summit meeting' sched-uled. The novelty of it all had been great for a short time at the beginning but had worn off a long time ago.

We settled down at a table and used our courtesy meal vouchers to buy bottles of beer, something Belgium does very well. It was five o'clock in the evening and already pitch dark outside. Two hours passed amid disgruntled chat of over-priced Christmas presents and the home-made alternatives you could get away with and the inevitable talk of what each one of us would do when finished nannying. Everyone had a plan. I didn't usually say a lot during that kind of conversation because everyone knew I'd been a nanny for years and just assumed that's what I'd spend the rest of my life doing. That worried me a lot. It was one thing when I despaired of a future that held nothing but dirty nappies and empty baby bottles but it was another altogether when everyone else thought that that was what was in store for me too. It was like a colour-by-numbers picture: the scene was already set and the dull colours dictated in advance. It was awful. Something had to change some time.

Another two hours passed. Only the passengers waiting for the flight to Dublin were left in the bar. Most were Irish. The courtesy meal vouchers had long since run out and we, the nannies, were reluctantly spending our hard-earned cash while others spent their not-too-hard-earned cash.

It was gone nine o'clock when a smartly dressed air hostess approached the table. 'The plane won't be here for another hour,' she told us, her voice full of sympathy, her face the picture of regret, 'but Sabena is happy to offer you complimentary drinks until the plane arrives.' She moved on to the next table.

I looked behind me at those tables who'd already

received the good news. It was a landscape of broad grins and greedy eyes. The prospect of free booze seemed to lubricate the happy hormones. If an Irishman was granted three wishes by a well-meaning leprechaun, I could guarantee that a bottomless glass would be the first thing he'd ask for.

One hour later, the plane still hadn't arrived and the stock of drink at the bar had all but dried up. The on-duty stewards and barmen exchanged worried looks. Some raised their eyebrows in amazement at the heap of empty bottles in each bin behind the bar and the clusters of empty glasses that covered each table. But they were the only ones worrying. Disgruntled passengers we were not. Someone had taken a fiddle out of their bag and was playing merrily in the corner. More dust-covered boxes of alcohol were fetched from the storeroom and the bottles were barely out when eager hands would grab them. There seemed to be far more pairs of hands than there were bodies. Even allowing for the odd person with three hands.

At half past ten there was a public announcement that the flight to Dublin would be boarding immediately, *immediately*. And there was no mistaking the immediacy in their immediately. The crowd swayed towards the departure gate amid lively shouts of disappointment. A few had to be helped along by less than able helpers. It was a great start to the trip home.

'Ladies and gentlemen, welcome to Dublin airport.

When you leave the aircraft, a shuttle bus will take you from the runway to the terminal. Thank you for flying Aer Lingus. We hope you had a pleasant journey and look forward to welcoming you aboard again.' I could hear the air hostess smiling.

It was March in Ireland. It was March in the rest of the world too but that seemed to matter less. *I was coming home.*

The fella sitting beside me had stripped down to his T-shirt as soon as we'd boarded the plane in Brussels. He must've thought he was on a charter plane to Ibiza and was getting ready for the blazing heat. Maybe it was just wishful thinking.

Hiding behind my veil of fuzzy curls, I peeped at him, pulling my denim jacket closer around me. The air-conditioning was blasting from the spout above me. He was flicking through the duty-free magazine and sighing longingly over the array of bottles. And not the perfume ones either. He had a deep agricultural tan. It started abruptly where the sleeve of his T-shirt ended and stood out in stark contrast to the gleaming white flesh I'd caught a glimpse of, hidden beneath his T-shirt sleeve, when he leaned forward to grab the magazine. He was Irish. There was no doubt.

'Heading home on holidays?' I asked idly. Conversation for conversation's sake.

'Nope. Heading home for good,' he answered, without even looking at me.

'Been living in Brussels?' I persisted.

'Nope. Flanders.'

'That's lovely.' You wouldn't catch *me* living in Flanders. 'Working?'

'Yep.'

'Great. What were you doing?'

'Boning meat.'

Meat-boners were clearly men of few words. 'Yeah?' I asked enthusiastically. I'd never met a meat-boner before. I'd met chicken-sexers but never meat-boners. 'And what? Did you decide to give boning a break? Break a bone?' I chuckled at my own wit.

Two weary eyes darted in my direction. 'The factory closed down.'

'That's bad luck.' I clicked my tongue. 'What are you going to do with yourself now?'

'Dunno.' He just didn't want to talk.

I leaned closer and tried to sound soothing. 'I suppose you're going to take some time off and think about it.' I'd just spent ten years thinking about what I was going to do, and instead of sounding soothing, as I'd intended, I think I somehow oozed superiority, which nearly made me laugh as I had nothing whatso-ever to be superior about. Superior was one thing I know for sure I was not. There was a list of whole other things, too, when I thought about it.

'Dunno.' He shut his eyes and let his head sink on to his chest.

Why didn't he just *tell* me what he wanted to do? He must have had some idea. Now that I did I reckoned mistakenly that everyone else did too. 'Are you going to try to find a job?' I probed.

'Dunno.'

'Maybe you should try something new,' I said, to help him out. And I was about to tell him I was heading home for good, too, and very seriously thinking about getting myself an education, when he suddenly exploded.

'Look, I've just lost me job.' He had the look of a man demented. 'Me wife and four children only have me to put food in their mouths. And I'm not in the humour to feckin' chit-chat. Okay?' He turned roughly in his seat to face me and glared accusingly, as if it was *my* fault. The middle-aged woman in front of him shuddered as his knees jerked violently against the back of her seat. 'Okay?' he shouted at me again, when he didn't get an answer.

I nodded silently, thinking that he should've just said that he didn't want to chat in the first place. Knowing that, I wouldn't have insisted.

'Settle down back there,' the middle-aged woman he'd kneed from behind quipped. She gave him a nasty look over her shoulder, her face squashed between the two seats in an unbecoming manner. 'Young fellas are all the same,' she told her neighbour, loud enough for us to hear. 'They think they own the place. It wasn't like that in my day.'

'It still isn't,' her youthful neighbour replied coldly. He was about twenty-five. She'd chosen a bad ally.

Beside me, the meat-boner was in spasm. He flung

off his safety-belt and shot out of his seat, clumsily clambering over me to reach the aisle.

I propelled him off me with an irate push.

The nerve in his jaw twitched threateningly. Predictably his abrupt spurt had captured everyone's attention. 'Have you seen me legs?' he shouted, at the middle-aged woman, and he stabbed his long, skinny limbs with a long, skinny finger. The veins in his neck throbbed threateningly. 'Have you seen how long me legs are?' he demanded again. 'Well, you try folding a string of uncooked spaghetti into a matchbox and see how far you get.'

Beneath her permed cap, the woman in front looked as if she was about to burst into tears. Obviously she liked being the aggressor, not the aggressed, and like most aggressors didn't take well to being the aggressed. I, on the other hand, usually played the role of the aggressed brilliantly. Anyway, I didn't feel a scrap of pity for her. I just prayed he wouldn't start on me. Just in case he looked my way, I busied myself with a loose thread on my jacket. The loose thread took on a sudden, enormous importance: I mean, the whole jacket might have come apart. I worked my fingers furiously, telling myself to mind my own business.

The next time I stole a glance up, it was really only seconds later – the longest I could last – the air hostess was standing, poised behind him. 'Excuse me, sir, instead of harassing this poor lady, could you please put your spaghetti limbs back into their box!' Her tone was icy underneath an Antarctic smile. She nodded towards his seat. 'Thank you!'

He had the decency to look slightly embarrassed. But only slightly.

'Well, you made a right fool of yourself there,' I spurted, foolishly breaking my silence, but unsurprisingly not stopping to think about it. 'I hope they don't think we're related.'

He sniffed and retorted, 'They wouldn't be able to tell if we were from the legs anyway.' He was looking at mine the way a disgruntled meat-boner might, trying to work out how long it would take him to rid my bones of all that flesh.

'*Huh*,' I said. I couldn't think of anything else to say. There was nothing *wrong* with my legs. They weren't as long as his, thankfully. They were a bit chunky but that was only because I'd spent too long cycling up hills when I was little. There were always hills wherever I wanted to go. Someone who wanted to make me feel good about myself whoever that might be, might say that they were shapely legs, and it would only be a little lie.

Ninety minutes of stony silence later, I stepped gratefully from the dry air of the plane and into the cool March breeze that rolled down from the Dublin mountains to lick my face in a moist welcome. The sun stood high and white in the sky. A proud sun. I stood at the top of the galvanized steps that fell from the plane to the runway below, and waited for my turn to go down.

Behind me, an older American couple, complete with bulging *fanny packs*, dissected their Irish roots and compared inherited traits. In Ireland we called *fanny packs* bum-bags.

The crowd was slowly edging their way forward when my eyes drifted past a huge sign, hanging behind the glass front of the viewing deck of Dublin airport. I'd just been looking around me leisurely, passing time. I hadn't really expected to *see* anything. My eyes darted back, wide with disbelief and I swallowed hard. There, spelled out in massive, wobbly letters, were the words, 'WELCOME HOM LOLA'. I hadn't had a proper education but I'd had more than enough to know that there was an E missing at the end of the middle word. Subtlety and spelling were *not* two of Elise's traits. I buried my face in my hands. I was coming home. And this was only the beginning. Returning to Ireland might mean finding my salvation but it also meant returning to the collective arms of my family, who lived outside the realm of the normal and didn't even realize it. Salvation might have to wait a while, I thought.

I pulled at the sunglasses perched on my head and tore them through the mass of dark, disobedient tangles where they were lodged until they covered my eyes, and worried that people could tell that the Lola from the sign was me. I only ever wore those sunglasses to keep my hair out of my eyes but today they were my disguise. The lenses were of a thick plastic. Looking through them gave me a warped version of the outside world that was still preferable to taking them off.

Through the welcome plastic blur, I noticed that the crowd in front of me had moved on and were now racing, without trying to look like they were racing, to the shuttle bus sitting on the runway, each determined to nab a seat for the two-minute journey to the terminal.

I shook my head at the scuttling sight and moved forward. Three more fuzzy steps to go before I reached Irish soil, and with a flicker of elation licking my gut, I felt a sharp tug as the heel of my shoe suddenly caught behind the open-backed step. With the clumsiness of an elephant wearing stiletto heels for the very first time, I toppled over and collapsed down the last three steps. Lola Flanagan has definitely arrived, I thought bitterly.

The hard, unforgiving tarmac came dangerously close to my face. Not looking forward to what I would see, the glares, the glances, and the satisfied look on the meat-boner's face, I gingerly tipped my sunglasses up and peered out into the daylight. Sure enough, everyone on the shuttle bus had seen me fall and was nailing me to the tarmac with gazes of curiosity and pity. Crucifying me to the spot. The meat-boner actually looked like he might be giggling.

I steeled myself to make a move just as the lady from the American couple behind me cooed, in a concerned, fine Southern drawl, 'Honey, are you Irish?'

'I certainly am,' I replied, wondering why she couldn't just ask me if I was OK, which would have been a reasonable question as I lay on the ground, instead of asking me if I was Irish, which didn't seem to be such a reasonable question. 'Why?' I kept the question short, in tone and in length.

'Well, y'all are mighty hospitable here in your country and you won't be mindin' littl' ol' me if I join you down there,' she said, as she clambered down on all fours to kneel beside me.

There was only one thing to do. I stared at her in pure and utter bewilderment.

'Y'all are so passionate,' she told me. 'I just love that passion.' She lowered her head, pursed her painted lips and fervently kissed the sticky tarmac. 'I saw you do that just now and I wanted so badly to share this moment with you. People don't do that in the US but I think it is a beautiful gesture, a truly beautiful gesture.' She was moved. Her eyes were watering and her lips had a faint black sheen to them. 'JD, sweetheart,' she called to her partner, 'I hope you've been filmin' me kissin' the Irish soil.'

Sure enough, JD was standing a few feet in front of us, his face hidden behind a sleek camcorder with so many buttons it looked like it could easily double as a life-support machine. 'I gotcha,' he assured her sweetly.

'Excuse me,' I muttered, and dragged myself up off the ground, picking bits of the tarmac from my knees and the palms of my hands.

JD made a chivalrous leap forward, as nimble as an eager mountain goat. 'Here, darlin', let me help you.' He held out a plump hand. 'Did my wife tell you that we're Irish, too? My granddaddy came from Mayo,' he proclaimed proudly, still holding my hand. He pumped it vigorously. 'JD Gallagher,' he said, introducing himself. 'Mighty pleased to make your acquaintance.'

'Lola Flanagan,' I mumbled, and tugged my hand loose. The big sign behind the glass window was bobbing up and down in waves of encouragement.

The driver of the shuttle bus, growing weary of the performance on the tarmac, thumped his horn impatiently and shouted through the open doors, in a thick Dublin accent, 'If youse three are waiting for Fader Christmas, he'll be along in December. Oderwise, geh in.'

There was no doubt in my mind, waiting for Father Christmas would have been much better.

Inside the heated terminal, we swarmed towards Passport Control and waited in line, most people exchanging patient smiles and knowing grimaces. The meat-boner was the first one through, his long legs bringing him quickly to the top of the queue. My turn came. I flashed my passport, hiding the 1980s photo with my thumb, and walked through.

I climbed the noisy escalator behind Passport Control. There was some commotion near the top. People were gathering in small groups. Heads nodded in pleasant surprise and cameras flashed excitedly. Straining my ears I heard the distinctive sound of the fiddle being played.

The sun-drenched corridor was lined with young Irish dancers. They wore heavily embroidered dresses in jubilant colours and dainty black dancing shoes. They lifted their nimble legs high, keeping their arms firmly by their sides, fists clenched tightly. As they danced, their tight ringlets bobbed up and down. The look of scrunched concentration on the small faces made me smile. I hadn't smiled since I'd landed on the tarmac and it felt like too long.

JD's camcorder whirred beside me.

A poster above the dancing heads explained that this was an Irish Tourist Board incentive to introduce visitors to the ambience of Ireland from their very first steps on Irish soil. I remembered the days when the Irish Tourist Board had had offices in a few of the bigger towns and its employees didn't stir from behind their desks. Things *had* changed.

They finished and bowed shyly.

I wondered why Elise had never bothered putting us into Irish dancing classes. It probably wasn't *French* enough, I thought. I told them they were brilliant, as I passed by.

I got my bags, grabbed a trolley and piled it high. Steering was treacherous. The little kids, sensing danger, scampered out of the way. The meat-boner swung a single bag over his shoulder and glided past me, still scowling. I ignored him.

The customs officials stood grinning at my efforts and the colourful medley of suitcases and bags that held all my worldly belongings, of no value to anyone but myself. They waved me through with a heartening, 'Not too far to go now, love.'

The sliding doors opened on to an arrivals hall that was teeming with people, anxiously peering at each face as we filtered through the doors, trying to spot the familiar one.

A small space opened up ahead of me. I jostled my way forward and claimed the abandoned spot. There I stood, looking into the expectant crowd, waiting for the Flanagan welcome committee.

A glimpse of brilliant colour skidding across the floor caught my eye. An elaborate yellow bow dashed between legs and careered around trolleys, yapping madly and heading in my direction. An excited frenzy of doggy hospitality. Coco, hidden beneath the folds and streamers of a yellow bow, was the first to find me, showing a rare display of affection for someone other than Elise.

'Hello, girl,' I said, bending down to swoop her up in my arms. She licked my face, her small pink tongue leaving an unpleasant smell of Pedigree Chum on my skin. I dropped her back on to the floor as neatly as I could.

'Lola, *chérie*, there you are. Ah, I am so happy. Let me look at you.' Elise held me at arm's distance and let her eyes travel up and down. 'You look *so* well,' she continued. 'A little bit round about *les fesses*, the bottom, but that is a problem from your father's family.' She smoothed her fine wool jumper over her petite frame.

My father looked at me and winked. The French were obsessed with weight, and thirty years in Ireland had not yet persuaded Elise to abandon this obsession.

Perri and Belle, both looking just as round as I did, were standing behind Elise, grinning and throwing their eyes up to heaven in gestures of mock incredulity. They'd heard it all before.

Perri, her hair cut short since I last saw her, was wearing her usual uniform – a tailored man's suit from Oxfam. Her skin still glowed and this made me feel like I'd spent the last ten years in a cave, no sun, no light.

Belle was the hippie chick. She wore her hair in long plaits with fresh flowers woven through them, an open-necked smock top and long, trailing skirt that revealed bare, dirty feet when she walked. It was *March*, I thought, her feet must be blocks of ice.

'C'mon,' my father suggested warmly. 'Let's go to the pub for a pint. Thirsty work, this airport-collecting business.' He pointed to the busy bar at the other end of the arrivals hall and stepped behind my trolley.

'Did you see the sign?' Belle asked, as she linked her arm through mine. Perri had caught up with my father, and Elise was babbling to Coco, the Chihuahua who understood French perfectly.

'Couldn't miss it,' I answered, grimacing. 'And Elise's spelling hasn't improved either.'

'Yeah, I know but she wouldn't listen to any of us.' She shrugged as if to say 'What else is new?'

The pub was jammed with Irish and foreigners alike, and a haze of thick smoke floated heavily in the air. Elise and Belle spotted a free table, covered in spilt beer and cigarette butts. In undisguised disgust, Elise pulled a white handkerchief from her suede handbag and handed it to Belle to start mopping, which she obediently did.

I left promptly. I'd done more than my fair share of mopping up messes over the past ten years. Elbowing my way to the bar, I wrestled my way to stand beside my father and Perri. Dad had his hand up in the air and was enthusiastically waving a crumpled ten-pound note back and forth with no sign of stopping.

I was puzzled and looked at Perri curiously. 'He thinks he gets served quicker in city pubs when they see the colour of his money,' she explained, in a whisper. 'He doesn't seem to know that everyone else here has money too.'

'What'll you be having?' he asked, when he turned and saw me.

'A pint of Bulmer's, thanks.'

'Ah, so, you're back on the old Bulmer's, are you?' He gave me a knowing look. Thankfully, a *fond* knowing look.

Perri poked me in the ribs and suddenly I was sixteen again and reduced to mumbling. 'Eh, what do you mean?' I stammered guiltily.

'I thought you'd have had enough of that stuff from your youth.' He looked at me from beneath his bushy eyebrows. 'I remember the day we brought your brother to Dublin for university. Yourself and your sister there drank a barrel-load of the stuff. Cuts the stomach out of you, it does, but sure you found that out for yourselves. The hard way, as best you know how.' He examined the ten-pound note he held, trying his best to look disapproving but struggling to hide his smile.

Perri and I stared at each other in amazement. He had never, ever mentioned the Bulmer's incident before.

Incredulously, I asked, 'How did you know?'

'Fathers know these things,' he said, and left it at that. 'Anyway, better not let your mother see you drinking out of a pint glass. You know what she thinks of girls drinking pints.' And in a fit of fatherly logic, he added, 'I'll get you two glasses to pour it into instead.' He turned his attention to the bar.

I could see Elise and Belle sitting at the table across the pub, Elise babbling and Belle smiling patiently. My father stood beside me waving his money and Perri was fixing her trousers. It *was* good to be home. For the time being anyway, I realistically reminded myself, before I started to tell myself that I had the perfect family, too.

Out of the blue, a loud male voice beside me exclaimed, 'That's a fine arse on you, girlie.'

'Excuse me?' I spluttered, and whirled around.

My admirer had a large beer belly that spilled generously over the top of his faded jeans, turned up on the outside to reveal a pair of pointed boots. A flamin' *cowboy*, I thought. 'There's no mistaking that for two eggs in a handkerchief!' he added.

I wasn't used to this kind of attention. I wasn't used to *any* kind of attention. 'Perri, do you hear this?' I asked incredulously, a little bit of me stupidly flattered but the other bits clearly outraged. After all, he was a disgusting specimen.

Perri nodded. 'Let me handle this,' she said flatly, stepping in front of me. She had been spurning men for years now and was brilliant at it, as well as enjoying it. 'Right, you,' she pointed a threatening finger at him, right between the eyes, 'take that back.'

'Will not, girlie. It's a free world and I'll say what I want to.'

Perri's eyes flashed with fury. 'Take it back,' she ordered.

'*No*,' he shouted.

Without saying another word, she grabbed his pint of Guinness from the bar and emptied it over his head. The thick black liquid flowed like lava over his flushed face and dripped from his beard. It did nothing to cool him down.

I looked on in a kind of tired dismay because I had known, just known, that we couldn't have left the airport without some kind of scene. It would've been too good to be true. This is exactly what I meant when I said that our family gatherings were never *normal*, my family was not *normal*. I think my father probably used to be, way before he met Elise and had the rest of us.

Now he looked over his shoulder and his casual glance turned to fury: he hated to see us misbehave. 'I can't bring you anywhere,' he hissed venomously at Perri. He turned to the cowboy and began a faltering apology, his face a bed of earnest folds. 'I am . . . very, very embarrassed and apologize on my daughter's behalf. She's, she's – '

'Don't bother,' Perri interrupted. 'Because I'm *not*. I'm not sorry.'

He leaned over towards the man, ignoring Perri, and whispered cautiously, 'There's a good reason for this, this groundless attack. You see . . .' He paused and glanced around him to make sure no one was listening but, of course, everyone who could *was*. 'You see, she's a lesbian,' he admitted, with a bit of a pained expression. 'It has to be that. My other daughters would *never* do that.' My father thought that Perri being a lesbian was the root of all her problems and was in the habit, a habit that had taken years in the making, of openly telling everyone. But that didn't mean it was something he was comfortable with. He had just been tutored by Elise for too long.

'Is she now?' the man scoffed, as the Guinness dripped from his face, but he didn't seem too bothered. He didn't seem bothered *at all*. He had the smug look of someone who'd just been handed a trophy. 'And there was I thinking it had something to do with the comment I made on your other daughter's fine arse there,' he taunted my father, looking around at his audience for approval. Some of them foolishly spurred him on. 'An arse made for squeezing,' he continued. He reached out a twisting hand towards me, a big, hairy shovel, fingers splayed.

My father moved forward to shield me and growled, 'The comment you made on my daughter's *arse*? The comment you made on my daughter's *arse*! Is that so?' And with that he drew back his fist and punched him in the gut, defending my – defending my – my what? Well, I *don't* know. There wasn't really anything to left to defend.

The punch didn't hurt the cowboy; it seemed to take more out of my father. He massaged his fist and looked surprised that he'd actually hit him. 'You hit like a feckin' pansy,' the cowboy mocked, rubbing his stomach lightly as if he'd been tickled. 'There seems to be only one man in your family,' he said, looking at Perri.

'And I *don't* hit like a pansy,' she told him, as she drew back a clenched fist and struck him squarely on the jaw. She didn't flinch but the cowboy looked like he'd had a bit of respect knocked back into him.

At this stage, I was the only one who *hadn't* hit him. The crowd around us at the bar, who'd all given up trying to pretend that they weren't taking any notice of what was going on, seemed to be looking at me *expectantly.*

Nervously, I glanced over at the table where I'd left

Elise and Belle. Elise was shaking her head, looking poised and disdainful. Coco, the faithful chihuahua, was actually *sneering* at my father. And Belle looked to be on the verge of helpless tears.

What in the name of God had I come home to? I thought despairingly. There was no way I was going to hit the bloody cowboy, especially not with a *priest* sitting in the far corner with a perfect view. Had the priest not been sitting there I might have felt obliged to deliver him a slap. But I could never resort to violence in front of a priest. And this one looked a little bit like Tom Hutherfield-Holmes!

4. Tom Hutherfield-Holmes
Visits Ballyhilleen for the First Time

1995

Tom Hutherfield-Holmes first made the journey across the Irish Sea three years ago. JP and he arrived in Ballyhilleen on a rare and unexpected visit one Hallowe'en morning. It was a dark, damp time of the year, and in Ballyhilleen it was even darker and damper. They arrived through the early fog in a sleek rental car that cut through the heavy haze with the ease of a newly sharpened blade. I just happened to be there at the time, having escaped from Brussels, babies and dirty nappies for a week and wishing that I didn't have to go back, that I had something I could escape to.

Perri wasn't around. She had swapped Ballyhilleen for Galway, where she was painting clowns' masks on the eager faces of children all over the town. Bright streaks of red and yellow paint and dabs of black and white. Little clown faces could be spotted running all over Galway, she'd told me on the phone. The paint only washed off on the third day. Perri couldn't afford the good-quality stuff. The kids loved it. The parents went mad. Elise and my father thought she was doing voluntary work in an old people's home there and sent her pocket money every week. She was doing better than I was.

Belle wasn't around at the time either. The abortion debate had once again reached a crescendo and she was off on a crusade around Ireland with a team of travelling nuns defending the unborn child's right to life.

There was just my father, Elise and me. And the big house still felt full. Elise could do that. Her presence took up all the empty space.

It was early Saturday morning. Elise and I were sitting at the kitchen table, swapping tales of living in the wrong country. I was busy moaning that I could never find a proper tea-bag in Brussels and Elise was complaining that the Irish always cut their lettuce into little bits instead of folding a leaf on to the end of the fork, the proper way to do it. I'd heard the same complaint a thousand times before. But then again she'd heard me moan about unsuitable tea-bags before, too. It was a kind of therapeutic moaning by mutual consent. A kind of family ritual.

Behind us, my father was fiddling with the tuning knob on the old radio. He was trying his best to find a radio station that played what he called decent music. He was shaking his head sadly. 'In my day, the songs had words to them,' he muttered. I'd heard that one before as well.

Outside, in the cold, foggy morning, a car horn could be heard bellowing insistently. The noise seemed to be getting closer and closer until it couldn't get any closer. It was right outside our front door. 'What the hell *now*?' my father bellowed, echoing the horn, and rushed to the door, with the radio tucked safely beneath his arm.

Elise paid little notice and continued to lecture me on the appalling eating habits of the Irish . . . They did this . . . they did that . . . they didn't do this . . . they should do that. Sometimes I think she forgot, clean forgot, that she had an Irish husband, had lived in Ireland for over thirty years and reared four children who were Irish. On the other hand, we could never forget that *she* was French. 'Elise, the *they* you keep harping on about is *us*,' I told her, slouched down on the kitchen table in a fit of sudden fatigue. We'd had this conversation before too, and she liked to pretend we hadn't. So now we would have to have it again.

'Who's *us*? *Us* who?' she asked, in a highly agitated voice.

'Not *you*,' I pacified her, '*us*. JP, Perri, Belle and me.'

'What?' She was horrified. She began to fidget with the soft scarf elegantly rolled at the nape of her neck. 'You are *French*.' She sniffed haughtily. 'All of you are *French*.' She closed her eyes, as if to dismiss some nasty thought. 'You have been brought up in Ireland, that's all.'

I was frustrated but adamant. 'We're not. We're *Irish*.'

She let out an indignant sigh and waved a neat hand in front of her flustered face. 'You even speak French,' she wailed delicately.

'So does Father Rourke but that doesn't make *him* French.'

'Aha,' she gasped shrewdly. 'Father Rourke. So this has something to do with him?'

'It doesn't,' I snapped, immediately regretting the hasty comparison I'd made with him. I sat up and folded my arms across my chest in a stubborn gesture. 'Anyway, he was only an example,' I muttered. 'And a bad one at that. His French is as good as my Latin.' My Latin was limited to whatever few words I'd stumbled across in the dictionary when I'd been trying to broaden my knowledge last year by learning a page by heart for three weeks. I could remember a few of the more impressive words I'd learned but the opportunity to use them never seemed to come up. And, to be honest, I wasn't always sure what to put either side of them either.

'But his name was the first one that arrived in your head, *n'est-ce pas?*' Elise insisted, in a satisfied voice. Her face wore a smug expression.

'No,' I barked. 'It wasn't.'

A fierce row was brewing when the kitchen door swung open and JP strode in triumphantly. My father followed him, shoulders squared, back ramrod straight and a proud smile across his face. The radio that he had been protectively clutching only moments before had been casually forgotten somewhere between the front door and the kitchen.

A third figure, gazing curiously all around him, followed them.

'Jean-Pierre,' Elise squealed girlishly, and kissed him adoringly four times with loud smacking noises, before holding him at arm's distance and studying him inch by inch. 'Have you lost weight?' she wanted to know, concerned that he might not be eating. 'Have you?'

'No, Elise, I haven't.'

'You seem a little pale,' she worried. 'Have you been working too much?'

'You know us City boys,' he joked charmingly. 'Work hard, party hard.' He winked at me.

I groaned inwardly. I knew *just* how hard JP played.

The third figure stood behind him, and as JP showed no sign of introducing him, he took a step forward and did it himself. 'Hello, everyone.' He smiled. His was a soft voice topped with an English accent. And if it was at all possible for a voice to tickle an ear then his definitely tickled mine. 'Tom Hutherfield-Holmes,' he continued. 'I'm delighted to meet you all.'

He looked delighted too, I mused contentedly, as he acknowledged each of us with a quick tilt of his head. 'I've heard a lot about you from JP,' he told us, somehow making it sound like JP had told him only good things about his family, and not the things that made us a real family.

I looked at him slightly suspiciously but almost immediately decided that I couldn't doubt his sincerity; his smile was open and warm, and his expression too honest. Anyway, Tom Hutherfield-Holmes was a treat to the eyes. All the clichés held true. Tall, broad-shouldered, tanned, thick blond hair. I just couldn't think bad of him and found myself apologizing to the part of me, the teeny part, that might be offended at my own shallowness. Someone like him would never ordinarily look at someone like me. But there he was, sharing a batch of his disarming smiles evenly between myself and Elise. Instantly, I wanted them all for myself.

Elise rushed forward excitedly. 'You naughty boys,' she tittered. 'You should have told me you were coming.' She stretched out her hand delicately to shake Tom's.

He took it and smiled at her. 'It's lovely to meet you, Mrs Flanagan.'

Elise cooed. 'Call me Elise,' she insisted.

My father leaned over my shoulder and muttered in my ear, 'Feckin' pansy.' It was Tom's yellow tie that did it for him, I think. I'd noticed the yellow tie the minute he'd walked into the room, a streak of sunshine hanging down the front of his shirt, but hadn't for one minute questioned its fashion-worthiness.

'Yeah,' I agreed in a whisper, secretly disagreeing. The tall Tom Hutherfield-Holmes did not look like a pansy to me. He sounded so sincere when he spoke to Elise that I was unreasonably willing him to tell me that JP had never mentioned that he had such a beautiful sister – just so that I could believe him. Because I would. But, of course, he didn't. For all his charm Tom Hutherfield-Holmes was probably not one to lie.

For the next while Elise and Tom drowned each other with buckets of mutual admiration. A few drops occasionally landed on me and I soaked them up.

My father had soon had enough. He grabbed his gnarled walking-stick and left with a resigned wave.

We watched him go.

JP turned to me. 'You look like you've put on a few pounds,' he remarked casually, then added, 'A few pounds too many, I think.'

I glared at him and mouthed a rude word, hoping that Tom Hutherfield-Holmes hadn't heard him but in any case he had the good grace not to examine me there and then. I'd no doubt he'd sneak in a look later when he thought I wasn't looking – manners or no manners.

He raised his eyebrows pretending to be shocked. '*Moi?*'

Elise frowned and looked at me. 'I hadn't noticed those few pounds, but now that you say it, I *do* see them.' Her voice went stern and a hard glaze slipped down over her eyes. Weight was not a light issue in our household. 'Lola, you must eat grated carrot with lemon juice for dinner until you have found your correct weight again,' she ordered me, pulling a face. 'No more of these crisp sandwiches.'

'It's only five pounds.' I tried to sound untroubled by the extra weight, as I had been up to the time where JP had suddenly pounced on them. But the five pounds now seemed more like fifteen. They had tripled under the weight of Elise's glare, and were still getting heavier. 'Funny how you didn't notice anything until JP brought it up,' I said defensively.

'You've been hiding it, haven't you?' JP asked, in a sweet voice, laced with arsenic, as unable as ever to resist the temptation to cause a little trouble.

'And it must be right if *he* says so, mustn't it?' I tugged self-consciously at my woollen jumper with the white furry cat stitched on the front, stroking its soft fake-fur ears for comfort but wishing I wasn't wearing it. It was one I left in the wardrobe in Ballyhilleen and pulled out for warmth whenever I came home. It wasn't the kind of jumper that would ever impress Tom Hutherfield-Holmes. 'It's only five pounds,' I argued, half-hearted. 'I don't know what all the fuss is about. *Five pounds.*' I held up a hand with the fingers spread. 'Five pounds of fuss,' I finally grunted.

Meanwhile, Tom Hutherfield-Holmes had given up pretending that he wasn't interested in our conversation and had turned to watch the three of us with a look of undisguised amusement.

With nothing to lose, certainly not my dignity at this stage, I brazenly held his gaze. 'And I suppose you're an only child?' I asked knowingly, sure that he wouldn't be looking at us with such amazement if he wasn't because he would know that this went on in all families.

Elise poked me sharply on the shoulder. 'Manners,' she hissed.

'Yes, I am,' he replied honestly. 'How perceptive of you,' he congratulated me. 'How did you know?'

JP sneered. 'Lola has a special connection with celestial beings.' He coughed loudly, as if making a grand announcement. 'Priests.'

'Really?' Tom asked.

'Have you and he,' I jerked my head towards JP to make the link, 'been friends for long?'

Tom studied us both, not too sure with which one of us his answer would get him into trouble. 'Yes, quite a while,' he confessed eventually.

'Then I shouldn't need to tell you this, but never,' I thumped the table with my fist, 'believe anything he says.'

Tom grinned and looked at JP.

'See? I told you,' JP said to him. 'I told you what she was like. Feisty little thing, isn't she?'

Humiliated, I stormed out of the kitchen.

JP and Tom went for a stroll around the village. They weren't gone long. As they walked in at the door past me, I noticed that Tom's trousers were splattered with delicate spots of mud, making an endearing symmetrical pattern up the back of both legs. I steadied myself. Since when had I found splashes of muck so appealing?

'So what did you do?' I asked JP, *nearly* ready to forgive him for earlier. I'd calmed down considerably. And I was thinking that it would be nice to have Tom Hutherfield-Holmes around for a few days. Maybe I could bring him to the pub and if I was lucky people might think that he'd come back to Ballyhilleen on a visit with *me*. The thought cheered me up immensely. Beyond his unquestionable attractiveness, a side to him that I was definitely aware of and should probably be immunized against for my own good, lay something else that drew me to him, something in his quiet but assured manner, and a playfulness I thought I could spot lurking behind his easy smiles. Fate had thrown him in my path and I wasn't about to hop over him and continue idly on my way.

'Nothing,' JP grumbled. 'We did nothing.'

'Did you meet anyone?' I persisted. Surely they did *something*, I thought, met *someone*.

Another mumble. 'No.'

I tried Tom. 'What did you think of Ballyhilleen?' I was hoping he liked it.

'It's nice,' he said. 'Smaller than I imagined.'

My voice quivered. 'Is that *all*?' Why was I so disappointed that he wasn't speaking volumes of poetry in praise of Ballyhilleen?

He tried to explain. 'I really prefer cities.'

Without meaning to, I clicked my tongue disapprovingly. Surely city boys could like the countryside too?

For the next few minutes they just sat there in a state of despondency while I peeled potatoes for dinner and wondered what I could say to cheer them up. Eventually JP spoke. 'We're going to head back to Dublin now,' he announced sheepishly. 'Our flight is only tomorrow night but there's nothing to do here.' He stretched out his hands, making empty cups.

I caught hold of a second knife and solidly slapped a potato into the empty hand. 'Peel,' I ordered, trying to blot out what he was saying. 'Just peel. That'll give you something to do.'

'We're going,' JP replied emphatically, dropping the potato.

Tom was nodding apologetically. They'd already made up their minds.

I stopped peeling. 'You can't do that. You'll upset Elise and Dad. I mean, I don't mind, couldn't care less,' I lied, because I *did* care. You go, I wanted to yell at JP, but leave me *him*, leave Tom for me.

Somehow I forced a couldn't-care-less snigger. But the snigger turned to a sanctimonious gargling. 'When I come home, I stay home,' I lectured JP. 'I don't go running off just because there's *nothing to do*,' I mimicked him. And sometimes I wished I could. In fact, it was more than sometimes. I seemed to spend most of my life wishing I could run off somewhere.

Tom was still nodding sadly, as if he understood how I was feeling, when he couldn't have known.

'You *can't* go,' I declared flatly. JP wasn't getting his own way and he wasn't going to cut short Tom's stay. I'd even changed out of the furry cat jumper and pulled on a black polo-neck top that I was sure made me look five pounds lighter at least, though neither of the two of them seemed to have noticed.

JP glared at me. 'Well, we *are* going.'

Elise walked into the kitchen. 'Going where?' she wanted to know, too calmly to have understood that he meant going *away*.

'He's leaving,' I said grimly.

Her face crumpled in disappointment.

I shot JP a murderous glance. I would be stuck at home for days to come trying to cheer her up and watching my father mope around the house. And then they wouldn't even be upset when I left to go back to Brussels.

'But you've only just arrived,' Elise pleaded with him.

'I know,' he muttered, 'but I've just had an urgent message on my pager.' He held up a small, square object and stuffed it back into his pocket before Elise could realize that it was a cigarette case. 'Work problems,' he lied, 'and I have to go back to London immediately.'

I fought the urge to point out to Tom that *this* was what I meant when I said never to believe anything that JP said. But I couldn't. I didn't want to upset Elise further and I didn't want Tom to think I was just being spiteful.

Elise turned to Tom and said hopefully, 'Would *you* like to stay on a few days?'

'That's a great idea,' I said enthusiastically. 'Elise would be thrilled,' I added hastily, in an attempt to unhinge my words of the all-too-apparent enthusiasm that hung on them.

'I'm afraid I can't,' he apologized.

JP stepped in deftly. 'Tom has to come back with me. He's my right-hand man.'

Lies, I nearly snorted. Tom had probably never worked a full day in his life.

JP put his arm around Elise's crestfallen shoulders. 'Maybe I'll make it back before Christmas,' he promised. 'And I'll bring Tom.'

I knew he wouldn't.

And he didn't.

Visits had been few and far between since he had left for college nine years earlier.

5. The Bulmer's Experience

1986

At the age of seventeen, JP left home to go study at UCD, University College Dublin. Elise and my father drove him up in the well-used family estate car. He only brought one bag with him and in it were two pairs of jeans, one pair of army trousers, two jumpers and four T-shirts. Nothing that needed ironing. Nothing that needed delicate handling. He was wearing his jacket. I don't even know if he brought any underwear with him. He said it drove the women wild, naked skin. He used talk like this and he was only seventeen.

I was old enough to know that if he *did* bring any underwear he would wear the same ones all week. I thought it was *disgusting.* I thought *he* was disgusting.

The Flanagan girls stayed at home to celebrate JP's departure. There was no tearful farewell. He didn't say goodbye. Instead he slapped us each on the head.

JP had turned slapping into an art form. He made the slaps look caring and brotherly but they were sharp and hurt like hell, and if you complained, you'd be accused of making trouble. Elise would say, '*Mais non, ma petite*, don't be silly. He is your brother. He *adores* you.' Brothers might adore sisters in France but here in Ballyhilleen they embarrassed you in front of your friends, they fancied their older sisters and slapped you on the head. Good riddance to bad rubbish, we said. We were happy to see him gone.

We heard the wheels of the car crunch forward on the gravel outside the front gate of the house and shifted into full celebration gear. Being a teenager, I knew that celebrations called for alcohol. We had all tasted alcohol well before then, during the long summers with our cousins, aunts and uncles in France.

The French had a very relaxed attitude towards serving alcohol to children. They'd been giving us red wine diluted with water to drink with our meals from when we were little more than toddlers. I'd expected red wine to taste like Ribena but it didn't. During those long summer days, I'd also discovered Breton cider. Far more drinkable than wine. All coolness and light it was.

Today I was going to learn the hard way, the *best* way I learned according to my father, the difference between Irish cider and French cider. Irish cider could kill you while French cider just tickled the senses.

I was sixteen, Perri was thirteen and Belle was ten, and I decided that today, to celebrate, Perri and I would be allowed to drink cider. Belle could only drink Shloer, a fizzy apple drink for teetotallers.

Perri and I set off for the off-licence down in the village. It was the middle of September but there was still a hint of summer in the sky. We instructed Belle to stay at home and get the kitchen ready. 'We'll time you,' I told her. I was very good at giving instructions.

Belle always did things much quicker when she thought she was being timed.

Dublin was at least a three-hour drive away, one hundred and forty miles, so I reckoned that we had a good eight or nine hours of freedom ahead of us. In my careful calculations written down on a sheet of paper, I'd included the return journey to Dublin, time for eating, as the men in our family had hearty appetites and could not be denied food, and, of course, goodbye time. Had it been only my father and JP on the excursion to Dublin, this would have taken three minutes.

'Do you have everything, son?'

'I do.'

'Good lad.'

'Right.'

'Be sure to call your mother now.'

'Yeah.'

'Right. Good lad.'

And that would be that. But with Elise there I'd had to include an hour for the goodbyes. I knew she had been busy writing a going-away poem for my brother. She wanted to read it out for him, as he stood outside his new digs, where he was about to start his adult life, as a kind of symbolic gesture. I figured JP and my father would spend ten minutes persuading her not to do it. Elise would summon the tears. They would give in and she would read the poem. Another ten minutes. She would want to explain the significance of every word she had chosen. Another ten minutes. Then JP would get a long lecture on vitamins, personal hygiene and how no one would ever replace him. Maybe one hour wasn't enough.

It was only a fifteen-minute walk from our house to the off-licence on the main street but during that time we had to plan how we would persuade Mr O'Sullivan to sell the two of us alcohol. I was in the same class at school as Mr O'Sullivan's daughter, Concepta. My father used to say that Concepta was as broad as she was long but that you would have to love her. I *didn't*. But I wasn't thinking about that today. My big problem was that Mr O'Sullivan knew I was definitely not over eighteen.

I was wearing my mini-skirt and a tight T-shirt with *I want, I want, I want* written all over the front. I thought it made me look older. You know, sassy.

Perri was wearing her stretch denims and a T-shirt saying *I'm bad*. Nothing could make her look older.

'Hiya, Mr O'Sullivan,' we sang. Big innocent smiles and wide, wide eyes.

'Well, how are my two favourite girls? In for some bull's eyes and apple drops?'

Yep, I thought. We're in for *liquid* apple.

'Well, Mr O'Sullivan.' I took a step forward, about to tell a venial lie that might condemn me to a few months of purgatory when I died. I was blushing. Fortunately, Mr O'Sullivan seemed to think that I was intimidated by talking to a grown-up. 'Elise sent us down because she had to take JP to university in Dublin and she said that when she gets back she would surely be upset and desperately need a drink of French cider to cheer her up.' I was a genius.

'Your poor father,' he said. 'Losing the only other man in the household. Sure who will he have to talk to now?'

Mr O'Sullivan did *not* understand our household. My father talked to Elise more than he talked to JP, more than he talked to the rest of us. He seemed to get a second tongue when it came to Elise. He told her everything.

'My father will talk to my mother, Mr O'Sullivan, who is going to be *heartbroken*, that's the exact word she used, *heartbroken*, because this is the first time any of her children will live away from home,' I explained slowly, because he needed to realize that my mother really needed the cider to cheer her up.

'Well, now, I couldn't have that happening, could I?'

'No, Mr O'Sullivan.' Together.

'But you know, girls, as well stocked as I am, I don't have any French cider. Tell you what, though, I'll give you two flagons of Bulmer's. There's enough there for Elise to have a bath in. It's a fine Irish cider. Couldn't expect you girls to know that, though, could I?'

'No, Mr O'Sullivan. Thank you, Mr O'Sullivan.'

'And I suppose you'll be wanting that put on your father's account?'

'Yes, Mr O'Sullivan.'

''Bye, Mr O'Sullivan.'

The two bottles clinked merrily as we skipped and ran back to the house.

'The bottles are glass, Perri. If we get caught, if Mr O'Sullivan tells, we're going to say that we were getting them the cider as a surprise, and that the bottles fell and broke on the way back to the house. We *didn't* drink them. OK, Perri?' I sounded confident. I had it all thought through.

Peri nodded. 'OK, Lola.'

'What took you two so long?' Belle moaned, when we got back.

'There are things at ten years of age that you cannot understand, Belle. Things like how to get what you want from an adult, which can sometimes take a little bit of time. I'm sixteen and very good at it. I'll teach you when you're older. OK?'

'OK, Lola. What did you get from Mr O'Sullivan?'

'Bulmer's. He says it's like French cider. But you can't have any.'

'But I want to celebrate JP's going away to Dublin, too.'

'OK, but one glass only and then you're drinking Shloer.'

'OK, Lola.'

The kitchen table was covered with an odd assortment of glasses, packets of biscuits, bags of crisps and coloured paper napkins. Belle had collected daisies and dandelions from the garden. They were floating helplessly in crystal vases that were much too big for the delicate posies.

Perri had disappeared. 'Where's Perri gone now? Do I have to do everything myself?' I sighed. Secretly, I *liked* doing everything myself, I *wanted* to do everything myself, and threw fairly savage tantrums – Elise called them *crises* – when anyone else tried to take over.

'Perri's gone to get some straws because she said that one of the boys in your class told you that you get hammered if you drink through a straw.' Belle cocked her head to one side. 'What does hammered mean?'

'Hammered is what I will do to you if you don't go and get her. Your sister's got a real problem. I've read articles about people like her.'

'You mean Perri is famous?' Belle gasped.

We closed the curtains in the kitchen in case any of the neighbours decided to call round to check that we were behaving ourselves properly. We tied them together in the middle with wooden clothes pegs, even though the kitchen was tucked away around the back of the house, because if the neighbours knocked on the door and there was no answer they would come round to the back for a nose. Curtains closed, we would be safe to get up to no good.

Solemnly, we took our seats around the table. Perri poured the Bulmer's.

'Look at the bubbles,' Belle enthused.

I sniggered. 'That's a very intelligent comment, Belle.'

'Lola, pass the straws round.'

I hesitated. 'It doesn't seem sophisticated to be drinking the Bulmer's through a straw, does it? I mean, I bet you don't see Karen what's-her-name drinking her Bulmer's through a straw and she's *very* sophisticated.' Karen what's-her-name lived beside Concepta O'Sullivan and barely talked to anyone. 'Did you know she's off to live in New York? She says Ballyhilleen's just too small for her. Concepta told me.'

'Yeah, well, that one's got her head so far up her arse she could take her own tonsils out. Good riddance. Fortunately, she's not the same size as Concepta or she'd have to pay a fortune in excess baggage.' Perri was wheezing with laughter she was being so funny.

Belle looked at her with admiration.

'That's an awful thing to say about poor Concepta,' I said. It was awful but true. It was just awful to say it and *laugh*.

'*You* call her the Enormous Conception, so what's the difference?'

'*She* calls me Worzel Gummidge.' She called me that because of my fuzzy hair.

Perri pulled a sympathetic face. 'Anyway, to get back to the straws. You said Eddie Reilly told you that if you're drinking alcohol and you want to get hammered really quick, like, you should drink through a straw.' She rubbed the *I'm bad* felt letters on her

T-shirt. 'And if you're really desperate you should put a small pinprick in the straw. Are we that desperate?'

'Forget it, Perri. And don't listen to your sister, Belle.' I wagged a finger at her, like I'd seen Elise do. 'There's no need to go pricking holes in perfectly good straws. Eddie Reilly is a real gobshite and we're not using straws till we know how to drink properly.' And that's that, I thought. 'Imagine you're eighteen and down in the pub trying to suck your Guinness through a straw. You'd look really smart then. A real *gobshite*.'

Belle's hand was flat against her mouth. 'You said *gobshite*,' she muffled. 'I thought you gave up swearing, Lola.'

'I *did*,' I insisted. 'I only swear on special occasions now.'

So, it was decided to put the straws back in their bag.

All three of us had our glasses full in front of us and the smell of fermented apples filled the air. The kitchen was half dark. No sunlight escaped past the curtains. I lit two candles. Between the two candles stood the bottles of cider, the brown glass flickering in warm tones.

'Remember, Belle, you're only allowed one glass. Perri and I will have the rest.'

'OK, Lola.'

The cider tasted much stronger than the Breton cider I'd tried. The taste was still strong towards the end of the glass, but nice too. We didn't talk during the first glass. I think we were all thinking how grown-up we were.

Perri finished her glass first. It seemed that she attacked alcohol with the same impatience that she attacked everything else and the pale liquid had quickly disappeared. She was singing at the end of the table.

'What are you singing, Perri?' Perri had a great voice. Well, we weren't sure if it was altogether great but it *was* loud and rasping.

'I'm singing "*The minstrel boy to the war has gone, In the arms of death you'll find him . . .*"'

'That's a bit morbid, isn't it?' It reminded me of music class and sitting in the dunces' row with Concepta O'Sullivan.

'Yeah, I'll change. It's just that I remember all the words to that one.'

Belle continued to sip her cider and scrunch her nose up.

'I don't think I like this stuff,' she complained.

Perri grabbed the glass. 'That's OK, Belle. I'll finish that for you.' She tipped the pale liquid into her mouth and smacked her lips.

Belle poured herself some Shloer and decided that she was in charge of filling up our glasses. She did the job well because within half an hour the first flagon of cider was empty. Emptied into our glasses.

And sure enough my head had begun to spin and my cheeks were feeling very hot and prickly. French cider didn't make me feel like this, like jelly. With this puzzling thought in mind, I went to put my glass back down on the table and it missed, or did it? I wasn't quite sure. Did the glass miss the table or did the table miss the glass? I erupted into a furnace of giggles. 'I'll need a new glass, Belle. Just as well you put two dozen out on the table, isn't it?' Two dozen, two dozen. Now, that *was* funny.

'I didn't. I only put . . .' she counted aloud ' . . . thirteen out.'

'What in the name of God possessed you to put thirteen glasses out on the table when there are only three of us here?' Perri quizzed, sounding like she'd never been *that* thick when she was ten.

'The extra glasses were in case the neighbours came around and saw through the curtains and wanted to come in for a drink with us.'

'Yes, brilliant idea. I think they'd love to sit down and have some Bulmer's with us. I mean, they wouldn't think this was strange or anything. This probably happens in their houses, too. We should maybe get out Elise's special Waterford crystal, just in case.' Perri could be savage. 'Lola, this sister of ours should be put into a special school for the over-intelligent,' she declared.

Belle looked like she was going to cry. Not that *that* would be strange.

'Ah, leave her alone,' I slurred. 'She's only ten . . . no, eleven . . . no, ten . . . ten, ten, ten. More cider, pleeeease.'

Suddenly, the Bulmer's-charged emotions were on the loose. 'Belle, I love you. Perri, I love you too. I think I may even love JP. I am going to call him tonight to tell him I love him. I think that's a great idea. Do you think he'll say "I love you" back?'

Perri gaped. 'I think he'll puke, Lola.'

'But we don't say "I love you" often enough,' I gulped. 'None of us do. Belle, say "I love you" to Perri.'

Belle was willing. 'I love you, Perri Werri.'

'Perri, now tell Belle that you love her too.'

'Love yoo-hoo too-hoo.' She tilted her head backwards and balanced her empty glass on her forehead. 'Happy now, Lola?' Her voice sounded stretched. 'Your little family all loves each other.'

God, this was *brilliant*. 'I'm so happy now, I'm ready for another drink.'

My family was great. Why did we all fight with each other every single day? On the spot, I decided never to bicker with any of them ever again. We should do this more often. We should do this every day. The five packets of biscuits were empty but I couldn't remember eating any of them myself. But then again I couldn't remember Perri or Belle eating them either.

My tongue was too big for my mouth.

Belle had become bored with the Shloer, Perri and me, and was doing her homework for Monday.

Perri was practising her singing with the sweeping brush in front of her mouth. '*Oh, Lord, it's so hard to be humble, When you're perfect in every way, I can't wait to look in the mirror, 'Cos I get better-looking each day . . .*' and on she sang.

Belle had a little friend with her doing her homework too. 'Belle, who's that little girl sitting beside you?'

Belle glared at me. 'There's no one sitting beside me, Lola,' she sulked. 'And talk proper. I can't understand you.'

I stood up to see if there was any Camembert in the fridge. I really wanted a slice of Camembert. Smelly, runny Camembert with the white powdery crust that I'd eat as well.

But the ground wasn't where it was meant to be when I put my feet down. I crumbled on to the floor. Not ladylike. Not good. Karen what's-her-name wouldn't do this. 'Where's the floor gone, Perri?'

Perri was wrapped around the sweeping brush. 'You're not on the floor, Lola. You're on the ceiling.' She began to sing. 'Lola's on the ceiling. Lola's on the ceiling . . .'

With a wisdom beyond her ten years, Belle wearily lifted herself up off her chair and decided to make tea and sandwiches. 'I can't even get my maths exercises done with the noise the two of you are making,' she complained. 'This is no fun for me. You've ruined everything.'

I started to cry. Big Bulmer's tears.

Hours and hours later I heard the muffled sound of Elise and my father coming home and forced open my eyes just long enough to see a slit of light from the bedroom door. Our father checking that we were tucked up safely in bed.

I *supposed* I was still alive. I didn't feel that I should be. Someone had replaced my eyelids with rough sandpaper, wrapped my tongue in a wad of fur and stuck a tambourine inside my head.

This was all JP's fault. *God*, he was going to pay for this.

I didn't know then that that day would come twelve years later. The bottom would fall out of JP's world. And land on top of us all. And just when I'd finally decided to come home.

6. Me, Father Rourke and the Marriage Proposal

1977

This fascination, in the most obsessive sense of the word, that I had with priests had started at a very young age. Most fascinations probably do, so this one was no different. The parish priest in Ballyhilleen was Father Rourke, a mild-mannered man with a ruddy complexion and a lilting Kerry accent, and he used to descend on our primary school once a week to spellbind his junior congregation with talk of God the Almighty, Heaven and Hell. He travelled on a cloud of reverence, that was sure.

God the Almighty was a powerful father who never got cross. Heaven was the place we all wanted to be, sitting beside the angels and singing hymns all day long. But the idea of hell had us shaking in our shoes. 'I'm not going there,' I lisped fervently every time.

We sat cross-legged on the floor in front of him, gazing up at him in blatant adoration while he conducted his crusade to educate a class of awestruck seven-year-olds on how to be good Irish Catholics.

Each one vying for his attention, we tried to outdo each other by asking the most complicated questions we could come up with.

Concepta O'Sullivan's hand shot up eagerly the minute he walked into the room. She always wanted to be the first with her question. 'Father Rourke, how could the Father, the Son and the Holy Spirit be the same person?' She smiled proudly at her difficult question, gloating.

'Father Rourke, why was Mary a *Blessed* Virgin?' Frances Mullrooney frowned. 'Am I *Blessed*?'

I folded my arms and quizzed, 'What does *Virgin* mean?'

'Father Rourke, what size nails did they use to screw Jesus to the cross and did He cry, I mean, really *roar* crying?' Gerry Fields demanded, thirsty for all the details.

Father Rourke solemnly answered our questions, one by one, and he answered them as if they were the most important questions he'd ever been asked, his blue eyes twinkling softly. He always remembered our names and gently began his explanation with, 'Well, now, Concepta,' or, 'Well, now, Frances'. And at that moment, you felt like you were the only person on this earth who really mattered.

My favourite question was the one about the Blessed Virgin conceiving without sin. I asked about that nearly every time. No amount of explaining could make me understand it. Elise would smirk when I asked her about conceiving without sin and Father Rourke's unhurried explanations about Mary being visited by the Holy Spirit only confused me more.

By the end of the first year of Father Rourke's visits, he had my seven-year-old heart firmly in his grip.

I would be Father Rourke's wife, that I'd decided. Elise had told me that he didn't have one, that priests weren't allowed to have wives. She added that she thought it was a silly rule because all men needed a woman to look after them. I was sure that Father Rourke needed *me* to look after him. I was only seven but I could do everything that a big girl could. And I could fit my hand in through the letter-box from the outside and open the front door if he forgot his key, and a big girl couldn't do that. When I went to live with him, I would bring some of Elise's frilly things with me to dress up in, to make him happy.

Concepta O'Sullivan wanted to be Father Rourke's wife as well but she wanted to wait until she was a big girl and could work in her daddy's shop, so she could bring him bottles of whiskey for free. We'd once heard Mr O'Sullivan say that Father Rourke liked his whiskey.

It was at breakfast one Saturday morning that I told the rest of the family that I would be leaving them soon to go live with Father Rourke in his big house.

'I have something to tell everyone,' I said seriously, in between mouthfuls of steaming porridge to put hair on my chest. I tried again, louder. 'I want to say something important.' The porridge struggled to stay in my mouth.

'What's wrong, Lola?' my father asked, spreading generous layers of creamy butter on a thick wedge of bread. He loved his butter.

'I'm off to be Father Rourke's wife.' I bent towards the table and licked up some porridge that had escaped and fallen on to the rough surface. My tongue felt all prickly.

He stopped buttering his bread, his knife held mid-air. 'Are you now? And do you think that Father Rourke would like to see you licking your porridge off the kitchen table?' He shook his head. 'I don't think so.'

'I'll pack your suitcase for you,' JP added quickly. He seemed worried that I might just change my mind if I found out that Father Rourke wouldn't let me lick the porridge off the kitchen table.

Elise plucked Belle from her high chair and walked towards the table, winding her with small pats to her back. 'But I told you, Lola, that priests aren't allowed to have wives.' She gave me her beautiful, beatific smile, the one that I spent hours in front of the mirror trying to copy.

'You said that was a silly rule,' I whined.

'Yes, I think it is,' she agreed. '*Mais c'est la vie.*' She shrugged her shoulders. I tried to copy that too, in front of the mirror.

'I think it's a silly rule,' I said determinedly, and finished licking the porridge off the table, ignoring my father moaning about my table manners.

Every man had to have a wife. Adam had Eve, who

72

fed him on green apples that made him want to put clothes on, and Joseph had Mary, though she had conceived without sin through the Holy Spirit, who visited her in a dream.

I ran upstairs and pulled my small plaid suitcase from under my bed, in the draughty room I shared with Perri at the top of the old house.

Perri's small hand pushed open the bedroom door. She sidled up to me. 'What you doing?' she asked, seeing the suitcase propped up on the enormous patchwork quilt. Elise had sewn it by hand and each square was something she remembered from when she was little: summers spent running around the vineyards of the Loire valley down by Vertou, Clisson, Le Louroux-Bottereau, where Muscadet wine came from; food-covered tables lying in shadowy stone courtyards; fishing trips to the banks of the river Erdre; happy days on Belle-Ile, at their family holiday home, an old fort standing at the top of a craggy cliff overlooking a secluded sandy cove. Her childhood was there, stitched together.

'I'm going to be Father Rourke's wife and I'm off to see him,' I answered clearly, 'to tell him.' I opened the suitcase again and threw in my money-box. I couldn't leave home without my pennies. The coins rattled loudly as I swung the case from the high bed to the floor.

'Put on your good clothes, like for when we go to mass.' Perri walked over to the wardrobe and grabbed hold of my navy sailor dress and matching cap, my good outfit. 'Do you want me to come too?' she asked.

Perri always wanted to do what I did. 'No, because I won't be coming home again and you're too little to find your way back on your own,' I explained, while I pulled on the dress. Finished, I turned to look in the mirror. Dark curls shot out from under the peaked admiral's cap, framing a pale face that was missing two front teeth and home to a freckled nose that turned up at the end. The eyes that stared back at me were coloured with green and brown flecks and always reminded me of a speckled hen. The white-collared sailor dress stopped about four inches above two knobbly knees that bore the scars of daily mishaps. On my feet I wore bright red wellies.

Perri was staring at me from her bed, where she sat swinging her legs over the edge and plucking at some loose threads. 'You look lovely, so you do.'

'Father Rourke is going to get a big surprise when I tell him that I'm coming to be his wife, isn't he?' Carefully, I smoothed the front of the dress with a flattened hand, wanting the pleats to be perfect.

'He's going to be very happy, I think.' Perri nodded.

I didn't say goodbye to Elise before I left the house. I didn't want her to ruin my plan. With determined steps, I walked down the gravel drive, turning back at the end, when I reached the big iron gates, to see Perri waving happily to me from the bedroom window. She opened the window and leaned out. 'Will you be at school on Monday?' she shouted.

74

'Yes,' I shouted back.

'I'll bring your sandwiches so.' Perri had just started school and loved her shiny lunch-box.

'No, it's all right,' I yelled. 'Father Rourke will make me sandwiches.' I could taste the soft, fresh ham sandwiches he would make me every day, before walking me down the road to school. 'I'll probably have a bag of Tayto, too.' I loved crisps.

Father Rourke lived in a big house beside the church. Winter or summer, there was always a streak of smoke coming from the chimney. It was hard to keep the house warm, I'd heard him say once.

It wasn't very far away but it seemed like the distance to Dublin with short legs. My cap kept on slipping off my head and my wellies were beginning to rub off the back of my heels. I didn't have on any socks and they'd soon be red raw. My arms were aching carrying the suitcase.

A short cobblestone path with tufts of grass peeping up between the stones led the way to Father Rourke's front door. Standing on the very tips of my toes, I reached up and grabbed the brass knocker. Swinging by my spindly arms, I boldly banged the knocker against the door, and waited.

Expecting Father Rourke to open it, I was disappointed when Mrs Henehan appeared from behind the wooden panels. I looked at her crossly. Mrs Henehan had a sweeping brush in one hand and a dirty cloth in the other. She wore a scarf knotted over her hair curlers and a flowery nylon dress with a thin patent belt around her middle. Mrs Henehan didn't have a waist, she was the same round shape all the way down.

My bottom lip was trembling. I desperately wanted to ask Mrs Henehan what she was doing in *my* priest's house. Mrs Henehan already *had* a husband.

'Please, I would like to see the priest. Please. Thank you. Please.' I tried to squeeze in every polite word I knew.

She sneezed, sending a misty spray over my head. 'He's busy doing tomorrow's sermon. Tomorrow's Sunday. You can't see him.'

'But it's very important. I have to see him,' I pleaded.

'Well, you can't and that's all there's to it. Go home and don't be bothering poor Father Rourke.' She used the end of the sweeping brush to poke me in the shoulder, trying to prod me back down the path. 'Be off with you.'

Behind her back, I caught sight of Father Rourke walking from one room to another, intently studying a book he was holding. Probably the Bible. 'Father Rourke,' I shouted through the door, as loudly as I could. 'Father Rourke, come out here, would you? She's being very mean to me, so she is.' A big toothless grin spread over my face.

'Hello, there, Lola,' he said, kneeling down in front of me and snapping shut the book he was holding. It had a big cross on the front of it and looked very important. It *was* the Bible. 'You're looking very smart today.' We shook hands, and my small, dusty hand was swallowed up in his big, clean one.

'Thank you, Father,' I said. 'I have to talk to you. It's very important.'

'Come on in, Lola.' He stood up and stepped to one side.

'But, Father,' Mrs Henehan brusquely interrupted, 'you're *surely* too busy?'

'I'm *never* too busy to see someone who needs to speak to me, Mrs Henehan,' he chided her.

'Your nose is only out of joint,' I said to her, as I swept past, using one of my father's favourite phrases. The look on her face told me it had been the right thing to say.

Father Rourke smiled and asked Mrs Henehan to bring some tea and biscuits into his study.

She seethed, *seethed*.

In the sitting room, he pointed to a brown leather chair. 'Sit down there, Lola.'

I dropped my suitcase down beside the chair and took my cap off and put it on my knees. 'Can I take me wellies off, Father? They're a bit sore on me feet.'

'Of course you can.'

I kicked them off and watched them land on the floor. I would remember my socks the next time. 'Father, I've come to tell you,' I gushed, 'that I'll be your wife.' I left a silence too short for him to say anything. 'I've brought things with me, so I don't have to go home again today.'

As was his habit, Father Rourke treated these words

as if they were the most important words he had ever heard. He was sitting opposite me and leaned across. 'Well, Lola, I'm sure that some day you'll make someone a grand wife, but it's not going to be me.'

The tears sprang up in my eyes. Maybe my bladder was too near my eyes, just like Belle's. 'But why not? I'm a big girl and you need a wife to take care of you. Why can't I be a wife?' I wailed miserably.

'Yes, you *are* a big girl, but you need to be a *much* bigger girl before you can become a wife,' he explained gently, 'and I've got Mrs Henehan to take care of me. She does all my washing and cleaning.'

Beseechingly, I looked at him from behind a wall of tears. 'But Mrs Henehan has a husband. Didn't you know?'

'Yes, I know, Lola. She's my housekeeper. That's her job. I'm a man of God and men of God don't have wives. We're married to the Church.'

So, that was it. He was married to the Church. He wasn't going to let me live with him in the big house. I wasn't going to play in the chapel whenever I wanted to. I wouldn't get to listen to everyone's confession, sitting on his knee in the confession box, and he wouldn't be making me ham sandwiches every day for school with a bag of Tayto.

I started to sob. 'I can't walk home again. Me feet hurt and, anyway, Mrs Henehan never brought in the tea and biscuits.'

At that moment, I heard my father's voice in the hallway, apologizing to Mrs Henehan for disturbing her from her jobs around the house and, no, he hadn't come about her Paddy's problem with stray cattle, he was looking for his eldest daughter, Lola.

Mrs Henehan told him that I was in there all right, after making a right song and dance to see the priest. She was getting me into trouble as best as she could.

'Good morning, Father Rourke,' my father said, striding into the room. 'Sorry about the little visitor. She was gone before we knew it.' He turned to glare at me. 'Lola, get over here now, little lady.' He pointed sternly to the floor beside him.

I pulled on the wellies and scuttled across the rug.

'We'll be seeing you tomorrow at mass, Father.' He propelled me out of the door ahead of him. I didn't dare sneak a look back at Father Rourke.

His bicycle was parked at the end of the path, propped up against a tired rosebush. After tying my suitcase to the back carrier with some thick brown twine that he pulled from nowhere, he swung his leg over the bar and pulled me on to my special red saddle, in front of his own.

'I'm sorry, Daddy. I'll never do it again, so I won't,' I cried. 'I'll never bother the priest again.' I knew I was in trouble and sobbed all the more loudly.

'What are we going to do with you, Lola?' he asked me. 'What is the poor priest to think? First, you go parading yourself around in front of him in your mother's bits and pieces, and now you go begging the poor man to take you in. I don't know what kind of a home he thinks you come from at all.' I could feel him shake his head behind me.

'I'm sorry, Daddy. I'll never do it again. I mean it. I don't want to be put over your knee when we get home. Me feet are too sore from the wellies.' I gazed over my shoulder at him, holding my admiral's cap down on my head with one hand and hanging on to the handle-bar with the other. 'I think you probably scared the priest,' I fretted nobly.

'Ah, Lola, you'll break my heart,' he whispered into my ear, in a soft voice that a father only uses to a daughter, every syllable drenched with love.

7. The Foxy Lady

Monday, 9 March 1998

I stretched lazily, happily hidden from the world beneath the warm blankets. Brilliant rays of sunshine sneaked into the room. It had the makings of a bright March day. Beside me, in the sagging double bed, Perri snored softly.

By the time we'd staggered back to Perri's flat last night, after a lengthy eight-course dinner in a local Chinese restaurant with Elise, Dad and Belle, to celebrate my homecoming before the rest of the family made the arduous one-hundred-and-forty-mile, three-and-a-half-hour trip south back to Ballyhilleen and I stayed in Dublin with Perri, we had been too tired and too full of food to set about emptying the tiny box room that was going to convert into a dolls'-house-sized bedroom for me. Fortunately, I didn't need much space because when Perri had described the room as a shoe box, she hadn't been exaggerating.

Last night, I'd climbed happily into the double bed beside Perri, rolling straight into the dip in the middle of the mattress while Perri hung comfortably over the side of the bed.

The flat, with its lino-floored kitchen, big square sitting room and fold-down sofa, one proper bedroom and a poky box room that I would inherit, was in the south side of Dublin, tucked away on the third floor above a drinkers' pub called the Tipsy Tinker, run by a cantankerous fool, Charlie Barry. Charlie was better known as Whiskers. He had a big, bushy beard.

The outside of the building had a definite run-down look to it. Inside was a bit better but not by much. Its near-dilapidated state was the only reason that Perri could afford her own flat in Dublin. That and the fact that Charlie Barry seemed blissfully unaware that he was at least twenty years behind with his rates compared to what the rest of Dublin was paying these days. Needless to say, Perri didn't see why she should enlighten him. For the low rent, she gladly put up with a lot. The washing-up water went down the kitchen sink only to resurface through the plug hole in the shower. As a result, you could find yourself standing in the shower with spaghetti hoops wound around your toes.

Ever mindful of Perri's safety living on her own in the Big City, my father decided for all of us that the rampant decay was a blessing in disguise as the building wouldn't attract any unwanted attention from the gougers who, according to him, freely roamed the streets of Dublin.

But just to be on the safe side, two weeks after Perri had moved into the flat last year, he'd arrived on a surprise visit, his chunky toolbox and three sturdy safety locks in hand. He slipped into the flat easily. Not a trick he had picked up in Ballyhilleen, where everyone left their doors open.

When Perri got back to the flat that evening, she found the three new locks firmly fixed to her door. There was a note telling her that she would be safe from now on. The keys to all three locks were left with Whiskers Barry for her to pick up downstairs. Perri had since claimed that Whiskers had made copies of the keys for himself. She swore that her underwear went missing.

Five days after that, my father was back in Dublin dressed in a paint-splattered boilersuit. Whiskers Barry spotted him arriving. He was armed with eight litres of matt emulsion, bought on special offer from Mickey Spillane at the hardware shop in Ballyhilleen, his entire collection of well-used paintbrushes, a plastic bag of stained rags and a bottle of methylated spirits. He wouldn't have thought to check the colour of the paint.

He let himself into the flat again, using the spare set of keys he'd quietly kept for himself five days earlier, for emergencies, of course.

By the time Perri showed up at the flat, her bare walls were lime green. Every room of the flat had been painted lime green. This time there was no note to say who'd been but the carefully folded leaflet with tips on how to avoid getting mugged and a thick slab of Ballyhilleen cheese on the kitchen table were all the clues she needed. She didn't speak to him for three weeks until he came back up to Dublin and painted the whole flat white. My father hated it when one of us wasn't speaking to him and I'm sure he would have done the walls in gold leaf if it meant that Perri would talk to him again.

The flat's one good feature was a rooftop terrace. Admittedly you had to squeeze yourself out on to it through the small window in Perri's bedroom. A two-foot-high red-brick wall ran along the rim of the terrace and there was an old garden bench and lots of empty wine bottles.

The digital clock radio read 9.30 a.m. Reluctantly, I dragged myself out of bed, slipping my feet into Perri's unused pink fluffy slippers, a present from Elise when she was still convinced that she could inject a bit of femininity into Perri even if she was a *woman's* woman.

Wearing the slippers, I climbed out through the bedroom window and on to the rooftop terrace. There was the muffled sound of voices and cars from the road below. I sat on the bench, arms wrapped around my legs and chin resting on my knees. A delicious smell of freshly baked bread wafted up from the bakery three doors down. My stomach rumbled. My heart sang. At that moment, for a fleeting instant, it didn't matter to me that I didn't have a job, had practically no savings and would have to think of something to do very quickly now that I had achieved the first part of my plan. And I needed money before I could get an education.

I sat there a while listening to Whiskers Barry whistle some rebel tune in his flat below Perri's. I'd met Whiskers Barry once or twice before.

Perri poked her head through the window, eyes

barely open and her voice still groggy from sleep. 'What are you up to out there?'

'Just thinking.'

'Hang on, I'll come out.' Perri hauled herself through the window, wearing only an Iron Maiden T-shirt and baggy knickers that looked like they'd come off the smalls rail in Oxfam. She wandered over to the bench where I was sitting. She didn't seem to notice the cold air. 'So, whatya thinking about, then?'

'Two things,' I told her. 'Getting myself a job and an education.'

'The two go hand in hand,' she replied wisely. 'I have neither,' she added, less wisely.

'I can't afford to stay without a job for long.' Maybe four days, I thought.

'So, you managed to save a lot working as a nanny, then?' Perri laughed. 'We were all wondering when you'd begin sending the money envelopes home.' Her expression was suddenly serious.

I *hoped* she was joking. 'Don't tell me JP sends money home?' I gasped, my heart sinking. The answer might just be yes as JP was capable of grand gestures. And the opposite too.

Perri lifted my despair with a lively pat on the back. 'Don't worry,' she assured me, the serious façade slipping to reveal a grin. 'He doesn't even send his dirty washing home. And we all know that that would probably come before any money ever did.'

In the building opposite, there was a sudden blurred movement behind the dirty panes of a window. I stared intently for a moment to see if I was mistaken but there it was again. 'There's someone spying on us from over there,' I announced, with conviction, pointing straight at the window, at the dim outline.

'Ah, him, he's always there,' Perri answered, in a flat, unexcited voice. 'Nothing better to do, I suppose. I consider it a charity to let him gawk,' she carried on casually, standing up to turn her curvy rear end in his direction and wiggle it in an outrageously lurid manner, baggy knickers flapping in the wind.

I was appalled. 'Stop goading him,' I ordered her.

Flopping back down beside me, slightly out of breath as a result of the contortions, she panted, 'I might be able to wangle you a few hours at the school, if you're interested in teaching English to groups of ungrateful foreign adolescents for minimum wage and maximum effort.' She raised an eyebrow questioningly and grinned as she guessed what my answer might be.

'If all else fails, I'll keep it in mind.' I'd heard far too many stories of Perri's students and her penny-pinching boss to be even vaguely tempted even if I did have nothing else to do. 'While I'm deciding what to do with my life, I want a hassle-free occupation that pays the rent with money left over for a few pints and the odd extravagance,' I decided aloud. 'Is that asking too much?'

'Yes,' she assured me gravely, with all her twenty-five years' experience of life, 'it is. That's only for the lucky ones.' Hesitating for an instant, she added in a voice heavy with mischievous overtones, 'There's a private club down the road where they're always looking for dancing hostesses. Flexible hours and a stress-free environment.' A laugh. 'What more could you want?' She winked at me and made an exaggerated effort of licking her lips. 'Luscious.'

'What would I have to do? Wait on tables, serve drinks, bop a bit from lap to lap?' I closed my eyes and pictured an expensively furnished, dimly lit room, champagne and dark suits, nimble, doe-eyed temptresses, and me. 'I could do that,' I told her confidently.

'No, no.' She sighed, reading my mind easily. 'Close your eyes again and picture bare lightbulbs, overweight punters and second-hand spangled bikinis.'

I did as she said. The second picture was very different from the first but still wore an attractive hue brought on by the two simple facts that I needed a job I could actually do and I needed to earn some money fast. 'I could do that, too,' I told her. What the hell? I thought. May as well be hung for a sheep as a lamb. 'Would it be *really* sleazy?' I wanted to know, never having been inside one of these clubs whereas Perri probably had.

'Yeah,' she admitted. 'But at least you'd be a *performing artiste.*'

I brightened up. 'Yeah, you're right.' The idea of being an *artiste* held a sudden appeal. The best excuse ever for being broke. I ran a hand through my hair. 'I bet I'd be a bigger success blonde, though,' I said seriously.

'What?' Perri cried, looking at the dark mess on

my head. 'Well, before you take any drastic action, let's see how well you can perform,' she advised me. 'Strip off there and give me some action.' Perri grabbed hold of an old garden brush that was propped up against the side of the bench. 'Here, use this as a prop.'

I peeled off the T-shirt I'd slept in and the jumper I'd hastily pulled on to shield me from the cool air, but I left on my knickers with the tired daisies, pulling the back up between the fleshy cheeks of my rear end to create a make-do thong. The March air nipped at my bare skin.

Perri pulled a face. 'Only a mother would love you,' she commented wryly.

'Music, please, maestro,' I ordered, and stood with one leg wrapped around the long handle of the brush and an arm flung behind my head. It was what I thought was a suggestive pose. The figure behind the window disappeared. So much for the suggestive pose.

Perri could sing. She really *could* sing. She began a raunchy number from her seat on the bench. Her loud, husky voice drifted down the side of the building and in through the open window below, where Whiskers Barry had finished whistling his rebel affiliations and was having his first drink of the day. His eye-opener, he called it.

'Put a sock in it, Perri, for feck's sake,' he roared out of the open window. He followed it with a long, vulgar belch. 'There, that's what I think of yer bloody crooning, ya whore, ya.' Whiskers could have made Billy Connolly blush if he really put his mind to it.

But that morning he was just being his charming self.

Perri pretended not to hear Whiskers's ravings. She sang louder while I gyrated for Ireland. When the song came to an end, after three encores instigated by Perri, I was panting heavily and my face was covered in a fine film of sweat. 'Well, what d'ya think?' I gasped anxiously, because with nothing else on the cards a dancing job at the Foxy Lady Club could be just what I needed.

She beamed at me. 'I think we've found you a new profession. The Foxy Lady down the road won't know what hit them.'

I tugged at my hair reminding her of what I'd said earlier. I didn't like it anyway so surely it wouldn't matter to me if it was blonde.

'Do you *still* fancy the idea?' she groaned, but didn't try to dissuade me. She would love to see me looking like a piebald pony.

'Absolutely,' I replied, suddenly determined. 'And *you* can do it for me. We'll get dressed and get a home kit. And then I'll go down to this place this evening and get an audition.' I had it all worked out. My life was going to *change*. That very day.

'You're on,' Perri shouted, and leaped up from the bench. 'God, Dublin was such a boring place without you.'

'You should try Brussels,' I moaned. In truth I doubted if Dublin had been boring without me but it was nice to think so for a split second.

*

We got to Dunnes Stores in the city centre by the middle of the morning and headed with determined steps straight for the hair-care counter, where we spent a good forty-five minutes discussing the advantages of ammonia-free hair-colouring. Neither of us knew what we were talking about but we still had an awful lot to say on the subject.

Perri fingered my dark strands soberly. 'Your hair is really dark,' she said stating the obvious. 'So,' she continued knowledgeably, 'I don't think it's an ash blonde that we're after.' She put three boxes back on the shelf. 'You don't want a red blonde either, do you?'

'Nah, too cheap,' I said.

She put another two boxes back on the shelf. 'That rules out these ones.'

'How about summer blonde?' I suggested.

'Nah. It's too early in the season, only March yet.' She held a box up hopefully. 'This one?'

I shrieked. 'I don't want hair that colour. That's only for tarts.' The model on the front of the box had bright yellow hair. Even her beautiful face couldn't make it look better.

'OK, OK.' Another box was shoved back on the shelf. 'You're left with these two.' She offered me two boxes.

I studied them both carefully. 'That's the one,' I decided, and pointed to the box that claimed to transform dark brown hair into honey-blonde locks. 'That's definitely the one.' I examined the price label.

'You do realize I'm saving about sixty pounds with this kit? In real terms, Perri, that's around thirty pints of Guinness. A-bloody-mazing.'

'That's six suits from down at Oxfam,' she calculated. 'Grand job.'

I smiled at her. She smiled at me. But, of course, we would be smiling. I'd only been back in the country for one day.

Whiskers Barry was standing on the street, announcing to no one in particular that the pub was open, as we sauntered down the road from the bus stop, shopping-bag swinging optimistically. He had his back to us and an expanse of pale, flabby flesh was prying its way out from above the waistband of his trousers.

Perri pulled me into a doorway to wait until he had disappeared back inside. 'It's too early in the day to face that,' she whispered.

Once we'd reached the flat without being waylaid by Whiskers, I wrapped a shabby towel around my shoulders. 'Down to business,' I declared.

Perri pulled out the plastic gloves and paper instructions. 'I can't go wrong,' she assured me. 'They've even drawn the instructions,' she mused. 'Just as well, I wouldn't have known what a head looked like.'

We both laughed. It would be my last laugh of the day.

Fifty-five minutes later, I was bending over the side of the bath, rinsing a purple coloured mixture from my head. 'Tell me it's not purple,' I gurgled, through the running water.

'It's not *purple*,' Perri reasoned. 'Here, take this and blast it dry.' Perri pushed the hairdryer into my hands. She was acting as if she was hoping the hot air might blast the colour right off my head.

But it was too late. By then I was staring at my reflection in the mirror, desperately twisting my head to see if the cap of yellow, brass-like colour would change. It did. From every different angle, it looked an even brighter yellow, brass-like colour, with a dollop of saffron here and there. 'I'm not sure I want to see it dry. It looks awful enough wet,' I yelled, and glared accusingly at Perri. 'It's awful, isn't it?' I cried.

'Well, it *is* awful but, on the other hand, it's definitely blonde.' Holding my shoulders, she spun me around several times and studied me carefully, trying to disguise a smirk. 'It'll be brilliant for your new career. You'll need a stage name and you can just call yourself the Brass Babe, or Wella Yella.' Her face was a picture of strained contortions as she forced herself not to laugh, to fight back the hysterical laughter I *knew* she was only just keeping a lid on.

'You're right,' I decided emphatically. 'Who gives a damn?' I tried to admire myself in the mirror. 'No one in Brussels had this colour hair,' I said, eventually finding one good thing about having a hair colour that would put a brass knob to shame.

'No one in Dublin has either.' She coughed.

*

The Foxy Lady was hidden down a dingy side-street, a quick fifteen-minute walk from the flat. At least, I won't have far to go to work, I told myself, quite certain that I would get the job, no problem. A neon sign blazed 'The Foxy Lady Club – Men Only'. The window was dark and grimy, and a small handwritten ad read, 'Exotic Hostesses Required. Apply within, 5 p.m. – 6 p.m. No experience necessary. All sizes considered.'

I stopped for a moment as sudden doubt entered my mind. What was I doing here? A stern inner voice reminded me immediately that I was broke, desperate and severely lacking in qualifications for any other job. Not that I was qualified for this one either but fortunately they weren't looking for qualifications or experience.

I rang the doorbell and waited.

'Yeah, whatya want?' The door was pulled open by a middle-aged man, dressed in a light blue suit of a seventies cut and a black open-necked shirt. He wore a silver cross and chain around his neck. His trousers were pulled too high and his round stomach stuck out from below the tight belt rather than above it.

'I'm here to audition for a job as an exotic hostess,' I told him, in what I hoped was a professional voice.

He looked me up and down, taking in the high-heeled shoes, the short skirt and, no doubt, the slightly – but only slightly – chunky legs. He snorted a few times and invited me in.

My eyes adjusted to the darkness inside. A scattering

of bare tables was clustered around a half-moon-shaped stage in the middle of which a tall pole stood erect. The club was empty.

'Sandy,' he shouted, towards the stage, 'get yourself out here now, now, now.' He clicked his fingers impatiently three times.

Sandy appeared, at her leisure, from behind the heavy drapes at the back of the stage, obviously used to her boss's frequent demands and rude manner. She was encased in a tattered bathrobe and wore heavy makeup. She was blonde and she wasn't even youngish. 'Whatya want, Paddy?' Her voice was bored. Momentarily I worried that mine would become bored one day too. Damn. I worried that it was bored already. Flat and dead with no edge to it, just like Sandy's.

'Take *her* backstage,' Paddy bellowed, nodding dismissively in my direction. 'And get her ready to do a number for me.'

Sandy's jaded eyes met mine, the makeup caked to the black bags. 'Come on, you, follow me. Want a fag?' She pulled a pack of Carroll's from the torn pocket of the faded bathrobe.

'No, thanks. I don't smoke.' And I almost felt bad about it, as if I was insulting her by not smoking, although she didn't look that easy to insult.

'Ya don't, don't ya?' She bestowed a knowing, bitter smile on me. 'Well, that'll all change if you come to work in this dump,' she guaranteed me ruefully.

'Where are we going?' I was following Sandy down a narrow hall that stank of cigarette smoke. It had

94

such an air of neglect about it that the smell of stale smoke was the only sign that life still passed this way.

We walked into a small room that was cluttered with empty cigarette packets and buckets of cheap makeup. A bare bulb gave the room a harsh light. 'Welcome to Paddy's paradise. This is the room us girls get to share to make ourselves beautiful for the shows.' She cackled humourlessly. 'There are ten of us in all, new ones come and go, and we're all packed in like sardines. Paddy won't spend the money to do up one of the other rooms. Stingy out.'

I listened to her, before I asked eagerly, 'So, what's it like to be an *artiste*?' Unbelievably, I still wasn't put off. And Sandy herself had obviously seen a few full moons at the Foxy Lady Club so something had to be keeping her there. With her skills she could probably work anywhere. The money must be brilliant, I reasoned.

'*Artiste*?' she choked. 'Listen, love, I don't know where you got your info but we don't do paintin' and drawin' here.' The cigarette hung from between her red chapped lips. She was shaking her head, ash flying. 'Take these.' She nudged towards me a shiny loincloth and two miniature triangles held together by a fragile thread. 'Put them on,' she ordered flatly. She stared openly at my hair. Her gaze was a cruel concoction of pity and repugnance. 'Who did that hair for you?'

'My sister,' I confessed.

'Bloody awful it is too.' Sandy filed her talon-like nails for a few minutes while I changed, then turned to scrutinize me in the teeny spangled outfit, shifting self-consciously from foot to foot. 'I've seen worse,' she declared, 'but you won't get away without the Pan Stik.'

'It's OK,' I said, thinking I wasn't going to let Sandy near my face with Pan Stik. 'I'm wearing my own foundation.' It was actually tinted moisturizer but I worried that that mightn't imply enough camouflage for Sandy.

'The Pan Stik is for your arse and thighs, love,' she pointed out. 'Turn round,' and with rough, well-practised movements, she began to paint me with a thick layer of it. It was several shades darker than my skin. 'You won't notice the colour under the spots. We won't worry about your face for the moment, Paddy's not really interested in that.'

Thank God, I thought ruefully.

Sandy walked me back up to the stage where some fuzzy synthesizer music was playing, vying for dominance with the muffled noise of a radio coming from the back. She fiddled with a few switches, her long nails scraping against the plastic fittings and suddenly the stage was bathed in a bright blue light. 'Now, you'll have to dance for about three minutes,' she instructed me. 'Then Paddy'll tell you whether you're in or not.' She sucked on her cigarette. 'He'll probably get Marge, that's the ball and chain, to come out of the office and have a gander as well. She makes the decisions here.'

That's when the doubt really kicked in and I started to tell myself that changing nappies might've been a good career after all. I had a sudden picture of Elise and my father sitting out front, *not* the proud parents. My father had his head buried in his hands while Elise wrestled with the higher question of why I would want to do this to myself. The dye had burned my hair and it seemed to be sizzling on my head. 'Oh, *God*,' I moaned, cursing Perri for persuading me that this was a normal thing to do and cursing myself for having needed no persuasion whatsoever. But the prospect of a paid job was dangling seductively before my eyes so somehow I found the strength to stand my ground and resist the urge to run.

'Right, get on with it,' Paddy shouted. A plump, black-haired woman in a clingy catsuit was sitting beside him, a bundle of what might have been voluptuousness around twenty-five years ago. It had to be Marge, I guessed. He snapped his fingers. 'One, two and a one, two, three.' He grinned at Marge. Marge scowled. I guessed Paddy loved these auditions and auditioned as many girls as he thought he could get away with.

Vehemently, with all the fervour of someone who hadn't prayed for years but suddenly needed an almighty favour, I prayed that this would be one of those moments that I would look back on and laugh about, that I might one day see the funny side. I knew it might take thirty or forty years.

In jerking fits of rhythmic discomfort, I swayed, shimmied and crawled across the small stage, tossing my head from left to right, silently begging for the music to stop or a fire bomb to come through the front door. I felt like a scraggy circus pony. Needless to say, the boundless confidence that had spurred me on only that morning on the rooftop terrace was gone. If only I'd given this a bit more *thought*, I silently screamed at myself.

'Use the pole,' Paddy bellowed usefully from the first row. 'Use the feckin' pole.' He looked despairingly at Marge.

'Yeah, get up off your hands and knees. It's not beggin' out on O'Connell Street you are.' She sniggered delightedly. I was sure she thought she could do better. In fact, I was sure she *could*.

Hesitantly, I pulled myself up off my hands and knees, black dust stubbornly sticking to my bruised knees, and undulated sheepishly over to the pole, where I slid up and down, my head hanging low, in such acute embarrassment that Paddy had the mercy to interrupt me. 'We've seen enough of ya, ya useless tart. Get back to the convent and don't be wasting our time.'

Mortified, I ran off the stage and stumbled down the hall to the dressing room, eerily empty without Sandy. I flung the shiny loincloth on to the floor and quickly pulled on my clothes, desperate for escape. Paddy and Marge were nowhere to be seen as I bolted through the main door, not caring who heard the sobs of self-pity that erupted forcefully from my throat.

When I burst though the door of her room Perri

hopped up from the bed. 'Well, how did it go?' she asked enthusiastically.

'I've just had *the* most humiliating experience of my entire life,' I wailed, looking for sympathy. 'Look at what they did to me.' I whipped off the skirt and showed her the thick layers of paint.

'Mud treatment?' she asked, confused.

I shook my head. 'Pan Stik.' I wailed again. 'Oh, Perri, I didn't feel like an *artiste*, I felt like a slag. And what's more,' I gulped, 'I didn't even get the job. I was useless. I was humiliated. Hu-*mil*-iated.' I flung myself on to the bed.

'Calm down, calm down,' she said soothingly, rubbing my hair. I could nearly hear the brittle strands snap. No job, no money, no education and, now, no hair. 'Tell you what,' she cooed, 'tomorrow I'll see what I can do to get you a few hours' a day teaching English and we'll get some brown hair dye and forget that all this ever happened. OK?'

'OK,' I nodded miserably, somehow believing that it was possible to believe that this never happened. 'I'm very grateful. And if we could just not tell anyone about it.'

'OK,' she agreed. 'Let's go down to Whiskers and see if he can recommend a strong cure for humiliation.'

8. A Run-in with Father Des Murphy

Friday, 13 March 1998
Saturday, 14 March 1998

As we were saying goodbye to the rest of the family on the previous Sunday evening, after the lengthy Chinese homecoming meal, Perri and I outside her flat in Ranelagh, Belle leaned out of the window of the battered estate car and promised she was going to come up to Dublin at the weekend. Ballyhilleen was only a bit more than a three-hour bus journey away heading south but she managed to make it sound like an event similar to man walking on the moon. I think she was afraid that she might miss something if she didn't come up. I didn't know what that could be. I certainly wasn't going to be making a fool of myself any more. I was finished with that kind of juvenile behaviour.

We'd listened to her excited shouts as the car rolled down the road, until her voice was nothing more than muffled radio interference. The rumpus drew Whiskers Barry from his three-legged throne behind the bar of the Tipsy Tinker. He stumbled outside and stood on the cracked footpath in full battle stance, arms akimbo and nostrils flaring, cursing Belle and all related to her. Thankfully Perri and I were able to creep unnoticed into the building through the door behind him while he lost himself in his ranting.

It was now Friday evening, and Perri and I were sitting in the kitchen of the flat, sipping cups of tea and noisily munching a packet of Jaffa Cakes, waiting for Belle to arrive off the bus and seeing who could fit the most Jaffa Cakes into their mouth at the same time. Perri won. She got four in. So, not only had she sleeker hair than me and golden skin but she also had the bigger mouth. Inexplicably, Perri seemed to think that this was something to be proud of. She tried to explain why it would be but she still had the four Jaffa Cakes in her mouth and there was only a messy eruption of crumbs.

We swapped contented glances. Perri and I were getting on like a house on fire and I'd been back six whole days by then.

The humiliating incident down at the Foxy Lady was nearly forgotten, or at least, never spoken about and I'd wisely dyed my hair back to a darker brown colour, and while it didn't look exactly natural, it was a lot better than the technicolour disaster I'd had. There were still streaks of saffron, but they were really only noticeable when the naked glare of the sun hit my head or under a bright light. Needless to say, I avoided both like some slimy creature from the underworld but it wasn't always easy.

A few of Perri's friends had called around one

evening and they thought the saffron streaks were mad. Perri made me stand under the kitchen light so they could see them properly. One of them *fancied* me. I swear she *actually* fancied me. I knew when someone fancied me because it didn't happen that often, so I couldn't help but notice, and *she* fancied *me*. I was *terrified*. But secretly pleased that someone had liked my hair.

On Monday, I was going to start a three-week contract with Vocab-U-Lary, the language school where Perri worked. She'd wangled me an interview with the school director, John Dooley, earlier in the week, in an attempt to whitewash the Foxy Lady incident. He didn't really *want* another member of the Flanagan family working for him but Perri had hinted that she might feel it a 'moral obligation' to tell Mrs Dooley the true extent of Mr Dooley's forty-five-year-old assistant's hands-on role.

The affair was stale news around the school and everyone knew that his wife knew all about it and was frankly relieved that it spared her the sporadic carnal encounters with her husband that had once punctuated her life, or so Perri told me. But John Dooley lived in a different world. He was convinced of his cleverness in keeping his bony mistress a secret for all these years. Anyway, I got an interview the next day.

Sitting confidently behind his imposing desk, with no idea that he looked like an impostor, John Dooley said he had two simple questions for me, adding slyly that even a Flanagan should be able to answer them.

I panicked, fearing he was somehow related to Paddy at the Foxy Lady Club and had learned of my exotic hostess audition, the fiasco I'd condemned to my past even if it wasn't that far past. They both had the same wax-like skin and stretched plastic smirk. They *could* be family. Everyone was related to everyone else one way or another in Ireland. I collapsed against the hard plastic back of the chair. My white shirt, my special *interview* shirt, donated by Perri, stuck to my skin in clammy anticipation of his two simple questions.

His first question was whether I had a TEFL, Teaching English as a Foreign Language, diploma, a prerequisite for teaching at the school, an absolute necessity, he'd stressed. Hesitating for only the briefest moment, I smiled confidently and assured him that I did. It was a blatant lie, of course. I had no diplomas.

The second question, he'd said, was of a more personal nature but it had to be asked, it had to be asked. Mr Dooley was studying his thin fingers closely, counting the lines and folds, looking suddenly uncomfortable and even more of an impostor behind his impressive desk.

I folded my arms and crossed my legs, curling into a defensive huddle, in front of him.

He coughed, started to speak and stopped again. Then, he reached across the cluttered plane of his desk, taking a blank sheet of paper. He glanced at me, he couldn't have failed to notice the confused expression, and scribbled a few words on the sheet, in a jerky scrawl. Folding it neatly in two, he leaned across the desk and handed the pristine piece of paper to me.

I thanked him, as you do, and opened the note. On it was the question he couldn't bring himself to ask. *Do you share your sister's sexual orientation?* I scribbled one word, that word naturally being *no*, on the same bit of paper and handed it back to him. It struck me that John Dooley was probably the kind of man who had sex through a carefully cut hole in his bony mistress's nightie.

Of *course* I knew what was on John Dooley's mind. He was remembering his embarrassment when the parents of Bea, Perri's Spanish student, had called him to say their daughter had come home boasting that she'd been involved with her teacher in Ireland. They thought he should know. And they were furious.

Dooley calmly told them that their accusation was absurd, he told them that he didn't employ *those* kind of people and sent for Perri to deny the accusation, leaning back in his chair awaiting glorious vindication. John Dooley would love glorious vindication. But Perri, in true flamboyant, righteous style, had gleefully admitted to her extra-curricular activities and reminded a by now very perturbed Mr Dooley that they were both over the legal age of consent and it was really none of his business.

Mr Dooley found the whole incident very distasteful and Perri was fired on the spot for breaking school rules – the rule had been added there and then.

A few days later, Elise swooped down on Dublin

to the aid of her victimized little girl, who had been badly mistreated at the hands of a narrow-minded *monstre* hiding behind a desk in Dublin. Elise paid an unsuspecting Mr Dooley a visit. I'd pitied him fleetingly when I heard about this.

She came dressed in her most chic of finery, pure, undiluted Gallic charm oozing from every well-scented pore, her accent more pronounced than ever, as happens when she becomes emotional. Sweeping into John Dooley's office, Coco tucked safely under her arm and hissing, she demanded to know why he was making such a fuss over a little kiss or two. She confided in him that her daughter had told her all about his skinny *floozy*, this was a word she'd picked up from my father, and accused him of trying to destroy her daughter's life because he felt threatened by her *sexualité*. Elise assured him that she would allow no person to do that.

Mr Dooley shrank back into his chair, and did not doubt what she said.

My father was sitting outside in the car, illegally parked, with his old policeman's cap on his head and the engine running. Elise emerged triumphant and they took off back to Ballyhilleen. Perri got her job back the next day.

'I wouldn't have asked that question, except for the little problem we had with Perri that I won't mention, but I'm sure you know all about.' Dooley ventured an explanation, looking pained that he couldn't just write it and push it across the table to me.

Frankly, I desperately needed the job, needed the money, so I didn't point out to him that the school also took on boys, should my urges, which were more or less fully reserved for the deity, propel me towards the students. 'Of course, I *fully* understand that, Mr Dooley.'

'Well, then, that's that.' He rested his forearms on the desk. 'I think you'll do nicely, Lola. You begin on Monday at two o'clock. Three hours every afternoon, Monday to Friday, for three weeks. Here are the details of your group. Fifteen French students from the Paris area.' He handed me a brown manila envelope. 'Read them carefully. You'll need to do up a study plan and course outline by Monday, but then you'll have no problem doing that with a top-notch TEFL diploma under your belt, will you?' Plastic smirk.

'No problem at all, Mr Dooley. I've had a lot of experience in that particular area,' I lied again. What else could I say? I couldn't really mention that I had absolutely no experience, didn't even have much of a proper education, and had reverted to teaching only after failing an audition to become an exotic hostess. I didn't even *want* to teach. I supposed I *could* tell him that I could change a nappy in fifty-five seconds flat, using only *one* hand.

'Now, Lola, this is a total immersion programme and even though you speak fluent French, I would ask you to speak only English with the students and it would be better if they didn't know you spoke

French at all and were obliged to converse in English. Do you have a problem with that?'

'Absolutely not, Mr Dooley. Total immersion is fine by me.' I'd have to remember to ask Perri to explain the total-immersion concept. I was sure it had nothing to do with holding their heads under water. 'What level are the students?' That sounded like a fairly adept question, I congratulated myself.

He looked pleased that I'd asked the question. 'Basic,' he told me.

I smiled at him. 'Well, that's always more of a challenge.' Good, I reckoned, I should be able to teach them *something* if they knew nothing.

'Yes, indeed. You'll need to use various pedagogical methods and techniques to stimulate the learning process. You have individual reports on each of the students in the envelope I gave you.' He stood up and held out his hand, indicating an abrupt end of the interview.

'Thank you very much for your time, Mr Dooley.' Could you please explain what 'various pedagogical methods' there are and, eh, why a 'learning process' needs to *be stimulated*? 'I look forward to starting on Monday.'

'Goodbye, Lola. Please convey my best wishes to your mother. A formidable woman.'

Belle arrived at the flat flustered and flushed. The fresh flowers that decorated her long plaits had wilted during the bus journey to Dublin and were hanging limply in her hair. She gushed breathlessly, sounding even younger than twenty-two, as she explained that Kevin Brady had driven her to Dungarvan, a few miles from Ballyhilleen, to get the bus to Dublin in his new, second-hand Ford Escort that he had bought the day before. Belle said that he was driving past the school and had come to a screeching halt when he saw her rushing out of the gate, struggling with her weekend bag and the picnic basket Elise had packed for her to bring to Dublin in case we weren't eating properly, which we weren't.

A group of Belle's seven-year-olds, dishevelled after a day of boisterous play, had been waiting outside and cheered merrily as Belle climbed into the car. Belle was absolutely convinced that she was fulfilling an important role in society, educating the little people of today to become a caring, giving and happy generation. She patiently taught them to share their toys with each other, to express their anger by other means than biting and to appreciate the majesty of the fields. These were lessons she felt older generations had lacked. I thanked God her power was confined to a small classroom in Ballyhilleen.

Inside, the car smelt of cow manure. A wonderful, earthy smell, Belle claimed. Kevin worked on his father's farm, a man of the land and the only man for Belle, only he didn't know it yet, though our whole family had known for years.

'Well, spit it out. What did he talk to you about?'

Perri asked, opening the third pack of Jaffa Cakes and pouring Belle a cup of cold tea.

Belle smiled blissfully. 'He said he was going to Cork next week with his father to buy some new machinery,' she enthused, picking the dead flowers from her hair.

I forced two Jaffa Cakes into my mouth. I still couldn't match Perri's four. 'And?' I muffled. Neither I nor Perri could match Belle's enthusiasm.

'It's not very far from Ballyhilleen to Dungarvan,' Belle replied defensively, her trembling voice portraying her disappointment. 'We didn't have *that* long together.'

'It's *fifteen* miles of conversation all the same,' I argued.

'I think I talked too much,' she finally admitted. 'I was *excited*. I told him that I'd moved into the Portakabin at the end of the garden . . . because I wanted to be independent.' Belle was very proud of this. 'And I was telling him *all* about it and suddenly we were there.'

I swallowed the biscuits in my mouth. 'In other words, you didn't let him get a word in edgeways during the whole time.'

'No, Lola,' Belle insisted, her voice shaking even more. Kevin Brady was always an emotional subject. 'I was working myself up to asking him if he wanted to drop by sometime for a cup of camomile tea and it took a lot of talking to get there.'

Perri groaned.

'Anyway, Dad ruined everything,' she spluttered. 'Kevin will never come near me again. We passed him on his bike down by the chicken factory and when he saw me in the car with Kevin, he shook his fist so hard I thought he was going to topple off the bike, and then he shouted, "Leave my daughter alone. You're nothin' but a common thief." I was mortified.' Belle looked heartbroken.

'What did Kevin say?' I wanted to know. My father strongly disapproved of Kevin Brady. He'd caught him trying to leave O'Sullivan's off-licence with a bottle of whiskey in his pocket that he hadn't paid for. Kevin was only thirteen at the time but my father had never forgiven him. He was a man of the law and there was no excuse for criminal behaviour in his books.

Belle's eyes were watering. 'He just said, "Your father has it in for me. I wouldn't mind but that one time with the whiskey is the only run-in I've ever had with the law." That's what he said. He didn't even get mad.'

We all nodded. Kevin Brady was the quiet kind.

Perri made a suggestion. 'Listen, if you *do* ever manage to sneak him in without Dad seeing him, would you ever give him something other than *camomile* tea?' She sighed in exasperation. 'I mean, you *do* want him to come back again, don't you?'

'Yes,' Belle sobbed. 'OK.'

Some things hadn't changed, I discovered. Belle

still spent as much time emptying her bladder through her eyes as before I'd left home.

The next morning, we had breakfast on the roof terrace, under a cloudless, cold sky. We ate the soda bread that Elise had sent up with Belle, which made a welcome change from the usual packet of Jaffa Cakes. Afterwards there was the usual bickering about who would shower second. Nobody wanted to go first because they would have to clean the water from the kitchen sink out of the shower tray with bits of yesterday's beans floating around in it and nobody wanted to go last because there would be no hot water left.

In the end, Perri decided she'd go second because it was her flat so I had to go first and Belle went last. When she finally emerged from the bathroom, smelling like one square mile of lush rainforest, Perri and I both gasped loudly in dismay. Belle was dressed in a long skirt that looked suspiciously like it was made of brown sacking.

'Is that a *sack*?' I gaped.

'It's *recycled* sacking,' she answered primly. 'And if more people made an effort to use recycled material, the earth wouldn't be in such danger.'

'All my clothes *are* recycled . . . from Oxfam,' Perri snorted indignantly.

Belle caressed her sacking lovingly.

Perri and myself exchanged worried glances.

'It's a great idea,' I said tactfully, wanting to avoid

a time-consuming show of tears. 'Let's go. Are you going to put on any shoes, Belle?'

'No,' she replied stubbornly, and we left it at that.

As it was such a fine day, we'd decided to walk to St George's Arcade, a nirvana of second-hand shops, cosmic jewellery stands and organic foodstuffs near the city centre. We were meandering down a side-street, near Grafton Street, when Belle stopped to examine the soles of her feet for the first time since she'd left the flat. They were black with dirt and the odd cigarette butt was stuck to them creating a lumpy pattern.

'It's fine to go barefoot in Ballyhilleen, Belle, but you're really not proving your allegiance to saving the world by trampling around Dublin with bare feet,' Perri preached. 'You could find yourself with a syringe stuck between your toes.' Dublin had a serious drug problem. Perri hauled Belle through the door of a small shop we happened to be passing.

I followed them. Inside, the shelves were crammed with all sorts of junk and at the back of the shop, a wire basket full of brightly coloured flip-flops. Perri knew all the strangest of places in Dublin.

She steered Belle towards the tall wire basket. 'Cheap and cheerful,' she insisted, and forced a pair of flip-flops into Belle's hands.

Once more outside, we stood squinting at the sudden bright light after the darkness of the shop. I knew my saffron highlights would be glistening majestically in the glare of the March sun but there was nowhere to hide. Three pint-size teenagers with shaved heads and pierced noses, dressed in identical baggy tracksuit bottoms and oversized sweatshirts, brushed by.

'Jaysus, would ya look at da bloody bag-lady?' the last one sneered, as he rubbed himself against Belle.

Perri stepped out in front of him and clipped him firmly on the head. 'That'll teach *you* some manners.' Perri's tolerance of jeering males was low and I wasn't surprised that she'd hit him.

He looked Perri up and down disdainfully, taking in the pinstripe trousers and jacket, the chunky brogues. 'Wha' da hell are you?' he asked brazenly, spitting at her feet, with well-practised accuracy.

Determinedly, I stepped in for I *knew* how to deal with children. I'd done it for long enough. 'Look here, you little gouger,' I grabbed hold of the tip of his ear and squeezed hard, 'take your scrawny arse and – '

'Excuse me,' a man's serious voice interrupted me. 'You girls should really be ashamed of yourselves.'

Abruptly I let go of the ear and spun around. Standing before me was a young priest, dressed in black trousers, a black shirt and traditional white collar. He was wearing a fitted leather blazer. A look of open disgust clouded his handsome features. '*What's* going on here?'

The fella whose ear I'd been pinching burst into tears. 'Father, thank God you came along. I was on me way to visit me granny in the ho'pital when these three hopped on me for no reason.' His shoulders were shaking and enormous sobs racked his thin frame, as he threw himself into his performance with the utmost conviction.

'That's not true, Father,' Perri shot indignantly. 'He was verbally abusing us, *verbally abusing* us. Do we honestly look like we go around harassing kids?'

The priest cautiously eyed Belle's recycled sacking and strong arms, a result of lugging feisty seven-year-olds around the school playground. Then, his eyes homed in on my saffron highlights, gleaming brazenly in the sunshine. 'Well,' he said, looking at me intently, '*you* look like you could have a fierce temper.'

'That's out of a bottle, Father,' Perri assured him.

'I swear, Father, they were beatin' me up. I'm always gettin' bullied 'cos I'm so small. I'm so little.' He was practically shrinking before my eyes such was the potency of his charade. The tears were beginning to disappear and his two friends were shouting at him to hurry up. They called him Razor. 'Me friends are callin' me. I'm off. Ta for savin' me skin.'

The good-looking priest held out an arm. 'Before you go, I want to give you my name and I want you to get in touch with me if the bullying doesn't stop.' The handsome priest, genuinely concerned about Razor's vulnerability, pulled a card from his back pocket and gave it to him. 'The name is Father Des Murphy and this is the number you can contact me at.'

Razor scurried down the street. Behind Father

Murphy's back, we saw him toss the card into the dry gutter.

'Are you a *real* priest?' Belle blurted.

Father Murphy eyeballed her. 'And why is that *so* hard to believe?'

The colour rose in Belle's cheeks. 'I didn't mean to be rude, it's just that you're kind of young and, em, kind of, em, good-looking for a priest.' She was twisting her plaits around her fingers and looking at him with barely disguised admiration.

A smile creased his face and laughter lines appeared around his eyes. He looked like he laughed a lot. 'I'll take that as a compliment.'

'You can indeed,' I gushed, before I could stop myself. My fingertips tingled with the urge to touch him, just to pat him on the arm, or stroke his neck, something, anything.

Perri nudged Belle. They both stared at me. There I was, standing beside Father Murphy, reeling back and forth on my heels, smiling up at him and tapping one hand lightly on my chest, as if warding off a dizzy spell.

'Well, ladies, I'll bid you farewell. God bless.' He sauntered off in the same direction as Razor had only a few minutes before.

I strained my neck to catch a final glimpse. 'Father Des Murphy,' I sighed. 'Now there goes one fine man.'

Perri corrected me flatly, 'One fine priest, I think you mean, p-r-i-e-s-t.'

'He can save my soul any day.'

9. The Return of JP at Twenty-nine

It was a quarter past nine in the evening and we were
thoroughly exhausted from a day spent roaming the
streets of Dublin, trawling around the shops and
trying to spend as little as possible, which I had come
to the conclusion was surely more tiring than spending
money. We escaped on to the rooftop terrace to savour
the night stillness. The light had long faded and the
air was chilly. I knew we should've been complaining
about the cold but we'd grown up in an old house
where there were nearly more draughts than bricks so
the cold just washed over us like a familiar friend.

Belle was sitting on the bench with her feet plunged
into a basin of hot water, contentedly wriggling her
toes, steam rising to her knees. She was trying to mend
the damage that traipsing around the city, first barefoot and then in a pair of cheap flip-flops, had done
to the soles of her feet. They were red and tender and
I was surprised because Belle went barefoot a lot but
she swore to me that the streets of Dublin were harder
on the feet than the streets of Ballyhilleen.

Perri was kneeling on the ground in front of her,
measuring generous helpings of red wine into tall-
stemmed glasses that had been a present from Elise,
after Perri had once offered her wine served in a jam

jar. Elise had been speechless. Money had been scarce at the time, that had been Perri's excuse.

I was lying on the bench with Belle, my head resting in her lap. The three of us were still getting on. We were either maturing or it was the calm before the storm, I mused. We were all still getting on. I'd been there nearly a week. In my hand, I held the unopened brown envelope that John Dooley had given me at my interview with the details of my group of students. Perri assured me that I had nothing to worry about as far as teaching was concerned. It was a cinch. Those were her words. *A cinch.* Her only advice to me was to insist that everything was an exception to the rule and therefore could not be explained. I imagined hordes of students swarming around Europe thinking that ninety per cent of the English language was made up of exceptions to the rule as Perri's legacy to the world.

When we'd arrived back at the flat earlier in the evening, Whiskers Barry had pounced on us as we sneaked past the pub door trying to will ourselves invisible and avoid a confrontation with him. 'Come 'ere, ye three whores,' he'd roared, spotting us immediately and slipping out from behind the bar, scuttling precariously towards the door. 'Yer brother was here lookin' for ye. Botherin' me was what he was doin', with all his feckin' questions.' Whiskers had a near empty pint glass in his hand, and the dark liquid inside splashed in angry waves against the side of the glass as he swayed.

The three of us looked at each other with raised eyebrows and simultaneously turned to Whiskers. 'JP?' we chorused incredulously.

Surely not, I figured. It was hard to believe. JP had been living in London for years and only came back to Ireland to visit when Elise complained bitterly enough that she never saw anything of him. He rarely turned up unexpectedly. The last time had been years ago with Tom Hutherfield-Holmes in tow. A high-flying job and a busy lifestyle left little room for spontaneity. Well, not the kind of spontaneity that would foster a trip home but that would allow, perhaps, for a spur-of-the-moment weekend skiing trip to the Alps.

Whiskers was staring at Belle's sacking. 'That's what I'm tellin' ye.' His eyes never strayed. 'Anyway, what kind of name is that, for feck's sake?' he scowled. 'JP sounds like a brand of tea-bag.'

Haughtily Belle informed him, 'It's short for Jean-Pierre,' trying to hide her discomfort at the way he was devouring her.

Whiskers snorted sceptically. 'Humph, short for Fairy Poofter more like.' After a few hiccups, he wobbled towards Belle, who quickly took several stunned steps back. ''Tis a grand rig-out you're wearin',' he proclaimed. His eyes were glazed but there was no mistaking his blazing admiration for Belle's soft curves, the very ones Elise thought we all had too much of. She would be horrified to think that Whiskers Barry of all people might covet them.

Belle looked even more uncomfortable. 'Did JP say when he'd be back?'

'I'm only tellin' ye what I know,' he told us sourly. 'And how many more of ye are there in that family? I'm sick to the teeth of the lot of ye. I told him I'd set the dogs on him.'

Perri tossed her head and stormed past him. 'You don't have any dogs, Whiskers,' she shouted back at him, over her shoulder.

'Yeah, you were out,' he swiftly retorted, then swivelled once more towards Belle and growled, 'I hope you don't grow up to be like your sister.' He turned towards Perri's disappearing figure. 'Ya flamin' whore, ya!'

Sitting up on the rooftop, several hours later, JP having still not reappeared, Perri was giving us her logical explanation and blaming JP's apparent apparition on Whiskers's inebriated imagination, when suddenly the doorbell rang. The low tinkle was barely audible up on the rooftop but Belle heard it and scampered to her feet, spraying water everywhere and hurtling my head from her lap. She dived nimbly through Perri's bedroom window and arrived back beaming several minutes later, with JP in tow, who was looking uncharacteristically sheepish, clumsily hauling his tall frame through the window.

'I don't *believe* it. What are you doing here?' Perri asked, stunned and probably a bit annoyed that Whiskers had been right all along.

'I heard Lola was back and thought, what the hell,

the whole family may as well be here.' He tried to be jokey, but his voice was flat and his expression pitiful, his usual cockiness cast aside. He looked as if he hadn't had a decent night's sleep in a month and his ordinarily impeccable clothing hung loosely in deep creases.

Instinctively, I knew something was amiss and I was worried. 'What's wrong?' I asked, quietly and seriously. It was easy for me to dislike JP when he was being arrogant and selfish, but like this, well, it was much harder. Anyway, I didn't really dislike him. We had had a special bond since we were children. I was sure it was because we'd spent three years together on our own before the arrival of Perri. At times like this, when he needed me, the bond quickly resurfaced and all the other times when that bond had been difficult to find were quickly forgotten.

He rubbed his bloodshot eyes and answered, in a deflated tone, 'Everything.'

Perri grew more concerned then, too. 'What's happened, JP? Tell us,' she urged him.

He slumped on to the bench, leaving the three of us standing in front of him, forming a protective sibling arc and frowning down on his slouched shoulders and the back of his head as it tilted forward and he hid his face in his hands.

'God,' he muttered, 'I'm in a right mess. A complete gobshite, that's what I am . . . I just walked straight into it,' he continued, and shook his head in disbelief. 'And they took as much as they could get . . . They got everything in the end . . . everything I had.' He was looking up, his eyes pleading with us to understand whatever it was he was trying to tell us but none of us had figured out what that was.

His words made no sense to me – to any of the three us, if the blank expressions on either side of me were any indication. To be honest, I was a little bit relieved that I wasn't the only one who didn't seem to understand what was going on. Briefly, I wondered if this – this breakdown had something to do with the financial markets of which I knew nothing.

Belle sat down beside him, wrapped her arm around his shoulder and, with the persuasive, sympathetic voice of someone used to reconciling bloodied, warring seven-year-olds, said gently, 'Why don't you tell us what happened from the beginning? Take your time, we're listening.' She sounded so persuasive that I almost began to tell the story of my own incertitude about life at that moment and the feelings of inadequacy that had been plaguing me like restless ghosts for some time.

But instead, intuitively knowing that no short explanation would explain the scale of JP's distress or his bewildering retreat to Ireland at the age of twenty-nine, I sat down in front of the bench where Belle and JP were huddled together and said nothing. The Dublin night lights cast dim shadows on the unlit rooftop, where we sat in near darkness waiting for JP to begin.

He took a deep, unsteady breath. 'Well, here goes.

Friday night, two weeks ago, I was in the mood to party, you know.'

Nothing shocking there, I thought, JP partied most nights of the week. I glanced at Perri and Belle and could tell from the casual look on their faces that they were thinking the same thing.

'Tom and myself decided to go to a private men's club he knew. An *exclusive* private club,' he clarified, seemingly for me, 'in case you've got visions of a seedy, lap-dancing place.'

And indeed a vivid image of the Foxy Lady did leap to mind, right after a startlingly perfect picture of Tom Hutherfield-Holmes had flashed before my eyes and a shiver of excitement had run through me at the mention of his name, despite what had happened the last time we'd met. The humiliation I had suffered at the Foxy Lady, at the hands of the slime-encrusted Paddy, only came second to the humiliation I'd felt the last time I'd met Tom in London when I was visiting JP. It was an incident I had hoped never to remember. But from time to time it crept up cruelly on me, from the dungeons of my memory, to remind me of the fool I'd made of myself. I'd thrown myself at him and he'd thrown me back ... in the nicest possible way. But it still stung. At least had he been cruel I could've labelled him a bastard and consoled myself with the misguided but comforting thought that he'd mourn his loss some day. But what could I fight the 'niceness' of his rebuke with?

'It's a bit of a tradition in the city, these clubs, like

mass on Sundays in the Flanagan house,' JP continued, grimacing wryly, which reminded me that I hadn't been for months and I wondered if I could track down where Father Des Murphy said Sunday mass.

JP continued soulfully, 'Anyway, we went to a few of the wine bars first, then Sid suggested we stop off at his place for a few drinks before Tom and I headed off to the club.' He turned to Perri. 'You remember Sid, don't you? You knocked him off the bar stool when you came over to London last year.'

'Oh, yeah,' Perri said, with a degree of distaste. 'Then *I* was the one who got kicked out when he'd been the one hassling me. There's no justice in this world,' she concluded.

JP looked about to commiserate but decided to continue with his story. 'Anyway, Tom and myself headed back to Sid's pad.' He looked at us. 'One of those things that seemed like a good idea at the time. We left about an hour later, fairly plastered by then.' He paused for an instant, combing through his memories. 'I can remember taking a cab,' he recalled, 'and Tom was arguing with the taxi driver about hunting.'

Belle shook her head grimly. 'I don't agree with hunting.'

'And what do you think you're doing to Kevin Brady?' Perri inquired, of Belle's keen pursuit of the farmer's son.

'The difference is,' Belle parried, '*he* would be happy to be caught. I know it.'

I smiled at her conviction.

JP coughed loudly to get our attention, suddenly eager to get on with his story. It just seemed to be taking so long. 'Go to the club. More champagne. Then,' he declared dramatically, 'trouble reared its ugly head ... well, actually, the head wasn't ugly, quite distinguished, in fact.' He laughed ruefully and I thought I could decipher a note of hysteria. Elise usually laid claim to any bouts of hysteria in the Flanagan household and JP's lapse had me very anxious about what was to come.

He had our full attention now. 'This – this gentleman,' he spat viciously, leaving me in no doubt that we weren't really talking about a true gentleman, 'struck up conversation. I just thought it was chit-chat – jobs, the usual. Then he suggested that we go on with him to a club he knew for a little behind-the-scenes gambling. I felt a lucky streak coming on, didn't I?' He shook his head again as if he couldn't believe it himself.

'But what did Tom say?' I asked him. Even though Tom had led a fancier lifestyle than JP, he somehow seemed more grounded than JP and I would've been surprised if he'd let JP get into anything that he thought unwise. But maybe I was placing too much responsibility on Tom's shoulders. Maybe I just wanted him to be better than JP.

'Fair dos to Tom,' JP granted, and I was relieved, 'he was dead set against the idea and tried to talk me out of it. He swore there'd be trouble one way or another . . . and, wouldn't you know, he was right. But

I ignored all the advice and left with this man I'd just met in his gleaming Jag.'

'Talk about thick,' Perri scoffed.

'You think I don't know that?' JP replied, in a tortured voice, and shrank back on the bench.

Belle threw Perri a condemning look. 'Go on. What happened then?' she encouraged JP.

'When we got to the club I was a bit worried because I didn't have that much cash on me but my *new friend*,' he nearly choked on the words, 'said he was very well known there and would personally vouch for me.' He looked at us sorrowfully. 'I have to say I did get a bit of a kick from it at the time.'

Perri threw her eyes up to heaven. 'I'll bet that didn't last long,' she commented, in the voice of one who knew all there was to know about short-lived thrills.

'No, it didn't,' JP agreed. 'Inside were tables with every kind of game you could imagine, packed with gamblers. I was feeling lucky . . . and drunk.'

'But you said you had no money,' Belle reminded him. 'How could you pay for anything?'

'Huh,' JP grunted. 'I had a ten-thousand-pound credit in no time, personally guaranteed by the guy who'd brought me there I can't believe it now. How could I have been so thick?' He rolled his head in his hands. 'Anyway, during the next hour or so, I lost a bit, won a bit. The thrill of winning thousands of pounds in one turn of a wheel was addictive,' he rushed to tell us. 'I wasn't even thinking of the money

I could lose. A little while later, I was about five thousand pounds down.' He nodded sadly.

This was beginning to sound ridiculous. 'How could *you* have been so stupid?' I asked him. 'You, of all people, with a proper education.'

'I've asked myself the same question a thousand times, Lola.' His fingers raked his hair almost savagely. 'Suddenly, the ten thousand quid was gone. Every fucking penny of it.'

I gasped. It was such a vast amount of money to me that I couldn't understand how it could all disappear in such a short time.

'But I was still sure I could win big,' he continued. 'You know, cover my loss and more. More chips miraculously appeared in front of me . . . the big win was just around the next corner . . . I could feel it . . . I placed all my chips on red thirteen,' he chanted, as he replayed the scene in his mind. 'The wheel seemed to turn for ever. Then, I lost everything. Funny how I remember that it was red thirteen, isn't it?' he asked us.

Belle stared at him, her mouth gaping open, while Perri looked at him sadly, as if she had known this day would come. I'd never seen her looking so prim.

'I don't believe it,' I cried. 'Tell me you're joking.' I was trying to imagine what my father's reaction would be to having a gambler in the family. I knew my father was proud of me for all the innumerable tiny reasons why a father is always proud of his little girl. But it was the stories of JP's successes with which he regaled the crowds on a Friday night in O'Sullivan's. He would be devastated.

The hounded look returned and he stretched out his hands. 'I wish I was, Lola. I really wish I was.' His voice dropped. 'The guy that had brought me there steered me away from the table and we went into a small room with two leather couches on either side of a roaring fire . . . It reminded me of the flames of hell. And suddenly everything changed. He pushed me on to the nearest couch and explained, in very clear terms,' he told us, in case there was any doubt of the severity of the situation, 'that I would have to pay back the money, including interest and the five-thousand-pound joining fee, which was the first I'd heard of it.' JP searched each of our faces and came to rest on mine. 'I was shocked. It came to thirty thousand and he wanted it within forty-eight hours.'

Belle, Perri and I stared at him incredulously, lost for words, something that rarely happened.

'I mean,' he continued, when none of us spoke, 'I tried to explain that I didn't have that much available cash, you know. I asked him if I could repay him in instalments and he just laughed.' JP imitated the chilling laugh for us. 'Definitely the kind of laugh that made you understand he wasn't amused and the situation wasn't funny at all, if you see what I mean.'

I did and I shivered.

'Then I remembered that my annual bonus was due. It would cover the amount I owed several times over. You can't imagine how relieved I felt . . . but it wasn't due quick enough. I only had *forty-eight hours* to come up with the cash.' He calculated quickly. 'That's two thousand eight hundred and eighty minutes.'

'Is that legal?' Belle wanted to know. 'It can't be,' she decided.

'Belle,' JP stated, 'the whole set-up was illegal.'

Belle looked appalled.

'Anyway,' JP declared, 'it got worse. These two goons came in, and if they wanted to intimidate me, they did a good job, I can tell you that. Both of them had shaved heads and looked like they belonged in a maximum-security prison wing. Apparently, these two were the "business associates" who would collect the money. No funny business. And you know what? I had to agree. Funny business was definitely not an option.'

'Yeah, you were right. Better not mess with *that kind*,' I agreed, too. My experience of *that kind* was coloured by a fertile imagination and the television, and I had no trouble imagining what they might be capable of. They would have no compunction whatsoever about rearranging JP's face for him. And while I often thought it unfair that JP had seemed to get the whole family's share of good looks, I certainly wouldn't want that changed at the hands of bloody madmen. Most of the time, anyway.

'Well, it was a little late for that, not messing with that kind.' He sighed. 'Needless to say, I didn't sleep a wink, trying to work out how I would get the money. I mean, I didn't have enough time to do anything.' He spread his hands uselessly. 'The two goons who'd escorted me back to the flat told me they were well connected in the police force and would find out immediately if I got the police involved . . . Anyway, that would have been pointless. I'd had far too much to drink and the whole evening was a haze in my mind. I didn't have any names and I certainly didn't have an address for the club.'

'Sounds like a pro job to me,' Perri decided expertly.

For once in his life, JP readily agreed with her. 'Yeah, I figured they must do this quite often. I walked straight into it.'

Belle was on the verge of tears for him. 'You poor thing,' she sobbed, 'what an ordeal.'

Her sympathy was the catalyst JP needed to tell what happened next because there was more to come. 'The problem I was faced with was finding the cash at such short notice and I completely panicked . . . That's when I had the most stupid idea I've ever had – though at the time it was as if God Himself had thrown me a lifeline.'

'Did this bit take even more stupidity than the first bit?' Perri demanded, and I felt her sympathy for JP waver.

'Afraid so,' he reluctantly admitted. 'Eli Jones, that's where I work,' he explained needlessly – I'd heard so much about Eli Jones over the years that I could tell you where the coffee machine was on every floor, 'is investing heavily in new technology. There is stiff competition in the marketplace, and we hoped that by using state-of-the-art technology we could gain a slight edge, you know. It was a major cash investment. The risk was that this new technology hadn't been tested in real-life situations, though it had been successful in simulated scenarios.' He registered our blank looks but proceeded anyway. 'We needed to move quickly, ahead of the other financial institutions. If the technology worked out, we would pay handsomely for exclusivity rights and, hopefully, use it to our advantage. But we needed to assess its exact capabilities beforehand, and quickly.'

I scrunched my nose and JP decided not to dwell too long on the finer details of this technology. 'As head of the department, I'd been cleared for immediate access to funds and expense approval. I didn't need higher authorization for sums under a hundred thousand pounds.'

Suddenly Perri folded her arms across her chest. She'd guessed where this was heading, though I still hadn't.

'I could invent a problem with a supplier or contractor who was suddenly demanding a thirty-thousand-pound cash advance. Everyone knew the tight deadlines we were working against and the pressure we were under to take a decision on this one. True, it wasn't a regular occurrence, but if I carried it off, well, no questions would be asked.'

'You didn't?' I gulped, as I finally realized what he'd done.

'I *had* to,' JP justified himself. 'So, on Monday

morning, after another sleepless night, I went to see the finance guys and told them that I needed thirty thousand for a supplier who was demanding a cash advance on some equipment.'

Perri responded quickly, 'The balls of you!'

JP accepted the reproach without comment. 'When the finance guys said it would take a few days to process, I leaned on them a bit and stressed that someone would be answerable to the big bosses for missing deadlines, implying big trouble for them. A few phone calls later and the money was on its way. Hey presto.'

Perri's voice was loud and harsh. 'Hey presto, my arse!' I wasn't sure why she was being so indignant. It wasn't as if Perri wouldn't be capable of coming up with such a plan herself. I reckoned that she was upset because she knew that once he'd told us the story we would somehow become involved, too.

'Perri, I *know*.' JP sounded exasperated. 'You think I'm proud of what I did? You think I *like* sitting here and telling you this? Believe me, I am in a living hell.'

None of us doubted him. Well, I certainly didn't.

'There's just the end to come, now,' he said. 'As I sat in the flat that night, waiting for the other fuckers to arrive, I couldn't believe that I had just defrauded Eli Jones of thirty thousand pounds. My God, I'd practically taken the money from them. But my intention was to take the money from my bonus in four weeks' time and go back to see the finance guys.' He paused thoughtfully. 'I'd planned to say that as a sign of his good faith and renewed interest in doing business with us, the supplier had returned the cash. Yeah, yeah, I know what you're thinking, all a bit unbelievable, but I really thought I could make it work ... at the time I was desperate. It seemed straightforward enough.'

'All going well, that is,' I ventured, because he wouldn't be sitting here in a heap if all *had* gone well.

'Yeah, all going well,' he expelled a long sigh, 'which, *of course*, it didn't.'

Perri raised her eyebrows. 'How did they find out?'

'They didn't exactly "find out", more like were told. I told them myself. You see, my conscience stepped in.' JP didn't sound pleased with his conscience. 'I decided to explain the situation to my boss. I had a really solid relationship with Frank and I thought that he'd appreciate my honesty.' He nodded convincingly at me and I nodded back, a lot less convinced. 'Especially considering that if I'd kept my mouth shut, I would probably have got away with the whole thing,' he added quickly. 'I'd also be paying the money back so I figured I'd be reprimanded and the chances of a promotion would disappear for a few years.'

I really couldn't believe that he'd decided to confess to taking the money and expected just a light rap across the knuckles. 'That was a bit optimistic, I think.'

'It sure was, Lola, but I was in a very fragile state of mind, don't forget. Predictably, Frank went ballistic and immediately called a meeting of all senior directors.

What I did was wrong. No excuses. I should have explained the situation to him straight away.'

'Bummed out on all fronts, eh?' Perri said.

JP ignored the jibe. 'I knew then that everything was *not* going to work out as planned. Appreciating honesty and overlooking a theft are two very different things. And I should've known that.'

'They are,' I said.

'The senior directors called for my immediate dismissal and voted to press criminal charges. There was also some talk of cancelling my bonus but that would mean that I couldn't pay the money back so they dismissed that idea. Very sporting of them.' He laughed ruefully. 'They pay me so I can pay them.'

Belle put her arm around his shoulder. 'Are they going to press charges?'

'Have you skipped the country?' Perri accused.

'No, no, no,' JP insisted. 'Despite his none-too-pleased views on what I'd done, Frank fought my corner and persuaded the directors to accept my immediate resignation and not to press criminal charges, on the proviso that I sought professional help for my *gambling problem*. You see, he didn't believe that such a fiasco could be the result of *one* gambling expedition. They think I have a gambling problem!'

'Well, do you?' I had to ask. It was all so unbelievable.

'No.'

'Oh, how the mighty have fallen,' I heard Perri sing happily.

'Fair enough, I deserve that,' JP conceded. 'But I have no intention of telling Elise and Dad the truth. I'm going to say I needed a break. Dad would be devastated to know that he had reared a thief.'

'Well, he's already got a lesbian and a failed exotic hostess in the family,' I told him. I looked at Belle in her crumpled sacking but didn't add her to the list as she'd been tearful enough since JP had arrived.

'I've got it,' Perri shouted suddenly, jumping to her feet. 'Tell them you were being sexually harassed. It'll guarantee you lifelong sympathy and they won't want the gory details.'

JP smiled genuinely for the first time that evening. 'That's a bloody brilliant idea, Perri.'

'Sure, 'tis a grand idea,' slurred Whiskers Barry, who must have let himself into the flat with the spare set of keys he always denied having and was peering at us through Perri's bedroom window. Bulging out of his shirt pocket were a pair of knickers. They were *mine*. 'Can I be sexually harnessed, too?' he wanted to know.

I prayed that he hadn't left me a pair of his underwear in return for mine. There was only so much I could take in one week.

10. The Confession in Ballyhilleen, and Kevin in the Portakabin

Friday, 20 March 1998
Saturday, 21 March 1998

My father peered quizzically at JP from across the kitchen table in Ballyhilleen, swirling his whiskey around in a tumbler that he rocked loosely between his thumb and forefinger. He took a long sip and smacked his lips. 'Explain it to me again now, son.'

JP settled back into his seat. 'I really don't want to go into all the details. I just don't feel up to it,' he lied, in a pained voice. 'It's too raw.'

Elise's forehead creased with genuine concern for her only son. '*Mon pauvre chéri*,' she whispered.

As JP's accomplices, Belle, Perri and I sat solemnly around the table, each of us shifting restlessly in our chairs at the enormity of the lying going on but knowing that there was no other way.

I was waiting for my father to leap from his chair and shout, 'I know a cock 'n' bull story when I hear one. You lot are lying through your teeth.' Then he'd turn angrily to JP, eyes flaring. 'You good-for-nothing,' he'd hiss, pointing a rigid finger at JP. 'You were fired for helping yourself to your employer's money. I know you were. Old Flaherty down in the village has a second cousin who lives in Dublin and her next-door neighbour's daughter is married to an English fella whose brother works for Eli Jones and I know everything there is to know. *Hah!*' It could happen.

It was the Friday evening after JP had turned up at Perri's flat and we had unanimously voted to go with him when he went down to Ballyhilleen the following weekend, enduring the three-and-a-half-hour bus journey, to explain his return. Lying barefaced to Elise and my father about why JP had fled London made me feel uneasy. But it was nothing compared to the unease that I would feel sitting here telling them the awful truth.

'Well, I just can't fathom it.' My father sighed, perplexed. He turned to look at Elise. 'I never thought I'd live to see the day that a fella would be forced to leave his job because some woman was up to her funny stuff.'

Eager to add authenticity to JP's story, Perri joined in. 'Oh, yes,' she gravely assured my father, 'there's even a big Hollywood film about it, sexual harassment.'

'Yeah, there was an awful lot of rumpus at the time,' I told him, pausing to look at him seriously. 'Stirred up quite a few hornets' nests.' I gave him a knowing look and prayed that he didn't look back at me too hard and catch me lying. He'd always been fairly good at that.

He was stunned. 'Is that so? Who was in the film?'

'Michael Douglas,' Perri answered.

My father raised the whiskey glass to his lips and paused. 'A good actor, that fella. Was it fact or fiction?'

This seemed to be an important question. 'Oh, I think it was based on fact,' I lied.

He faced JP and drained the last of his whiskey. 'And this woman who came after you was one of the big bosses?'

'Yeah, right up there at the top,' JP replied earnestly, and I nearly believed him myself.

My father slammed the glass on to the table. 'The cheek of her. And no one would believe you when you tried to complain?' He was outraged.

'No, they all thought I'd lost the run of myself completely.'

'And so you left?'

'Yes.'

'Well, I'll be damned.' Standing up, he walked over to JP, put a firm hand on his shoulder and said, 'Good to have you home, son. It's a shame about the circumstances.'

JP looked relieved that he had crossed the hurdle. He stood up and gave my father a clumsy bear-hug. My father looked enormously pleased. He steered JP from the kitchen and they headed off to the pub to wet JP's return.

When the door shut behind them, Elise exploded. '*La pûte . . .*'

Belle flung her hands up to her mouth in shock. 'Uh-oh, you're not allowed say that word,' she chastised Elise. 'That's a bad word and you know it.'

'Well, that's what this – this creature, this thing is, a *whore*,' Elise declared unabashedly. Her hands were gesticulating madly, her painted nails angry flashes. 'Poor, poor JP. Imagine how he must be feeling. I tell you, I would like to go to London and find this person.' Furiously she began to wipe the doors of the kitchen cupboards with the tea-towel she'd grabbed off the drying board, obliterating imaginary smudges.

Perri and I exchanged worried glances, knowing full well that Elise would not hesitate to make the trip. She would savour a confrontation with the woman she thought had ravaged JP's life.

'Well,' I said calmly, 'I don't think that would be a good idea.'

Elise stopped rubbing momentarily to question me. 'Why not?' She was waiting for a good reason, hand poised in mid-air.

Because, I thought, there's a nasty surprise in store for you in London. 'Because,' I reasoned, 'JP wants to put this whole thing behind him.'

Unconvinced, she began rubbing again.

'Yeah, why else do you think he decided to move back to Ireland?' Perri added.

Belle joined in the persuasive tirade. 'As his mother, you are the *one* person, the *one* person who can really help him.' Elise loved to be reminded that she was JP's mother.

Belle grimaced behind her back.

I decided to play the trump card. 'Besides, if you go over and sort it out, JP would end up going back to London. Whereas this way he stays put in Ireland,' I told her coolly.

Three anxious faces stared at her back waiting for her reaction.

She stopped her scouring and turned around. 'Yes, of course,' she purred. 'I hadn't thought of that.' A triumphant smile crept across her face. 'He stays, then. I won't go to London. *Voilà*.'

'Well, thank God for that,' I exclaimed, feeling very relieved.

I opted to sleep out with Belle in her brightly decorated Portakabin at the bottom of the garden. This had been her home for two months now and she reckoned that she had come a long way in her quest for independence. She was hoping the next step would be a home shared with Kevin Brady, who lived in blissful ignorance of Belle's higher plans for him.

The Portakabin had a main living area, a separate bedroom and a small bathroom with a tiny cubicle shower, toilet and sink. I was still sharing a bed with Perri in Dublin while JP stayed temporarily in the box room, so I was enjoying the Saturday-morning solitude of Belle's lumpy settee. The week had been exhausting. Trying to get my life together was exhausting. Having no money was exhausting. Trying to get everyone else's life together as well was exhausting. It was all exhausting.

On Monday, I had shown up at the language school one hour early for class to hand over the rough course outline I'd invented to John Dooley, expecting him to throw it back at me and call me a fraud. But he'd glanced through it and seemed satisfied. The next fifty-five minutes were spent pacing around the small classroom waiting for my group of French students to arrive and wishing I could change their nappies just because that was something I *knew* how to do. I spent the time dreading their arrival and at the same time wishing they would hurry up so I could get on with it.

Just before two o'clock, a bunch of adolescents streamed into the room, chattering in French and exuding a young Parisian sleekness. I motioned for them to be seated and breathed a sigh of relief when they obediently took their places.

As Perri had helpfully suggested, that morning we would kick off with a brief introduction, a what's-your-name-waste-time game, as she called it. Perri was a constant source of useful hints. She didn't take teaching English seriously, she was just whittling away the time while she figured out how to get her singing career off the ground. I took it very seriously. I didn't have a fall-back career now that my exotic-hostess plans had turned sour. And I had no money.

I turned around to write on the board and heard a young voice say in bewilderment, '*Dis-donc, t'as vu les fesses qu'elle se paye?*'

I stopped writing and spun round, ready to let them know in French that the size of my arse was of no educational concern to them. Then I remembered John Dooley's insistence on total immersion and his firm order not to speak French. I had to content myself with a stern reprimand. 'No talking, please,' I chided severely, wanting to establish right from the start who was in control. That person being me.

As they glanced disapprovingly at each other, pursing shapely French mouths and raising perfectly groomed eyebrows, I could easily read their thoughts – they had been lumbered with the English teacher from hell, for three whole weeks. It would be hell for me too, I wanted to assure them.

On the board, in plain readable lettering, I wrote FIRST NAME and below that I wrote SIRNAME.

'Excuse me, I thought surname was spelled with a U not an I?' A voice challenged, in a *perfect* American accent.

Shocked, I stopped writing, keeping my back and infamous arse to the class. I honestly could not remember if he was right or not but there was no way I could admit to that. I mean, there was no way I could admit that I wasn't sure how to spell the blasted word. I closed my eyes and wondered how Perri would cope with this situation. Boldly, that's how I decided she would cope. I whirled around and informed them, 'That's how we spell it in *this* country.'

The question came from a dark-haired youth, sitting in the middle row, with his desk pushed beside the adjoining one and his arm flung casually around the clear-skinned, pretty girl beside him, gazing at him with tender admiration.

'Why are you speaking English?' I demanded.

He replied brazenly, 'Because you don't speak French.'

'I mean,' I said drily, 'why are you speaking p-e-r-f-e-c-t English?'

'I lived in the US with my parents for ten years. My father worked for an American company.'

'Right.' I took this in. 'And what are you doing in *this* class for those with only a basic knowledge of English?' I only wanted the ones with a basic knowledge because they had so much to learn that I couldn't help but teach them *something* – even if it was inadvertently.

'I wanted to be in the same class as Clarisse.' He looked passionately at the girl in his hold.

Clarisse smiled coyly at her beau.

I reached across the table for my attendance list and chirped, 'What's your name?'

'Laurent.'

My finger ran down through the names quickly finding one, a Laurent Ducros. 'Well, Laurent Ducros, we'll see about that.'

His face carried an unfazed expression, as if doubting my authority. A mistake to be sure, I fumed.

In four quick strides, I reached the classroom door. 'I'm going to have a quick word with the director and I'll be back. You, Laurent, start packing.'

Fifteen minutes later, I walked back into the classroom with a newly found intense dislike of John Dooley. 'The client is king,' he'd told me adamantly, and refused to let me uproot Laurent to another class.

I argued that he had deliberately lied about his level of English on his report and would learn nothing in my class. 'The client is king,' he had repeated. Then I threatened him with the wrath of Laurent's parents if they discovered that their son had enrolled himself for kindergarten English. This seemed to spark a reaction. Dooley solved the problem by pulling out his thick student file and placing a call to Madame Ducros. Madame Ducros thought Laurent should be left where he was happiest. This meant he stayed put and the client stayed king.

My face masked by bitter defeat, I stood at the top of the room with my shoulders back and hands firmly planted on my hips. 'Right, Laurent, *I* have decided you can stay.' I forced out a smile. 'Now, move your desk away from Clarisse's,' I hissed. 'This is a classroom not the back row of the cinema. You are expected to behave like an adult here.'

With a flash of inspiration, I landed Laurent with the job of writing new vocabulary on the board. This saved me from any more possible spelling mishaps and kept him disgruntled and busy.

Perri was disbelieving when I told her about my fluent English speaker. 'You won't get away with *anything* with him around,' she assured me, and took several steps towards me until her face was just inches away from mine and I couldn't dismiss what she was about to say. 'I pity you,' she mouthed, which pretty much summed up how I felt about myself.

Thursday afternoon, half an hour before the end

of the class, John Dooley came bursting through the door. Everyone turned to stare. He was clearly agitated. 'Lola, I'm in a bit of a fix,' he panted, a shaky hand straightening the wide-bottomed tie that had gone askew, 'and your sister has very kindly offered both your services.'

Behind him, Perri stood grinning importantly, brushing invisible specks from her suit collar.

'The French ambassador has invited me to a small gathering over at the embassy this evening,' he said, in a low, intimate tone implying that the French ambassador was a close friend.

I looked at him dubiously from under a raised eyebrow.

'But I can't go,' he all but wailed. 'Mrs Dooley is scheduled to see a specialist about her, em, her little problem and I'll never hear the end of it if I'm not there. I clean forgot all about it.' He grimaced. 'Mrs Dooley's appointment, that is, not the ambassador's little do,' he explained. 'It starts at five on the dot so you'll need to be on your way immediately.'

'Mr Dooley,' I began coldly, 'you seem to forget that I have a classful of students, or a classroom of kings, as you yourself might say, they being clients and all.' The opportunity to appear righteous didn't often present itself and I grabbed it. 'We have another half-hour to go before class ends.'

Mr Dooley snapped back to reality. He clapped his hands loudly. 'Class, you're all dismissed early. Dismissed early today. Irish tradition on certain Thursdays,' he bellowed. Mr Dooley had never actually taught and believed the louder he spoke the better the students would understand. 'Class dismissed,' he roared again, even louder than the first time, when no one moved.

They gazed at him, baffled. No one moved until Laurent translated. Then, the classroom was empty within seconds to the sound of scraping chairs.

'What do we have to do once we get there?' I asked warily.

'Just don't make a show of me,' he replied. 'Or yourselves for that matter.'

A short while later, Perri waved Mr Dooley's invitation in front of the security guard at the embassy who beckoned us through. We followed the sound of clinking glasses into a large reception room filled with well-dressed people who, at a glance, appeared to be mostly members of the French community.

Perri looked fine in her trouser suit, apart from the T-shirt beneath which read, 'A dog is for life. A student is for the summer.' On the other hand, I looked sorely underdressed in navy leggings and a plain white long-sleeved vest top. Fine attire for three hours in a sticky classroom but a disastrous choice for early-evening drinks at the French embassy.

Accosting a passing waiter, who was balancing a well-polished platter of champagne-filled glasses, we helped ourselves to two glasses each, one for each hand, and quietly hid in the corner, remembering Mr Dooley's instructions not to make fools of ourselves.

This was no 'little do', as John Dooley had called it. From the safety of our corner, we reckoned there must have been over a hundred people present. Black-suited waiters with aquiline noses, carrying silver platters of champagne and intricately delicate canapés, discreetly spanned the room. This was *formal*.

My attention drifted to the top of the room, where a distinguished-looking gentleman took the podium and, in the confident, smooth tones of a seasoned speaker, asked for everyone's attention. The room was hushed immediately.

The French ambassador welcomed his guests warmly and thanked everyone for being present. Over the next ten minutes he spoke earnestly in French of his desire to build a lasting relationship between the people of France and Ireland, and his deep commitment to supporting Irish business. Not that it seemed to need supporting, these days, I mused.

Perri stifled a yawn and I nabbed two more glasses of champagne. The waiter was unimpressed with my mode of dress. 'Does Mademoiselle usually wear her underwear for official engagements?' he sneered, in a whisper.

'Mademoiselle doesn't usually wear her underwear at all,' I answered back, and sipped my champagne thinking some people carrying trays had a real nerve considering they only carried trays.

He walked away.

'Plonker,' Perri said.

'Yeah.' I nodded.

I opened my mouth to lambast him a bit more now that I knew Perri would agree with me when she poked me violently in the ribs and said, 'Ssssh, listen!'

The French ambassador was saying, 'John Dooley is from the Dublin-based language school, Vocab-U-Lary, which has taught English to more than three thousand French students over the last fifteen years.'

'What's going on?' I mumbled.

Perri shook her head. 'Dunno. He's saying not to forget that the Irish people have a beautiful language of their own . . .'

'Wha'?' I yelped.

'As many French people present here this evening have never had the opportunity to hear Irish spoken and its beauty,' he continued, 'I have asked Mr Dooley to say a few words in his native language.' An efficient-looking assistant with rolled hair rushed up to the podium and whispered in the ambassador's ear.

Mr Dooley had conveniently forgotten to mention his little *arrangement* with the ambassador to us. Well, there would be no speech in Irish now that he wasn't here, I promptly decided.

The efficient-looking assistant scuttled back to her position. The ambassador smiled. 'Unfortunately,' he announced, 'Mr Dooley is not able to be present with us this evening due to unforeseen circumstances.'

Perri and I breathed a sigh of relief. Even with the best of intentions, neither of us would have been able to stand up and deliver an impromptu speech in Irish. Apart from the occasional word to confuse foreigners abroad, we hadn't spoken a full sentence since we left secondary school in Ballyhilleen. And I'd left Ireland before it had become a cool thing among young people to be able to do. Just another thing I'd missed out on. The revival of our own language.

'However,' our host continued, 'he has kindly sent two colleagues, whom he has assured us would be very pleased to oblige. Ladies and gentlemen, please welcome,' he glanced at a small white card, 'Lola Flanagan and Perri Flanagan.'

The guests clapped enthusiastically.

Perri choked on her last mouthful of champagne and dropped her glass.

I giggled nervously.

Rows of heads swivelled our way. We'd been spotted.

'Lola, Perri, please do come up.' The ambassador beckoned, smiling congenially in our direction.

The obliging crowd parted to clear a path to the podium. We had no choice but to advance forward, as slowly as we could without actually coming to a complete standstill.

'Now what?' I muttered frantically to Perri.

'Dooley, the *bastard*,' she hissed, and licked her lips nervously. 'What can you say in Irish?'

I answered truthfully. 'The Our Father and that's it.'

She groaned. 'Well, it's got to be that, then.'

'No way,' I said vehemently, beneath my breath, smiling at a guest who had offered their hand in greeting. 'There are surely other Irish people here who'll *know.*'

'You don't have a choice,' she insisted. 'I'll make up a translation.'

We were within a few paces of the podium. '*You* do the prayer and *I'*ll do the translation,' I argued.

'No way,' she quibbled, and shot in front of me to reach the ambassador first. 'Pleased to meet you, sir,' Perri greeted him. 'My sister will speak and I'll translate.'

A wave of nausea nearly sent me reeling.

'Very well, I will leave you the podium.' The ambassador beamed. He switched on the microphone before stepping down.

I paled and my mouth went dry.

Perri and I stood side by side, leaning into the intimidating microphone. I coughed tensely. Several guests flung their hands over their ears. I hoped against hope that there would be no Irish guests there, and if there were, I hoped they had been educated outside of Ireland and had never learned to say the Our Father in Irish. 'Ár n-Athair atá ar neamh,' I began warmly. Our Father who art in Heaven . . .

Perri translated. 'It is an honour for us to be here today.'

'Go naomhthar d'ainm: Go d-thigidh do ríogacht,' Hallowed be thy name, thy kingdom come . . .

Perri nodded in agreement with my words and then said boldly, 'My sister and I have strong links with your country.'

And so we continued right to the end of the prayer.

The smiling ambassador expressed his gratitude with a nod, as he took to the podium once more.

We fled fast.

There was a loud banging on the door of the Portakabin. The insistent knocking roused me from my journey through the past week. Still lodged in a nylon sleeping bag, I hopped over to the door. 'What are you doing here?' I shouted. I didn't mean to shout or appear rude but the sight of Kevin Brady in our backyard, at a quarter past nine on a Saturday morning, did beg the question to be asked. My father would kill him if he happened to look out of the window.

'Belle was telling me the other day when I gave her a lift to the bus that she'd moved out of the big house . . . and I was just passing by . . . and thought I'd drop in to see how she was getting on,' he said casually. 'I've finished the milking.'

He was risking his life if my father caught him. 'Well, *Kevin*, come in, why don't you?' I said loudly, hoping Belle would hear and have time to calm herself. I knew his sudden appearance would send her reeling to a place where sanity was forgotten. Stepping out of the sleeping-bag, I shouted over my shoulder, 'Belle, *Kevin* has popped by to say hello.' I couldn't have stressed *Kevin* any more than I did.

'Chance would be a fine thing,' Belle chortled, in disbelief, from the bedroom.

I smiled at Kevin and shrugged. 'You try.'

'Eh, hiya, Belle,' he shouted, in the direction of the bedroom, leaning forward on one foot.

The bedroom door swung open with a bang and Belle had to prop herself up against the frame. 'Kevin!' she exclaimed hoarsely.

'I'll put the kettle on.' I yawned, as both of them looked at each other, wondering what to say next. Standing watching the water spurt from the small tap, I noticed a thick rope, knotted at the end, hanging to the side of the sink. Giving the rope a mighty yank, I asked Belle what it was.

She rushed over. 'Don't pull it whatever you do!'

'Too late. Sorry.'

She put her hands to her face. 'Oh, no.'

Kevin stood by in bewilderment.

'What's the fuss anyway?' I asked, confused.

Her shoulders fell. 'It's security,' she gushed miserably. 'Dad installed it. The rope runs all the way to the house and rings a bell. It's for emergencies. He'll be out here any minute, gunning for an intruder.' She turned to Kevin, crestfallen. 'You've got to go,' she implored him. 'He'll kill you if he catches you here.'

'Right you are,' Kevin said, and promptly disappeared.

Belle and I stood and watched him vanish deftly around the corner of the house, just as my father, clearly agitated, came thundering towards the Porta-kabin, a barefoot JP in tow – albeit reluctantly. 'Right,' he shouted. 'Where's the gouger?' He was short of breath and red in the face.

'Sorry, Dad,' Belle moaned. 'False alarm.'

JP and Dad turned to go back into the house, my father relieved and JP muttering obscenities beneath his breath. I followed them and glanced back over my shoulder long enough to catch a glimpse of Kevin Brady bravely slipping back into the Portakabin.

At that same moment, JP's mobile phone leaped to life in the pocket of his shirt. My father eyed the small black object suspiciously. 'Could never fathom those things,' he told me, as I hobbled up the garden path behind him.

'Tom, me old mate,' I heard JP roar joyously into the phone. My heart bolted. He could only be talking to *Tom Hutherfield-Holmes*. I'd first met him when he'd visited Ballyhilleen with JP but I'd seen him once more since then, in London, and the thought of our last encounter made me blush furiously. I was torn between dashing straight into the bathroom where I could splash icy water on my face to put out the flames that licked my cheeks and neck or hiding behind one of the bushes to glean what I could from their conversation. There was no choice, really. I waited until my father had disappeared indoors and crouched behind an overgrown hedge, balancing unsteadily on my hunkers but determined to hold my position. Just listening to JP talk to Tom made me feel part of his world, closer to him. I had tried to forget how good I'd felt being around him the last time we met in London because I knew that it wasn't the kind of something I could ever hope to build anything on. And while my brain could understand the logic in what I tried to tell myself, my heart couldn't, or just plain wouldn't, for no other reason than it was doing what it wanted to do. Hearts can be such traitors at times.

11. The Weekend in London

April 1997

As a grand gesture, because he was well capable of such grand gestures when it suited him, *and* because he'd completely forgotten to get me a Christmas present a few months earlier, JP offered to pay for me to come to London for a weekend, adamantly insisting down the phone line to be given this chance to display his generosity.

He didn't really need to insist as I would've readily agreed to the trip at the mere hint of an offer, always eager to escape nappy-changing for any length of time and to any destination on offer. The usual destination was Ballyhilleen. But London was far better.

In eager anticipation, I packed a weekend bag before I even knew when I'd be going. JP had assured me that he would look into it straight away. Fortunately, the ticket arrived a few days later so I didn't have that long to wait, pulling my toothbrush out of the bag every time I needed to wash my teeth, puzzled at how it always managed to make its way to the bottom between brushes.

Enthusiastically I ripped open the envelope to find a ticket for a return journey in First Class on the Eurostar. I inhaled deeply, feeling an inexplicable sense of self-importance stemming from the plain white envelope when I read that I'd be travelling First Class. Me, Lola Flanagan, in First Class, I mused happily. In my mind, it was a measure of JP's affection for me. In his mind, it was probably a brilliant way to offload some of the guilt he felt at having forgotten my Christmas present.

Needless to say, I'd never travelled First Class before. Because of the meagre wages, we nannies tended to take the cheapest seats going. I had never travelled on the Eurostar before either, which I figured would be like rolling along the sea-bed in a state-of-the-art canister with windows. The novelty and pretentiousness of travelling First Class appealed to the bit of me that liked to be made to feel important but never was. All the same, I was slightly nervous about all sorts of watery ends I imagined I might encounter during the trip when we actually crossed beneath the Channel.

The ticket arrived with the early-morning post on Wednesday, only four days after I'd spoken to JP, and it was booked for that very Saturday morning, coming back on Sunday evening. Saturday wouldn't come fast enough and Sunday would surely come too soon.

Early Saturday morning, after hours of waiting impatiently for the sun to rise so that I could get up too, I climbed on the yellow tram that ran to the Gare du Midi, huddling my weekend bag protectively between my feet, away from the professional pick-pockets who rode the trams for a living, and trying to flash the First Class ticket I held tightly at every opportunity.

Strangely, I seemed to forget constantly at what time the train was leaving and had to look at the ticket and check every five minutes or so, closely examining back and front, waving it about proudly. I even caught myself asking the person sitting next to me to check the departure time for me, and *class*, in case I'd misread the information all along. They seemed to think it was strange, too, as they eyed me warily with more than a hint of disbelief.

The Eurostar terminal at the Gare du Midi was an impressive add-on of glass and steel that made the old part of the station look even older. I arrived with just enough time to find my place in the right carriage and sat down, impressed by the spacious seating arrangements around me and the tiny reading lamps on every table. It was empty except for a well-dressed older couple, who sat across the aisle reading the morning newspapers in a kind of well-practised silence.

A dark-haired steward immediately offered me a choice of champagne or orange juice. I took a glass of both. Then, a second of each, and a third and fourth one of champagne. If this wasn't what everyone did when travelling First Class on the Eurostar then I could never have guessed, as he quietly handed me glass after glass, his face a mask of professional nothingness. I was determined to dull my senses before we began our journey under the sea. Besides, to refuse free champagne, already poured into glasses, would've been extremely bad manners, an unforgivable waste.

The train left the station punctually at the time indicated on my ticket, and double-checked by me at least ten times and one other person too, and we reached Lille in less than an hour, by which time I'd had both the continental breakfast and the traditional English breakfast served by the same steward with the expressionless face. By then I was wishing that some sort of emotion would register on his face as the less expression he showed the more I felt obliged to manifest, as I grinned in abundance and thanked him profusely each time he walked past my table.

We left Lille as soon as the handful of people waiting on the platform had boarded the train. My eyes grew heavy and the gentle rocking of the train, with the warmth subtly infused into my body by four or five glasses of champagne, lulled me into a lazy sleep until a sudden loud voice announced that the train was about to enter the Channel Tunnel, in three different languages, as if we would be taking three different entrances. This was it. I gripped the sides of my seat, waiting for the roar of the sea, and glanced nervously at the couple sitting across the aisle who rustled their newspapers simultaneously and smiled calmly.

It went dark outside, my ears popped faintly . . . and then . . . then nothing. That was it. I was almost disappointed that I felt no sense of danger, no matter how hard I tried, nor could I see the sea menacingly close in around me in a final curtain call. Either the champagne had dulled my senses, as I'd hoped it would, to the point where they couldn't be relied on as senses any more, or this was not the fearsome experience I'd expected. There were no fish swimming past the window, seaweed did not grapple ferociously with the iron works of the train, and face masks and oxygen tanks didn't come tumbling from the ceiling. Maybe First Class was less of an adventure than sitting in Economy, where I'd usually be ensconced, and where I was sure that by now I'd have been offered a pair of courtesy rubber fins and instructed to kick like mad to get to the other side.

It was over in less than twenty minutes and we surfaced in England, with not a drop of sea-water dripping from any crack or crevice.

JP was waiting for me at the taxi rank outside the Eurostar terminal at Waterloo. He had his back to me but sensed my approach, swivelling round to face me, a broad grin lighting the handsome features that needed no lighting whatsoever.

'Lola,' he shouted delightedly. 'There you are.'

'Here I am,' I agreed happily.

He looked over my shoulder. 'Tom!' he called out. 'Tom! Here she is.'

I turned to look in the same direction and saw Tom Hutherfield-Holmes striding towards us from the door into the terminal, waving as he deftly wove a path among the other passengers.

'Here I am,' I repeated, as soon as he'd reached us. He hadn't changed since I'd first met him two years earlier in Ballyhilleen when JP and himself had cut their visit short to escape the quietness of the village, which wasn't really quiet at all. I'd been immediately taken with him that time, somehow liking how I saw myself when I looked through his eyes. A part of me wondered whether his instant appeal had anything to do with the assumption I'd made the moment I set eyes on him that someone like Tom Hutherfield-Holmes would never be attracted to someone like Lola Flanagan. The very same part of me had wondered, too, if this simple equation might not be at the root of my obsession with priests. A safe obsession because it could only ever be one-sided.

I gathered my weekend bag into my hands and flung the strap across my shoulders. Immediately Tom stepped forward and insisted on carrying it, managing to make me feel like it would be an absolute pleasure for him. From the corner of my eye, I saw JP look at him sceptically, but I knew that if the girl walking between them had been anyone other than his sister, JP would've pulled the bag from Tom's hand and insisted on carrying it himself.

We took a taxi to JP's apartment, which was on the top floor of a modern building that overlooked the river. Inside, it was sparsely furnished in leather and steel, and the odd ethnic-looking object, shaped like different internal organs, that seemed to serve absolutely no purpose other than to break the hardness of all the leather and steel. The whole place reeked of money.

We'd barely arrived when Tom decided enthusiastically that he would take us for a sushi lunch. I wasn't keen on the idea, never having eaten sushi before, but I didn't like to appear too unsophisticated to swallow raw fish so I clapped my hands appreciatively, seal-style, and made the favourable noises I figured would be expected of me. Tom slipped a small mobile phone from the pocket of his jacket and walked to the far side of the room to call a taxi.

'Why don't you just do a quick omelette here?' I suggested to JP, in an urgent whisper once Tom was far enough away, eager to escape raw fish for lunch.

He looked at me in surprise, placing his hands on his hips. 'What? Cook?' he spluttered.

'Yeah,' I said, nodding encouragingly, 'you know, just something quick.'

The idea seemed absurd to him. 'Here?' He swallowed, looking around him uncertainly.

'Yeah,' I insisted, not understanding his reluctance. I suddenly wondered if this beautiful building had a strict no-cooking policy.

JP pointed to the gleaming kitchen with its angular layout. 'That is *not* a kitchen to cook in,' he told me, puzzled as to why I seemed to think it would be.

The sleek stainless-steel appliances shimmered enticingly, begging to be used. 'They look perfect for cooking,' I argued.

He threw back his head and laughed. 'Lola, *no one* cooks lunch in London,' he told me. 'And I don't cook at all,' he said, with determination, glancing towards the kitchen area again. 'Sure I couldn't splatter all that shiny stuff.'

Tom had finished his call and crossed the room again, flicking shut his mobile phone and popping it back into his pocket in one fluid movement. 'The taxi will be here in fifteen minutes. Shall I show Lola to her room?' he asked JP, who nodded.

'Yes, do,' I readily agreed, eager for some time alone with him, just the two of us, so I could bask in his undivided attention. I followed him down a long corridor with lights that shone upwards from the floor like tiny beams from a subterranean moon, slyly admiring the contradiction of Tom's strong walk with the boyish habit he had of lightly scratching his head as if he was lost. It was a habit I'd only just noticed and it made me want to rush up to him and take his hand reassuringly in mine. Of course, I knew that he needed no reassurance. The quiet confidence I'd first noticed in Ballyhilleen was still there giving him a gentle air of someone who was completely at ease with himself but felt no need to prove it. Quite the opposite to me.

My room was at the very end of the corridor. It was tastefully decorated in umpteen different shades of expensive white. Until I walked into that room, I never knew that there was more than one shade of white.

With a casual ease, Tom threw my bag on to the bed and flopped down beside it, stretching out comfortably, his arms folded behind his head. Foolishly I blushed at the intimacy of seeing him lying on the bed where I would sleep. The perfect planes of the cotton throw were in happy disarray.

'It really is great to see you again,' he said, studying my face with what looked like genuine pleasure, as far as I could tell. I pressed my nails into the palms of my hands to try to stop myself blushing again under his frank regard. Unfortunately, the skin was long hardened from the arduous use of detergent and bleach in Brussels and the effect was . . . well, it wasn't even really an effect, I didn't feel a thing except the tingling of my cheeks.

He continued to look at me as I reddened. 'I've been trying to persuade JP to get you to come over for a long time.'

'Have you?' I asked eagerly, more than a little curious to know why he wanted *me* there, when he could probably have had anyone he wanted, and trying to dampen the flickers of hope that I could feel begin their merry dance. There was nothing special about me.

'Yes, and your mother too,' he added. 'I felt so bad about our short visit last time. The way we rushed off.'

My chin dropped on to my chest with a crestfallen nod. 'Oh.' The flickers of hope brought their merry dance to a complete standstill.

'JP hasn't managed to persuade Elise to come over yet,' he explained. 'But it's wonderful that you're here.' He sat upright and clapped his hands together playfully. 'We're going to have some real fun.'

My voice went flat with disappointment as the chasm widened between the kind of fun he meant and the kind of fun I desperately wanted. 'Yes, I'm sure we will.'

I was sure that JP hadn't even mentioned to Elise that he'd like her to visit him for a weekend, too worried that once she arrived in London he wouldn't be able to make her leave again soon. And JP would be uncomfortable having someone around who knew him too well, for too long, as they might puncture the groomed image of himself that I was sure he'd conjured up for his London friends. That was probably why he'd booked me to leave the very next day, so I couldn't do too much damage.

Tom didn't notice the sadness that had invaded my voice like an unwanted parasite. 'I'll leave you to freshen up,' he suggested brightly. 'Not that you could get much fresher,' he added, eyes twinkling merrily. 'Anyway, take your time. The taxi won't be here for another ten minutes.' The room seemed less white once he'd gone.

Glumly, I looked at my watch and brooded. Ten minutes was *not* the amount of time I took when I was taking my time. No, ten minutes was the very least amount of time I needed. Ten minutes meant I had to rush.

Panicking, I unzipped my bag and pulled out a new outfit I'd bought in a warehouse in Brussels where they slashed the prices. I didn't know what people wore to lunch in London but this was a stretchy black velour tube skirt that came down to my ankles and a matching fitted top with a band of sheer material in the middle. At the time, I'd thought it simple and stunning, an outfit that could take me anywhere, even to lunch in London. Now with only eight minutes left before the taxi arrived, I wasn't so sure. Nevertheless I put it on because I had no real choice and gingerly took a step backwards to look at myself in the mirror hanging on the wall. It was a waste of time. The mirror was a minimalistic six inches from one side to the other. Whatever way I turned I was only half a foot wide.

I grabbed my toilet bag and rushed into the *en suite* bathroom. Dark grey marble and *more* stainless steel. Turning on the water in the Y-shaped stainless-steel basin, I combed handfuls through my hair to dampen the wilful curls. With streams of water dribbling down my forehead, I added a slash of a deep berry colour to my lips. If I'd had more time, and more skill, I would've painted myself a face worthy of one of the great masters for Tom Hutherfield-Holmes. I examined my reflection in the round mirror that hung rigidly from the ceiling on a stainless steel bar. The damp curls were now pressed against my head in obedient waves and the dark lipstick stood out starkly against the paleness of my skin. There was something very vampirish about the reflection that stared back at me. I moaned loudly as there was a knock on the door and JP called out, 'Taxi's here.'

'Be right there,' I answered, pulling on a pair of knee-high black boots.

When I walked into the lounge area, JP greeted me with a look of amusement mingled with curiosity while Tom assured me that I looked very styled. I decided to take it as a compliment but couldn't help noticing that he'd said styled and not stylish, and wondered what the difference was. If there'd been a decent-sized mirror in the bedroom I would probably have known.

The sushi bar was in Soho and I spent the next forty-five minutes artfully washing down bits of raw fish with mouthfuls of chilled white wine. During this time JP and Tom were engaged in heaping lavish praise on the suspicious-looking small parcels that continually arrived at our table brought along by yet another suspicious-looking small parcel dressed in a shimmering kimono that would need to be surgically removed at the end of her shift.

After lunch JP generously decided that he would treat me to a new outfit for going out in that evening – I think he was disturbed by the thought that I might wear the one I had on me. The one Tom had called styled – but not stylish.

The three of us sauntered towards Covent Garden. I walked in the middle but felt myself continually drawn to the side of the path where Tom walked, veering constantly his way and reluctantly hauling myself back to the middle again.

'Lola,' he said, after I'd bumped into him for the fifth time, 'am I standing in the way of your magnetic north?'

JP grinned but thankfully said nothing.

'No, no,' I assured him, making a conscious effort to position myself exactly in the middle of the space between the two of them.

At JP's insistence, we entered a small clothes shop with about five items hanging insolently on each rail – the kind of place I'd never dare enter on my own, or with anyone else I knew. JP and Tom were greeted with hot hellos from the two sales assistants, who seemed to recognize them.

JP propelled me towards the fitting room at the far end of the shop and said to one of the sales assistants, the prettier one, 'Could you pick out some clothes for my sister?'

Both sales assistants looked at me in my black tube skirt and smiled sympathetically.

I was mortified. It was clear what everyone thought of the clothes I'd picked out for myself.

'Yes, of course,' she answered, teasing her raven-coloured cropped hair with her fingers. She made it look like it was a totally different question she was answering.

'We'll definitely be able to help you,' the other one, the thinner of the two, added, wedging her slight frame into their conversation.

The fitting room had two plush armchairs to each side of the louvred door. JP and Tom followed me down to the back of the shop and sat on the chairs while I checked furtively that they wouldn't be able to see in through the painted slats once I was on the other side.

'I think she likes you,' I heard JP tell Tom and I panicked wildly for one moment, certain that he was talking about me, wondering how he'd been able to guess and praying there was a fire exit in the dressing room. But then I saw him throw his head towards the pretty sales assistant and I knew who he really meant. JP relaxed back on to the soft cushions of the armchair expectantly and waited for Tom to insist that it was *him* that she really liked. I knew him well enough to be able to tell this.

But Tom looked bemused. 'Not interested,' he murmured, and smiled at me just as I'd finished examining every slat. He might not fancy me either, I thought gaily, but that didn't stop me liking the way he looked at me. I returned his smile with a shy grin and disappeared into the fitting room to wait for the sales assistants.

JP decided to make it easier for Tom. 'Maybe it's *me* she likes?' he suggested coyly.

Tom chuckled. 'Why would she like you?' he teased JP. 'You're an ugly mutt with a job that's barely one step up from the photocopying machine, the black and white photocopying machine,' he pointed out jokingly, 'and you talk with a funny accent.'

I was readying myself to roar with laughter when JP quickly counter-attacked with a ready-made list of all the reasons why she would like him – and most of them I couldn't argue with, even though I did interrupt with the obligatory grunt of disbelief every now and then.

The sales assistant handed me a bundle of flimsy clothes on dark wooden hangers. I eyed the bits of material dubiously.

Reluctantly I tried on the first dress. It was made from a wispy material and looked far too long for the width. And as soon as I viewed myself in the mirror I discovered that I was right. The dress was cut to flatter a seven-foot matchstick.

'Come out,' JP ordered me.

'No,' I said adamantly, and frantically pulled off the dress over my head before he could make me show myself in it.

The fit of the second dress was no better and the colour was worse than the first. This one was a flesh-toned deathly white, making me look like a specimen that had escaped from the morgue. I stared incredulously at the mirror as I tried hard to convince myself that this could be called fashion. But I just couldn't.

'Come out,' he tried again.

'*No,*' I hollered, cringing at my own reflection.

The next outfit was a powder blue skirt that floated out at the knees and a low-cut knitted top that clung to my chest invitingly. I might be persuaded to leave

the fitting room in this one, I thought, happily examining my reflection.

'Are you going to come out and let us see this one
or not?' JP teased, trying to peep through the slats.

'OK, I'll come out,' I agreed, and pulled on the
knee-high black boots I'd worn into the shop. 'Well?'
I demanded, with a lot more confidence than I felt
walking out of the fitting room.

Tom was trying not to stare at my chest, though I
was willing him to, while JP wasn't even trying. 'You
can't wear that,' he announced firmly, his eyes locked
on the two well-formed mounds tightly encased in
their delicate layer of powder blue. 'And when did you
get *those*?' he wanted to know, sounding very unhappy.

I ignored him and turned to Tom. 'What do you
think?' I asked him boldly, feeling uncharacteristically
daring.

'Fabulous outfit,' he declared appreciatively, and I
beamed at him gratefully.

'She's *not* wearing that,' JP insisted sullenly. 'And
I'm the one paying.'

I scowled at JP, knowing that I could never afford
to buy the clothes for myself.

Tom laughed at JP's stubbornness and warned him,
'If you don't buy them for her then I will.'

I was ecstatic and tried a few different poses in
front of the mirror.

The pretty sales assistant walked towards us with a
pair of very high-heeled sandals swinging from one
hand and a coat with a soft feathery collar hung over

the other arm. Both were the exact same powder blue as the rest of the outfit. 'Try these on,' she suggested helpfully.

I slipped into the fitting room and came back moments later wearing the sandals and coat. I was so pleased with my own reflection, and it was such a novel feeling, that I couldn't drag my eyes away from it.

'That's better.' JP perked up. 'At least, they're covered . . . I mean, she's covered.' He turned to me. 'Do you like it?'

'Oh, yes,' I breathed, hardly able to believe that such an outfit could be mine.

'We'll take the lot,' he decided, swiftly whipping out his credit card and looking enormously pleased at his own level of generosity.

'Thank you, thank you, thank you,' I sang.

Tom needed to make a few phone calls and decided to head directly back to his place once we'd left the shop, me proudly carrying three bags. Well, he wasn't heading back to *his* place, he was heading for a hotel where he was staying for a month while his place was being redecorated. He told me this as if it were the most normal thing in the world to do, which I didn't think it was. I remembered the time in Ballyhilleen when a pipe burst and the whole house needed to be repainted and new carpets put down. We'd all lived in the garage for a week and slept with our coats on.

JP and I went back to his apartment where we emptied our trunk of childhood memories for a few hours. Towards the end of the afternoon I told him I had some shopping to do and disappeared for about an hour.

When I came back I enthusiastically handed over the presents I'd bought for him to thank him for the ticket and the beautiful new outfit, even though I knew he didn't really expect anything. In a vast home-decorating shop I'd luckily happened on nearby, I'd carefully chosen six scatter cushions in vibrant colours for his living room, to add a bit of warmth, I reckoned, to all that flat leather and cold stainless steel. There was fuchsia, mango, fern, indigo, citron and saffron. It had taken me ages to decide on the colours and I was especially pleased with the rainbow effect they'd create in his sprawling living space.

Pulling cushion after cushion out of the bag, JP wore the horrified expression of a magician who expected to pull a fluffy rabbit out of his top hat but all he got was a skinned rat. He tried to hide it, as he gathered all the cushions and marched down the artfully lit corridor, doing his best to convince me that the one place in the apartment that could really do with a bit of colour was his walk-in wardrobe. Dejected, I traipsed down the corridor after him. Those cushions had cost me half a week's salary, I thought miserably, as he promptly stuffed them on to the highest shelves trying to persuade me that they looked just right there.

We met Tom at eight o'clock that evening in a bar called K90. JP and I were already sitting on high stools at the bar and sipping wonderfully creamy cocktails that brought on hazy feelings of well-being by just looking at them. I was wearing my new powder blue outfit, though I had been strictly ordered by JP not to take the coat off, a command I certainly didn't intend to follow, and my hair was twisted into a simple knot that got looser every time I turned my head, which was a lot as I'd never witnessed London on a Saturday night.

The berry lipstick of earlier that afternoon was replaced by a very light natural-coloured lip gloss. But I'd studiously applied so many layers that I felt my bottom lip was hanging over my chin and I should be careful not to trip over it as I toddled along in my new sandals with their four-inch-high heels.

Tom laid a hand lightly on my shoulder. 'You look beautiful, Lola,' he said softly, and left his hand on my shoulder. He turned to Tom. 'So do you,' he joked.

'Do I?' I asked eagerly, pouting my thick, sticky lips. 'Do I really look beautiful?'

JP shook his head. 'Don't get her started,' he moaned. 'She's had to look in every mirror and every window we passed on the way here. She's even been doing her best to catch a glimpse of herself in that,' he said drily, pointing to the shiny cocktail stirrer sitting innocently in my glass.

'I have *not*,' I stormed defensively. I wasn't about to confess in front of Tom that I *had* been trying to study my reflection in the narrow rod.

Tom stepped in before a family row could erupt. 'She has every reason to look in mirrors tonight, JP,' he said, sounding very reasonable, and very believable.

My confidence immediately soared several notches higher on the confidence scale.

'Lola is an attractive girl,' he continued, rubbing my back in a soothing motion that might have been either friendly or brotherly. But I preferred to read far more into it than that. 'I don't think she realizes it, though.'

JP was looking at me dubiously. 'She's all right, I suppose,' he agreed, somewhat reluctantly because he was used to being the one in our family who laid claim to the good looks. Not that I had suddenly developed looks of my own: I was just looking good that night in my expensive powder blue outfit with Tom's hand on my back.

As Tom was speaking I could feel my back straightening and my shoulders being pulled back by an invisible hand. He really didn't have to say all that much to make me feel good about myself, I realized.

The barman slid down the bar towards us and we ordered more creamy cocktails. I heard JP ask for a small mirror, too, but I chose to ignore him and turned to Tom. 'What's the name of the hotel you're staying at?' I asked him. 'Is it nice?'

'It's a small hotel near Portman Square called the Manor House,' he told me, 'and it's very nice. If you'd been staying any longer, you could've come round for a drink, or ten.'

'I'm going back tomorrow,' I told him mournfully.

'Yes, I know.' He sighed and I wondered whether

he was sighing with polite disappointment or real disappointment.

'Duty calls, you know,' I said sarcastically.

He seemed to pick up on the dissatisfied undertones in my voice and chose his words carefully. 'Looking after children is a very responsible job, Lola.'

'Yes,' I lied, 'it certainly is.' You had to be *very* responsible to change nappies, mop up vomit and get up at four o'clock in the morning because a wide-awake three-year-old had had enough sleep to do him for the rest of the year.

'And I'm sure you do a wonderful job,' he insisted.

I didn't have the heart to contradict him. Besides, I didn't want to because suddenly I began to think that maybe I did do a wonderful job, maybe I was capable of doing a wonderful job. Tom Hutherfield-Holmes believed so firmly that such things were possible for me he had me nearly believing them myself.

Delighted by this discovery that I could be won-derful, I sipped my cocktail, humming contentedly into my glass while JP commandeered Tom's attention towards a table of four girls sitting behind us whose carefully unstyled hair and sheer makeup looked so natural that I could tell it had taken hours of artful preparation. At least when I looked natural, I was natural, I consoled myself. And when I didn't look natural, I definitely wasn't natural.

Our barman was called Franc from Paris but it didn't take me or JP long to discover that he was really a Frank from Sligo who, for the sake of his career, had adopted a French accent and punctuated his sentences with French words. JP and I thought that adding a French word or two to an English sentence was perfectly normal. That was how it was in our house all the time. If the French word could get the meaning across better, or sounded better, then you'd stick it into the sentence.

Even my father, whose knowledge of French hovered at a level less than basic, was prone to asking Elise for a mid-morning *café au lait, demi-écremé sans sucre*. Perfectly normal.

Our dinner plans evaporated as we sat at the bar savouring the mix of cocktails that Frank expertly laid before us. I was enjoying the full attention of Tom and JP, whose eyes had become slightly too glassy to look far beyond me. My powder blue coat slipped down from my shoulders and sat in soft folds around my hips. JP didn't notice but I caught Tom looking away quickly and concentrating a bit too much on the ashtray on the bar.

'Hey, you,' Frank shouted at me, 'do you have a licence for those?' His gaze dropped admiringly to bosom level.

I tittered proudly.

Another hour or so passed in sipping cocktails at the bar. The place was now so crowded that every time someone wanted to pass Tom had to take a step closer to me. Every part of me, from head to toe, tingled delightfully when he brushed against me. It had to be impossible, I told myself forcefully, *impossible* that I could feel such sparks when he came close to me and that he would feel nothing at all. Yes, he *had* to feel something too, I easily persuaded myself. So gently, almost imperceptibly, yet very perceptibly, I placed a hand on his thigh with a light stroke . . . and waited confidently.

Beside me I felt him stiffen uncomfortably and slowly move back out of my reach. Then he smiled at me in a bittersweet way that told me he guessed at what lay behind the caress but that he was going to pretend it was just an affectionate gesture between friends. Then he glanced at JP to make sure he hadn't seen.

My heart sank to the floor in a rush of misery. He hadn't smiled at me in any kind of encouraging way, the way I'd persuaded myself he would. That damned *kind* smile he'd bestowed on me was not what I wanted. I felt the tears of shame and rejection well up in my eyes and blinked them back. I should've known better. Lola Flanagan dressed in expensive powder blue, sitting in a trendy bar, was still Lola Flanagan.

'I have to go home now,' I blurted.

JP and Tom both looked at me in surprise. 'But it's too early,' JP argued.

'I'm jet-lagged,' I replied, unconvincingly I knew, unable to look at Tom, wondering how I could've misread all the signs. It couldn't only be Frank's creamy cocktails. He'd been so nice to me, so complimentary, surely that had to have meant something. He couldn't be like that to everyone. Why did he have to make me feel so bloody special ... and then so bloody worthless?

The next afternoon, a few hours before my train was due to leave, a group of JP's friends called round to the apartment to say hello. They were accompanied by Tom who, as usual, looked genuinely pleased to see me. This time I'd steeled myself not to read anything more into it other than simple pleasure at seeing a friend. It wasn't easy because I wanted it so badly to mean much more. Everything about him appealed to me: his unassuming confidence, his eagerness to listen to me when I spoke, how he made the bad in my life sound good. All these things and more. And, without resorting to plain trivia, he was gorgeous.

Cautiously I watched him move around the room, exchanging a quick word with everyone there, making sure he forgot no one. It was clear that he was popular among his friends. He caught my stare and smiled. And even though I knew there was nothing to it, I couldn't stop myself feeling special. I felt special when he looked at me, I felt special when he talked to me. God, I realized shakily, I even felt special just being in the same room as him.

And all this was going to get me nowhere very quickly.

12. Aunt Potty and Concepta O'Sullivan in Ballyhilleen

Saturday, 21 March 1998

I managed to scuttle into the kitchen as JP was bringing the conversation to an end, and a few minutes later my father sat opposite me at the kitchen table waiting for an answer to a question I hadn't wanted to be asked.

'Ah, no,' I groaned, 'I don't want to visit Aunt Potty.' I was on my own with my father. Cornered.

Aunt Potty was in fact Great Aunt Potty. At ninety-two, she was my father's only living aunt. The other five aunts and four uncles were snugly tucked up in Ballyhilleen's overcrowded graveyard. There weren't a lot of plots left in the graveyard but one had already been reserved for Aunt Potty. That was fifteen years ago and the plot still lay cold. Aunt Potty was in no hurry. I couldn't remember her real name. We had always called her Aunt Potty on account of the porcelain potty she'd always kept under her bed that we'd discovered full to the brim one morning as children. It was no secret that Aunt Potty was gone with the fairies. She was, in fact, gone potty.

She had been in a nursing-home for the last ten years and I didn't want to go. It smelt funny there and anytime I went near the place it somehow reminded me that the distance between myself and Aunt Potty was not that great and I'd better hurry up and do something with my life.

My father didn't say anything, he just looked at me with a sad, hurt expression.

I couldn't bear it. I couldn't bear the guilt. 'Don't give me that look. I'll go,' I conceded sullenly.

When we got there Aunt Potty was propped up in an armchair, surrounded by pillows. On the opposite side of the room she shared sat her elderly roommate, toothless and sucking noisily on her bottom lip. Her bulk spilled out over the sides of her chair.

Aunt Potty made a vague attempt to pat her wiry hair into place. 'See that one over there?' she asked loudly, once we'd reached her side, giving a shaky nod in the direction of her roommate. 'She's expectin',' she announced, 'and I don't see no husband comin' in here to visit either. Well, she needn't think I'll look after that baby.'

Aunt Potty's roommate bared her smooth gums in surprise. 'I'm just a big girl,' she lisped innocently. 'I've always been a big girl.'

Her days of being a girl were long gone, I thought sadly. Mine would pass, too. They were probably already on their way.

I looked at my father, who shrugged helplessly. 'Here you go,' he said to Aunt Potty, dropping the half-bottle of whiskey we had brought her on to her lap. 'A little something to wet your whiskers.' He stopped abruptly and looked about him uncomfortably as he tried not to stare at the wiry whiskers that sprouted from Aunt Potty's chin. He rued his words.

Her weepy eyes lit up at the sight of the whiskey. She fumbled clumsily around to the side of her armchair and pulled three used paper cups out of a creased plastic bag hidden under the chair. 'You pour then, like a good lad,' she instructed him, 'and don't be afraid of it either.' She smacked her lips and pointed across the room. '*She* can't have any while she's still carrying that illegitimate child.'

My father dropped some of the amber liquid into each of the stained cups. It landed with a loud plop.

I stuck my nose into the cup and sniffed deeply for comfort. Then I leaned towards him and whispered, 'Does she know who we are at all?'

Aunt Potty sipped her whiskey through a straw and suddenly seemed to notice me for the first time since we arrived. 'Who are *you*?' she demanded.

'Lola,' I answered quietly, 'Seamus's daughter.'

'Who's Seamus?'

'That'd be me,' my father explained softly.

A young nurse in a starched uniform came into the room pushing a wheelchair and smiled warmly at Aunt Potty. Aunt Potty quickly hid her empty cup beneath the woollen blanket covering her knees. 'Here's the maid now,' she told us.

'Mrs Doyle, time for your walk.' She smiled sympathetically at us. 'You'll have to say goodbye to your visitors.'

Aunt Potty looked at us vaguely. 'Oh, they've nothing to do with me, pet,' she said in alarm. 'They're from the adoption agency . . . you know, for the baby across the way . . . yer woman expectin', over there.'

'Ssh now, Mrs Doyle. That's no way to be talking about poor Mrs Molloy.'

Aunt Potty looked at her in surprise. '*Mrs* Molloy? *Mrs* Molloy?' she screeched. 'Who'd marry her? She hasn't got a tooth in her head.'

I heard the screaming the minute I opened the car door and dashed around the side of the house, down the path to the Portakabin, jumping over the stray briars that tumbled on to the pebbled path. Angry voices, one high-pitched, one deep, both frantic. Belle and Perri were arguing ferociously.

My father ignored the commotion and calmly headed into the house, whistling gaily as he went. Blazing rows had been a feature of everyday life during our childhood and I think he'd wisely given up taking any heed a long time ago.

Gasping for breath, I flung open the door to the Portakabin. Perri ducked and tripped over a pile of school copy-books as Belle, usually of a calm nature, threw the cutlery tray at her, sending an assortment of odd knives and forks flying into the air.

I stepped into the turmoil, relishing the chaos, a reminder of how things used to be. 'What's going on here?' I demanded, because I *could* demand. I was the eldest there.

'Piss off and mind your own business,' Perri shouted rudely from the ground. Her face was flushed a shiny pink with anger. She grabbed at a fork that had landed with a dull thud in front of her and leaped up. She fixed Belle with a vicious stare. 'I'll teach you to throw cutlery at me,' she threatened, crouched low and advancing slowly towards Belle.

Belle was ready to do battle. 'Come on, I dare you. Come on . . .'

I jumped between the two of them at the same instant that Perri lunged at Belle with the fork. I felt a sharp pain in my arm as the fork bit through my jumper. 'I don't bloody believe this,' I yelled at Perri, my arm smarting.

'Now, look what you've done,' Belle screamed at Perri. 'You're dangerous, you are.'

Perri was unrepentant. 'Serves her right for interfering. She always sticks her nose into everything.' She snorted.

I reached out and snatched the fork from Perri. 'We'll see how you like a taste of your own medicine,' I said, and stuck the fork into her fleshy arse.

Perri yelped in pain, one hand rubbing the spot. 'For Christ's sake, Lola, feck off, would you? This is between Belle and me.' She turned to Belle. 'Look, all I'm trying to say to you is to be careful that Kevin Brady isn't only after what he can get. I'm not saying he *is*, I'm just saying be careful that he's *not*,' she preached, sounding like the untainted maiden she wasn't.

'So, all this is about Kevin Brady, then?' I should've known.

'Perri says that Kevin is only interested in me for what he can get and that's not true,' Belle wailed.

'I did *not* say that,' Perri insisted.

Belle glared at Perri venomously. 'You did *so*.'

'Oh, come on, Perri,' I added, 'I heard you.' She had, of course, said just that.

'I said *might*, *might* only be out for what he can get. Well, *someone* has to warn her about men.' She looked at me as if it couldn't possibly be me to do it, and I wondered if I needed to remind her that *she* was a *lesbian*.

'Anyway, I've already told him I don't agree with sex before marriage,' Belle piped up. 'And he says he respects me for it,' she added slyly.

Perri and I swapped looks of disbelief.

'That doesn't mean he's not going to try to get you to change your mind,' I warned her wisely, wondering where the wisdom came from.

'So, no sex before the wedding?' Perri asked in amazement.

Shaking her head adamantly, the long plaits jumping over each shoulder in turn, Belle answered, 'Absolutely not. And I haven't told him we're getting married yet.'

There was only one place to go on a Saturday night in Ballyhilleen and that was the pub. Everything happened at the pub. The O'Sullivan family had the local monopoly on alcohol. They had the off-licence and the pub. Of course, there were a few other pubs but Mr O'Sullivan dealt with them in his own way. There was only one off-licence in the village and that was O'Sullivan's, and if you didn't show your face in the O'Sullivan pub often enough, you would find it very difficult to buy a bottle from the off-licence. Mr O'Sullivan had a simple policy. And that's how it worked.

We headed off for the pub at around seven o'clock. I walked slowly with JP while Perri and Belle, their differences forgotten, wandered ahead in front of us.

O'Sullivan's was full of familiar faces, older but still familiar. The wooden chairs were the same, the pictures on the wall, though slightly faded, were still the same, and the wrought-iron coat-stand had been around so long that it had come back into fashion again. I relished the familiarity of it all, knowing that it probably wouldn't be long before that same familiarity began to get on my nerves.

On the way down, I'd decided that I was going to tell everyone in the pub what I was doing when they asked, as they were sure to do. I would say that I'd moved back to Ireland and I was teaching in a private school in Dublin. And it would feel good to be able to say something other than minding people's children. They didn't have to know that it was only for a few weeks. Teaching sounded like such a . . . such an intelligent profession. Needless to say, I wouldn't be mentioning anything about the failed exotic-hostess audition – it'd be different if I'd actually got the job.

Over the years, the story of minding children in Brussels had grown lamer and lamer and as a result I'd given O'Sullivan's a wide berth on my last two visits home. But I was ready to face them again now.

Among the familiar faces was one I hadn't seen for several years but recognized immediately: Concepta O'Sullivan's. My old rival for Father Rourke's affections. I knew it was her despite the shaved head, pierced nose and black clothes. She was still a big girl, even bigger than she'd been at school. She was sitting at the bar chatting to Gerry Fields.

During our teenage years, and for years before that too, Gerry had been the Ballyhilleen heart-throb. Boyishly handsome, cocky and conceited. He was a brilliant athlete and, with no trouble at all, I could still picture him running down the school pitch with his hurley held high, clearing a path ahead of him with bloodcurdling war cries. A sixteen-year-old lithe warrior, at the time.

Well, he'd changed. The fresh good looks had disappeared. He was ruddy and bloated. Years of guzzling pints had taken their toll, I supposed.

As we edged closer I could hear Concepta, the Enormous Conception, assuring Gerry that she was the only one in secondary school who *hadn't* had a crush on him.

Gerry looked at her with open disbelief. He was standing confidently, feet wide apart, both hands behind his head, rocking back and forth. 'Is that so?'

he asked, in dismay. The reality of his faded youth and a distant athletic physique had not yet dawned on Gerry Fields, who still wore a heavy cloak of arrogance that he couldn't afford.

Concepta, of course, was lying through her teeth. She had been in my class in school and her collection of Gerry Fields pictures from the sports section of the local newspaper was the biggest in the class.

JP was getting the drinks. I rubbed my hands together with glee. 'Bulmer's, please,' I ordered. 'A pint.' Elise wasn't around to stop us drinking from pint glasses.

Perri mouthed, 'How ya?' to Concepta. 'Bulmer's for me, too,' she told JP, and turned to me. 'She looks great,' she enthused, glancing back at Concepta.

'Yeah,' I agreed blankly, thinking Concepta did *not* look great. But then again neither did I so I said nothing more.

Belle had arranged to meet Kevin at the pub and was glancing nervously around her. 'I'll have a pint of Guinness. No, I won't,' she changed her mind, 'I'll have a gin and tonic. No, no,' she changed again, 'make that a Southern Comfort. Straight. No, with ice.'

JP nudged Belle. 'Stop panicking. He'll be here.'

Perri took a swig of her pint. 'Here he is now, just coming through the door. Don't look.'

Predictably, we all turned round to stare. Kevin had made a real effort. The creased blue denims of this morning were gone and he had on a pair of creased black denims. The denim jacket was still the same but his fair skin had the sheen of a fresh shave.

Belle swung back again, blushing. 'Act normal,' she pleaded with us, as if we knew how.

'Right so,' Perri agreed, and downed the rest of her pint in one swift swallow, belching loudly when she got to the end.

Belle gasped and looked like she might cry. She glared at Perri.

Kevin shook hands with JP and nodded to the rest of us, shifting from one foot to the other, doing a nervous little jig.

'Let's find a quiet corner,' Belle suggested to Kevin, 'where people have manners,' she added, eyeballing Perri, and as she turned to go, making sure Kevin had his back to her, she kicked her hard on the shin.

By my count that was twice in the same day that Belle, who shunned all violence, had attacked Perri. And both times to do with Kevin Brady. That was what frustrated passion must do to you, I decided.

At once, Perri opened her mouth to protest but I wagged a cautionary finger in front of her face. 'You deserved that,' I told her.

JP dragged his fingers through his hair in exasperation. 'Don't get your knickers in a twist, Lola,' he advised me. 'He's a lad and that belch will have impressed the hell out of him.'

'From the mouth of a *girl*?' I asked sarcastically.

He looked at Perri. 'I don't know if I'd really call her a girl.' He shrugged.

'Stop talking about me as if I'm not here.' Perri shook her empty glass at JP. 'Your turn, I do believe.'

Furious, JP slammed his empty glass on to the bar. 'I'm warning you two, right here, I'm not going to be your wallet for the night.'

'I don't think you're in any position to do any warning, JP.' I handed him my glass and smiled sweetly. We knew his secret and for that he would end up paying dearly. 'A bag of Tayto, too.'

Perri and myself sniggered gleefully as soon as his back was turned, thinking we were on to a really good thing.

'How ya?' a voice interrupted us.

'Concepta O'Sullivan,' Perri replied, and eyed her from top to bottom, 'as large as life.'

Concepta gave a throaty laugh and her great chest heaved. She slapped Perri on the back. 'And you're as subtle as ever, you mad cow.' She looked at me. 'How's tricks, you?'

'Ah, you know yourself.' I sounded like old Paddy Mulroney down the road who was ninety-two and crippled with arthritis. 'Actually, I've been abroad. Just moved back to Ireland and living with Perri in Dublin. I'm instructing teenage foreign Philistines in the intricacies of the English language.' I threw my eyes up to heaven. So much for the great teaching career I was going to lead everyone to believe I had. The truth had popped out.

Perri pulled the same kind of face. 'Me too,' she said. 'And hating every minute of it.'

Concepta folded her arms across her impressive chest. 'I'm in Dublin myself. Ranelagh,' she told us, and turned towards Perri. 'Whatever happened to the great singing career you had in store for yourself?'

It had been common opinion in the village that Perri would follow the path of greatness, Ballyhilleen's answer to Dana. But it hadn't happened yet.

'I had to put it on hold for a while,' she told Concepta. 'Only temporary, though.'

Concepta nodded.

Perri continued, 'But lately I've been thinking about putting an all-girl band together.'

Perri had been talking about this a lot during the past week, to the point that I no longer really listened.

'Yeah?' Concepta asked, adding keenly, 'I play the drums and all.'

I stared at her. 'When did you start to play the drums?' I remembered having spent more time in the dunces' row in music class with Concepta O'Sullivan than anyone else. It was a constant battle to see who could reach the furthest depths of hopelessness. I always won, me and my recorder, but Concepta was always a close second.

She seemed to understand and laughed loudly. 'I started taking classes about five years ago. I had to do something with these arms.' She threw her powerful arms into the air and gave her imaginary drum-kit a frenzied roll.

'Whoa, easy, girl,' I joked, and looked at Perri, expecting to see the same scepticism mirrored on her face but she was looking at Concepta with admiration tinged with curiosity, and something else too. I couldn't put my finger on it.

'Let's get together,' Concepta suggested brightly.

'You're on,' Perri agreed enthusiastically.

'Drinks,' JP mumbled, an overflowing pint glass of Bulmer's in each hand, three bags of Tayto clenched between his teeth, and dangling in front of his chin.

JP didn't acknowledge Concepta's presence and Concepta looked right through JP.

Perri took her glass and, grinning unabashedly at Concepta, said, 'Thanks for offering, JP. Concepta'll have a double vodka and orange.'

JP shot Perri a murderous look and she returned it with an equally sinister stare. 'Do I have to pay, if it's for you?' he asked Concepta grudgingly. Her father owned the pub and I'm sure he could see no reason why he'd actually have to part with money to get her a drink.

Concepta grinned. 'Aw, I'm sure he'll make an exception and allow you to cough up a few shillings. Everyone knows you're rolling in it.'

'Not any more,' JP muttered, and turned to the bar.

I was left on my own. Perri and Concepta had moved to one side and were standing nose to nose busy discussing the Dublin music scene, which I knew nothing about. Their conversation was animated and full of a rapid kind of gesturing that would have sent the body language experts into a frenzy. There was a definite spark between the two of them that I wanted to put down to a mutual passion for music and, perhaps, a tendency towards weirdness.

I closed my eyes briefly and beckoned in a flight of fancy that had been flirting with my mind ever since our chance meeting with Father Des Murphy in Dublin the weekend before.

The wide-shouldered, impossibly fine-looking priest was standing before me, tearing feverishly at his white collar, trying to oust the shackle, the tiny beads of perspiration glistening on his forehead betraying his heightened emotions. His voice quivered as he told me, in earnest, impassioned tones, how he had somehow tracked me down, that he was willing to turn his back on the Church and forget his vocation, to be with me, to stay by my side.

I sighed contentedly and opened my eyes but I was still on my own. It had been a great few seconds. Belle and Kevin were leaning against the wall on the other side of the pub. A few steps away, Concepta was sipping the double vodka and orange JP had reluctantly bought for her. JP had disappeared.

I got tired of eavesdropping on the conversation between Perri and Concepta, and trying to lip-read the intimate-looking chat between Belle and Kevin, and looked for JP. I scanned the crowd and further down, spotted the back of a head that looked familiar in its confident tilt and disobedient, wavy mane.

JP's elbow was propped up on the bar and trapped between his bare arm and the rough wood of the bar was a small blonde wearing a navy cardigan over a nurse's uniform. No, I decided, she wasn't trapped, she was willingly embedded.

I marched over. 'Hey, hey, hey, big fella,' I gushed adoringly, and waited for his reaction.

JP swung round to see where the flattery was coming from, his eyes dulling with disappointment when he saw it was me.

'Sorry to interrupt,' I continued, in a sweet, innocent voice. 'I was fed up waiting.'

The nurse looked from one of us to the other, a slightly bewildered expression clouding her face. She smiled at me apologetically and made to walk away. JP put out a hand. 'It's OK,' he said to her reassuringly. 'She's my sister.'

'He says that to all the girls,' I told her, doing my best to look hurt but accepting of my lot and forcing my bottom lip to tremble.

'Sue, meet my sister, Lola,' he said, stressing the word *sister* far more than was necessary and nodding from Sue's direction to mine. 'Lola,' he spat my name, 'this is Sue.'

Sue smoothed the creases out of the skirt of her crisp white uniform, as if trying to ease the tension out of the situation. 'Look, I'm going to head off now.' She turned to me and explained, clearly embarrassed, 'I just popped in for a quick drink on my way home from work for a few days. I'm nursing in Cork and, em, I've had the drink so, em, I'll hit the road now.'

'You don't have to go. She really is my sister.' He looked at me for confirmation.

I said nothing.

Sue grabbed her bag from the floor. 'Nice to have met you, Lola.' She threw an icy glance at JP and left.

'Well done,' he snarled at me.

Picking imaginary dirt out from behind my nails, I feigned an air of naïveté. 'I don't know what you're talking about.'

'You know bloody well what I'm talking about.'

'"Ah, don't go, she really is my sister,"' I mimicked. 'Don't worry, it's only a teeny dent in the smooth exterior of JP Flanagan, the man who . . .'

JP wasn't listening to me any more. He wasn't even looking at me. His eyes were fixed on some point over my right shoulder. 'What the hell is going on over there?' he exclaimed.

I followed his gaze to where Perri and Concepta were practically locked in an embrace, they were so close to each other. In a small country pub, public displays of affection between a man and woman were rare enough but you never saw a woman hug another woman. Not in Ballyhilleen anyway. And not the publican's daughter and the village sergeant's daughter. There were no telling nudges or knowing looks, for the moment.

'I *knew* it,' he bellowed.

A few nearby heads turned.

'Sssh,' I urged, and swallowed the last drop of

lukewarm Bulmer's in the bottom of my glass. '*What* did you know?'

JP was trying madly not to point and looked like he might be in the throes of a seizure. 'That other fat cow over there with the shaved head,' he whispered. 'She's a lesbo!'

I looked over again. Perri and Concepta were drawn together and surrounded by an undeniable aura of complicity and togetherness. I didn't want to agree with JP straight away out of sheer stubbornness. Besides, there was no way *Concepta O'Sullivan* could be a lesbian. I'd sat beside her in school for years. I'd *know*, for God's sake. 'You're only put out 'cos she didn't fawn all over you,' I said, remembering how JP's appearance had gone unnoticed by Concepta, which, in hindsight, was a bit unusual.

JP was undeterred. 'I can see the headlines now – "The Village That Breeds Lesbians",' he declared dramatically.

'I thought you men liked that sort of thing, two women together.'

'Yeah, well, we do,' he admitted, 'but only when we're playing a *vital* role.' He paused. 'If you know what I mean.' He grimaced. 'And definitely not where my sister is involved. God, the thought of it, I'm glad I'm moving out of that place next week.' Perri had ordered JP out of the flat because he was beginning to take up too much space for himself. 'I, for one, wouldn't want to be around for any of Perri's little romps.' Over the years, JP had clung to his conviction

194

that lesbianism was not a true sexual orientation, just another means that scorned women had thought up to get back at men. In other words, he couldn't really deal with it.

For the third time, I turned to look at Perri and Concepta. Well, I thought, sharing a flat with Perri meant that I would *definitely* be around for these romps, as JP called them. I hadn't really thought about it before . . . in any depth. Yeah, I'd known for years that Perri was gay. It was no secret. But living abroad had meant that I didn't really come face to face with *it*. Now, there was every possibility that I would come face to face with *it* at three o'clock in the morning, treading naked from bedroom to bathroom. Fleeting pictures of some naked, faceless lover invaded my mind and I pushed them back out again. I didn't want them.

Growing up, I'd noticed that Perri wasn't interested in boys like everyone else. But I'd just put it down to her being a tomboy. The first time I saw, with my very own eyes, that Perri had a real soft spot for girls I was nine and Perri was six.

13. The Nativity Play

1979

In the primary school in Ballyhilleen, with its well-polished tiled floors that you weren't allowed to run on, one of the highlights of every school year was the nativity play at Christmas time. Mary and Joseph were the really important roles but the part of the old grey donkey was nearly as popular. Nobody wanted to play the man at the inn who turned Mary and Joseph away. The licking up to the teachers to get the best parts started in early November.

It was before school on a very chilly morning. A wet mist swung low over the fields around the house. I pulled open the kitchen door and ran across the backyard to the garden shed, where my father was trying to repair the hairdryer flex Belle had chewed. She was not yet three and didn't know any better. Perri had watched her do it. She was six and did know better. And now she was sulking because she wasn't allowed go to the birthday party on Saturday any more.

The dirt-coloured duffel coat that I hated passionately but had to wear billowed out like a cloak behind me. I was running fast. My sudden appearance made my father jump and the long-handled screwdriver fell to the concrete floor with a sharp clang. 'Daddy,

Daddy, can I have something to bring in to the teacher?' I pleaded breathlessly. I was sure my nose was bright red because it stung. It was probably shining, too, because I rubbed Vaseline all over my face to protect it from the cold. That was an idea I had thought up by myself. Elise was horrified and swore it would make my face hairy.

My father bent down to pick up the screwdriver. There were scraps of wire everywhere. He looked at them puzzled, he looked at me puzzled and scratched the top of his head with the end of the screwdriver. 'Is it her birthday?'

I launched into a flustered explanation. 'No, it's the school play next month and I want to play the Virgin Mary and Miss Ryan is picking the parts tomorrow and she'll only pick a nice girl to play the Virgin Mary,' I paused to breathe, 'and I want to bring her a present so she'll know I'm a nice girl.'

'Well, there aren't many flowers around this time of year, pet. Why don't you ask Elise to help you bake a cake when you get home from school?' he suggested helpfully.

'No, it's too late for that. I want to bring one in today.' He didn't seem to understand that it was urgent. 'She's picking the parts tomorrow. I need something *today*.'

'Ah, Lola, why do you leave everything to the last minute?'

I pouted. 'Elise always says "Put off today what you can do tomorrow."'

'She's got her days mixed up and her words back to front, it's "Never put off till tomorrow what you can do today." But that doesn't get us anywhere now, does it?'

Shivering, I pulled the duffel coat around me. A fierce, whistling draught was sneaking in under the shed door and whipping around my ankles. 'No.'

'I have it,' he shouted suddenly and clapped his hands, 'the perfect present.' He kicked aside the coloured wires and stepped across the shed to where a plastic Quinnsworth bag was hanging from a hook. 'The very thing. Crubeens. Fresh from the Brady farm. Martin Brady is a good man.'

Crubeens were pigs' trotters and, boiled up, were considered a very tasty dish. I didn't like the fatty flesh but I loved to lick the bones, once my father had eaten the meat. Elise hated them. My father didn't understand the fuss. After all, she ate frogs and snails.

Curious, I peered inside the bag. I had never seen raw trotters before, except attached to the pig's leg, of course. Pictures of footless pigs dancing around Brady's farmyard leaped at me. I shuffled backwards away from the bag. 'Yuck.'

He handed the bag to me. 'Not at all. She'll love 'em. I'm telling you.' He patted my head with the hand that hadn't been holding the bag. 'My daughter the Virgin Mary.'

In the end, I wasn't picked to play the Virgin Mary even though Miss Ryan had been delighted with the bag of fresh crubeens and I was nastily labelled teacher's pet. Perri got the part because she could sing and I couldn't. Gerry Fields was going to be Joseph. I was the innkeeper's wife and, worse, JP was the innkeeper. We would have to pretend to be married and I hoped we wouldn't have to kiss or hold hands. At least, we got to play the innkeepers that gave Mary and Joseph room in the stable, not the ones who turned them away.

We practised twice a week in the school hall. There was very little talking in the play and a lot of singing. Most of us knew the words to every Christmas carol anyway. One side of the stage was scattered with straw. This was the stable.

JP refused to put his arm around me during rehearsals. I didn't want him to anyway but Miss Ryan tried to make him. 'JP, put your arm around Lola . . .'

'No.'

' . . . and when Mary and Joseph pass by to go into the stable, look at her lovingly.'

JP was furious. 'I will *not.*'

'I wouldn't touch *my* sister if you paid me,' Gerry swore to JP.

'That's enough of your impudence, Gerry Fields. Do it now, JP Flanagan. I'm losing my patience.'

'You can't make me.'

Miss Ryan gave up.

Perri and Gerry fought incessantly, too. Perri sang louder and better than Gerry, and she wanted to stand next to the donkey every time. The donkey was

Deirdre Walsh, a new girl in Perri's class who had waist-length pigtails and a cute American accent. Deirdre and her parents had been living in America since Deirdre was born and they had just come back to Ballyhilleen. Nobody could understand why they had left America to come to live in Ballyhilleen.

Everyone was in costume. Perri had on a long blue nightdress with a crochet shawl around her shoulders. I wasn't sure they did a lot of crocheting in Bethlehem but I didn't say anything in case Miss Ryan thought I was being smart. Gerry and JP were wearing dark blankets and I was tightly wrapped in a sheet that took a lot of unwinding to escape. Deirdre Walsh was wearing a grey leotard, grey wool tights and a donkey's mask with pointed ears. Perri was beside her and they were linking arms.

Miss Ryan sounded annoyed. 'Perri, how many times do I have to tell you to stand on the other side of the crib? You are the Baby Jesus's mother not the donkey's.'

'Yeah, Perri,' Gerry grunted unhappily, from across the stage, 'you're my wife. You're meant to be beside me, doin' what I tell you and feedin' the baby.'

'I don't want to be your wife. You're a boy,' she replied, and turned to Miss Ryan. 'Miss Ryan, I don't understand something. I don't understand why I can't stand beside the donkey. Why can't Mary be best friends with the donkey?'

'Perri, do you want me to ask someone else to be Mary?'

'No,' Perri whimpered, and walked slowly over to stand beside Gerry at the crib. She didn't even look at him when she got there.

Miss Ryan turned her back to sort out the wings that had fallen off the angels and Perri scurried across the stage, back to the donkey.

There was an almighty scream. 'Perri, get back to your place.' Miss Ryan looked at her crossly.

Perri lifted her nightdress up above her knees and ran back to her place.

Gerry didn't greet her kindly. 'You're a loser, Perri Flanagan, and the next time you run away, I'm going to beat you up, so I am.'

Perri didn't look scared. 'I hate you,' she bellowed. 'Deirdre is much nicer.'

Miss Ryan was now holding the naked doll that was going to be Baby Jesus. 'Now, now, Perri, Mary doesn't hate Joseph and you shouldn't hate anyone either. God wouldn't like it.'

It was the night of the nativity play. Our big night. Perri, JP and I were the first ones to arrive at the school hall, early for a last dress rehearsal. We huddled together on the cold stone steps outside the back entrance to the hall and heartily ate the picnic Elise had prepared for us for later, when we would be hungry.

There was the odd screaming match and usual tearful outbursts, but the rehearsal before the show went smoothly. JP agreed to smile at me, once, and Perri spent longer standing beside Gerry than she did

Deirdre. Deirdre and Perri had now taken to swapping clothes and we never knew whether Perri would come home from school wearing the same clothes as when she left the house in the morning. The two of them touched tongues a lot, too. They liked the furry, slimy feel. Elise thought it was all *charmant*.

The heavy velvet curtain went up at seven o'clock. Miss Ryan was wearing a long velvet skirt and a white, high-collared blouse. She stood to the side of the stage energetically mouthing the words to every song. Each row was filled with adoring grandparents, proud parents and mocking older brothers and sisters.

The last song of the play was 'Silent Night'. Perri started to sing on her own in a clear and confident voice. Then Gerry joined in, trying to sing louder than she did. Everybody sang the last verse together. The clapping lasted for ages before the curtain swished down. Nobody moved. Still the clapping continued and shouts for more, more.

The curtain heaved and was lifted up from the dusty floorboards, bits of straw hanging from the end.

The quiet music for 'Silent Night' began. We all waited for Perri to start singing again. Nothing happened.

My eyes moved from the darkened outlines of the audience to where Perri and Gerry were standing. Gerry stood on his own, looking furious, fists clenched tightly by his side.

Perri was on her knees and had her two arms flung

around the donkey who was down on all fours and neighing madly with delight.

'I'm not going back over there ever, Gerry Fields,' she roared into the crowd.

14. Concepta and Perri Get It Together in Dublin

Monday, 23 March 1998

I walked down Grafton Street on Monday afternoon, shoulders stooped, heading for another tedious week at the Vocab-U-Lary School of Languages and frantically trying to find an inspired idea for that day's lesson. Desperately I racked my brains. Nothing happened. Sighing aloud, I decided there and then that I did not have a natural flair for teaching. There was no point denying it, I was a hopeless teacher.

'You're late,' Mr Dooley growled, as I passed the open door to his office.

'It's a matter of definition,' I replied, determined not to let him rile me. 'And in my definition I'm bang on time.' Looking at my watch, I counted that I had two minutes left to get to the classroom before I'd be late even by my own definition.

He placed his two hands flat on his tidy desk and levered himself out of his chair, looking vexed. 'Your sister never showed for her class this morning,' he announced angrily. 'Lucky for her, neither did anyone else.'

I bit my lip to stop myself telling him that I already knew. 'I haven't seen her,' I lied.

I continued down the long, dark corridor.

Concepta had taken the bus back to Dublin with us yesterday. At Elise's insistence, JP stayed behind in Ballyhilleen to be mollycoddled. Back at the flat, I moved all my belongings into the tiny spare room. The bed was hidden under a mountain of clothes and the carpet was strewn with books and shoes. Perri and Concepta stayed up until the small hours of the morning, drinking cheap wine and plotting the rise to stardom of this new all-girl band they'd decided to put together. They needed another member and were busy drafting an ad to stick up, as I headed to bed, depressed that tomorrow was Monday, but keeping my dark thoughts to myself so as not to taint their happiness. I congratulated myself on my own generosity.

I slept fitfully, wriggling uncomfortably between the jumpers, jeans and T-shirts weighing down the blankets. I didn't hear the front door bang during the night. That meant that Concepta had stayed over. She hadn't gone home. And I had an idea that she hadn't slept on the couch. It was an uncomfortable idea.

Some time after the sun was up, I realized that Perri was on the phone. The walls of the flat were cardboard and I could hear every word. She was trying hard to mask the fatigue and hoarseness in her voice. 'Mrs Murphy, Perri Flanagan from Vocab-U-Lary,' she said, with a put-on perkiness. ' . . . Yes, I'm fully aware that it isn't seven o'clock yet but could you possibly let

José know that this morning's class is cancelled?' She stopped to hiccup. 'No, no I'm feeling fine, in perfect health. Em, I have rather unfortunately double-booked myself. We'll reschedule.'

Perri had all the telephone numbers for her students' host families for such emergencies. It was the first task she set each class.

After the fifth call, all in the same vein, I fell back to sleep.

'Lola, Lola, it's nearly noon. Get up.' Perri began to pull the clothes off the bed. 'Come on, get up. You've got to go to work.'

'You're one to talk,' I muttered drowsily, remembering this morning's hastily cancelled English lesson.

'Come on,' she cajoled. 'There's coffee and Jaffas. Mmmm, you like that, don't you?' she tried to tempt me out of bed. Leaning against the door with a towel wrapped around her and smelling of soap, she radiated happiness. She could have been an ad.

'Why are you in such good humour?' I rubbed my eyes with two tightly clenched fists.

'Ooh, it's all coming together.' She bounced over to the bed again, brimming with an animated energy. 'Family life . . .' She looked at me lovingly.

I closed my eyes.

' . . . the band,' she continued happily. 'And my love life.' There was an expectant pause.

I pulled the faded pillow over my face. Perri was waiting for me to say something. 'I'm thrilled for you,' I muttered through the feathers. Please, I thought, please don't tell me any of the details. Nothing. None of them.

Perri was jumping on the bed and laughing. 'Can you bloody believe it? Concepta O'Sullivan, of all people. God, if someone had told me last year, last week, Saturday, even, that I would end up falling for Concepta O'Sullivan, I would have laughed them out of it. I just can't believe it. And she's into music, too.' Perri sighed contentedly.

I couldn't believe it either. The Enormous Conception. 'So, eh . . . so her size doesn't bother you, then?' This was the first question that came to mind, and a big mistake.

Perri stopped jumping. 'What kind of stupid question is that?' she asked crossly, before a huge saucy grin lit up her face. 'Actually, now that you mention it, all that softness, it's kind of,' her eyes glazed over, 'well, it's very carnal.'

Thanks be to God JP was in Ballyhilleen, one hundred and forty miles away, I thought. He could never take this. I could barely take it myself.

Laurent Ducros, the bane of my short teaching career, was not in the classroom when I reached the end of the corridor dead on time for the lesson to begin. His chair was empty. I nearly cried with relief. 'Today, it's grammar,' I told the class.

There were several groans from the ones who understood what I said.

Once the class was finished I sneaked past Mr Dooley's office. As a teacher, it was my responsibility to report absences to him immediately. Reporting Laurent's truancy would mean that Mr Dooley would pursue it and Laurent would undoubtedly be in class tomorrow and the next day and the next. But if I said nothing maybe he wouldn't show up for the full week. There was no real decision to be made. I burst into the bustle of Grafton Street and headed towards O'Connell Street to catch the bus.

When I got back to the flat Concepta was still there. I could hear her voice as I shoved the key into the lock. Had she altogether forgotten where her own flat was?

Sitting opposite Perri and Concepta at the kitchen table was JP, sipping a cup of tea and looking conspicuously uncomfortable. I nearly laughed aloud. He jumped up instantly when I walked in. 'Come on,' he said grabbing my elbow. 'Let's go.'

'No, I've only just got back.' I kicked the door shut behind me. 'What are you doing here, anyway? Why didn't you stay in Ballyhilleen?' I asked him.

He pulled a face. 'I couldn't take it. All that attention centred on me. I told them I had a job interview.' He had his back turned to Perri and Concepta, and his face contorted as he mouthed unintelligibly at me.

I ignored him and seconds later he left on his own in a huff.

'He's a bit homophobic, your brother,' Concepta pointed out, as if we hadn't noticed. 'Are you OK about this?' She waved a finger between Perri and herself, indicating the link in case I'd missed it.

'Um, oh, yeah, it doesn't bother me,' I told her, forcing a smile. This wasn't a discussion I wanted to have. Every time I looked at Concepta, my mind played tricks on me. Either she was sitting there in her school uniform, looking like she did when we were twelve, or she was stark naked. It was very disturbing.

Concepta wisely changed the course of the conversation. 'So, how did class go?'

I stuffed a Jaffa Cake into my mouth. There were always Jaffa Cakes on the kitchen table. Perri knew someone who worked in the factory and we got the boxes that failed quality control. 'I'm not cut out for this. I just know I'm not.'

'Get another job, then,' Concepta suggested.

'But I don't have a proper education, or any real qualifications,' I said honestly. There was no point trying to hide it. 'And there are so many twenty-three-year-olds running around waving first-class degrees that I wouldn't have a chance.'

'Why don't you go back to college, then? You always did *fairly* well at school.'

'Except at music,' we both said together.

'I can't afford not to work,' I continued.

'You could work part-time. I've a friend at UCD and she does bar work. You could do that. They're looking for bar staff all over the town. You can even choose your own hours, there's such a demand. I can see it now . . . Lola Flanagan, the prize pint-puller.'

Her strong arms were pulling dozens of imaginary pints.

Perri came in on the end of the conversation. 'I'm sure we could persuade Whiskers to give you a job in his "establishment" downstairs, if I was to use my enormous influence with him.'

'I suppose I *could* do Business Studies or something,' I decided.

'No, no. Too boring. You need to do something with a bit of pep to it. You know, a bit of oomph.' Concepta clicked her fingers. 'Drama, for instance.'

'I need to do something with a guaranteed job at the end of it. Accountancy, for instance.'

Perri put a hand on Concepta's shoulder. 'Oh, for God's sake, Lola, you don't want to be an accountant. Nobody wants to be an accountant any more.'

'You're right, I don't. But that's just the problem, I don't know what I want to do. I just know that I want to do something.' I hadn't spoken aloud about myself for ages and I was quite enjoying it. At last I was getting a chance to air my thoughts. There and then, I decided to take a step towards the future. I would get the information I needed from some of the colleges around. Then I would decide on a course and do it. I could almost convince myself it was that easy. When I lifted my head to tell Concepta and Perri about what I'd decided, Concepta was standing up and seductively, at least in her interpretation of the word, moving her generous hips, clad in enormous black combat trousers, in slow circles. 'I suppose an exotic-hostess position is out of the question.' She roared laughing.

I glared at Perri. Concepta *knew* about the exotic-hostess audition. Sisterly bonds had been broken. That was lust for you. I decided to keep my resolutions to myself.

Perri and Concepta drifted out soon after to stick up the ads for the new band member. Just minutes after they left JP arrived back. 'You timed that well. They've just gone,' I told him.

'Yeah, I know.' He sounded relieved. 'I was downstairs in the pub helping Whiskers finish a bottle of Paddy's.'

I rolled my eyes. 'You're such a coward. They haven't got anything contagious.'

'Ah, Lola, I know,' he mumbled. 'Don't go on. The whole thing makes my skin crawl. Anyway, I'm only being honest. And Concepta O'Sullivan of all people, I mean, *Jesus*,' he swore. 'She's all flesh.'

I felt that I should stick up for Concepta. 'She's actually very nice.'

'Yeah, nice and *butch*,' he scoffed scornfully. JP liked his women girlie and his girls womanly.

'You should try expanding your outlook. Take your blinkers off,' I suggested drily.

He looked at me dubiously. 'My outlook would never expand that far . . . not to include the likes of Concepta O'Sullivan,' he claimed unreasonably.

'What is your problem with Concepta?' I snapped.

'I don't have a problem with Concepta.'

I eyed him in disbelief. What had we spent the last few minutes arguing about?

' . . . I just don't know why she had to pick on Perri,' he said sanctimoniously.

'Pick on Perri?' I echoed incredulously. 'Nobody picks on Perri if she doesn't want to be picked on.' And he didn't really care anyway. Then suddenly I lost all patience with him and shouted, 'I wouldn't worry about any of these things if I was you.' My hands gripped the side of the kitchen table as I leaned over it. 'You're out of here this week! Gone. History. *Du vent.*'

Up to then, I hadn't taken sides when Perri threatened JP with eviction from the flat, which happened a lot. But I did now. She was right. We'd be better off without him. I stuck a threatening finger under his nose. 'Have you got the message?'

JP slapped away my finger. 'I've already got someplace else lined up, in Dalkey,' he boasted, looking around him disdainfully. Dalkey was out on the coast. A lovely place to live. Expensive lovely. 'I'll be glad to be out of this place. It's a dump here.'

'You were happy with this dump when you had no place else,' I interrupted him sulkily. I'd love to live in Dalkey.

'And as for the lot of you living here,' he snorted, 'you'd make the inmates at St Eunice's look sane.' St Eunice's was a well-known loony-bin in Dublin – home to some of the most deranged minds in Ireland, the others seemingly housed in a small flat above the

Tipsy Tinker. And with that he walked out and slammed the door. Seconds later, he stormed back in. I hadn't even had time to move away from the table, still smarting from the St Eunice's comment. 'By the way, I bought that for you.' He slid a book at me across the table. 'Thought it might help with your lessons.' And with that he walked out again, slamming the door even harder.

That door wouldn't take much more slamming, I reckoned, before glancing at the cover of the book. *Teaching English to Foreigners Made Easy.* I grimaced. That was JP for you. He could slap with one hand and stroke with the other.

15. The Resuscitation in St Stephen's Green in Dublin

Friday, 27 March 1998

JP moved out of the flat and into a spacious apartment with two bedrooms in Dalkey, or so Elise told us. We'd had to quiz her for the details, as JP refused to speak to either Perri or me. He was annoyed with Perri for being a lesbian and thought that I could do with learning some manners. The effects of his humbling experience in London were wearing off and his usual audacity was back in place. I hadn't even had a chance to thank him for the book.

Perri and Concepta had decided to hold auditions to find their new band member on Friday evening in the Tipsy Tinker. Five girls had called the flat after reading the scrawled ad looking for a guitarist that they'd stuck up around Ranelagh. In an uncharacteristically organized fashion, Perri gave each of them a time, at thirty-minute intervals from each other, to be at the Tipsy Tinker and told them to bring along a cassette of their work, hoping to let them know that she meant business. I didn't know what to expect.

Friday afternoon, the girls met me outside Brown Thomas on Grafton Street. I'd finished teaching for the afternoon. As Concepta was spending all her time at our flat, we'd quickly become friends again.

'He's back,' I moaned to her, reaching out to help myself to a crisp from the bag Perri held in front of her. 'He had the flu, that's all.'

Perri quickly pulled the bag back. 'Who's back?'

'Give me a crisp and don't be so stingy.' I snatched the bag from her. 'Laurent Ducros, the know-it-all I was telling you about, the one who speaks fluent English and sits there for three hours solid waiting with his tongue hanging out to correct my spelling or grammar or whatever. Do you know what he had the cheek to tell me today?' I continued determinedly. 'He told me the Irish can't pronounce their Rs properly. I can't take much more of this.'

'What did you do?'

'The ultimate punishment. I moved Clarisse to the other side of the classroom.' I explained who Clarisse was. 'Clarisse is Laurent's girlfriend, his *petite-amie*, and they're like Siamese twins joined at the hip.' I bunched up my fist. 'If you were to hit Laurent, which I am very tempted to do, Clarisse would get the bruise.'

Concepta gave me a sympathetic look.

'Hey,' Perri gasped suddenly. 'Isn't that the priest who read us the Riot Act for bullying that Ballymun brat the other week?'

'Father Murphy?' A delicious frisson shot through me. 'Where? Where is he?' I looked around but couldn't single him out from the throng of sprightly shoppers and unhurried tourists that filled the width of Grafton Street. 'Tell me quick,' I panted. 'Point him out, Perri.'

Perri grabbed me by the shoulder and whisked me round to face the opposite direction and pointed her finger.

It was then that I noticed the false nails. Long, square-tipped, deep purple and threatening. She caught me looking. 'Oh, those,' she said casually. 'Concepta likes to have her back tickled and scratched.'

My right hand flew up involuntarily to stop her going any further. 'I don't want to know.'

Her finger was still poised, newly acquired talon pointing towards the end of Grafton Street. A few heads turned involuntarily to see where she was pointing. 'Here, just follow my finger.'

I obeyed eagerly and suddenly, amid the tangle of heads, I saw a flash of white collar sitting piously on a black shirt. I recognized the purposeful gait. 'It's him,' I breathed, and handed the bag of crisps back to Perri. 'I can't eat any more of these. I've just lost my appetite,' I said, very seriously.

Beside me, Concepta's round face was creased with laughter, as she stamped her feet struggling to contain the raucous roars waiting to erupt. With a seemingly tremendous effort she composed herself enough to speak. 'So, old Father Rourke is free from the shackles of your affections, then? I thought you'd grow out of that, your fixation with the clergy.'

'Well, I haven't,' I snapped. 'I'll see you in Whiskers's before seven.' The first audition for the new band member was at seven and I had promised to be there. Why they wanted me I did not know. I could barely distinguish between the sound of the piano and the trumpet.

Slinging her bulging backpack over one shoulder, Perri came to an abrupt halt. 'What? Where are you off to?' she demanded, slightly annoyed but working herself up to getting more so. 'We didn't come all this way into town to meet you for nothing, you know.'

Concepta playfully snapped the braces holding up the men's trousers Perri was wearing. 'Ah, look, it doesn't matter, Perri. It's no big deal. We were coming in anyway.'

Perri decided that Concepta was taking sides and had an unpleasant look on her face. 'Yeah, but the point is that we wouldn't have made plans to come into town in the first place if we hadn't already arranged to meet Lola. Would we?' She was facing Concepta with her hands planted on her hips. Her usual battle stance. I was familiar with this. In Concepta's place I'd give in.

But she stood her ground. 'Well, we had to get a cassette deck for the auditions this evening anyway,' she argued. 'Come on, Perri, don't be childish.'

Perri never reacted well to being called childish, which she was frequently on account of stubbornness and her tendency to lose her temper.

'Childish?' she roared. 'I'm not being childish. Me,' she stabbed her chest, 'at least I've had the guts to be honest with my parents and tell them that I'm a lesbian. Oh, yes, I'm proud of what I am, Concepta O'Sullivan, I don't need to hide it.'

Concepta looked upset: for all her straight talking and brazen attitude, she had not yet summoned up the courage to break the news to her parents that she preferred to dance at the other end of the ballroom. She was an only child and thought she would surely break her father's heart. Besides, she didn't have a fairly broadminded French mother either. It was a sore point and Perri shouldn't have used it as fighting ammunition, I decided.

But that wasn't my problem. If I hurried, I calculated, I could still catch up with Father Murphy. Of course, I didn't know what I would do once I had caught up with him. I'd improvise, I supposed, then wallow in embarrassment.

Perri and Concepta were staring at each other. Concepta's eyes betrayed her hurt and Perri's face was set in an obstinate cast of stone.

'Just kiss and make up,' I advised them. I just wanted to run down Grafton Street. They both jerked their heads towards me in surprise. 'Not here, of course,' I added. 'Go home.'

Suddenly Perri's face softened, and Concepta looked relieved.

'I'll leave you to it, then.' Without waiting for them to reply, I turned and walked away.

The irony of the situation hit me. Some of my most vivid memories of Concepta were of her and me vying for Father Rourke's attention in our younger days, fighting tooth and nail over every glance or morsel of conversation shot our way. And there I was, eighteen years later, standing on one of Dublin's busiest streets, stuck in the middle of a heated argument between Concepta and her new lover, who happened to be my sister, and about to run down the crowded pedestrian street, chasing after yet another priest. At least Concepta had moved on. But I just couldn't help myself.

Resolved to seize the moment, I broke into a quick run. The short, fitted skirt that clung to my thighs was not ideal for running. My leather shoulder-bag, stuffed with everything from an English dictionary to a family-size tub of Vaseline, bounced along enthusiastically. In a fit of impatience, I pulled it from my shoulder and stuffed it under my arm. By the time I reached the end of Grafton Street, the zipper of the skirt had clumsily worked its way around to the front and my shirt was flapping loosely about my hips.

Tucking the shirt in haphazardly, I peered into the shifting crowd. Again, the white collar on its black background leaped at me like a flag. He walked into Stephen's Green. Slowly now, I followed at close pace, keeping my eyes firmly fixed on the back of his head. I began to memorize it. A halo of shiny brown, three velvet kinks rolling down the back of his head, a cluster of fragile tendrils shaping his nape. Ooh, God is good, I mused.

I must be careful not to lose him now, I thought. I'll wait a little before I approach him, just until I get my breath back, and then I'll walk up to him and say something funny. Something funny and intelligent. Something funny and intelligent, and spiritual.

A young voice called out expectantly, in a distinctly American accent, 'Hey there, Ms Flanagan. Yo!' Laurent Ducros was lying on the grass, wrapped in a fiery clinch with Clarisse, which was all the confirmation I needed that the articles I'd read on rampant teenage sex were unfortunately true. I was sure the grass beneath them would be scorched to a cinder when they stood up. 'Come on over,' he yelled.

I stopped walking but made no attempt to head over to where they lay entwined, chewing gum and blowing bubbles. Enormous bright pink bubbles.

'Come on over,' he repeated loudly, removing himself from Clarisse's arms.

Predictably Clarisse wilted.

I looked ahead. Father Murphy had stopped to tie a shoelace. His foot was propped up on a bench and he was bent over, focused on the length of string. Strong thighs, round buttocks and a smooth back. I was assailed by a barrage of unholy thoughts.

Reluctantly, I turned my attention back to Laurent. 'I can't come over. I'm allergic to grass,' I hissed back at him, desperately. With an inclination of my head, I silently beckoned him over to me, not wanting to attract Father Murphy's attention before I was ready for him.

Laurent jumped up and wandered over to me. 'Whatcha doin'?'

'Just hangin',' I replied nonchalantly, trying teenage talk to make myself feel less conspicuous.

'Cool.' He paused thoughtfully. 'You just looked like you were in a real hurry though, like real intent on something.'

A brittle laugh. 'Laurent, you stayed in the US too long,' I admonished him. 'You let all those techno espionage and murder mayhem films they produce by the cartload over there go to your head.' I sneaked a sidelong glance. Not my first either. He was walking on.

'Hey, now,' he chided playfully, eager for a bit of fun. 'You're not gonna tell me that you haven't been staring at that priest up there all this time that we've been standing here shooting the breeze.' Laurent had also learned how to talk loudly from the Americans.

'Keep your voice down,' I warned him, before quickly glancing to my right again.

He was disappearing into the distance and I stood there watching him.

'Blast,' I muttered. There was a definite edge of frustration to my voice. It should not have surprised me that Laurent picked up on it.

'Hey, what's the big deal?' Laurent looked too, puzzled. 'You're following him, aren't you?' He sounded pleased with himself. 'Whatty do? Run away with your Bible after a prayer meet?'

He blew a big pink bubble. I stuck my finger into it and it flattened on to his face. 'Hey, whatya getting so upset about?'

'Nothing,' I grumbled.

'You haven't got the hots for him, have you?' He slapped his hand hard on his thigh.

'Of course not,' I denied emphatically. 'I mean, no way. No, absolutely no. No question. Not if he were the last man on earth. No, definitely no. And he's a *priest.*'

Laurent eyed me suspiciously. 'What was it that guy Shakespeare said? Yeah, "Me thinks the lady doth protest too much," or something like that. He's got my vote.'

'Don't be ridiculous,' I quipped.

Laurent looked confused.

'OK, OK, I'll admit I *was* following him. But it's not what you think.' It's not a dazed twenty-eight-year-old, running through the park after a strange priest she met just once. 'I know him.' A little. 'We've met before, except not really in good circumstances, well, they weren't bad either, they were just eventful, well, no, not really eventful, more unfortunate. Yes, unfortunate circumstances, and now I'm just trying to get a chance to make a good impression.'

'Hey, why didn't you say so? I can help.'

'No.'

He continued enthusiastically, 'How do you fancy being the Good Samaritan? Where's he gone? I have the best idea.' Laurent scanned the park. 'I can't see him.'

'I've lost him,' I declared gloomily.

'No,' Laurent said adamantly. 'He's probably made

for the other side. Let's cut him off.' He ran across the grass, Clarisse forgotten. 'Hey, sorry about your allergy,' he yelled back.

'All in a good cause,' I panted.

'Just follow my lead when the time comes,' Laurent instructed me.

An uneasy feeling invaded my gut, but then disappeared. He *must* know what he's doing, I thought. Kids today are so good at these kind of games. Plus he's French. Smooth. And he spent years in America. Bold. By the time we reached the path, I had easily convinced myself that I was in the best of hands and together we would produce a spectacular worthy of an Oscar, or at least an Oscar nomination. Whatever that spectacular would be, because I still had no idea.

Laurent stood in the middle of the path and examined the scene from different angles. 'Cameras and action,' he yelled. With that he lay flat out on the ground, feet facing in the direction from which he figured Father Murphy would come.

Passers-by stared openly but didn't stop. Thankfully. Another mad American.

He lifted his head from the ground. Tiny dark pebbles stuck to his hair. 'I can see him coming.'

I quickly looked around and sure enough he was heading our way. Long strides devouring the path. 'What do you want me to do?'

'You're going to pretend to be giving me mouth-to-mouth resuscitation,' Laurent urged. 'Quickly.' He lay back down, eyes closed. 'You can make believe you found me here, on the ground, out cold and you're trying to revive me. A great image to impress with.'

I leaned towards him and hesitated. 'You'd better not enjoy this.'

'Relax, I'm *not* going to enjoy it. OK?' He looked as if he just might.

Going down on my bare knees beside him, I placed a hand on either side of his head.

His eyes were closed.

'You had better *not* enjoy it,' I whispered fiercely again. Why was I doing this?

He opened one eye and glared at me. 'I'm sacrificing myself for you. Get on with it.'

Remembering a few of the more convincing moments from hospital programmes, I pinched his nose hard to shut off his air supply and tilted his head backward. The pebbles were digging into my knees. I glanced up. It was time. Father Murphy was only a few steps away.

'*Laissez-le tranquille,*' a wild, panicked voice came from nowhere, ordering me to leave Laurent alone.

Laurent sat up at once like some great puppet master in the sky had pulled on his strings. Clarisse leaped on to my back and grabbed a fistful of my hair. Father Des Murphy stood gaping before us.

It was one of those golden Kodak moments.

Laurent threw me a contrite look and pushed himself up off the ground. '*Enfin, du calme, Clarisse. Je t'explique . . .*' He plucked Clarisse from my back and, in hushed tones behind me, began to explain the favour he was doing me.

Clarisse responded with a sheepish grin. '*Désolée.* Sowwy.'

'You'll be sorry at exam time,' I muttered, under my breath.

Father Murphy was studying my face.

I tried to look different from the last time we met, sticking my chin into my chest, shoulders slumped and toes pointing inwards. I was hoping that he might not recognize me. All these contortions took tremendous effort.

Recognition flashed blatantly in his eyes. 'You,' he accused.

Such was my concentration on changing my appearance as much as I could without resorting to the use of a scalpel that I nearly screamed from the unexpected shock of being identified. I felt like a criminal.

'You,' he continued, 'I remember you and your friends . . .'

'They were my sisters,' I interrupted. At least, he would know I had a family.

'Yes, you and your sisters were engaged in a clever bit of bullying, weren't you?' he persisted contemptuously. 'And what do I find today? I find you kneeling on another poor boy in broad daylight, physically abusing him, pinching him, strangling him. Fortunately,' he turned to Laurent and Clarisse, 'his friend came along and she half your size.'

'I can explain. It's all a big misunderstanding . . .'

'Again,' he noted sarcastically. He dug his hands into his pockets and looked around him. 'Where are the guards when you need them?'

Panic bile rose in my throat. 'No, no, let me explain, please,' I begged, turning for Laurent. A few staunch denials from him would help. He was gone. 'He's gone,' I choked.

'Well, you hardly expected him to hang around.' His voice was scathing and his eyes bored into mine. Absolute unveiled disgust. At times like this he undoubtedly wondered if there was a God at all, and if there was why did he allow the likes of me to roam the country freely?

I took a deep breath. 'Look, I'm their teacher. They're here to learn English. We were doing a role play . . . and they got a bit carried away.' This was a different shade of the truth, not really a downright lie. 'Kids, eh?' I laughed uneasily. Maybe I needed to add a dash of absolute truth. 'Well, Father, you can check with the school, Vocab-U-Lary. The director there is John Dooley and he'll verify my story.' He'd fire me, if he found out, and he might even be right to do so. Even Elise wouldn't be able to save me from this.

Father Murphy didn't look fully convinced of this story. 'Right, I'll give you the benefit of the doubt,' he said suspiciously. 'Let there not be another time.' He ran a shapely finger behind his hard, white collar.

I resisted the urge to grab it and put it in my mouth. 'Theoretically, there wasn't any *other* time.' Thick, thick, thick, me, me, me.

With a curt nod of his fine head he walked on.

Humiliation, bitterness, anger, betrayal . . . These were a few of the feelings bubbling furiously in the cauldron inside my head. Somehow, the mechanics of my mind managed to switch the blame for the whole incident to Laurent and Clarisse, and the thought of revenge made me feel a bit better.

Laurent wasn't the first French fella who'd made a fool of me, I thought viciously. No, the very first one had been Thierry Corbineau. I had been sixteen, naïve and willing. Suddenly it seemed logical to me that Laurent Ducros should be the one to pay for what Thierry Corbineau had done to me twelve years earlier. What I'd felt at that time went beyond slight bruising to the deepest pit of my emotions to where those lonely feelings of humiliation and rejection lurked unwanted in every sixteen-year-old.

16. The Summer of Humiliation on Belle-Ile

1986

The car engine purred softly outside the front door. Two butterflies played daintily around the side mirror, flirting with their light reflections, or so it seemed to me.

My father had been sitting patiently in the front seat, drumming his fingers on the warm steering-wheel in a soft, unhurried beat, for the past forty-five minutes. He was waiting for everyone else to get in, which we did, but at different times, and then crawled back out again when we remembered something else to bring. July was dawning brilliantly and we were off to Belle-Ile for three whole weeks.

Belle-Ile, a small island, sat off the west coast of France. Wild and wonderful. *Sauvage*, Elise called it. Her family, my grandparents, had a holiday house there. The house wasn't really a house, it was a reno-vated fort that had been in their family for years. It stood majestically at the top of a craggy cliff and overlooked a secluded rocky beach from where a capricious sea spread out in a never-ending pool to reach the mainland. The fort had long open slits, not windows, and during the summer nights nervous lizards made frivolous guest appearances. The walls and floors were an ominous grey stone but during the long summer days they provided a cool shelter from the warm sea breezes that pirouetted the nooks and crannies of the old building outside.

'Get a move on, all of ye, we'll miss the ferry.' My father's patience was finally ebbing. 'We'll never make it to Ringaskiddy on time,' he huffed sternly.

Elise stuck her head out from behind the front door. She had donned a straw hat with a great floppy brim to protect her face from the wicked rays of the sun should they penetrate the car windows. The wrinkles that graced Elise's face were the fine lines of motherhood not age, or so she told us, and maybe character, too. 'Please, *chéri*,' she addressed my father, 'don't shout.' She pulled the brim of the hat up so he could see her disapproving, almond-shaped eyes. 'Really, it makes everyone so nervous when you shout all the time.'

It should be said that my father rarely shouted. Elise often shouted, in English or French, depending on the height of her Gallic agitation. But she *chose* not to remember those moments and thought it so rude of people around her to shout.

'Elise, I'm in the car. You're in the house. I have to shout to make myself heard,' he shouted reasonably.

Elise's hat reappeared. 'That's not true, *chéri*,' she argued. 'You could just *throw* your voice, like me.'

As I was the only one in the car at that moment, he looked at me in despair. Shaking his head, he opened the car door purposefully and stepped outside. The gravel crunched beneath his feet, heralding his arrival to those still loitering inside. He breezed by Elise and a few minutes later reappeared with JP, Perri and Belle in tow. They had had a spanking of words. A brazen look shadowed JP's adolescent features, Perri was sulking, shoulders back and head held high, and Belle's bottom lip was sticking out and quivering.

'Lock the door now and get in the car,' he called back over his shoulder to Elise, in a low, firm voice. He was careful not to shout.

The car, heavily laden with holiday luggage, and now a ton of bad feeling too, meandered down the drive, hovering dangerously low to the ground.

Sitting inside the car was like being in a sauna without the roomy wooden benches, the invigorating eucalyptus vapours and the refreshing knowledge that you could get out whenever you wanted to. Elise refused to open her window. 'I can't possibly. The sun is so wicked this time of year, eh?'

'The RSPCA wouldn't let you treat dogs like this,' JP complained, stretching out the neck of his T-shirt as far as it would go and blowing furiously down on to his chest.

'Be careful you don't blow away that thick forest of hairs you've got hidden in there,' Perri taunted JP, more than a hint of sarcasm draping her words.

JP shot Perri down with a murderous glance. 'Drop dead.'

Being seventeen JP was extremely proud of any

sign of upcoming virility and being thirteen Perri was deeply scathing of the whole manhood business.

My father stuck in a cassette of country music. He usually asked what kind of music everyone wanted, giving us a legitimate reason to bicker boisterously in the back. This time he didn't. The gratingly jovial sound of Box Car Willie and his guitar bounced off the roof and sides of the car and washed over us.

No one dared say anything but I could feel the strings of disapproval hanging ominously in the air, weaving a thick blanket that was ready to drop at any second.

Box Car Willie continued his spirited repertoire for the next hour. When one of his favourite songs came on, my father, who was tone deaf, would sing along to it, getting all the words in the wrong places and clicking his fingers to the wrong beat.

Perri, as the only one in the family who could sing, was so annoyed by this unintentional mockery that I could feel her go tense beside me, her arms rigid and lips pressed tightly together.

Finally, the music came to an end. I breathed a quiet sigh of relief and Perri relaxed.

My father looked at the cassette in surprise. *'Huh?'* and keeping one hand on the steering-wheel, he deftly turned the cassette back over and jabbed it in again.

Box Car Willie flooded the car once more. I could've cried.

Miles and miles later, Elise read a battered signpost, 'Three miles to Ringaskiddy.' Ringaskiddy was the ferry terminal outside Cork. We would sail to Roscoff from here then drive down to Quiberon where we would take another ferry across to Belle-Ile. We did this trip every summer. Sometimes it was harmonious, shared sandwiches, spirited games of I Spy and action-packed detailed holiday plans.

'I'm going to lie on the beach all day every day and come back black.'

'Me too.'

'And me.'

'Not me.'

Other times the trip was fraught with deafening silences, country music and no picnic stops. That was today's one. And the nearer we got to France the more French Elise became and the more blatantly Irish the rest of us appeared.

Bored from the tedious fifteen-hour ferry crossing to Roscoff, aching from the long road journey right down to the furthermost tip of the Quiberon peninsula and snappish from the pointless rows with JP and Perri that had steadily punctuated each leg of the trip, we reached Le Palais. The old port town announced our welcome arrival on Belle-Ile.

Elise chattered excitedly in French, twisting and turning in her seat, pointing eagerly to the cafés and local shops and waving at people she thought she might know. We took it in turns to mutter a response, all except my father. He just couldn't get his tongue around the French language and had enormous problems distinguishing between *bonjour*, *bonsoir* and *bonbon*. He couldn't. But it didn't bother him.

We headed away from Le Palais and wove our way along intimate country roads that hugged the unruly coastline. Twenty minutes later, the crowded estate car turned down a dry, dusty lane riddled with potholes. As always, there would be a blazing row every morning over whose turn it was to race up the lane, dust rising in dry puffs from heels eager to reach the neighbouring farm where we got our daily supply of fresh, creamy milk. Each of us desperately wanted to be the one because the farmer's wife, Marie-Paul, made sinful fruit tarts, laced with liqueur. And she always insisted we stay for an enormous slice, taking a seat on the worn wooden bench in her friendly kitchen. My mouth began to water.

Our estate car ground to a halt in the courtyard in front of the fort, and we all poured out. I closed my eyes and tilted my head back, letting my face bask in the gentle warmth of the sun. When I opened my eyes again, my grandparents were rushing across the courtyard, arms outstretched ready to embrace the first one to reach them. JP and my father made a sudden move to unpack the car. Elise, Perri, Belle and I raced across the yard, all tiredness and stiff joints forgotten.

Each of us received four kisses. Right cheek, left cheek, right cheek again and then the left cheek again. Between the two of them, my grandparents kissed us thirty-two times and we hadn't even been there three minutes yet.

My grandmother called lightly to JP, who was trying his best to crawl into the empty car boot to avoid the inevitable kissing palaver, her eyes twinkling with affection. '*Jean-Pierre, mon petit lapin, viens embrasser ta grand-mère.*'

Reluctantly, dragging his feet through the small, round pebbles underfoot, JP crossed the courtyard and surrendered to the affectionate assault of my grandmother.

Then, it was my father's turn. He was hiding behind the car, pretending to examine the tracking on the tyres. I could hear him mutter to himself.

My grandmother wondered aloud whether he had forgotten about them. '*Alors, Seamus, tu nous as oubliés?*' She pronounced Seamus as Saymush. Cocking her elegant head to one side, she pursed her lips in a typically French expression of pouting disapproval.

My father understood not a word of this sentence, except his own distorted name but he *could* recognize a matriarchal summons. 'Come, come,' she beckoned, in heavily accented English.

Hitting the grimy bonnet with his hand, as if in congratulations for having endured the journey, he rounded the front of the car hesitantly. 'Just checking the tyres. Long trip, you know. Best to do it straight away,' he said lamely.

Elise looked at him, steely.

He grasped the unspoken warning immediately.

'Martine,' he addressed my grandmother, injecting a generous measure of warmth into his voice, 'a pleasure to be here again, an absolute pleasure.' Disguising the awkwardness I *knew* he felt, he leaned towards my grandmother and sprinkled her cheeks with the obligatory four kisses.

Then it was time to eat. It was always time to eat here. My grandmother clapped her smooth hands together like cymbals. '*On mange.*'

JP soon discovered that Solange, the daughter of the farmer who supplied us with milk, had blossomed since we first met her years ago. She was now as captivating as the wild flora that dotted the island, and fully versed in the power of her natural charms. JP was enthralled and made only fleeting appearances at the fort for food.

Most days Belle kept my father company. At ten she was still a daddy's girl. They did odd jobs around the fort and took long walks picking berries. Every day Belle tried to teach him a few new words of French. He would make appreciative gurgling noises and forget them immediately, like water passing through a sieve.

Elise spent a lot of time in the company of her mother, catching up on family news, discussing what had become of old friends and making trips to the market where they would fill round baskets with small bags of tiny shrimps, delicate mountains of soft plums, crusty baguettes, creamy cheeses, thick rolls of country *saucisson* and chunks of pâté, perfect ruby red tomatoes and flowery shrouds of lettuce.

Perri and I divided our time between the beach and Le Palais. Sitting propped up on the rocks of the cloistered beach, huge brightly coloured towels spread like a magnificent carpet beneath us, we held heated contests to see which one of us would brown the quickest. I don't know why I bothered because Perri had inherited an olive-skinned complexion from my grandfather, the *French* grandfather, that is. I smeared myself with baby oil and lay shimmering in the sun as my skin turned a delicate pink, horrifying Elise into shrieking.

When boredom crept up on us, or on the rare overcast day that made us spurn the beach, we would ride to Le Palais on two old rust-riddled bicycles that lay forgotten at the fort most of the time.

We were into the third, and last week, of our holiday. The long hours spent at the beach had turned my skin a very light golden colour, the pink glow had disappeared. I tirelessly kept the colour well oiled to make sure that it didn't peel before I got back to Ireland and could show it off in the village.

The wheels of my bike wobbled shamelessly and the wind caught my hair in a vicious grip, as I now freewheeled down the hill into Le Palais, skin shining. The shop fronts and house doors sped past in a colourful blur.

Perri was beside me, her two legs stretched out at a shameful slant, higher than the handle-bars of her bike. Her feet were bare and her toes wiggled madly.

'Wheeeeeeeeeee.' The pedals of her bike were spinning furiously.

A young fella stepped on to the road. He was looking straight ahead and didn't see us, or hear Perri's boisterous whooping. I was heading straight for him . . . I couldn't avoid him . . . There was nowhere to go. Perri was concentrating hard on balancing to my left, her legs splayed acrobatically, and a row of parked cars sat stubbornly to my right. I pulled hard on the brakes of the bike. They squealed loudly. I roared. He jumped back just in time, and Perri and I sped by.

In that instant I noticed dark hair, tawny skin, navy Fred Perry style T-shirt, faded ankle-length jeans, no socks and brown leather deck shoes. And the furiously indignant look on his face.

Perri looked at me and shrugged. 'Oh, well.'

We propped the bikes against a post, down a narrow, shaded street near the port. The spindly pile of iron would sit idle until we returned. A solitary figure stood at the near end of the street, a dark outline against the backdrop of the hazy afternoon sun, rigid arms, squared shoulders, chin tilted stubbornly upwards.

We drew nearer.

'An apology would do well,' the solitary figure muttered angrily, glaring directly at me. 'If you had been driving a car, I would be dead now.' He was good-looking even in anger.

'Well, good thing she wasn't, then,' Perri replied

antagonistically, baring her teeth before I had the chance to say I was sorry. 'Or maybe it's not,' she decided.

I must have looked suitably mortified because a reconciliatory hand shot across towards me. He introduced himself confidently. 'Thierry Corbineau, *le fils du boucher*.' The son of the butcher. He was maybe two years older than me. I didn't know who the butcher was but he made it sound like everyone else did.

Shaking the hand offered, I replied shyly, 'Lola Flanagan, and this is my sister, Perri.'

His green eyes twinkled roguishly as he glanced from Perri to me, capturing my regard with his mischievous gaze. 'Flan-a-gan,' he slowly pronounced every syllable and never had an F sounded so fluffy and light. 'That's not a French name, is it?' he asked, knowing that it wasn't.

'No, we're Irish,' I boasted. And grinned.

He folded his arms across his chest and looked impressed. 'You speak really good French,' he praised, and took in the dark wayward curls, lightly tanned skin and eager face in one sweeping glance. He licked his lips and smiled broadly.

Perri interpreted the smile as a leer. 'God, he's so full of himself,' she grumbled in English.

Thierry wanted a translation. 'What did she say?' He waved at Perri. A trivial, dismissive wave.

'She said it's thanks to our mother,' I lied and, at the mention of Elise, remembered my posture and stood straighter, pulling my shoulders back and proudly sticking my chest out. 'She's French, our mother,' I explained.

His eyes immediately dropped from my face to the soft mounds nestling innocently behind a simple cotton T-shirt. The strength of his blatant stare disconcerted me, but at the same time a sliver of a thrill shot through me. I was proud of that stare and too naïve to know that any chest would have had the same effect, not just mine.

Perri wasn't pleased. 'That fella would want to pick his chin back up off the ground or he might end up with a severe case of lockjaw,' she quipped.

'Yeah, I know, terrible, isn't it?' I replied, not meaning a word of it.

'Are you here on holiday?' Thierry asked.

'Yes,' I replied, hoping our paths might cross again before the end of the week. 'We're leaving on Saturday.' It's only Tuesday now, I thought. There's still time.

'Where are you staying?'

Perri sighed impatiently.

'With my grandparents, out at the old Beneteau fort.'

'I know it,' he said. 'Solange's parents have the farm next door, don't they?'

Perri sighed again and mouthed, 'Solange, Solange, Solange.' She was fed up hearing about Solange. It was the first word out of JP's mouth every morning.

I ignored her and continued to look at Thierry with a hopeful expression while wondering how *well* he knew Solange. Her name seemed to slip off his tongue with the fluid ease of familiarity. Tiny bubbles of jealousy simmered. Solange, the tart.

'There's a small beach near the fort,' he continued. 'Do you want to meet up there later for a walk?'

Trying to feign indifference, I replied with a casual, 'Yeah, OK,' and blew a stray tendril of hair off my face. My sweating hands were bunched into tight fists hidden in the pockets of my shorts. I dug my nails into the soft palms willing myself not to blush. 'What time?' I asked, displaying a hint of eagerness and not daring to face Perri, knowing very well that the scathing look thirteen-year-olds were brilliant at giving would be etched across her face.

'Eight o'clock.'

'OK, see you then.' I turned towards the pier. 'Come on,' I urged Perri.

'What are you walking like that for?'

'Like what?'

'Like you've got a load of fleas in your pants.' She began to imitate the wiggle I had put on to impress Thierry.

'At least I've *got* an arse,' I said. Perri was still skinny.

'Yeah, and you haven't learned what to do with it yet.'

'Just 'cos I don't walk like a matchstick man wearing a pair of runners.'

'You're just annoyed that I'm browner than you are.'

'Ah, grow up,' I snarled.

*

Elise didn't appear too pleased when I told her I was seeing the butcher's son on the beach for a walk. '*Le fils du boucher?*' she repeated.

My cheeks burned. 'There's nothing wrong with being a butcher's son,' I said defensively.

Standing at the sturdy wooden kitchen table, my grandmother, stirring mustard, vinegar and olive oil into a vinaigrette, overheard and shook her head. '*Tel père, tel fils.*' Like father like son, she claimed.

I looked at Elise inquiringly. She explained rapidly that the butcher had been *un sacré coureur des jupes*, one hell of a lady's man, in his heyday.

'*Avant l'arrivée de la bouchère, bien sûr,*' my grandmother added. It was all before the butcher's wife appeared on the scene.

I still needed Elise's permission to go out after dinner. 'Well, can I go?' I pleaded.

She eyed me suspiciously and shrugged reluctantly. 'I suppose. But don't tell your father you're meeting a boy.'

'I won't, promise.' Before running out of the kitchen, I ran my fingers across my chest. 'Cross my heart and hope to die.'

At half past seven, I closed the heavy door to the fort behind me. With painstaking detail, I'd constructed an intricate story about looking for shells that I told my father. Wearing a short-sleeved baby pink T-shirt underneath a sleeveless white towelling boilersuit, whose trouser-legs were tucked into baby pink socks that peeped out from above white canvas ankle boots, I skipped down the dusty track that led to the tiny beach.

The layers of frosted lip-gloss with which I had coated my lips felt sticky and tasted awful. Never mind, I consoled myself, I've got a real date, a proper date, with someone I don't really know, not just some clumsy trip up the fields with one of the Ballyhilleen fellas.

It hadn't rained in days and my pristine ankle boots were quickly covered in a fine film of ochre-coloured dust. I spat on to my fingers and rubbed vigorously. The stubborn dust darkened and didn't shift. I spat again. The dark stain spread some more. I worried that my feet would be a right turn-off and decided to keep them hidden.

I came to the end of the track, clambered down over the tall rocks and dropped on to the pebbly sand below. Fine grains stuck to the dampened stains on the once white ankle boots. The boilersuit bottoms had popped out of my socks. I carefully pleated each one and tucked them back in.

Making sure that Thierry hadn't arrived so that I wouldn't be caught looking impatient, I glanced at my watch. A million tiny butterflies flapped their delicate wings in my stomach. Ten minutes to go. Good, I thought, I had time to think of some interesting things to say. A bit of fodder to fill the blank spaces. Chewing on my bottom lip, I racked my brains. Blank. Come on, I chastised myself, think, think. Still nothing. I began to despair. He was going to think that I was a right dimwit if I couldn't come up with one thing to say to him. Envious, I suspected that the girls who hung around Le Palais didn't plan their conversations.

There was a dull thud as a pair of feet landed on the sand behind me. '*Salut.*'

'*Salut.*' Caught in a wave of sudden awkwardness, I wondered bleakly what to say next. Back in Ballyhilleen we could compare teachers, grumble about too much homework, dissect the last school disco, lament the failures of the village hurley team, swap stories on neighbours. In the absence of conversation, I was sure the only thing he would notice were my dirty ankle boots. I dug my feet into the coarse sand and smiled painfully.

But Thierry was too busy talking about himself – his scooter, his father's shop, his military service – to notice. He continued his tireless one-man conversation effortlessly. It became clear that he really enjoyed talking about himself. I didn't mind, though. His complete self-absorption gave me the time to stare at him, unnoticed. He was definitely the best-looking fella I had ever seen and I easily forgave him his narcissism. I didn't really blame him.

He paused suddenly and looked at me. His gaze travelled the length of my body but I didn't sense the same admiration as earlier in the day. 'What are you wearing?' There was an edge to his voice.

'It's called a boilersuit,' I replied hesitantly. I tried to explain that they were all the rage in Ballyhilleen.

'Don't French girls wear them?' I asked hopefully.

With indignation, he firmly pronounced, 'Never.' His eyes scrutinized every inch of my favourite outfit. 'No, they would never wear this,' he declared tactlessly.

Great, I thought miserably.

Suddenly he changed the subject. 'Do you swim?'

I nodded. An enthusiastic, eager nod.

The eyes that had looked at me with blatant disapproval only a few moments ago lit up. 'Let's go, then.'

'I didn't bring my swimsuit,' I objected lamely.

'You don't need one. Stop acting like a little girl.' He put his arm around my shoulders and leaned close. 'Come on,' he whispered. In one swift movement, he peeled off his T-shirt. 'What are you waiting for?'

'Nothing,' I answered boldly, to mask my hesitation. Elise had brought us up to believe that there was nothing wrong with our naked bodies. JP, Perri, Belle and I had a carefree attitude towards naked bodies that our friends in Ballyhilleen thought hilarious but didn't share. I hesitated because I knew what Elise would think about the combination of naked bodies, the butcher's son and a deserted beach.

Thierry was walking to the water's edge, wearing only a pair of dark boxer shorts. He looked back over his shoulder. 'Are all Irish girls as slow?'

I began to undress until I was standing shivering in only my white cotton teen bra and matching knickers. Both were tinged yellow from too many hot washes. Determined to prove that Irish girls weren't slow, I

244

marched down to the water's edge and stood beside him. 'I was just giving you a head start.'

Hand in hand, we waded out into the sea and plunged under the soft swell. Coming to the surface at the same time, Thierry put his hand behind my neck and pulled me close to him. 'Close your eyes,' he whispered.

'OK.' I could feel the warmth of his lips before they even touched mine and then he kissed me in a way that was gentle and strong at the same time. The kiss of a man, I thought. I'll never kiss a boy again.

His mouth left mine and my lips felt naked before the trail he was carefully drawing down my neck and across my shoulder exploded into fireworks. With his too-eager fingers, he slid my bra straps down my arms and crushed me against him as he released the clasp at the back. 'Lola, Lola, look what you do to me,' he murmured. His hand was on the small of my back drawing me even closer to feel for myself what I *was* doing to him. Using his fingertips, he traced hypnotic circles on my skin. The soft pattern covered my stomach and hips. Deft thumbs tugged at the sides of my knickers.

I froze. 'Can't we just go on kissing?' I pleaded.

He looked deep into my eyes. 'All things progress, Lola,' he answered. They taught philosophy in French schools.

'They don't have to, do they?' I insisted, feeling myself stiffen. The warm feeling was evaporating.

Ripples of dissatisfaction ruffled the smooth

surface of the water, as he took a step backwards. 'No, they don't,' he replied coolly, 'but then we don't have progress.'

I folded my arms defiantly.

'Ah, I know what this is all about.' The cross expression on his face dissolved. 'This will be the first time, won't it?' he probed delicately.

'Yes, I mean, no.' The water was definitely getting colder.

He looked puzzled and raised his eyebrows.

'Yes, this would be the first time,' I explained, 'but, no, it's not going to be the first time. Not here, not now, not with you.'

'What do you mean?'

'I don't want to. I'm not ready. I don't really know you and I'm leaving again in a few days.' The nuns at school would be very proud of me for being so righteous and I felt quiet pleased with myself. Then I remembered that I was standing naked in the sea with a naked man I hardly knew. No, I decided, they wouldn't be proud of me. 'I just wouldn't feel right.'

Slowly Thierry realized that he was not going to get his way and turned resentful. 'You felt right enough to take off your clothes and come into the water with me. You felt right enough to kiss me and let me touch you and now, this.' He threw his hand up in the air in disgust. 'I am not a little Irish boy you can turn on and off when you want. I am French. I need to satisfy my desires. This is not good for me.'

'It's not going to *drop off*, you know,' I ridiculed him.

'You know nothing, and I mean *nothing*, about these things,' he spat.

'Enough to know when something isn't right – '

He interrupted, 'When something is not right? When something is not right? You know nothing.' His face turned a dark red beneath his tan. He strode through the water.

I stood motionless.

'You, you don't deserve that I show you what being with a man is all about,' he shouted angrily from the beach, pulling on his jeans. 'Go back to playing with little boys.' He scooped up my clothes. 'You will regret this.'

I watched, horrified, as he ran up the beach and climbed over the rocks with my clothes in his firm grasp. 'Where are you going?' I cried in vain. 'Come back.' There was the sound of his scooter as he left, and then nothing. The water was freezing now. I walked out slowly and stood at the edge.

With the water lapping around my ankles and the chilly night breeze whipping my bare skin into a landscape of sharp goose pimples, I crumbled. Thierry wasn't coming back and I was trapped on a beach, in the middle of nowhere, no clothes and freezing to death.

I heard loud voices.

'I don't see her. You said she would be on the beach. I don't know what possessed your mother to let her go off and meet a stranger. She could be dead by now.' My father.

Perri had let the cat out of the bag.

'Take it easy, Dad. It was only the butcher's son.' I knew Perri would be throwing her eyes up to heaven.

'That's all very fine for you to say, Perri. You don't shoulder the responsibility of being a parent.' His voice grew louder with emotion. 'You don't know how it feels to know that your daughters are at the mercy of every Tom, Dick and Harry of this world, and none of them decent, honourable men.'

'OK, OK, I get the message.'

'Do you? I wonder about that.' The words were tinged with a tired despair at Perri's insouciance.

The voices got nearer. Perri and my father climbed down over the rocks.

'Oh, my God,' roared my father, rushing towards the spot where I was huddled on the damp sand. 'Where is he? I'll kill the bastard.'

Perri asked the obvious question. 'Where are your clothes?'

I looked at my father, a look of embarrassment and shame. 'He's gone and he took my clothes with him,' I whispered, 'but nothing happened, I *swear*, nothing happened.' The tears flowed.

'The bastard,' he choked.

'I knew it,' Perri scoffed. 'I told you but would you listen? No, you wouldn't. Little Miss Lola Know-it-all. Typical.' Her great wisdom of thirteen years erupted.

I shot her a glacial look.

Taking off his knitted jumper, my father told me

quietly to put it on. 'I know none of this is your fault, Lola, you poor thing,' he added, and started to rub my arms vigorously to dispel some of the cold. 'Look at you, my little girl left naked on a deserted beach.' A stony expression descended on his face. 'It's all his fault.' He spat the word *his*. 'And your mother's. She should never have let you out.'

At my father's insistence, we went home the next day . . . three days early. A foul-faced JP sat huddled against the car door, livid that he had been torn away from Solange and refusing to speak. In the front, Elise sniffed her discontent into a tissue, upset at having had her holiday rudely cut short and not talking to anyone either. My father was so wound up about the whole thing that he threw his Box Car Willie cassette out the car window and lapsed into a deadly silence that lasted the entire twenty-five-hour journey home. And me, the whole experience had been far too humiliating for me to consider speaking, ever again.

17. The Auditions in the Tipsy Tinker

Friday, 27 March 1998

Red-faced with shame, I escaped from St Stephen's Green once Father Des Murphy was safely out of sight, and hopped on a crowded bus back to the flat. Such was my shame that I was sure everyone could tell. They all seemed to be looking at me. Thirty minutes later, I was standing at the door of the Tipsy Tinker. Perri and Concepta were huddled in a dark corner at the far end of the long, narrow pub, lost in their own world where there was only enough room for two. I looked at them enviously.

Whiskers was standing behind the bar, chatting to some of the regulars. He seemed in a rare fine humour, telling anyone who would listen, which was everyone as you wouldn't want to get on the wrong side of him, that he was off fishing for his next holidays. He was swearing that he was going to pull the biggest salmon out of the river Moy. He'd grab the bastard with his bare hands if he had to, he promised them. 'Jaysus,' he declared, 'there'll be both eatin' and drinkin' on her.' I could hear him clearly from where I stood.

Still holding the door open with a foot stuck out

behind me, I shouted down the back to Perri and Concepta, 'I'll be right with you. Two minutes.' A few heads turned as my voice made its loud journey down the length of the pub.

Before the first of the girls arrived to be auditioned, I wanted to run upstairs to the flat to check the post. As I'd promised myself, I'd called a college for course information earlier in the week. I hadn't told anyone about it yet. It was just for me. The college was a small private one in Ranelagh. I had seen an ad in the *Independent*. Someone had left the paper on the bus and I took it as a sign. These days, I was looking for signs all over the place. Of course, a small private college meant that there would be fees, too . . . but I decided to cross that bridge when I came to it. The name of the college had appealed to me. St Peter's Private College for Further Development. I knew someone called Peter in Brussels and he was very well educated, which I took to be another sign. He could speak five languages, he could. Of course, even the taxi drivers in Brussels could speak at least four. 'Gonna get myself educated,' I hummed, to the tune of some song I remembered about getting connected, nearly feeling the benefit already.

'Well, hurry up,' Perri and Concepta chorused, and smiled at each other in a way that locked everyone else out, including me.

'The first one won't be here for a good twenty-five minutes,' I reminded them, still standing at the front door and shouting. I could feel a cold draught sneaking in through my legs and Whiskers was throwing me angry looks from behind the bar.

'Put a sock in it,' he ordered, and looked at the regulars huddled around the bar. 'I know how to handle this lot,' he assured them.

I slid back through the door and raced up the stairs. There were two envelopes addressed to me. Nervously, I ripped open the official-looking one. The college had written back promptly with all the information I'd asked for. I flicked through the heavy glossy prospectus – no wonder they had to charge fees. Diploma in First-line Management, Diploma in Industrial Relations . . . I went on flicking until I came to a heading that could maybe mean something to me. Certificate in Women's Studies. Certificate in *Women's* Studies. Needless to say, I wasn't quite sure what I could *do* with one of those, but it sounded like the kind of thing a twenty-eight-year-old in control of her life would have. A Certificate in Women's Studies.

The other letter was from Belle. I stuffed it into my back pocket to read later. It could wait. I pushed the other one under my pillow to dream on later.

When I got back downstairs, Perri and Concepta were still huddled together. I walked towards them and clapped my hands together sharply. 'Quarter to seven, fifteen more minutes to go,' I said.

'Right,' said Concepta.

'Right,' said Perri.

'Remember,' Concepta continued, her two large hands held up as if cupping an imaginary head, 'we need someone who shares our taste in music, who can play the guitar,' she paused an instant, 'and who can read and write music because we're going to write all our own songs. No cover versions for us. That's for people who lack the talent to do their own stuff.'

Perri looked at her proudly. I thought they were expecting an awful lot from a few bits of paper stuck to the odd pole around Ranelagh.

'Any questions?' Concepta folded her solid arms.

'Explain why I'm here again?' I remembered promising to be at the auditions but couldn't remember why Concepta had insisted. I knew she had given me some kind of hare-brained purpose that had nothing to do with my musical talent, which was non-existent.

'You mean, why you're on this earth at all?' Perri looked at me with a feigned innocence, which she was no good at, mischievously pretending to misunderstand the question.

'You're here to represent the fans,' Concepta answered, ignoring Perri.

'But you don't have any fans, Concepta,' I told her.

'I *know* that,' she said condescendingly, as if I was a bit on the thick side, which I might have been. 'You're here to represent the fans-to-be.'

'Well, there's an idea,' I said, voice full of irony. 'You're giving your fans a say in the band before they're even fans and before you're even a proper band.' I stopped before I confused myself further.

'Yeah, great, isn't it?' she said, genuinely enthused, and not sounding in the least bit confused.

Just then I heard Whiskers say loudly, 'That's them down the back.'

We all turned our heads. Hesitating at the bar was a young girl, who looked like she had just changed out of her school uniform with the ridged marks of her socks still around her knees below the denim skirt she wore. She couldn't have been a day over sixteen. At the very most. And clutched her guitar case tightly to her chest. Had she not clearly come into the pub for the audition, Whiskers wouldn't have let her put a foot past the door. He was not keen on underage drinking. This wasn't from a moral standpoint, as he himself had begun drinking at the age of twelve, or so he told us, he just didn't want any trouble from the boys in blue. I could feel his unease creep towards us warningly as he began to slam bottles on to the bar, muttering to himself beneath his breath.

Hesitantly, the young girl walked up to the table with shy steps, her head tilted forward and a heavy fringe hiding her eyes.

'Straight out of a convent,' Perri grumbled.

I felt sorry for the girl, who was looking at us nervously. 'Be nice to her,' I warned Perri, who looked at me with such indignation that you would swear on your granny's life that she'd never been anything but. If you didn't know any better, that was.

She stood in front of us and cleared her throat. Her voice was soft and young, and the weak light in the pub gave her a fuzzy halo. 'Hi,' she stammered. 'My name is Maria. Maria Doyle and, em, I'm here for the audition, you know for the, em, the group, the all-girl band. I spoke to someone on the phone a few days ago and she said to come here for seven o'clock.' She'd spoken to Perri. She glanced at her watch. 'I know I'm a few minutes early,' she swallowed, pulling nervously on the zipper of her guitar case, 'but I could wait outside if you're not ready yet.' She smiled an obliging, angelic smile. 'And I've brought along the tape of me playing the guitar, like you asked.'

Concepta took the cassette she offered and said kindly, 'Well, let's have a listen.'

Perri sighed irritably. She would have asked her to leave straight away if she thought she could get away with it. Pure, saintly Maria Doyle was definitely not what Perri had in mind. Convent-educated she didn't mind, as long as she was a convent-educated deviant.

Concepta pulled a brand new cassette-player out of her backpack and slid it on to the table. I cast an admiring glance its way. 'Nice,' I commented. 'I bet that put a big hole in your pocket.'

She rubbed the expensive-looking black box lovingly. 'Nah, Perri nicked it this afternoon from the Ilac Centre,' she said.

Quickly Maria blessed herself. Clearly she didn't want to be privy to such information.

'You didn't,' I gasped at Perri. 'You would think that one thief in the family would be enough. Obviously not.' I was staggered. Only three weeks back in the country and I'd already discovered two criminals in the family. If my father only knew. It would kill him.

Annoyed, I turned to Concepta and jabbed her thick upper arm. 'And you let her do it, you . . . you?' I *nearly* called her a bloody fat cow but Perri would've exploded. 'You!'

She jabbed me back hard. 'As it so happens,' she said coolly, 'we were out of the shop before she told me she had it and we could hardly go back in and put it back on the shelf, could we? Just look on it as community investment in music.'

Maria Doyle was appalled: she was looking at Perri as if she belonged behind bars.

'Oh, for *feck's* sake,' I said, to no one in particular. I'd foolishly thought moving back would be *easy*. But here I was surrounded by a family of criminals and living with two lesbians. How would I ever get my life together when no one else had theirs . . . and didn't seem worried about it either? I should've done a stint with the missions.

Perri hit a button on the nicked cassette-player, her new acrylic nail scratching the plastic surface. It whirred into action. At least it works, I thought bitterly. It would have been really bad luck to nick a faulty one. We listened in a perplexed silence for a few minutes. We were listening to holy music, *holy* music, hymns.

'What is *that*?' Perri asked, not bothering to hide the distaste in her voice.

'It's, em . . . lovely,' I tried to insist.

Maria smiled at me gratefully. 'I play in the youth choir at Saturday evening mass in the cathedral and those are my guitar solos,' she answered Perri, humbly. 'I've only missed two Saturdays over the last three years.'

'No, no, no, no . . . *no*,' Perri snapped, and I kicked her sharply under the table for her insensitivity.

'We're looking for someone a little bit older . . . with a little bit more experience,' Concepta lied kindly, before Perri could say something awful.

Maria sounded relieved. 'Oh, that's OK. May I have the cassette back?'

Concepta handed her the cassette. 'Sure.'

She stood up to leave, tucking her prized cassette into the front pouch of her guitar case. Pausing an instant before she fled, she looked directly at Perri. I could tell there was an internal battle raging, the battle between keeping quiet or speaking up. I had a feeling she would've been more comfortable keeping quiet but felt duty bound to speak up. 'You need to get yourself to a church and confess your thieving,' she advised Perri piously. 'And if you really are sorry,' she continued earnestly, 'then God will forgive you.'

I stared at the fragile-looking Maria Doyle with new admiration. I had thought that young people like her, with convictions, morals and faith, didn't exist any more. A little voice in my head, the dubious one that causes me nothing but trouble, was sarcastically telling me to give it ten years and Maria Doyle would be having sex with the parish priest and spending the church collection on hard drugs. That's how bad that voice was.

Perri was unrepentant. 'Yeah,' she snorted devilishly, 'but will He give me the money to buy the things I need instead?'

Maria looked at Concepta and myself with . . . with something akin to devout pity. She spared a sad smile for Perri before leaving the pub.

The next two candidates didn't bother showing up, and Perri and Concepta began to moan that they would never find a third member. I was about to suggest that they scrap the whole idea and get proper jobs, or consider getting themselves an education like I planned on doing, when Whiskers's shouting grabbed my attention. 'I'm sick and tired of the lot of ye traipsing in an' out of here all evening.' He pounded his fist on the bar.

What was he talking about? I wondered, vaguely amused. There'd only been *one* other but Whiskers saw life through his own peculiar eyes.

'Don't you dare take that tone of voice with me,' a stern voice warned him.

Surprisingly Whiskers was reduced to a kind of whimpering. He pointed. 'That's them with their fat arses planted on the stools down the back.'

'And while you're at it, bring me a drink,' the voice ordered. 'Whiskey.'

'Right you are,' Whiskers replied eagerly. 'I'll bring that down to you.'

I squinted to get a better look at Whiskers's tormentor and saw a tall, slender girl with a torrent of red hair and a guitar. 'Yep, this one's for us,' I told Perri and Concepta.

Without looking up they both groaned. They didn't expect much but I had an unexpected good feeling about this one. For starters, she wasn't going to be intimidated by Whiskers Barry.

She strode towards us, her long legs gobbling up the stone tiles on the floor. She would've made a brilliant hurdler, if she hadn't chosen to be in an all-girl start-up band. She might have to try hurdling yet, I decided. 'Hey,' she announced, in a throaty voice, 'I'm your new band member.' She leaned her guitar against the back of my stool and stood with her hands planted confidently on her hips. 'What d'ya think?'

Concepta looked up and grinned, and began, 'I think you'll do just . . .'

'I *think* we'll listen to the tape first.' Perri cut her off curtly, giving Concepta an icy stare, tinged with jealousy.

'I didn't bring a tape but I'll play for you right here and now.' She grabbed her guitar and propped a leg up on a spare stool.

All three of us glanced nervously at Whiskers, waiting for his reaction.

She caught the look. 'Are you worried about the hairy git behind the bar?'

'Slightly,' I said.

Whiskers was walking towards us with a tubby glass in his hand. 'This is for the *lady*,' he said, implying that the rest of us were not ladies and handing the drink to the redhead, whose name we still didn't know.

'Thank you,' she said, in a sweet voice, looking straight at Whiskers. She moistened her lips.

I could have sworn that Whiskers blushed. The fleshy bits of his cheeks, which peeped out above his bushy beard, became an even deeper red than normal.

Pulling her long hair to one side and over her shoulder, she gave it an impressive flick with her hand and sent the flame-coloured locks flying in Whiskers's direction.

He gulped. He did. He *gulped*.

'Would it be a problem if I played a bit of guitar?' she asked him, and every word that came from her mouth was artfully coated in sugar-pink icing.

'No problem at all.' Whiskers gulped again. He pulled hard on the waistband of his trousers. They refused to budge over his belly. He moved away reluctantly.

'Now why can't you do that?' Perri asked me testily, as if Whiskers's everyday foul humours were all *my* fault. 'Why doesn't he act that way with you?' She was baiting me. 'I'll tell you why. Because you antagonize him the minute you walk through that door with your big fuzzy head.'

'I do not,' I replied vehemently. 'He fancies *her*.'

'That is a very frightening thought,' sniffed the redhead, a hand patting her flat chest in anguish. She stopped suddenly and folded her arms. 'You just have to know how to handle his sort. Flutter, moisten and flick,' she said levelly. 'That's my rule.'

'Well, you flutter, moisten and flick a lot better than I do,' I assured her, depressed.

'I give lessons,' she joked.

'I need them,' I said seriously.

Perri glowered at me. 'If you're finished feeling sorry for yourself why don't we let – ' She stopped abruptly in the middle of the sentence as she realized that she didn't know the redhead's name.

'Moira,' the redhead prompted.

Perri continued, 'Why don't we let Moira get on with playing?' Perri did a quick introduction. She nodded at me, 'Lola, my sister.' Then, she nodded at Concepta. 'That's Concepta. She's mine – ' a hasty cough ' – I mean, she's my girlfriend,' she corrected herself, staking her claim. 'And I'm Perri.'

Moira turned to Perri and said, 'She's a gorgeous thing but I won't be fighting you for her.' She winked outrageously at Concepta.

I roared laughing and Concepta clapped her hands gleefully. Gorgeous was not an adjective you would *ever* use to describe Concepta. Perri smiled, although reluctantly.

Moira began to play. Her head swung loosely. Perri nodded approvingly, and Concepta began to play her imaginary drums, her fists pounding the air in a furious tempo. I just sat and watched. After a few minutes all three of them came to a standstill. Concepta was eager to have my impressions, as the voice of future fans. 'Well, what do you think?'

'Very energetic,' I replied truthfully, wondering what she expected me to say.

'Yeah, brilliant,' she enthused.

Moira looked at Perri expectantly, waiting for her to say something, knowing somehow that the decision lay with her.

Perri couldn't contain her excitement and jumped up off the stool. 'Welcome to the band, Moira,' she cried, and gave her a hearty pat on her narrow back. Moira reeled forward and came within two inches of slapping her face off the table.

'Perri,' I said cautiously, 'you still have one more person to see.'

'We don't need to see anyone else,' she declared. '*You*'ll just have to tell her that the position has been filled.'

'I don't want to do your dirty work.'

'Just tell her,' she snapped.

Moira went off to the bar for a round of drinks to celebrate. I turned and watched her go. 'If I had legs like those you'd never catch me out of hotpants.' I sighed. 'Rain or shine.'

'I wear hotpants sometimes,' Concepta announced seriously, grabbing as much of her fleshy thighs as she could in her two hands.

'You *are* joking, I hope.' You could build a council estate on one of Concepta's thighs. I looked incredulously at Perri.

She raised her eyebrows questioningly. She didn't know if Concepta was joking either.

Moira brought back three pints of Bulmer's and another glass of Southern Comfort for herself. 'They're on the house,' she revealed proudly, setting the glasses down in the middle of the table.

'Have you been doing that thing again?' I asked her enviously, that thing that she'd earlier called flutter, moisten and flick, that thing that had transformed Whiskers into a mound of jelly in her hands. I wished I'd been able to do her thing earlier that the afternoon, in St Stephen's Green, when I really could've done with the effect it seemed to produce when she did it.

'Yep.' She sipped her drink. 'By the way, I bumped into a guy with a guitar at the bar looking for the auditions. I told him he was out of luck.'

'What was a *fella* doing coming here? The nerve.' Perri was outraged. 'The ad clearly said *girls only*.' She took a mouthful of Bulmer's. 'Bloody men,' she slurped angrily. Perri was easily irritated at the best of times, but when it came to male behaviour her aggravation knew no bounds.

Moira just smirked. I didn't think *she* had a problem with fellas.

18. A Home for Strays

Saturday, 28 March 1998

'The word Kevin has appeared *seventeen* times already on the first page alone,' I deliberated out loud, and flicked to the second, sweet-scented page of Belle's letter, which was a bit crumpled because it had been stuffed in the pocket of my jeans since yesterday, waiting to be read. I did a quick count. 'And ten times on the second page.'

'Give us a look.' Concepta leaned over. 'Jaysus, what's that smell?' she gagged, scrunching up her nose into a tiny wrinkled ball, no mean feat.

'That's Belle's rose-petal oil,' I told her. 'She makes it herself, in her Portakabin at the end of the garden.' I held my imaginary cauldron in the crook of one arm and stirred. 'And then she spends hours smearing it into her writing paper and letting it dry,' I explained, twisting a finger into the side of my head. 'She's mad.'

'I wouldn't open a letter that smelt like the air-freshener my granny used before they discovered that air-fresheners didn't have to smell worse than the smells they were trying to hide,' Concepta quipped.

'Yeah.' Perri snorted in agreement.

I tried to explain Belle's obsession with letters. 'Belle's what you would call a chronic compulsive letter-writer.' Anything that held Belle's interest for more than three minutes became an obsession. Letter-writing, Kevin Brady . . .

Perri was balancing on the back legs of her chair, sipping tea noisily. 'I got one hundred and thirty-nine letters from her last year,' she said. 'And it doesn't matter if you don't write back, they just keep on coming.' Her arm moved back and forth in weary waves. 'On and on and on.'

One hundred and thirty-nine letters, I repeated to myself, Perri got one hundred and thirty-nine letters. I was suddenly miffed.

'How many did *you* get?' Concepta probed, seeming to know exactly what was on my mind.

'Only one hundred and twenty-six,' I replied deject-edly. 'And I was the one living abroad, *starved* of news from home.' I was hardly *starved* of news from home since Graham Alexander Bell had literally opened the lines for Elise to stay in constant touch, but that was beside the point.

'News from home!' Perri barked. Turning towards Concepta, she began, 'Do you know that one of them was all of six lines long, *six lines long*, and gave me a very good description of the consistency of Coco's stools.' Coco, the beloved Chihuahua, whose health was a constant source of worry to Elise and Belle, and no one else.

'Huh?' Concepta grunted, puzzled.

'Stools,' she repeated. 'That's shite to you and me but *stools* to Belle,' Perri explained. 'Anyway, this one time, Coco's stools were green and runny instead of the usual solid mess, and Belle thought I could bring the description to a vet here in Dublin for a diagnosis. All this on rose-scented paper, too. It didn't seem right.'

'Yeah,' I continued sulkily, getting back to the letters, 'but they can't *all* have been about Coco, can they?'

Perri didn't answer. She wanted to know about Belle and Kevin. 'Has he wormed his way into Belle's drawers yet?' she asked jokingly.

'Oh, that'll be a done deal by now.' Concepta grinned knowingly.

'Loose morals are not a trait of the Flanagan family,' I told Concepta, and glowered at Perri. 'At least, not *all* of us . . . Well, not Belle, anyway.'

Perri made the sign of the cross over her groin area. 'She's saving herself.'

'Who's saving herself?' Moira wanted to know, walking into the kitchen, head swathed in a fluffy purple towel. She'd stayed the night at the flat. We were collecting strays, it seemed to me. She slept on the fold-down sofa in the sitting room, a present from the previous occupants who were afraid to move it in case it fell asunder.

Of course, the Enormous Conception had also stayed. She *always* stayed, these days, and I was more convinced than ever that she couldn't remember where her own flat was. I'd caught a glimpse of her wandering naked from the bathroom to the bedroom in the early hours of the morning and dashed back into my tiny box room so fast that I slapped off the bedroom wall opposite the door. It didn't bother me to see her in the nip. It was just the implications. The *implications*. The *pictures* it drew up in my mind. And that was what I'd been running from.

My eyes drifted lazily from Concepta to Moira. 'You two should just move in here altogether,' I joked, smug in the knowledge that the flat was way too small for that to happen. Way too small by far. And that suited me fine.

'We've already talked about it,' Perri told me. And she wasn't messing.

I stared at her in disbelief. 'You've *what*?'

'We've already decided that Concepta will give up her flat and Moira will move out of her parents'.' Perri studied my grim expression. 'It makes sense for all of us to be together. We have to *practise*.'

'*Practise* what?' I screamed at her.

'You won't even know we're here,' Moira assured me, with a wink. 'Unless, of course,' she paused thoughtfully, rubbing her pointed chin, 'unless, of course, the fold-down sofa creaks if there's two people *or more* in it?'

'Don't know. Never tried it,' I muttered. I was well peeved by now and couldn't decide if it was because Moira might get to find out if the sofa-bed creaked with two people in it before I did, or that they were moving into the flat and there wouldn't be a moment's peace ever again, or that I hadn't even been asked what I thought about it. At least in Brussels every time my host family had decided to add another baby to the household, they'd told me about it in advance – mind you, some things I didn't want to know about.

Moira pinched me playfully hard on the cheek. 'I'm only having you on. I won't try out the sofa-bed before you.'

'She'd swallow a brick.' Concepta laughed at me.

She's right, I thought miserably. I *would* swallow a brick. The sooner I got myself a proper education the better.

Perri dismissed me with a casual wave of her hand. 'She spent too long abroad and became gullible.'

Wait a minute . . . what was going on here?

'I hope it's not catching.' Moira shied away from me. Then she jumped out of her chair and started leaping madly around the kitchen, holding her towelled head in her hands and shrieking, 'Help, help me, I've caught it. I'm gullible, I'm gullible.' She pushed at the air dramatically, 'No, don't come near me, stay away. I'm gullible and it's catching.'

What was going on here? They were ganging up on me, that's what they were doing. I'd been there longer than those two bitches, I thought viciously, I had easily three weeks on them. Well, say something, then, I tried to tell myself, speak up for yourself.

Perri's face was creased with laughter and her feet were doing a frantic jig, her knees jerking up and down while Concepta beat the table with her fists, tears streaming down her round face.

I smiled woodenly, said nothing, wondered if St

Peter's Private College for Further Development also did a course on assertiveness, and hoped to God that Moira never got to hear about my weakness for priests, or worse again, the exotic hostess audition. 'You can stop now, Moira,' I told her flatly.

'I couldn't have kept up all that hoppin' up and down for much longer anyway,' she puffed, fighting to catch her breath.

It was only a few hours later and there we were back at the kitchen table. Perri, Concepta and I. I'd spent more time at that kitchen table than anywhere else since I'd moved back. And it wasn't even a nice kitchen table, just stained Formica, donated by Whiskers, so you can imagine that it was not an object of beauty.

Earlier on in the afternoon Concepta had reluctantly ventured over to her flat to get some things and give a week's notice to her landlord that she was moving out.

She wasn't gone long enough for me to enjoy the solitude when she was back with three bulging suitcases and screaming blue murder. She explained furiously, her mammoth chest heaving wildly, that the taxi driver had made her carry her own bags up the three flights of stairs to the flat. She was wild with indignation. 'The little fucker told me that I looked strong enough to carry all three cases on my *little* finger.' She flexed it.

I knew she was hoppin' mad because she called the taxi driver a fucker instead of just a fecker. Fucker is a nasty word, reserved for real rage, when no other word will do. But fecker is, well, it's lighter altogether, almost a gay word – in the happy, lively sense. That's the way it tended to work.

'They weigh a fuckin' ton, these cases,' she roared. Apparently the taxi driver had flatly refused to get out of the car to give Concepta a hand. A girl her size had to be as strong as an ox, he'd argued. In a fit of rage worthy only of Perri, Concepta pulled the side mirror off his car and handed it back to him, warning him that it would be his head next time. She told us all this in the same kind of nonplussed voice she'd use to tell us what she had for breakfast.

Brave talk, I thought, brave, *stupid* talk.

'I don't like using violence unless I'm really pushed, you know.' She turned to me because I was the only one she needed to convince. Perri thought violence against men was fine. 'You can see how I had no choice,' she tried to persuade me. 'Anyway, the mirror was practically hanging off. I just did the ignoramus a favour by handing it to him.'

'Really?' I replied, cynically.

'Yes, really,' she retorted. 'Besides, I told him I lived here with my three brothers.' She stuck up her fists. 'You know, just in case he ever thought about coming back.'

He'll be back, I thought anxiously, with his twelve brothers and thirty-seven cousins, all of them missing body bits from other scraps they'd been in around the city.

'I still have to bring my drums,' she said, as she eyed the near non-existent free space left around the flat critically. 'I might have to stand them in the shower,' she decided.

Later that afternoon Moira showed up with one big barrel bag that she flung into the sitting room, her room from now on. 'The folks send their regards. They're thrilled I'm moving out. They thought they'd never see the back of me.' She pulled out a round solid object wrapped in tinfoil from a straw bag that hung from her shoulder. It landed on the kitchen table with a hard bang. 'Mam gave me this for ye.'

We all looked at the shiny mound.

'It's a *Christmas* cake,' Moira explained.

'But it's nearly *Easter*,' I told her.

'We had one left over from last year.'

Concepta was ripping through the layers of tinfoil. 'I can smell it already,' she drooled excitedly. She took the almond-paste-covered fruit cake reverently in her two hands, stretched out her arms, held the cake above her head, offering it up in sacrifice. 'Somebody get me a knife.'

In no time at all the table was covered with a blanket of crumbs, raisins, sultanas and the lumps of almond paste that Perri had picked off the cake because she didn't like anything too sweet, except Jaffa Cakes. I ate the almond paste, hers and mine, because I loved everything sweet, priests and fair-haired Englishmen with soft voices.

An insistent banging on the door interrupted the

feeding frenzy that was going on. 'I'm not getting it,' I said, immediately wary. It could only be Whiskers up for another gawk at Moira, or the taxi man and his twelve brothers and thirty-seven cousins. Either way I wasn't getting up off my chair.

Concepta shifted uneasily on her own chair and grunted as she moved the waistband of her black floor-length skirt. Her bare stomach, a hill of rolling flesh, stuck out above the elastic. 'I can't move. I'm stuffed.'

'That's because you ate more than half of the Christmas cake,' I stated, in a voice that told her she only had herself to blame for feeling bloated. Then, sneaking a hand beneath my T-shirt, I undid the top button of my jeans then the second. They were just out of the wash, I told myself guiltily.

Moira lifted herself lithely from her chair. 'I'll go.'

I watched her willowy shape make its way across the kitchen to the front door. With one smooth movement she pulled open the door, as if she'd been living in the flat all her life.

'Well, hello-ho.' I heard two hands smack together appreciatively. 'What have we here? Thank you, God,' JP bellowed. I looked over my shoulder. He stood there, immaculately groomed, leaning against the door frame. If he'd been standing next to a prize-winning rosebush, I could've said that the rosebush paled in comparison. But he was leaning next to the door frame, so there was nothing I could say, except that he filled it rather well.

A navy linen shirt hung loosely over a pair of cream trousers. Not a crease in sight. Shiny hair, skin that was smooth where it was meant to be smooth and rough where it was meant to be rough, stretched over a landscape bone structure, and dancing, daredevil eyes. JP was beautiful. Yes, yes, Perri was attractive in a brooding, sultry kind of way, I was friendly-looking. Belle was Belle, but JP was just plain *beautiful*.

I'd accepted it by now. If there was one thing twenty-eight years did bring you it was a sort of calm acceptance of certain things once you *knew* they couldn't be changed. If I *could* change it, I would make me beautiful and JP friendly-looking. What twenty-eight years didn't always bring you was the ability to know *what* could and couldn't be changed, so if you got it wrong, you might end up accepting something you could've changed or fighting something you hadn't a hope in hell of changing. My lack of education, now that was something I thought I could change.

'Can I help you?' Moira asked, in a suddenly soft, slightly confused, little girl voice.

'You can help *me*,' Perri roared at her, 'by shutting the door in his face.' She refused to look at JP. 'Go on, slam it shut,' she urged Moira. Perri was still annoyed with JP, probably only temporarily, for his attitude towards Concepta.

Moira hesitated. She didn't know JP was in the bad books. She didn't even know who JP was. He stepped smoothly into the kitchen. 'Lesbians Anonymous?' he asked, with a wicked glint in his eye.

I shot him a withering look.

'Yeah, and no pricks allowed.' Concepta made no attempt to tuck her stomach back into her skirt. She leaned back in her chair leisurely, displaying even more flesh.

Moira was quick to reassure JP. 'Only two at today's meeting.' She tittered.

JP held her gaze far longer than he needed to and murmured seductively, 'Glad to hear it.' His presence filled the kitchen. A trait he'd inherited from Elise. Whereas I disappeared into a room when I walked in, the four walls swallowing me whole, the two of them managed to dominate the space there was.

'What are you doing back here only three days after you moved out?' I asked warily. We hadn't talked since he'd left. 'Oh, and thank you for the book,' I added. 'It was very thoughtful.'

'He didn't move out,' Perri reminded me, sour-faced. 'He was thrown out.'

'Ah, now, don't be like that, Perri,' JP pleaded playfully.

Moira was eyeing me suspiciously, thinking JP was a jilted lover of mine, since he couldn't be one of Perri's, returned to goad, or maybe even claim me back, which was a hoot because I'd never been claimed back in my life. But behind the suspicion lurked an unmistakable hint of admiration.

Perri continued determinedly. 'Disinfecting Dalkey, are they?' We knew that JP's new flat was in Dalkey but he refused to tell us where exactly. She persisted icily, 'Where is it? I want to know. What's the address?'

He remained adamant. 'I'm not telling you.'

The furrows on Moira's puzzled brow were deepening.

'Why not?' I demanded, unable to see the harm in it, now that he'd decided to speak to us again.

JP wagged his finger at Perri and me. 'Because I don't want you two showing up at all hours, pestering me, do I?' He gave Moira an inviting smile and raised his eyebrows suggestively. 'I might have company, after all.' There was a wicked glint in his eye.

The side of Moira's mouth twitched provocatively.

'You should be so lucky,' Perri jeered, glaring at Moira.

'You'll see.' He smiled. 'Now, if you ladies will excuse me I have to go powder my nose.' He stretched out his hand and rubbed the snub tip of Moira's.

She giggled.

'Slap him,' Perri advised her.

Concepta barely waited until JP had shut the bath-room door. 'That brother of yours,' she exclaimed. 'His head is stuck so far up his own arse he can see out through his mouth!'

'Your brother?' Moira gasped in delight.

'Don't even think about it,' I warned her stonily, but in a roomful of fairly ordinary people, two beautiful people are bound to be drawn together like magnets, I thought, so I couldn't really blame her.

At the light clang of a buckle falling to the floor inside and the rustle of material as trousers gathered around ankles, we all turned to look at the bathroom door. The walls of the flat were *very* thin.

Then I remembered that JP had been due at his first support group meeting for gamblers yesterday. That had been one of the conditions laid down by his employers when they agreed not to press charges against him. They were convinced that the root of JP's problem lay in excessive gambling. They couldn't believe a one-off foray into the clandestine gaming clubs of London could result in so much money being lost. And they wanted proof that he was attending the meetings.

'Did you go yesterday?' I asked him, through the wall.

He reappeared quickly and hesitated, looking around the kitchen uncertainly, not knowing who knew how much of the story and praying, I would've guessed, that Moira didn't know any of it. 'I went where I was supposed to go . . . saw the person I needed to see and . . . got what I had to get,' he replied cryptically, looking pleased at his own cleverness at not revealing too much.

I stared at him blankly. 'Was that a yes or a no?'

'Yes,' he answered, uneasily.

'So,' Concepta began, with the clear intention to humiliate. 'You went to your Gamblers Anonymous meeting, begged them to let you join up and then got them to do you some kind of certificate of attendance

276

so you could send it back to London and now you have no intention of ever going back there again.' She clicked her tongue disapprovingly. 'Oh, yes, JP Flanagan, I know all about your thievin' ways.'

I pretended to examine my fingernails, not at all surprised that Concepta knew all the details.

JP looked threateningly at Perri. Perri stared back defiantly, daring him to have to go at her. He thought better of it and simply shrugged his shoulders. 'I felt more of a fraud sitting there than I did taking the money in the first place,' he admitted. 'And I do *not* have a gambling problem.'

'Of course, you don't,' Moira cooed, concern etched across her face. 'Denial,' she mouthed at me across the table.

'With all that, I nearly forgot the reason I came over here in the first place.' It was as if an invisible fairy had waved her magic wand and sprinkled JP with cartons of stardust: his whole demeanour changed and a wide boyish grin spread across his face. 'Guess who's arriving tomorrow?' he demanded mischievously.

There was only one other person that I knew of, besides himself, who deserved such exaltation in JP's books. It could *only* be. 'Tom Hutherfield-Holmes,' Perri and I chorused.

'Yes!' JP yelped victoriously, pulling a clenched fist down through the air, arm bent at the elbow. He grabbed Moira, who was nearly as tall as him, and pulled her into his arms, slapping her fragile frame against his chest. With broad theatrical movements, he whirled her around the kitchen in a vortex of hops and skips, ignoring her mumbled protests.

JP and Moira may have been whirling around the kitchen but I was doing my whirling on the inside. *Tom Hutherfield-Holmes.*

'Cut it out,' Moira whined. Her grip on JP visibly tightened as he increased his pace and doubled his twirling, covering every spare inch of lino in the kitchen. It was making *me* sick just to look at them. Moira's ivory-coloured skin had turned a really sickly green, bringing back memories of another green face I'd seen years before. It was the time that we *made* Belle get on the big dipper in Tramore when she was seven and thought she was about to die.

19. A Day Out in Tramore

1983

'If you're *very* good,' my father began his bribe, 'as good as gold, I mean, I'll bring you all to Tramore for the day tomorrow. We'll go to eight o'clock mass in the morning and set off straight after that.'

'I'll be good,' Belle promised solemnly, aged seven. A solemn age.

'We should probably skip mass to avoid the traffic,' JP suggested hopefully, even though he already knew we *wouldn't* be skipping mass.

My father was staring at *me* in particular. And I knew why. I returned his stare uneasily, scuffing the kitchen floor with the toe of my old grey runners. It was Saturday evening and our turn to feed Father Rourke. He was coming over for tea at six o'clock, in time for the Angelus, which we would watch on the TV.

The minute the ceremonial RTE bells rang out Father Rourke would silently invite the family to bow our heads in prayer and we would. After the first ring, the battle of the legs underneath the kitchen table would begin. Belle's legs were still too short to play but Perri, JP and I had longer ones. The trick was to sit with a straight face and try to look like you were concentrating hard on the Angelus while you fought the war of the limbs under the table. And there was no flinching when a kick really hurt. The winner was the one who could make another cry. There was rarely a winner, just a lot of bruising.

My father held my gaze. He didn't know about what went on under the kitchen table but he knew full well about priests and me. 'I don't want you making a show of this family when the priest gets here,' he threatened. 'You're old enough to know better now.' He paused an instant, looking for more to say on the subject but thought better of it and finished up with, 'Indeed you are.'

'I swear to God, I won't say a word to him. Cross my heart and hope to die.' I did a quick sign of the cross below my left shoulder.

'Well, now, you don't have to go so far as not talking to the poor man. God bless us, if we can't talk to our own parish priest who can we talk to?' He looked around him for support and got none. 'Just none of your usual tricks, right?' He raised his eyebrows and waited for me to nod. 'I don't know what gets into that girl sometimes,' he muttered.

''Tis the bloody devil,' JP growled. 'Bleedin' Satan.' He was fourteen and put *bloody* and *bleedin'* everywhere he could. It made him look tough and all his friends were doing it too. 'Bloody bleedin' Lucifer.'

Maybe God was trying to tell me something, I thought. Maybe . . . maybe, I had a calling . . . maybe He wanted me to join a convent . . . maybe He wanted to dress me in black with a long stiff veil. Sister Paul always said that God worked in strange ways, and wasn't she herself dumped at the altar by a man, an American at that, before she discovered that she was meant to be a bride of God? Not that being dumped at the altar on your own wedding day by a foreigner wouldn't make you think of becoming a nun. And she was thirty-five at the time. And all the village knew about it.

I bowed my head and prayed very quietly so no one else would hear me: 'Please don't make me be a nun. Ten Hail Marys, five Our Fathers and one Glory Be.' I had discovered this shortcut last year. You didn't have to *say* all the ten Hail Marys, five Our Fathers and one Glory Be. You could just say the *number* you wanted to say. The result was always the same. I didn't *want* to be a nun.

'You'd better leave that bloody priest alone,' JP rasped, breaking my concentration. 'I'll break your bleedin' face if you even look at him,' he threatened. '*I* want to go to Tramore for the day.'

'I don't want to hear you using that kind of language, JP. We're not a family of Dublin gougers, here.' Gougers were the worst kind of people in my father's eyes. There weren't really any in Ballyhilleen but Dublin was full of them, he assured us.

'Why don't you go to bed now for the night?' Perri urged me. 'That way you'll miss Father Rourke altogether. We'll tell him you're sick.'

'I'm not going to bed now because I want my tea,' I replied obstinately. 'Anyway, if he thought I was sick he'd only want to come up and bless me,' I told her haughtily, because deep down I knew I *was* special to him. I just had to be.

My father held a warning finger up. 'Just you be careful, Lola.'

Father Rourke of the ruddy complexion, soft Kerry accent and merry eyes arrived promptly at ten minutes before six o'clock. He put his felt hat on the hallstand.

'Welcome, Father,' my father said proudly, for he always saw it as a great honour to be the one to feed the priest.

'Thank you now, Seamus.'

Elise moved forward elegantly, her delicate hand outstretched. 'Yes, yes, you are very welcome.' She beckoned Belle, Perri, JP and me forward. 'Come, *les enfants*, and say hello to Father Rourke.' *Faazer Roock*.

'*Vous êtes charmante, Madame Flanagan.*' He looked very pleased with himself. Father Rourke had a few words of French and with his Kerry accent had no problem rolling his Rs.

Belle ran up to Father Rourke and boasted, 'I'm going to be making my first Holy Communion soon and I've got my dress already.' She stopped to take a quick breath. 'It's upstairs and it's white with lots of frills and I've even got frills on my socks, too. And it's your job to put the Holy Communion into my mouth.'

'You're getting bigger by the day, Belle. Quite the little lady, now.' Father Rourke patted her head. 'You're a lovely little girl.'

Belle beamed and stepped to one side.

JP shook his hand, nodded and with one gruff word greeted the priest, 'Father.'

'Would you look at the height of you. You'll be a grown man soon. You'll make a fine garda, just like your father.'

JP scowled.

'Hello, Father Rourke.'

'Hello there, Perri. No doubt you'll be winning the school talent competition again next week.'

'Probably,' she replied confidently. This was before the nuns had bribed her to stay out of it.

I stumbled forward and looked down at my feet. 'Hello, Father Rourke,' I said gravely, and stood there in silence.

Father Rourke waited with an expectant smile for me to say more. I usually did, and when I didn't he seemed confused. 'Well, you don't have much to say for yourself today, Lola.'

'I'm on my best behaviour,' I told him miserably, dragging my eyes up from the floor.

Father Rourke smiled. 'So, that's what it is,' he said understandingly.

My father clapped his hands together to get everyone's attention. 'It's about time for the Angelus. Come on, and we'll go on into the kitchen.'

Elise, Father Rourke and my father sat at one end of the long kitchen table and Belle, Perri, JP and I sat at the other.

We had a good dining room with a mahogany table

down the hall. But we couldn't eat in there today because it had just been painted and my father was afraid the fumes would knock out the poor priest. It was never used anyway and smelt like a furniture shop.

Elise turned the telly on just in time for the Angelus. '*Voilà*,' she declared triumphantly. Elise loved watching the Angelus on the telly. She thought it was such a religious thing to do and so Irish.

Father Rourke tilted his head piously forward and blessed himself. We all did the same.

The clear ringing of the RTE bells interrupted the holy silence filling the kitchen. '*Dong, dong, dong . . .*'

JP licked his lips and gave the first kick. A hard one. Perri didn't flinch. She kicked back. I kicked too. Belle tried to kick but her legs were still too short and she walloped her small knee off the table. There was a loud whack. We stopped kicking while my father glared down our end of the table. Belle's bottom lip was trembling but she said nothing. He closed his eyes and continued praying.

The kicking began again. JP caught me in the ankle with a sharp blow and grinned maliciously. I felt my face grow red. The Angelus was over. No one had cried. No one had won.

Elise served dinner.

'I want sausages,' Belle complained, when Elise handed her the bowl of onion soup.

'No, you don't,' Elise answered firmly, and gave Father Rourke an apologetic smile.

He sipped his own soup. 'Lovely,' he murmured.

Next there was beef in a mushroom sauce. Perri pushed her plate away. 'I don't eat meat any more. I've decided to be a vegetarian.'

My father swallowed what was in his mouth. 'There are no vegetarians in this household,' he told her sternly. 'It's not normal. Eat your meat.'

Father Rourke prodded his beef lovingly and sighed contentedly.

The golden Tarte Tatin came for dessert.

Father Rourke mashed the last few crumbs on to the back of his fork. 'That was a grand apple tart, Elise. Lovely flaky pastry.'

I sucked in my breath and felt Perri nudge me. JP looked openly bemused and Belle's hand flew up to cover her mouth, too late to hide the gasp that had slipped out. My father closed his eyes and shook his head sorrowfully.

Elise couldn't stand her Tarte Tatin being called an apple tart. Even my father, who still couldn't see the difference between the two, except that one was the wrong way up on the plate, knew better than to call the Tarte Tatin an apple tart. It wasn't an apple tart. It was a Tarte Tatin.

Elise dabbed the corners of her mouth with a finger and forced a smile. 'It's actually a Tarte Tatin, Father,' she said.

'Well, you'll have to give me the recipe for Mrs Henehan. Her own speciality is spuds, you know. Boiled, roasted, fried, chopped, chipped. She's a dab hand with the old spud.' Mrs Henehan had been

Father Rourke's housekeeper for years now. No one else could have the job while she was still alive. There was a list, and once she died the next person on the list would get the job. Like that, there was no arguing. I hated her.

'Yes, of course, I'll write the recipe and give it to Mrs Henehan,' Elise said obligingly. 'Some time.'

I knew she was lying. She hated Mrs Henehan too, and would never give her the Tarte Tatin recipe. She would consider letting Mrs Henehan get her hands on it a worse sin than serving well-cooked beef. And that *was* a sin. We were the only family in Ballyhilleen who ate beef with the blood running around the plate. Elise refused to serve it any other way. It had taken my father ten years to get used to eating his beef like that and he still wasn't happy about it but said nothing because it wasn't going to change.

'I'll bring the coffee into the sitting room,' Elise said.

My father led the way, courteously guiding Father Rourke by the elbow, though Father Rourke knew full well where the sitting room was. I traipsed down the hall after the procession. Father Rourke sat in one of the flowery armchairs while my father sat in the other one opposite him. Belle, Perri and JP shared the couch.

I was about to flop on to the floor beside the couch when Father Rourke seemed to pat his knee. He doesn't want me to sit on the floor, I thought in delight. He's beckoning me over to sit on his knee.

286

Without hesitating, I stepped across the room to Father Rourke's armchair. Standing there, I caught the stern look in my father's eye. *He* asked, I thought defiantly. Perri, Belle and J P were looking at me oddly as well. *He* asked, I wanted to tell them.

Smiling smugly, I was about to drop down on to Father Rourke's lap when he coughed loudly. 'Lola,' he hesitated, embarrassed, 'you're too big now to be sitting on my knee.'

I was staggered. 'What?' I gasped, as I felt the tide of colour wash over my face. 'But you called me over. You *did*.'

J P was slapping his hand against his forehead. *Da-ah*!

Father Rourke looked extremely puzzled.

'I was going to sit on the floor but you patted your knee and I thought then that you wanted me to sit there,' I explained, wondering why no one else had understood that too.

Father Rourke laughed. A deep, amused rumble. He rubbed his knee. 'An old injury,' he explained, flexing his leg. 'God be with the days.' Another rumble.

I felt like a right eejit. 'Sorry,' I mumbled.

J P was now making throat-slashing gestures with his hand.

'No harm done,' Father Rourke assured me, and looked at my father, 'Sure she would have flattened me.'

'That she would have,' he agreed.

I turned to face him. 'It wasn't my fault,' I moaned,

avoiding Father Rourke's gaze. 'And I wouldn't have flattened him either. I'm not a heifer. And Father Rourke *did* pat his knee.'

'I did, I did,' Father Rourke was quick to reply.

'I know it wasn't your fault,' my father said soothingly, trying to lessen my embarrassment. 'Anyone could have made the mistake,' he added unconvincingly. 'An honest to God mistake, that's what it was.'

I swallowed hard. 'Will we still be going to Tramore tomorrow?'

JP's throat-slashing picked up pace.

'I'll tell you something, if your brother over there doesn't start behaving himself there'll be no one going anywhere.'

'I'd better bleedin' stop so,' I heard JP mutter behind me.

Tramore was about an hour and a half's drive away from us, beside the sea with loads of amusement arcades and rides. Every few steps there was a candy-floss stand or an ice-cream van or a chipper. It was brilliant. Belle, Perri, JP and I loved it. Elise hated it and it always cost my father a fortune, or so he told us.

We left after eight o'clock mass the next day, a Sunday. Belle had on the pink bottoms of one tracksuit and the red top of another. Elise took one distressed look at her and moaned, 'This is what happens when I let your father dress you. *Mon Dieu.*'

My father knew Elise well. 'We're *not* turning back to change her into some pansy frock.'

Elise feigned indignation and puffed.

Tramore was packed with holidaymakers. Loud disco music seeped through the doors to the arcades and mixed with the different music from all the rides. Elise put a hand to her forehead and groaned.

My father dug deep into his pockets and pulled out a wad of crumpled notes. He counted them out. 'Right now, here's three pounds for each of you.'

I gasped. It seemed like an enormous amount of money. 'Thanks, Dad.'

The others were pleased too.

'Lola, you're in charge of Belle's money. She's too small and she might lose it.'

'I will not,' Belle protested loudly. 'I'll mind it myself. It'll be practice for when I get my First Holy Communion money.'

'Right so,' he said to Belle. 'Look after it yourself but I don't want to hear any whingin' if you lose it.' Looking at Perri, JP and me he warned us, 'You're to stick together, all of you. Your mother and I are going to sit on the slip in peace and you can come down when you're finished.'

JP sneered at having to hang around with his three sisters. 'Bloody hell.'

Perri ignored him. 'Let's get some candy-floss.'

'Yeeeeah.' Belle charged towards the van that sold it.

'How many will it be?' the man in the white apron wanted to know.

'Four, please,' I said.

'I'm not having one of those big blobs of sugar,' JP scoffed. 'Bleedin' well grew out of that a long time ago.'

Belle looked at him as if he was mad because he didn't want any candy-floss.

The man in the white apron frowned. 'Three, then, it is.'

Belle stood on the tips of her toes and gazed up at him. 'Could we have three big ones, please?' she asked, awestruck.

'You're a lovely little girl and very polite you are, too. Your mammy has done a grand job teaching you your manners, hasn't she?'

Belle nodded eagerly and when he turned his back to whip the sticky pink floss around the wooden stick, she whispered, 'I want to be a candy-floss man when I grow up.'

JP sneered.

Perri slapped him hard on the shoulder and said in a very big voice for a ten-year-old, 'She's only seven, for God's sake.'

When we finished the candy-floss, we went on the ghost train and screamed solidly from well before the train started to move slowly into the tunnel to well after it came out the other side. JP screamed the loudest. A rasping, uneven scream punctuated with silences where his voice was no longer able to hit the crisp high notes it had only a few months ago. He was secretly proud of this, I thought.

With the deathly sound of howling ghosts and murderous screams still ringing in our ears, we sat pale-faced on the fence to the side of the tunnel and munched toffee apples from a nearby stand. The coating was hard. It was a real job to get your teeth through it. Belle had just lost her two front ones and had a big toothless gap. She grimaced as she tried to attack the toffee apple with her back teeth but couldn't. So she licked hers. It was going to take hours.

Behind us the big dipper, the best roller-coaster in the whole country, roared. The people in it must have been screaming their heads off but you couldn't hear them. The open carriages travelled fast along the dipping curves and the wind whipped the screams right out of your mouth and carried them off before anyone could hear. It left you with a dry, open, empty mouth. The really brave people would be sitting in the first carriage with their arms held high in the air and their hair frozen behind their heads.

Belle was listening to the roar behind her, too. She stopped licking. 'There's no way I would ever, ever, ever go on that. Ever.' She licked the toffee apple again. 'I absolutely couldn't.' Belle used the word absolutely a lot when she really meant something. She looked innocent and earnest. It reminded me of when I was seven and didn't want to go to hell.

But Belle *was* going on the big dipper. She was seven and it was time. Perri, JP and I had already decided earlier on. I felt a stab of pity for her. Maybe we wouldn't make her do it. I looked at Perri and JP.

They were both grinning. We *would* make her do it.

With Belle still licking her toffee apple, we headed for the dodgems. The little cars with the big rubber bumpers spun in circles trying to avoid as many other cars as possible, and bash into a few. There was a man in a box taking in money and giving out tickets and unfriendly advice. He pointed a finger at Belle. 'No food allowed in the cars.'

She held the toffee apple up in the air. The handle was covered in sticky dribble. 'Will you mind it for me?' she lisped, through the gap in her teeth.

The man in the box was busy and fed-up. 'I won't,' he snapped.

The woman beside him, counting out the money, nudged him sharply. She stuck her hand through the opening in the plastic window and gave Belle a motherly smile. Her teeth were smeared with the bright pink lipstick she wore. The little lines that crept up from her lips were filled with the same colour, too. 'I'll mind it for you, chicken.'

Belle gave her the toffee apple and grinned. 'You're lovely.'

The bright pink lips spread from ear to ear.

Perri and I climbed into one car, and JP and Belle took another. Belle waved happily from her seat. JP slammed his foot hard on the pedal. The car shot forward and slapped into the car in front. Belle stopped waving.

With his hands close together on the small steering-wheel, and his head bent forward nearly touching them, JP charged destructively at the other cars. He had a wicked look on his face. Undiluted mischief.

Belle was strapped into the seat but jerked forward every time JP drove the car into the rubber bumpers of another car. She spun her head wildly not wanting to lose sight of Perri and me. She even tried to get out of the car. Each time JP hauled her back.

'Car number nine,' the man in the box announced loudly, 'car number nine. Behave or you're out of here. Behave or you're out of here.'

Everyone heard and looked around for car number nine. JP swelled with pride. It was *his* car.

'Right, it's time for the big dipper,' Perri declared.

'I'm not going on that,' Belle protested. She shook her toffee apple, which she had got back from the woman in the box, from side to side. 'Absolutely no way.'

Perri caught her firmly by the hand and tugged hard. 'Don't be a baby. You *are* coming on it.'

'Bleedin' right,' JP added adamantly.

'I don't want to,' Belle whimpered.

'But you *have* to,' Perri replied. 'Isn't that right, Lola?'

'That's right,' I said. 'You'll love it. Come on.'

Belle looked at me, confused. She couldn't understand why I would make her do something she didn't want to do. Something that terrified her. But she trusted me. 'OK, I'll try it once,' she murmured, and her bottom lip trembled. 'For you.' She walked over to the bin and dumped her toffee apple.

JP held the tickets in his hands. 'We're off.'

Perri and JP ran up the ramp and climbed into the back seat of the front carriage. 'Hurry up,' they shouted.

I could feel Belle pulling on my arm. I glanced sideways. Her face was white. Her lips were whiter. 'It'll be fine. It's all part of growing up,' I told her. 'Learning to ride the roller-coaster like a big girl.'

She looked at me doubtfully.

'There'll be a lot worse than this,' I assured her. I took her by the hand and pulled her into the front seat beside me. She moved over in the seat and clung to me.

'Hey, hey, Belle.' Perri ruffled her hair from behind.

Belle slapped away her hand.

JP leaned over the back of the seat and said in a morbid whisper, 'Prepare to die.'

Belle's body stiffened. She turned to me rigidly and pleaded in a tiny voice, 'You promised it would be all right.' A small cold hand clutched mine. 'You promised,' she repeated.

I glanced down at her. I *had* promised. Her face was paler than before, nearly transparent now. Her eyes were wide with the enormous terror a seven-year-old can feel. I hung my head in shame. She was holding her breath, too scared to breathe.

I felt terrible, really ashamed of myself. 'Quick, Belle, we're getting off.'

We made to move but a voice stopped us: 'Please stay seated. The ride is about to begin.'

'No, Mr Roller-Coasterman, I want to get off,' Belle shrieked.

But his back was turned and he didn't hear Belle. He sliced his arm through the air. He was giving the signal to go. Go. Go. Go.

'He can't hear you, Belle.' I pulled her close to me. 'Shut your eyes tight.'

Making a deep rumbling noise, the carriages began to move like a great iron snake along the sturdy structure. They trudged noisily up a steep slope and ground to an uneasy halt when they reached the top. Right in front of us, the rails plummeted towards the ground. The first dip. The sturdy structure didn't seem so sturdy any more.

Belle's eyes flickered open. She looked relieved. She thought the ride was over. Then, her eyes fixed on the sheer drop in front of us. She opened her mouth to say something but the whole sentence was lost as we dropped into the hollow in front of us and roared up the other side.

For the next three minutes, as the roller-coaster thundered and dived, Belle didn't move once. She was as still as one of Father Rourke's church statues, a weepy expression frozen on her face. Her back was pressed hard against the leather seat. Her tiny hands, smaller than I'd ever seen them before, gripped the cold bar in front of her and didn't let go. Her face seemed to be lit by a green bulb tucked behind her skin.

This is all my fault, I thought miserably. I shouldn't have made her do it.

The iron snake's journey came to an end. Belle didn't move.

I gently nudged her. 'It's over. Time to get out.'

JP and Perri were already running down the ramp, towards the chipper. Belle climbed out shakily. '*Absolutely* never again.' Absolutely, her favourite word.

'I know,' I said. 'I'm sorry.'

She turned to me and, in a soft voice, said, 'It wasn't your fault.' She glanced after JP. 'It was his.'

I agreed with her because it made me feel better. 'Yeah, it was JP's fault. I mean, he's the oldest, he should've known better.'

Belle was unsteady on her feet and she was still *green*. She looked like she'd been born a sick child. Elise would have us cleaning out the shed for the next ten years if she found out about the big dipper. 'Better not tell Elise about this,' I said cleverly. 'Our secret?'

She turned her green face to me and nodded. She loved secrets.

I worried that she would stay green for ever and we would have to start calling her Kermit.

20. All That Money

It was Sunday morning, the day after JP had announced the arrival of Tom Hutherfield-Holmes. I was standing limply beside him, in the arrivals hall at Dublin airport, waiting for our dashing visitor to bound through the sliding doors. I *had* to be there. It seemed important that I should be the first one he'd see when he walked out. It would be a sign to him. My head dropped sleepily on to JP's shoulder with a dull thud.

I shivered from lack of sleep, *actually* shivered. The night before had passed in a smoky haze of after-hours drinking with Whiskers downstairs in the Tipsy Tinker. And the cool morning was a cruel mistake.

Whiskers had promptly kicked out the only five strangers in the pub at eleven o'clock on the dot, slurring his strict adherence to the laws of the country with not a smidgin of politeness. The rest of us sniggered knowingly at the poor eejits being shoved out of the door and reluctantly leaving. He firmly drew the bolt. We stayed put, and everyone else there, Whiskers's usual regulars of civil servants, the upstairs tenants – the number of which seemed to him to be increasing by the day but he couldn't be sure it wasn't just the booze – with a few students clapped and roared.

As the hours passed, the smoky haze became a dense fog. The length of the wooden bar was covered in empty pint glasses, overflowing ashtrays and crumpled cigarette packets, and Whiskers was slouched over one end. The laughing creatures of the night had become drink-spouting gargoyles.

I couldn't remember agreeing to the airport trip with JP, or why I'd told him I had to go. I hoped he didn't remember either in case I'd told him the truth. I had trouble gathering my thoughts. I was feeling tired and delicate, and the pounding in my head had reached new depths. There was an unpleasant, stale taste in my mouth. There was no doubt, I'd somehow spent the last twelve hours licking the floor of the Bulmer's brewery in Clonmel and not wound around a bar stool in the Tipsy Tinker.

I imagined my narrow bed in the tiny box room of the flat. The heavy blankets for warmth and comfort. And pure silence. The cosy feeling evaporated. Now that Moira and Concepta had moved into the flat there was very little quiet. Ah, feck the lot of them, I brooded. Feck lesbianism, feck music, feck Moira and her long legs, and feck alcohol. I was never touching a drop again. The thought of seeing Tom Hutherfield-Holmes again brought on sporadic feelings of well-being during which I perked up considerably, only to suffer a relapse seconds later.

JP was hopping impatiently from one foot to the

other. 'Where *is* he?' He fixed his stare on the small arrivals screen hanging from the ceiling. 'See there?' he asked for the fifth time, pointing at the flashing numbers. 'It says there that flight EI607 from London Heathrow arrived fifteen minutes ago.' He checked his watch again and concentrated on the sliding doors. 'So where is he? He should be through by now.' He looked at me expecting an answer or an explanation.

I shrugged. It was the best I could do.

Deep worry lines creased JP's wide forehead. 'You don't think he missed the plane, do you?' he asked. His mouth was pulled tight in a grimace.

With a tremendous effort, I managed to quiver, 'Probably not.' My voice didn't sound like my own. It sounded more like Whiskers's.

We waited another few minutes and I hazily thought about why Tom and JP had become such firm friends, two people who at first glance seemed polar opposites. On a day when my head was clearer the answer would've come much quicker but today I struggled. In the end, I concluded that JP's flamboyant side had recognized in Tom someone who would let him claim the limelight for himself but who would never fade into the background. JP loved to shine and liked to be surrounded by people who shone too but not the same way he did. And Tom, Tom seemed to relish the natural insouciance that followed JP everywhere he went.

It probably wasn't as simple as that but that was as far as I was going to get there and then. But when I thought more about it I realized that they weren't so different the two of them. Both were manly. And they shared other qualities too, in case manliness couldn't be considered a quality, though I thought it was. Both were generous, kind and genuine. Of course, all these qualities were just a bit harder to get to in JP, you had to dig a little deeper, but they were still there.

Suddenly, through watery eyes, I spied an impressive stack of matching suitcases piled high on an airport trolley, sliding purposefully across the smooth floor towards us. The brown leather mountain stopped a few yards in front of us.

From the side, I glimpsed the first inches of the sleeve of a navy blue blazer, pale pink shirt cuffs peeping out and a tanned hand with a large signet ring on the third finger. I perked up instantly and waited.

JP was grinning broadly. And waited.

Tom and JP hugged like two grizzly bears locked in a deadly embrace. They slapped each other's back hard. Then a few times more. I counted every second, waiting for the ritual to end.

'You old devil, you,' Tom enunciated smartly, and punched JP's shoulder. It was a rough, playful jab.

JP dipped to one side and retaliated with a sharp upper-cut. 'World middleweight champion, JP Flanagan,' he burst out, in the excited voice of a commentator, 'seizes the opportunity to lay on his opponent the kind of decisive punch that has made him king of the ring.' JP danced nimbly on the tips of his toes. 'JP Flanagan hasn't just *hit* his opponent, he has *hurt* him,' he sang. 'The man is damaged. The man falls. The crowd rises to their feet.' JP's voice had now reached a crescendo. Then, he dropped to a soft, admiring tone. 'Once again, ladies and gentlemen, JP Flanagan has proved what a first-class boxer he is.'

Without turning to look, I could sense the people around us staring. The two air hostesses with perfectly made-up faces standing beside me clapped enthusiastically. My cheeks stung with embarrassment. I was still waiting.

JP bowed graciously, soaking up all the attention. He was born to shine.

Tom and JP began to walk off. They were chatting in rapid bursts of dialogue, both at the same time, neither appearing to be listening to what the other one was saying, but they seemed really absorbed in the conversation anyhow.

'What about *me*?' I whinged pitifully, tired of waiting to be noticed and wondering if Tom Hutherfield-Holmes had seen me at all.

JP turned around and his thick eyebrows shot up. 'I'd forgotten you were even there,' he confessed truthfully.

'No wonder,' I said, cuttingly. 'It's like the return of the prodigal son around here.'

Tom listened to this outburst with an understanding look on his face. Armed with a devastating smile, he took a few steps back to where I stood. 'Lola, it's a pleasure to see you again.' He placed the palm of his hand gently behind my back and eased me forward. 'You look wonderful.'

And I *believed* him, even though I knew it wasn't true. He had such a way with words. He didn't even have to use that many of them.

We headed for the taxi rank. 'That's a lot of bags for a few days,' I commented casually, eyeing his expensive luggage with more than a hint of greed in my bloodshot eyes. I sighed inwardly, remembering the day I had arrived back in Dublin a few weeks ago. It already felt like a lifetime. None of *his* cases had to be held together with belts as mine had.

Tom looked a bit confused. 'I'm not here for only a few days,' he corrected me. 'I've decided to move to Dublin.' He slapped the side of a suitcase with the flat of his hand. 'Lock, stock and barrel.'

'So, that's what you've got in the bags,' JP joked.

They both chortled boyishly.

'But why?' I blurted, secretly thrilled.

'Yes, why indeed?' Tom paused. 'You see, Lola, I've never quite had a job as such,' he admitted easily. 'I've just been involved in managing my father's estate over the years. He has lots of properties that need overseeing and managing, and I'd always just helped him out.'

A shot of envy crossed JP's eyes. Being the son of the village sergeant didn't have the same ring to it.

'But,' Tom continued, 'I never really felt I was standing on my own two feet.' I glanced at his feet, finely shod in a pair of dark brown leather loafers.

'And now,' he declared, in his fine English accent, 'I've decided that it's time to launch myself in business.' He smiled confidently before adding proudly, 'With JP, of course.'

There was a look of smug satisfaction on JP's face. The fecker looked like he was marrying into royalty.

'Of course, with JP,' I said smoothly. JP must have known about this for weeks and hadn't mentioned a word. We were always the last ones to know about anything going on in his life, unless he needed us to spin lies for him. Then we were fairly useful, I thought bitterly. Sexual harassment, my arse. JP would've been leaning over that photocopier faster than you could say bottoms up!

Tom didn't seem to think it strange that JP hadn't told me, or any of us, that he was coming. 'I needed a business partner,' he continued jovially, 'and JP needed a job. Quite a marvellous coincidence, really.'

More chortling.

'Quite,' I agreed sullenly. JP could've asked me to help too, I brooded.

Tom's expertly cut fair hair, intelligent blue eyes, golden tan, expensive clothes and expensive attitude exuded success already. And JP's confidence and presence were a brilliant match. They didn't need me.

All those feelings I'd been battling with came flooding back. I felt like a failure. Before I could stop myself, I blurted out, 'I *myself* am going back to study.' Challenging JP's look of disbelief with a tilt of my chin, I went on haughtily, 'Didn't I tell you? I've got all the details. It's nearly arranged.' I nodded convincingly. 'I'm going to do a Women's Studies course.'

The letter from the college had arrived on Friday and it was hardly 'all arranged', as I'd said. It had only been a letter with information. And I hadn't uttered a word about it to anyone. Not to Perri, not to Concepta. No one. I was still trying to decide if I was brave enough to become a mature student. I hated the words *mature student*. It sounded like a serious illness.

My alcohol-battered brain spat words at me. Words like sacrifice, persistence, hard work. Truth be known, I was no good at these things. My father could even tell you, if you didn't believe me. I shuddered. I hadn't even been accepted at the college. I closed my eyes. I hadn't *even* applied yet. I willed my eyes open and hoped JP and Tom had disappeared up the skirts of those two air hostesses. But they were still standing there, studying me hard. All I had was the college prospectus. But at least it was a start, I comforted myself.

Tom was very supportive. His cufflinks sparkled as he threw his hands up in the air. 'That's marvellous, Lola,' he enthused, earnestly. 'It takes real courage to give up a job and go back to full-time study. Doesn't it, JP?'

If only he knew the job I would be giving up, I thought dismally.

JP frowned. His face was a picture of scepticism.

'I'm very excited about it. I've it all planned,' I lied. 'Whiskers is even going to give me a part-time job in the pub.' It was an inspired lie. Chemically enhanced inspiration.

'Is he now?' JP asked, his words drenched in sarcasm.

'Who's Whiskers?' Tom wanted to know.

'He owns the pub down below the flat where we live.' I deliberately left out all the nasty words that could be used to describe Whiskers. They might sully the gleaming picture I was painting of myself and my wonderful life.

JP snorted knowingly.

We jumped into a taxi. There was only a small queue on a Sunday morning. The driver was just finishing a twelve-hour shift and had seen one punter too many by that time of the morning. His face was grey and drawn, and his eyes were bloodshot. Like my own. The skin underneath them hung in loose folds. Like I hoped mine never would.

He hadn't a good word to say about anything. 'Yeez all think that the boom in Ireland is goin' to last another bleedin' fifty years,' he sneered, in a thick Dublin accent. 'Well, yeez can all mark me words. The Celtic tiger is about to roll over and die, so he is.' He roared loudly to make his point.

The three of us jumped at this heartfelt imitation of the dying Celtic tiger.

'And what with the feckin' Germans and Japanese buying property left, right and centre, the working man can barely afford to put a roof over his head in this town.' His eyes nailed us in the rear-view mirror. His voice rose indignantly. 'And the bleedin' priests of this country with nothin' better to do than father children.'

'I don't know what the world's coming to,' I commiserated and yawned. The commiseration was a lie. No priests had been trying to father any children with me!

JP poked me in the ribs. 'Don't encourage him,' he hissed.

I looked at Tom. He was staring at the driver, who had begun to shout yesterday's hurley results out the window of the car at another taxi driver. They were both stopped at green lights. We stayed there until they turned red and then we sped off.

The car screeched to a halt outside the Tipsy Tinker in Ranelagh. I climbed out stiffly. Thick, dark smoke was flowing from the exhaust pipe. Belle would have something to say about the environment. The back end of the car had disappeared under it completely.

I stood and watched the car pull away from the kerb. I waved even though I couldn't see the back window, which was hidden by the dense smoke. I waved just in case Tom could see me.

I climbed the stairs to the flat heavily.

It came as no surprise to me to find Perri, Moira and Concepta huddled around the kitchen table with mugs of steaming tea. I would've been surprised had they *not* been at the kitchen table. It was the only bit of space left in the flat. Their faces were pale because they hadn't been to bed yet. They had been the last ones to leave the Tipsy Tinker. But the conversation was animated. They were haggling over a band name. Concepta was beating the table with her imaginary drumsticks, a favourite occupation of hers I'd soon learned, and Moira was strumming an invisible guitar, which was quickly becoming a favourite occupation of *hers*.

'Well, did he arrive?' Perri asked. 'Tom Hutherfield-Holmes?'

'Yeah,' I replied sleepily. 'And guess what?'

'What?'

'He's not leaving again either,' I told her.

Perri looked puzzled.

'He's here to stay,' I explained. 'The Honourable Tom Hutherfield-Holmes and JP Flanagan are going into business.'

Perri was flabbergasted. 'Doing what?' she demanded.

'Don't know,' I realized. I'd been too upset that I hadn't been included in their plans that I'd forgotten to ask. Now that I thought of it Perri hadn't asked me to join the band either. I knew I couldn't sing or play any musical instrument, although I could've tried the triangle, but that was beside the point. She hadn't asked. Surely *someone* must want me.

The bathroom door opened slowly and the conversation died. The four of us watched as one of Whiskers's regulars, a civil servant from Sligo in an acrylic

V-neck and flannel trousers, stepped out into the kitchen gingerly, with a shoe in either hand. His clothes had a wet sheen to them. 'I'd best be getting home,' he spluttered bashfully. His chin was driven against his chest and he couldn't raise his eyes.

There could be only one culprit. 'You're a tart, Moira.' I shook my head sadly.

'It's not like that,' she insisted. 'He passed out downstairs and we brought him up here to sleep it off. We were just playing at Good Samaritans.'

'We have no spare beds so I put him in the bath,' Perri added. There was a cruel glint lurking in the corner of her eye.

'But you didn't have to turn the shower on him,' Concepta chided half-heartedly.

I turned to ask the poor civil servant if he would like a cup of tea but he'd gone.

Moira noticed too. 'Lola, would you give me *some* credit. My taste isn't *that* bad.' She scrunched her nose and grimaced, as if she had swallowed a whole bottle of cod-liver oil. 'Now,' she began thoughtfully, 'if it had been that brother of yours . . .' she rubbed a finger across her lips slowly and continued somewhat breathlessly ' . . . well, let's just say he wouldn't have had to spend the night in the bath *alone.*'

'Since you are living with us, his *sisters*, I would consider that to be treachery,' I told her firmly. JP was in my bad books again because of his business venture that I *hadn't* been included in.

'At the very least,' Perri added threateningly.

Moira pouted.

Everyone went to bed. Well, I went to my bed, Perri went to her bed, Concepta went to Perri's bed and Moira collapsed on to the sofa-bed. It was still morning. Barely.

When, some hours later, I stumbled bleary-eyed into the kitchen, Perri was on the phone. She held her hand over the receiver and mumbled in a groggy voice, 'Elise.'

'I'm not here, I'm out,' I mouthed, too tired to talk to Elise and feeling even more dejected than when I'd gone to bed.

'Yes, she's here,' I heard Perri say, as if she had recently taken a vow of honesty.

For crying out loud, I thought, lie, *lie*.

Perri listened for a few moments, nodding gravely. She held the receiver away from her face and turned to me. 'She wants *you* to know that Aunt Potty is on her last legs.'

'Tell her I'm sorry to hear that.' Ah, poor old Aunt Potty. 'Anyway, why does she want *me* to know?' I shrugged inquiringly, a generous heave of the shoulders, accompanied by a full pout and a display of hands. One of Elise's traits. I hadn't inherited it, I'd just spent so many years trying to copy it that I did it automatically now – and it looked nowhere near as good: it just looked like some nervous twitch.

Perri asked the question and listened carefully to the answer. Her eyes grew round in amazement. 'You're not *serious*,' she gasped.

I had a wild moment of panic where I knew for certain, I just *knew* that Aunt Potty had been diagnosed with a contagious disease. A deadly disease. And I had just been to visit her a few days ago. A sickness that inflicted terrible internal suffering but didn't disfigure you. No one would know you were suffering at all. God, wouldn't that be awful? No one would be able to see your suffering. There would be no point in suffering in that case.

In my head, I could envisage Father Des Murphy placing a cool hand on my forehead and whispering, 'She's a saint, an example to us all. All that suffering on the inside and not an ounce of self-pity.'

'You're not serious,' Perri repeated, agog. 'God Almighty, if I'd known that I would have gone to see her myself.'

So, whatever it was, it wasn't contagious. 'What?' I tried to grab the receiver out of Perri's hand but she kept a firm grip on it and pushed me away. 'What is it?' I demanded. 'Tell me.'

'Yes, I'll tell her,' Perri assured Elise down the line. 'One more thing. I've lost JP's new address. Can you give it to me again?' She scribbled a few words on the back of a brown paper bag and waved it at me victoriously. We now had the address he'd been so reluctant to give us. 'Great . . . Lovely . . . Yeah, we're all eating . . . Yeah, going to bed early, too . . . No. No need to send Dad up. The locks on the door are fine.' Perri gritted her teeth and rolled her eyes. She motioned for me to take the phone.

I shook my head adamantly.

'JP's fine . . . Yeah, saw him last night . . . Yeah, looks like he's getting over the London problem . . . And he's eating, too . . . No, I don't think he has a girlfriend yet . . . Yeah, it's a right shame.'

Concepta walked into the kitchen, scratching her oversized belly, and planted a firm kiss on Perri's cheek. 'That's my girl,' she croaked

Pretending to do a rigorous neck exercise, I looked away. That was the first time I had seen them kiss. And it wasn't even a proper kiss. But I was embarrassed none the less. And trying hard not to be. This was the reality of having a lesbian sister, I supposed. Just have to get used to it.

'Elise, this is *your* phone bill . . . I *know* it's the cheap rate . . . No, I haven't heard that Coco has been to the vet's again . . .' Perri looked at me helplessly, unable to persuade Elise to hang up.

'Be firm,' I advised, glad it wasn't me.

'Ah, there's the doorbell and Lola has disappeared,' she lied. 'Where's she gone?' She pretended to sound annoyed. 'Look, have to go, Elise. Talk again soon.' Perri put the phone down and rubbed her ear.

'Poor pet,' Concepta cooed soothingly.

'What about Aunt Potty?' I asked, eagerly.

'You're made, Lola,' Perri declared. 'You're a made woman.'

'Why?' I wanted to know. Desperately.

'Word has it,' she paused for effect, 'that Aunt Potty has changed her will and – '

'And what?' I cut in impatiently.

'Left everything to you,' she proclaimed.

'No,' I squealed.

'Yes,' Perri trumpeted.

A dismal thought appeared to blacken my fertile horizon. 'But she can't have very much, Aunt Potty, can she?'

'Spare a thought for the poor old lady, why don't you?' Concepta said scornfully, a bit too scornfully for my liking.

I glared at her. Concepta, I decided, could afford to be scornful about money. Her father, the publican, had plenty of it and she didn't have to share it with brothers or sisters.

'She *does* have money,' Perri insisted firmly. 'She got that farm when her brother died years ago and you know what they say, "Where there's muck, there's money."' She tilted her head to one side and squinted as if deep in thought. 'On the other hand, she's probably spent it all on that private nursing home,' she decided, spitefully. She definitely begrudged me getting the money. I'd begrudge her getting it too.

The excitement was hard to contain. I hadn't felt this charged since Ireland beat Italy in the World Cup in 1994.

'She's not dead yet,' Concepta warned.

Concepta was right. 'Yeah, let's not talk about it any more.' I'll just think about it. I wonder how I could find out how much money she did have?

Perri's head was hidden in the kitchen cupboard.

'Empty,' she pronounced, her voice bouncing off the bare shelves. She lifted her head. 'I've got a great idea.'

'She didn't say how much it was, did she?' I asked hopefully.

Perri ignored me. 'We'll go to JP's for dinner, out in Dalkey.' She grabbed the brown paper bag she had written his address on. 'Bet *his* cupboards aren't bare.'

Moira walked into the kitchen. Moira was so graceful that walking seemed too common a word to describe what she did. 'Has JP invited us over?' she asked. She made no effort to hide her delight as she waited for an answer.

'He has *not*,' Perri answered. 'We're just *going*,' she proclaimed self-righteously. 'He breezes in here whenever he feels like it. We'll just do the same.'

Moira flicked her hair and moistened those perfect lips. 'I'm ready.'

'I'm sure you are,' Concepta commented drily.

I couldn't quite figure out if they were talking about the same thing.

'Right, if everyone chips in, we can take a taxi. It'll be nearly as cheap as taking the bus,' Perri decided for all of us.

During the taxi ride, I whispered to Moira beside me that I was going to inherit a load of money soon. I had to whisper because I wasn't supposed to talk about it any more. But I was too excited not to tell her.

'It's like winning the lottery without ever having to buy a ticket,' she exclaimed enviously.

Suddenly I remembered to warn everyone that I was supposed to be going back to college.

'I told you it would be a good idea.' Concepta was pleased. 'Remember that conversation we had?'

'But I mightn't get in,' I moaned.

Perri nodded.

'And if I do, I mightn't even pass the *first* year.'

Perri nodded again.

Moira had a pensive look on her face. 'With that money . . . sorry, I know we're not allowed talk about it, but with that money . . .'

The taxi driver eyed me suspiciously in the rear-view mirror, wondering if he had Christina Onassis in the back.

' . . . you should pay your way into one of those private colleges.' She twisted in her seat to face us. 'I knew a girl who went to one of those colleges, and she said that because you had to pay to get in, they only failed you if you were *really* thick.'

I was very interested in what Moira had to say because since that morning I had decided that I really *did* want an education. 'Really?' And wouldn't it be great if I could *pay* for one? I know it would be defeating the purpose a little bit, but it would take all the stress out of exam time.

She nodded.

'So they only fail you if you're *really* thick?' That was that, then. I wasn't really thick, so I should be fine, even though it had been too many years worth counting since Sister Immaculate had taught me my multiplication tables.

Moira nodded again.

I looked at Perri triumphantly.

'She's not dead yet,' Concepta cautioned again. She pronounced each word carefully to make sure I understood. 'She's . . . not . . . dead . . . yet.'

'I know, I know,' I conceded grudgingly, 'but it's still a brilliant idea.'

'Let's celebrate.' Moira pulled a bag of sweets out of her pocket. They were black and white liquorice swirls.

Perri looked at me and waited.

'Liquorice swirls,' I squealed. 'I can't eat those.' I could feel a taste from the past rise in my throat.

'Tell 'em why,' Perri urged me. 'Go on, tell them.'

And so I did.

21. The Liquorice Swirls

1975

When we were children the family outing to visit the O'Driscoll family happened about twice a year with religious punctuality: once in the summer and once coming up to Christmas. They had a big farm about forty miles away. The Christmas trip was to swap tins of Rose's chocolates. It was my father who insisted on the Rose's. Paddy O'Driscoll and he had gone to school together as boys. Elise wanted to bring them a hand-decorated jar of gooseberry compôte. But my father insisted on the Rose's for Paddy O'Driscoll. Every single year. And Paddy O'Driscoll always gave my father the same tin of Rose's.

We set off in our dark purple Opel Cadet. Elise, my father, JP, Perri and I.

Even as children we knew something wasn't right between Mrs O'Driscoll and Elise.

Their conversations were always the same, though the words were different.

This time it was, 'Looking well, Elise. Ballyhilleen still agreeing with you, is it?' Mrs O'Driscoll said this in a flat, contemptuous voice with a nasty smile on her face. Mrs O'Driscoll had waited eight years now for Elise to pack her bags and take the first boat back to France. She didn't belong in Ireland. She belonged over there. With all the other fancy women. She never said those exact words but we all knew.

Mrs O'Driscoll reminded me of Mrs Henehan, Father Rourke's grim housekeeper and not my best friend. Neither of them had a waist. Elise had a tiny waist. And I wondered if that was the problem. Even at five years of age, I knew that a waist was very important to a woman. Elise told me so all the time.

Elise put on her pretend-nice voice. 'I must bring you some French cream for those veins.' She eyed Mrs O'Driscoll's cheeks in feigned concern. 'I always promise, don't I?' A pause. 'But then I forget,' she added, in a distracted voice, as if to let Mrs O'Driscoll know that the minute she walked out the farmhouse door she disappeared from Elise's mind.

Sometimes I felt sorry for Mrs O'Driscoll. Sometimes I didn't.

'Why don't you sit yourself down in that corner?' Mrs O'Driscoll pointed to the far end of her big kitchen. She wanted to make it seem like she was being polite but what she was really doing was letting Elise know she was in *her* house and *she* ruled the roost. Elise was banished to the old armchair with the threadbare arms in the corner. Like every other time.

Perri's tiny arms were wrapped protectively around Elise's legs and she was glowering at Mrs O'Driscoll, not happy with this adult game. Perri was still only two but nearly three. Being nearly three was very important to her.

Elise only agreed to sit there, in the corner, because it meant she didn't have to be too near Mrs O'Driscoll. She didn't usually do anything she didn't want to. It wasn't in her nature.

With a silent plea to Elise, sitting primly in the corner, to behave herself for a few hours, my father disappeared with Paddy O'Driscoll. He had his wellies on and his trousers tucked in. They were gone to walk the fields and talk about what ailed the world. On the way home again in the car he would pacify her by saying that it would be another six months before we had to come back again. Paddy and he were great friends.

Mr and Mrs O'Driscoll had children who were born the same year as all of us, JP, Perri and I, and every year in between. And some above, too. Like steps on stairs, my father used to say. I could never remember how many there were.

We children were expected to be friends because our parents were. Well, because our fathers were. But we didn't know them that well. And we weren't real friends. They were never all in the same place at the same time, even at mealtimes. They couldn't all fit. And they all had Irish names that Elise could never remember. So Mrs O'Driscoll would always pretend that she could never remember *our* names either.

A few of them came tearing into the kitchen, screaming and roaring and dripping muck everywhere. Mrs O'Driscoll slapped the head that came closest to her. 'Didn't I tell ye all before to leave the wellies outside?'

They ignored her as they opened cupboards and rummaged through drawers, looking for something to eat. They were always hungry, the O'Driscoll children. They'd eat the cross off an ass, my father used to say.

'Didn't I? she roared. Her red cheeks turned even redder.

'Yes, Mammy,' they sang, to keep her happy. They were well used to this chorus.

JP was standing with his arms folded, leaning against the table, trying to look like he was the most grown-up child in the kitchen. But he wasn't. Padraig was. He was at least eight and his face was hidden under a blanket of freckles. Padraig was wearing the bottom half of his pyjamas and a checked shirt that was buttoned up all wrong.

I cast a glance at Elise. She was looking at Padraig with an expression of sorrow and bewilderment on her face. I knew she would be.

Elise took pride in turning us out well and, while she still had a say, we were all dressed to her idea of perfection. Although sometimes I didn't want to wear what she chose, like the pleated skirt and starched shirt that made me want to stay clean so I couldn't go rolling in the grass. But I was only five and I didn't have a choice. Sometimes JP didn't want to wear his navy blazer with the gold buttons. He was already six. But he still didn't have a choice.

'Do you play hurley?' Padraig asked JP, between mouthfuls of dry bread.

JP preferred football because he was better at it. 'Yeah, I do.'

Padraig looked pleased. 'Come on so. I'll challenge you.' Crumbs went everywhere.

The O'Driscoll children were fiercely competitive.

JP looked at me. 'Are you coming?'

'No, I want to stay here.' Padraig O'Driscoll and his wooden hurley stick terrified me.

Perri held on to Elise's legs even tighter. She had to protect her from Mrs O'Driscoll *and* Padraig O'Driscoll.

Padraig grabbed two dirty hurley sticks from behind the door and a hard ball caked in mud, and charged out of the room, swinging the hurley sticks above his head and skilfully avoiding Mrs O'Driscoll's sweeping hand. His mouth was stretched wide open as he bellowed a well-practised war-cry.

JP followed slowly.

Mrs O'Driscoll spoke to a small girl standing beside her. She was littler than I was. 'Niamh, take this one out to the yard,' she ordered, pointing a thumb at me. 'There's a ball out there ye can kick around and here's something to stave off the hunger till dinner.' She handed her a few rough slices of chopped turnip. 'You're not to go further than the yard,' she warned.

'Yes, Mammy,' Niamh replied obediently.

'You go too, I've-forgotten-your-name.' She was talking to Perri.

Perri wasn't scared of Mrs O'Driscoll. 'No.'

Elise smirked at Perri's defiance.

Mrs O'Driscoll frowned and I thought that Perri was lucky she was over in the corner. Mrs O'Driscoll's left hand was itching. I could tell.

The yard was out through the back door. On one side of the big stone yard there was a gate that led to the hen shed and on the other side there was another gate that led to the milking parlour. I was very curious about the hen shed.

'Your mammy talks funny,' Niamh began.

'That's because she's French,' I replied, all knowledgeable.

'What's that?' Niamh climbed the rusty gate and was shouting at the hens busy pecking bits of grain on the ground. The hens ignored her. They had seen her and heard her too many times before. And all her brothers and sisters, too.

'It's another country,' I puffed, heaving myself up on to the gate. 'You're Irish,' I told her wisely.

'I'm not. I'm Niamh.' She began to jump up and down on the gate.

I started to jump as well. 'But you're Irish, too.' My voice went up and down. The gate was lurching.

'No,' she insisted, 'I'm just Niamh.'

'I'm Irish, too.' I didn't tell her that I was French as well. I wasn't sure I could explain why I *was* French because I didn't live in a different country. I just knew that Elise told me I was French.

She looked at me and explained very patiently, 'No,

you're Lola.' The way she said it reminded me of Sister Paul when I forgot the next line in my prayers.

I sighed. She was little and didn't understand. But she was eyeing me as if it was *me* who didn't understand.

'Get down off that gate this minute, ye little tippers,' Mrs O'Driscoll howled, nearly making me let go of the gate altogether with the fright she gave me. She was leaning out of the kitchen window and waving a wooden spoon. There was more of her outside the window than there was inside.

'Oh, don't tell me she's going to come out,' I gasped. I thought about using one of the words I'd heard my father use. But I didn't want Mrs O'Driscoll to hear.

She continued waving the wooden spoon at us and looked like she was trying to squeeze out of the kitchen window for sure. 'Ye'll end up knocking the teeth out of yourselves on those metal bars. And mark my words, Niamh O'Driscoll, you'll stay that way. I've enough problems keeping the lot of ye fed and in school uniforms without running to the dentist every second day.'

We clambered down off the gate.

'My brother says she's got eyes in the back of her head, so he does,' Niamh warned me.

I was amazed. 'But how can she see out through all the hair?' I was sure Elise only had eyes on her face. I'd better ask JP.

'I don't know how,' Niamh answered earnestly.

Now that Niamh had told me about her mother having eyes in the back of her head, I decided to tell her my secret. 'I'm going to marry a priest. His name is Father Rourke.'

'Come in and get your dinner,' Mrs O'Driscoll interrupted. She was hanging out of the kitchen window again. For a big woman she sure could bend. There were two dinners in the O'Driscoll house. One in the middle of the day and one in the evening.

We ran in. Niamh stopped to pull her wellies off. I stepped out of my muddy shoes. The toes of my white ankle socks were soggy.

My father and Mr O'Driscoll were sitting at either end of the table. My father patted his knee and said to me, 'Climb aboard and tell me what you've been up to.'

I smiled up into his face and explained that I had seen the hens. Farms were a mystery to me. I was little, and even though we lived in the country we didn't have a farm. I didn't tell him about Mrs O'Driscoll and the eyes in the back of her head.

Mrs O'Driscoll was busy piling plates with potatoes, bacon and cabbage. Her sleeves were rolled up to her elbows and she had a tea-towel tucked into the front of her skirt.

Elise was sitting at the table as well. 'Would you like me to help?' She didn't really *want* to help.

'No, no. You just stay where you are.' Mrs O'Driscoll looked appalled at the thought of Elise in a kitchen. *Her* kitchen.

'Where's my fork 'n' knife?' Perri yelled suddenly. 'I don't have a fork 'n' knife. Where's my fork 'n' knife?'

Perri didn't understand that you had to say knife 'n' fork because if you said it the wrong way round and fast it could sound like something very rude, that's what my father said. And that's what it sounded like now. *Feckin' knife.*

My father looked at Perri sternly.

'Where *is* my fork 'n' knife?'

Mrs O'Driscoll's bosom heaved and she looked very pleased that one of Elise's children was being rude. She had known all along that we weren't reared properly. 'Dear, dear,' she mumbled smugly.

'Lola is going to marry a priest,' Niamh announced unexpectedly.

My father sighed deeply.

JP stared. Padraig had thrashed him in hurley.

The older O'Driscoll children sniggered. And the younger ones looked at me in awe.

Mrs O'Driscoll looked at her husband pointedly as if to say, 'I told you so, Paddy O'Driscoll. Poorly reared children with no religion.'

Mr O'Driscoll bowed his head. 'Pass the spuds,' he muttered.

The cabbage was soggy and the bacon was too salty but I didn't dare say anything. I ate everything that was on the plate. I had to wash every mouthful down with a big gulp of milk. At least the milk was nice. They had their own cows.

When we were finished Mrs O'Driscoll handed Niamh and myself a bucket filled with sop. 'Go feed the hens,' she told us. It took the two of us to lift the heavy bucket. We staggered to the door. It was hard work on a farm. And I was very glad my daddy was a garda and didn't have any hens.

We put the bucket down and Niamh opened the gate. Most of the hens were wandering around outside the hen shed. She started to throw handfuls of the mess in the bucket on the ground. The hens quickly wobbled to the spots where it landed. 'Are there more hens in the shed?' she wanted to know.

I glanced at the low building behind me. 'Will I go in?' I asked excitedly.

'Yeah,' she said casually. She had been in the hen shed loads of times already.

I walked into the hen shed. There were wooden shelves on every wall. The hens' seats. A small twist of black and white on the ground caught my eye. The soft round mound was lying at my feet. I looked closely. It was a liquorice swirl. My favourite sweets. My *very, very* favourite sweets.

I looked around joyously. There were liquorice swirls *everywhere*.

The hens made liquorice swirls.

I bent down and picked up the liquorice swirl with my fingers. By now, I'd already decided that I would eat them all myself. It felt a little funny in my fingers, a little softer than it usually did, and it didn't have a wrapper.

I popped the liquorice swirl on to my tongue and closed my mouth.

Suddenly, a terrible thing was happening in my mouth . . . There was a nasty, nasty taste . . . a taste from the devil. I opened my mouth and, gasping, tried to push the mush out with my tongue . . . The devil's taste got worse. I began to cry . . . I couldn't swallow. I ran screaming out of the hen shed and bolted out through the gate, a hand over my mouth and the devil's taste trapped inside.

Niamh didn't know what was happening. She started to cry too. She raced across the yard behind me sobbing.

I burst into the kitchen.

Elise sprang from her chair in the corner.

I pointed to my mouth, again and again and again. '. . .' No words would come out. I tried to tell her that the devil's taste was in my mouth. I tried to tell her to get the devil's taste out of my mouth. The tears rolled down my cheeks. I hopped up and down on the kitchen floor.

She leaned close and dragged my hand away from my mouth. The smell hit her. Her hand shot up to cover her nose. 'What has happened?' she asked, appalled.

I tried again to tell her that the devil's taste was in my mouth. 'Ugh, ugh, ugh . . .' I panted feverishly.

Mrs O'Driscoll took three steps across the kitchen, looking puzzled, but not concerned. 'Jesus, Mary and Joseph,' she exclaimed. 'I'd recognize that smell anywhere. She's been in the hen shed. She's eaten hen shite that one.'

Elise lacerated Mrs O'Driscoll with the look she gave her. Her hen shed, her hen shite, *her* fault. She tucked me under her arm and rushed over to the kitchen sink. Turning on the tap, she urged me to open my mouth and she began to scrub inside with gentle fingers. It took a long, long time for the devil's taste to go away.

That was our last visit to the O'Driscoll family. And I never ate liquorice swirls ever again.

22. A Nice Start to the Fourth Week in Dublin

Monday, 30 March 1998

With a tremendous effort, the sun squeezed itself through the tiny window of the box room. The soft rays prodded my face, a reminder that it was Monday morning. I kicked back the blankets and groaned as I swung my feet over the side of the bed. I *made* myself get up, along with all the others *making* themselves get up across Dublin.

Quietly, I tiptoed into the dark hall, sneaking past the sitting room where Moira was sprawled across the sofa-bed, and Perri's bedroom where she and Concepta generously filled the narrow width of the bed, a carefree mound under a yellow sheet. They slept soundly.

Concepta swore she worked in a pub in Temple Bar, the Mecca of nightlife in Dublin, some nights. She kept telling me it was a real bustling place, but bustling or not, she was never there. She was always *here*. She seemed to be able to arrange her working hours to suit herself, which meant she never worked. I was sure that Eugene O'Sullivan was sending funds up from Ballyhilleen.

Moira was between jobs, as she put it, and made weekly trips to the dole office.

And Perri had just decided to give up working for John Dooley at Vocab-U-Lary altogether to concentrate on her music career. I wouldn't be the one to point out that she didn't *have* a music career as yet. JP would be sure to do that.

I knew what my father would call them. A shower of wasters, that's what he would say. Of course, I wasn't really much better. But that was only momentarily. At least I got up in the mornings!

The others slept for most of the day then spent all night tirelessly yabbing about what they would do when they'd "made it". In three short days, this band had somehow blossomed into their whole future. They even had a name now. Free Birds. I thought they should've called themselves Free Bats, given their sleeping habits. Between the lot of them, they had so much belief in themselves that I didn't question their success, not aloud anyway. I knew better than that. But, deep down, the little bubbles of doubt simmered away. At least, let them not get anywhere before I do if they are to get anywhere at all, I prayed.

I made myself a cup of tea and used the last Lyons tea-bag that was left in the jar, watching carefully as the perforated bag stained the clear water, pulling it out before the water got too dark. That way the others would be able to use it too, I thought sensibly. I left it to dry on the draining-board. Aunt Potty used to hang her tea-bags out to dry on her clothes-line. Elise thought it was a terrible stingy thing to do. I can remember agreeing wholeheartedly with her at the time but now the thought of *one* tea-bag being used for only *one* cup of tea seemed ridiculous.

Deliberately avoiding looking at the bed too closely in case I might *see* something, I crept through Perri's room with the steaming cup of tea in one hand and the letter from the college firmly clenched in the other. The chair beside the window wobbled as I climbed clumsily on to it and dragged myself out through the window to the roof terrace.

Sitting on the old bench out there, the cup of tea between my knees, I read the letter again, devouring every word inviting me, *inviting* me, to submit my application to St Peter's Private College for Further Development. Just reading it made me feel like I was achieving something. I sighed contentedly. Then my eyes flicked to the paragraph about the fees. *Thousands* of pounds. Well, not *that* many thousands, but there was no way I could afford them as things stood. But if Aunt Potty died and she really had left me some money – I felt a bit mean thinking about old Aunt Potty like she was an automatic cash machine but I did it anyway – then, it *would* be possible.

I yawned loudly, my jaws tearing back to let the tiredness out. There was a good reason why I was tired. It had been on the riper side of four o'clock in the morning by the time we'd arrived home from JP's new flat in Dalkey. He hadn't seemed too surprised to see the four of us standing on the doorstep the night before. 'Come in,' he'd immediately invited us, standing to one side to clear a way for us.

We rushed in. He patted my arm in a friendly, welcoming gesture as I walked by, but then his eyes moved on to Moira, who was artfully returning his lustful stare.

The flat was on the ground floor of an old town-house, maybe Victorian or Georgian, definitely old. It was a proper flat compared to Perri's hovel above the Tipsy Tinker. But it didn't yet have that lived-in feel that Perri's most definitely did. JP's flat would probably never have it.

Tom sat on a dark brown leather sofa, his face a picture of concentration, as he flicked through the sheets of paper he held in his immaculate hands. The Mexican-style heavy chest that served as a coffee table in front of him was hidden beneath tidy piles of more papers.

Perri spotted the kitchen. 'I hope you've got food here,' she said, disappearing.

Concepta nodded enthusiastically and there was a cacophony of slamming doors as Perri rummaged freely through the cupboards. 'I'll just check what Perri's doing,' I said, and ran into the kitchen, the rumbling in my stomach dictating my speed. I ran fast.

Perri had gathered a pile of food in front of her. There was a sliced pan, layers of cold meat, a slab of butter and a tub of grated Parmesan. Everything else seemed to be hidden behind gleaming cupboard doors.

There was talk and laughter coming from the other room as Moira charmed Tom with her story of the audition in the Tipsy Tinker. Even in the kitchen I could hear Concepta slap her hand against her thigh when Moira said something funny.

Suddenly JP stuck his head over my shoulder. 'You're some fibber, you are,' he accused half-amused. 'College, my *arse*,' he added, with a disbelieving laugh.

Perri overheard. 'She *is* going, you know,' she said firmly. 'It's all set.' Perri would say anything to rankle JP, even if it meant siding with me.

'Yeah, it's all set,' I repeated.

Perri dug a hand into the bag of bread and pulled out a stack. She began, slice by slice, to cover each one with a thick coat of butter. 'I suppose *you* thought you had the monopoly on education in our family,' she shot at him. JP was the only one out of the lot of us who went to university. She flicked out the crumbs that had stuck behind her new nails. 'Oh, and by the way,' she added, in an innocent voice, 'Moira's not interested in you. She thinks you're a right gobshite.' Perri pursed her lips regretfully. 'I asked her for you,' she lied, so sweetly. 'I only wanted to help.'

'Mind your own bloody business, Perri,' JP exploded, and stalked out of the kitchen muttering to himself. JP did not like to hear the word no and he didn't like Perri, or anyone else, telling him what he was or wasn't going to get, and I had an awful suspicion that he was going to *get* Moira.

As I sat a thick slice of cooked ham on each square of buttered bread, I warned Perri to keep quiet about Aunt Potty. I didn't want JP to know that I might be in the money. He wasn't getting his hands on any of it, and I had a suspicion that he might try. And after all, she *wasn't* dead yet. The money wasn't mine yet.

JP still had my confirmation money that I'd loaned him sixteen years ago. It had come to eighty-four pounds – a fortune at the time, a fortune at *this* time. He'd had no problem whatsoever in coaxing the money out of me. But at the age of twenty-eight, I was a good deal wiser.

In a flash, the interest I had in helping Perri make sandwiches evaporated. I let the ham drop on to the kitchen counter and urgently shouted over my shoulder, 'JP, what about my confirmation money? I want it back.'

It was the start of the last week in Dublin for my group of French students. They were eagerly heading back to Paris on Saturday, carrying with them a few more words of English than when they first arrived. And most of those, I felt pretty sure, had been learned outside the classroom and couldn't be used in any kind of decent situation. I wasn't sure if I'd managed to teach them anything, other than a hatred of grammar and the knowledge that the English language was full of exceptions to the rule, which couldn't be explained.

I waited in the classroom. Clarisse and Laurent deliberately avoided my eyes as they stumbled through the door awkwardly, making a disastrous attempt at hiding their embarrassment after the scene in St Stephen's Green on Friday afternoon.

Even though I had fully convinced myself over the weekend that they were to blame for the whole incident, I was feeling a bit embarrassed. I tried to hide this discomfort by shouting at them, 'Sit apart, you two.' To opposite sides of the room, my hands pointed. Let's be honest, I told myself, I *had* been chasing Father Murphy through the park, so it wasn't at all surprising that I was feeling embarrassed. But it wouldn't stop me trying again, I realized suddenly. And the thought of *that* nearly made me head straight for the Liffey. But they'd already closed the door. I'd stopped trying to find a reason for this obsession with the clergy a long time ago when I'd been unable to find any logical explanation – probably like with most obsessions. I just knew it made me behave irrationally but I was powerless to fight it. Anyway, I consoled myself, as obsessions go, it was a fairly harmless one.

The three hours of class dwindled by, as slowly as ever. The clock on the wall behind me clicked on the minute, every minute, and I heard every one acutely. The usual spate of high-pitched screaming matches, seat-swapping, ferocious pucking, and clothes-pulling punctuated the afternoon. I didn't care. And then there were the regular interruptions by John Dooley, who liked nothing better than to check up on me unannounced, sticking his head around the door and grinning like a nasty surprise. I'd stopped caring about that too.

But my tolerance levels were sinking fast. Another four days of this was likely to send me to an early grave. I could take Aunt Potty's plot, if she didn't end up using it. I'd need it before she did.

'Listen carefully, everyone.' I clapped my hands to get their attention. 'Behave yourselves.' I waited. 'You all understand the word "behave" now, don't you?' I'd had to say it often enough, I thought wearily. I scribbled the letters on the blackboard in strong frustrated strokes. BEHAVE. 'OK, you all B-E-H-A-V-E until Friday – that's another four days,' I flashed the right number of fingers at them, 'and I will bring you out on Friday evening.' I spoke slowly and over-pronounced every word enticingly. There was nothing like a good bribe.

I waited expectantly for a reaction and gave up after two minutes of puzzled silence. I snapped my fingers impatiently at Laurent. *Snap, snap.* 'Translate for them, would you?' I pleaded, turning my back to them and rolling my eyes at the mute blackboard, wondering if I had been an eejit at the age of sixteen, too. Of course, I had. I still was.

Speaking French in the classroom was against John Dooley's rule of total immersion, of course, and I only used English – but I cheated the whole time anyway: I let Laurent speak in French. It was so much easier than filling the blackboard with ridiculous drawings and doing a half-witted Marcel Marceau impersonation to explain some elementary word. And the result was just the same. They never remembered anything.

We were well suited, I mused. I was a hopeless teacher and they were hopeless students.

Inevitably, I turned to face them again, my face once more a mask of teacherly patience, and caught the end of a flurry of nods of approval as Laurent finished explaining what I'd suggested.

'Good?' I probed, dipping my head up and down questioningly.

A few responded with grins and three braved a rendition of the word 'good'.

'Goud.'

'Goode.'

'Gooth.'

'Settled, then,' I announced cheerfully. But the smile on my face froze and the mask of teacherly patience slipped. Fourteen of the fifteen pairs of clear French eyes staring at me had glazed over in puzzlement. Muttering to myself, I began to scratch the word SETTLED on the blackboard. The stick of chalk broke in half, as I jabbed away in exasperation. *Why* couldn't I have got the lap-dancing job at the Foxy Lady? I set about trying to explain what settled meant, in words they might understand, which didn't leave me with a lot of options.

I gave up and prepared to break John Dooley's total immersion rule. '*Soyez sage d'ici jusqu'à la fin de la semaine et je vous emmène tous au resto vendredi soir. On pourra s'éclater un peu. D'accord?*' I really wanted to make sure they understood that Friday night's outing hinged on a show of good behaviour for the rest of the week. And I'd have to keep my side of the bargain and make sure they had a good time.

It took several seconds for it to register that I'd just spoken to them in perfect French, but when it did the room was immediately hushed into a stunned silence. Then they started to bombard me with all sorts of surprised questions in rapid French.

Laurent Ducros looked at me with a new-found respect.

As I crossed O'Connell Street bridge after the lesson, my stomach began to complain loudly from the lack of food. Three young girls in skin-tight, patterned hipsters giggled knowingly at me as they brushed by, proudly displaying their concave stomachs. Professional non-eaters by the look of it, I promptly decided. One of them was showing so much stomach that the tops of her legs were nearly on display. Without really meaning to, I frowned disapprovingly at them. They stopped giggling, and three brazen stares pinned me to the railings of the bridge.

My stomach continued making unnatural noises and attracting the amused attention of passers-by. I responded with an apologetic grin every time, each one more strained than the last. The bridge seemed to go on for ever. Guided by a roaring stomach, my feet propelled me towards a mini-supermarket I spotted in the distance.

Less than three minutes later I was standing in the queue behind two Japanese tourists, who had emptied the entire wire tray of bananas, with a fistful of change in one hand and a six-pack of Tayto cheese-and-onion dangling from the other, silently fuming because I had wanted some of those bananas too. I studied them closely. They were wearing wide-brimmed canvas hats, long-sleeved blouses carefully buttoned up to the neck, cotton Bermuda shorts, woolly tights, white lace ankle socks and flatter than flat runners. They were not going to risk the struggling rays of the pale spring sun pricking even a midget-sized area of uncovered skin.

Suddenly I felt a set of fingers dancing lightly on my shoulder. It was a nice feeling and I let the fingers dance a second longer than I should have before I turned around, expecting someone to say, 'Sorry, wrong person.'

Tom Hutherfield-Holmes stood behind me. 'Hello,' he said warmly, a playful smile on his face. He smelt of a hypnotic mixture of warm sand and clear sea-water. 'I saw you come in,' he said.

I smiled back, 'Hiya,' and was immediately struck by how out of place he looked standing there, beaming down at me, in the mini-supermarket. He was too tall, too well dressed, too tanned, too something and too everything. It was strange because everyone else seemed to think so too, as they stared inquisitively at him, wondering what someone like him was doing somewhere like this, not that there was anything wrong with the place, smiling at someone like me.

The dainty Japanese women in front of me with the armloads of bananas and the well-protected skin, glossy heads coming to somewhere between his elbow and his shoulder, were busy dissecting him in rapid, song-like bursts and casting shy glances his way. *Stop it*, I ordered them silently, with such an unexpected surge of possessiveness that I almost clamped my hand over my mouth in case the words tumbled out of their own accord. If it was at all possible to look at yourself in disbelief, I was doing just that. Where did this sudden *possessiveness* towards Tom Hutherfield-Holmes spring from? I knew very well where it sprang from!

'How are you?' he asked, tilting his head towards me attentively as he spoke, his fair hair falling to one side. He asked the question as if he really wanted to know the answer, not like he had just bumped into JP's sister and was making polite conversation. He was looking straight into my eyes as he asked, with clear blue eyes that were rimmed with an unusual greyish purple, piercing the cool, unfazed façade I was trying to build. A perfect circle around each eye was slightly less golden where his sunglasses had shielded the smooth skin from the blinding sun on the slopes of the Swiss Alps, where he had been skiing just before he came to Ireland. But you would only notice if you were looking really closely. Like I seemed to be.

I swallowed the sudden urge to giggle nervously and wondered why it was that I was looking at him like that at all. 'Yeah, I'm fine,' I answered, taking a bit too long.

His eyebrows creased questioningly and he shifted legs, gracefully swapping the weight of his body from the right one to the left. The muscle at the top of his lean leg rippled beneath the material of his dark denims, rippled *invitingly*.

Reluctantly, I dragged my gaze upwards, amazed at the height of my own reluctance, and thought that I'd better try to explain this strange behaviour, which he probably didn't think was strange for me at all. This being said, I wasn't about to give him the real explanation. 'Just a bit hungry,' I told him, as if that explained everything, and meaningfully waved the long sack of crisps.

'Are you thirsty, too?' Deftly he tucked his starched shirt into the top of his jeans. It was already immaculately tucked in. His fingers slid momentarily behind the denim in an unintentional tease.

'I'm always thirsty,' I gobbled.

'Why don't we go for a drink?' he suggested.

I stared at him and gritted my teeth hard to stop my jaw from dropping to the ground at the unexpected question. The only reason I could think of why I *should* go happened to be the same reason why

I *shouldn't*. I was worried that I was beginning to fall for Tom Hutherfield-Holmes, have *real* feelings for him, not just the light-hearted butterfly emotions he'd sparked in me from the start but dangerously *real* feelings. The others, who found all things about him a bit too ostentatious for their liking, would not understand it. They'd laugh at me. Even when I tried, I just couldn't see the ostentatious part of him. I never had. Not that I had any intention of admitting any of this to them, but still. And I mean, if I was going to fall for him hard, why hadn't I fallen from the beginning? Why now? Why today? Or maybe I had fallen? And why was he asking *me* to go for a drink with him when he could have had his pick of the city? That was the hardest question to answer.

As I mulled over these weighty, weighty questions in my head, finding no answers that made any sense to me, I realized that he was *still* waiting for an answer. The whole queue seemed to be waiting. The Japanese were doing a much better effort at being discreet about it than the Irish, each one of whom looked like they wanted a say in the answer.

I nodded eagerly. 'I don't think I want the crisps any more,' I decided, and dropped the plastic sack into the oblong basket beside the door that held the packets of biscuits they were trying to sell off for 33p. It was strange that no one ever wanted the coffee creams and the manufacturers kept on making them.

'You're very like your mother,' he commented unexpectedly.

A wave of pleasure washed over me. My cheeks tingled with colour. Not a lot of girls would like to be compared with their mother, but I most certainly did. Even now, in her late forties, Elise was a beauty. No matter how hard I had tried over the years, I didn't look a bit like her and I knew it. But that someone else might think I did – well, that was grand.

A round plump security mirror was perched high up in the corner, over the cash register. Purposefully, I leaned forward and caught my reflection. Suddenly, it was as if I was looking at myself through rose-coloured spectacles. The wild curls that I had cursed ever since I knew how seemed to have become a mane fit for a temptress, the pale skin that I had always wanted to swap for Perri's darker complexion was transformed by a pearly glow, the eyes in the reflection sparkled back at me beguilingly and the mouth was made beautiful by the smile it wore, if only at that instant. Still, though, I looked nothing like Elise.

'So which bit *exactly* reminds you of Elise?' I quizzed Tom, as we walked out the door.

He studied me for an instant, reaching out graciously to take my overnight bag, full of books, from my shoulder, and said, 'It's more of an air, really.'

I dug my hands into my pockets while I considered this. 'More of an air?' I repeated. 'So nothing in particular?'

He paused. 'Yes, to the first, and no, to the second.'

I decided an air was good enough. 'Well, you're the

first person who has ever found *any* similarity between the two of us at all,' I said happily.

We took a few steps in an easy silence.

'It's really admirable that you are going back to college,' Tom began. His face wore the same honest expression that I'd noticed before. '*Really* admirable.'

It wasn't *that* admirable but it felt good that he thought so, somehow reassuring, a sign that I was doing the right thing for once. But what was Tom Hutherfield-Holmes doing to make me feel so confident and so lovely all of a sudden? I pondered this for a few minutes, as we continued to walk down the street. Truth be known, he was walking, I was floating.

Yet again, I could not find an answer. 'What were you doing wandering around like a lost soul on your own anyway?' I asked him.

He shrugged. 'JP wanted the flat to himself for a while. I think he was expecting, um, um,' there was a sheepish pause, as he looked at me, 'um, a visitor.'

'What? A guitar-swinging visitor with long red hair who answers to the name of Moira?'

He gazed at me in amazement. 'I thought that was a secret,' he gasped. He seemed honestly shocked that I knew about Moira and JP's spate of horizontal high jinks.

'That's about as secret as Charlie Haughey and Terry Keane,' I laughed. Charlie Haughey and Terry Keane, the politician and his long-standing ladyfriend, was one of Ireland's best known secrets.

'Who's Charlie Haughey and Terry Keane?' he wanted to know.

'What?' I choked. I thought *everyone* knew who Charlie Haughey and Terry Keane were.

'I'm only joking,' he quickly reassured me. 'Of *course* I know who they are.'

But I knew that he didn't. The expression on his face wasn't quite as honest as it had been. But that didn't matter. 'Surely the politicians in England are just as bad for that kind of thing?'

He picked up on my meaning. 'Yeah, they are,' he laughed loudly, 'but they don't hold the monopoly.'

We stopped in front of a bar called the Tunnel. The two bouncers on the door had on identical leather jackets, black T-shirts and smart black trousers stretched across thick legs, the crease visible only from the knee down. They wore earpieces and professional scowls. They greeted Tom with a stiff handshake and didn't even look at me. When I'd spent the odd weekend in Dublin before I left Ireland ten years earlier, bouncers were human and friendly, and at the end of a night they were usually more drunk than any of the punters, and it was very reassuring.

We stepped into the bar, and even for a girl without a proper education like myself, it wasn't difficult to figure out why it was called the Tunnel. The Tunnel, I mused to myself, and looked around. By the end of next year I'll be able to spell it frontways and backways, I joked, still to myself, of course, and grinned at how funny I thought I was.

Tom caught the tail end of this satisfied smirk. 'What's so funny?' he wanted to know.

'Just thinking that it was aptly named,' I informed him cleverly, as I surveyed the long narrow passage once more, with its low curved ceiling, and clever sunken lighting. 'Very . . . very . . .' I hesitated, willing the right word to appear, wanting to make a good impression. 'Very nineties Dublin,' I concluded.

'Indeed,' he agreed readily.

The square board hanging behind the bar gaily announced that Happy Hour was between five and eight. The chalked message explained that you could have two cocktails for the price of one. I glanced at my watch. It was half past seven. Half an hour of Happy Hour left. That was enough happiness for me.

'Two Slippery Nipples?' Tom's voice broke through my reverie.

I looked at him alarmed. Was he *really* asking me if I had two slippery nipples? I was stunned. How in the name of God did we get on to the subject of slippery nipples? And to think I had taken him for a real gentleman. 'That's none of your business,' I snapped, then added for good measure, 'Anyway, not at the moment, thank you very much.'

'But they're great,' Tom argued. 'Lip-tingling good.' He smacked his lips together, and quite nice lips they were, too. But I wasn't going to allow myself to think like that.

'Lip-tingling good. Lip-tingling good,' I mimicked his words, head bent to hide what I was doing. Where

the hell did he get that from? *I* had been had, I decided, and I was furious. I looked around to make sure no one else was listening to our conversation. I would have been mortified. But the barman caught my eye. 'Is that Two Slippery Nipples or not?'

Tom shrugged apologetically and answered for me, 'The lady's not keen.'

'Damn right,' I fumed, and vowed never to admit that I had been on the verge of being keen. All this crude talk had turned me right off. My illusions came crumbling down around me. I snorted half-heartedly, annoyed at myself and more annoyed at him. The only gentleman I'd met since I'd set foot back in this country was Father Des Murphy.

Tom looked confused. 'A bottle of St Emilion and two glasses, then, please.'

'A safer bet,' the barman said.

Without waiting for him, I stormed over to an empty table and furiously dropped on to the chair. Slippery nipples, my arse. What does he think I am? As I heatedly continued my silent lambasting of Tom's sullied character, I picked up the small sheet of paper lying on the table and absentmindedly began to skim the page, tutting to myself as I went. That's when it hit me. Oh, the shame and the embarrassment. There it was, as clear as day, Slippery Nipple, *cocktail* of the week. A Slippery Nipple was a *cocktail*? A Slippery Nipple was a cocktail! I moaned in disbelief and buried my burning face in my hands. What I really wanted to do was kick myself. A nice sharp kick on the shin for being so stupid. But Tom was walking towards the table with a bottle, two glasses and my bag. What must he think of me now after jumping on my high horse over a *glass of alcohol*?

'I just don't like Slippery Nipples,' I blurted.

'That's all you had to say,' he told me, and gave me a reassuring smile.

I was saved.

I loved the sound of his voice and waited impatiently for each new word. By now I couldn't remember a time when I didn't like his voice. It seemed to be there from the start . . . when I first met him, in Ballyhilleen, when my father had called him a pansy because he was wearing a yellow tie, and then that dreadful weekend in London when I realized how much I cared and he didn't, and at the airport a few days ago, when he was happily indulging JP's antics.

Like a dense fog that seems to appear from nowhere, the bar filled up around us, as Tom kept me entertained with stories about his parents and his childhood. It all sounded very normal despite the money they had, and when I told him so he warned me, in a very serious voice, that money wouldn't make you happy. Needless to say, I didn't believe that for one instant but I nodded anyway. As there was no money in my family, there was just no way that I was going to believe that having loads of it didn't make you happy. One day, I would have money. But first things first. An education. An education for Lola.

For him, I tried to make being a nanny for ten

years sound glamorous, which was nearly impossible because there was nothing glamorous about dirty nappies, creeks of vomit and endless fights with the Portuguese housekeeper, with the pidgin French, over whether cleaning up the vomit was actually under her jurisdiction or mine. I lost every one of these fights.

Then I told him about the French embassy, and the fools Perri and I had made of ourselves with our little speech in Irish, leaving out the bit about the fight with the waiter in case that might cast me in a bad light, as the kind of girl who couldn't be brought anywhere. That made him laugh and my chest swelled with pride. Well, I was secretly sticking it out anyway, hoping to get his attention, but up to now he'd been too much of a gentleman to allow his gaze to wander, or for it to be caught wandering in any case.

His infectious enthusiasm for my stories spurred me on to tell him about how JP going away to university had been responsible for my first hangover on Bulmer's cider, and how I'd had my first real taste of humiliation on Belle-Ile at the age of sixteen. I even told him that I'd once planned to marry the parish priest.

He told me that there had been times in London, especially at the beginning, when JP had been miserable because he missed us all so much. I found this hard to believe because it didn't fit with the picture of JP that I had in my head, a picture that had been twenty-eight years in the making. But Tom, in his earnest way, assured me it was true and admitted that he'd nearly been envious of JP at those times because he'd always wanted brothers and sisters, if only to miss them when he was away. I told him he could have mine.

We finished the bottle of wine and the barman magically appeared with a second and a knowing smile, then a third and an evil smirk.

We left the bar at ten o'clock. It took us ten minutes to find the door, and that wasn't because there were people blocking it. I did ask whether he thought they had moved it since we arrived. He did think so.

Outside, the bouncers were busy explaining to a gang of fellas with heavy northern English accents and garters around their heads that it was the policy of the bar not to accept stag nights. We stood on unsteady feet, willingly rocking into each other, and watched as they ran around the corner, slipped the lacy garters from their heads and sneaked back in one by one, tagging on to any group going into the bar.

'Clever boys,' Tom slurred.

'Not them mean boys in the leather jackets, though,' I slurred back.

Tom turned to me and wrapped his arms around me protectively, and it just seemed so natural that I let myself sink into his chest. He pulled me even closer, and bound together like that, we staggered up the street.

We traipsed down Grafton Street. I pointed to Vocab-U-Lary. 'I've got a very important job there teaching very important French people how to speak very important English.' At this point, I was having difficulty with the English language myself. Tom seemed to understand me perfectly. I didn't know where we were headed but I would have been happy to walk the streets until dawn.

Tom stopped suddenly. 'I have an idea.'

I tilted my face up to his and it must have been clear from the eager expression plastered across it that I would agree to anything. He didn't even tell me his idea, he just said, 'Come on.' A bit husky, his voice was too.

I chirped in agreement.

The night air was doing nothing to clear my head. The gentle breeze was only adding to the intoxication. I breathed in deeply. That lovely smell was there again. The one I'd first noticed in the mini-supermarket. 'Do you take your bath in sand and sea-water?' I wondered foolishly aloud, not too clearly, and buried my head deeper in his chest. He must do, I decided. I could hear shells crunch beneath my feet.

We meandered down the side of St Stephen's Green, looping from footpath to road, our legs entangled because we *had* to walk wrapped up in each other's arms, as if it were the first, or last, time we would ever meet.

'Why do you fancy me?' I was dying to know, not for one minute believing that three bottles of wine might be playing a potent Cupid. I *was* gorgeous. Everyone else was as ugly as sin. Perri, Elise, Moira, they all had faces like the back of a bus, the whole lot of them. I couldn't remember why I didn't always think that. Of course, it would be *me* that he would fancy. I preened myself for the glowing answer I was sure to get.

Tom didn't disappoint me. 'You're clever, funny and attractive.' At least, that's what I *think* he said.

I purred softly in delight, and then I remembered that he'd actually spurned my advances once. 'Then why didn't you do something that time in London when I felt your leg in the bar?' I blurted out and sobbed, 'You didn't want me then.'

'Lola, Lola, I thought you were drunk,' he explained tenderly, slurring endearingly while trying to sound serious and sincere at the same time. 'I didn't want you to regret anything. I knew there'd be other times for us.' He held my chin softly in his hand. 'I really did want to kiss you then,' he confessed. 'I want you to know that. And I still do.'

I laughed and gleefully admitted, 'The drink made me bolder but it didn't make me feel things I wasn't already feeling. Anyway, I think I might be drunk now too.'

'Now is different.'

'Now is great.'

Tom stroked my face lightly with the tips of his fingers. 'JP told me you were only interested in priests.'

JP's a bastard at times, I wanted to tell him, but he was still stroking my face and all I could do was purr. Every tomcat in the neighbourhood would soon be on our tail. I wanted to explain about the priests, I wanted to let him know that I never did anything I shouldn't have with any priest, that it was just a harmless . . . thing, a thing that he might cure me of. But it wasn't the right time. All those words would never come out in the right order, if they came out at all.

Tom tugged on my sleeve. 'Here we are.'

We had stopped in front of a small hotel, on the edge of St Stephen's Green. We climbed the steps to the front door unsteadily, Tom leading and pulling me in behind him, not wanting to let go for fear that I might run away, I supposed, or fall down in a heap. 'A double room, please,' he asked the receptionist. 'For one night only.'

At those words, my heart took a sober painful leap. For one night only.

Tom squeezed my hand reassuringly, as if he could read my thoughts, and I smiled at the back of his head. 'The night of a thousand nights,' I warbled unintelligently, not sure what I meant, but thinking it sounded fittingly romantic. 'The night of a thousand nights,' I repeated.

Tom cast me a fleeting worried glance over his shoulder and landed his credit card on the desk.

I was grateful that I had my overnight bag with me. Maybe it looked like we weren't two people who had met in a mini-supermarket off O'Connell Street bridge, shared three bottles of wine and decided to find a hotel room for the night. I hiccuped tellingly. Then again, maybe not, I decided.

'Room twenty-four.' The receptionist pointed to the stairs. 'Third floor.'

The only thing I noticed about room twenty-four was the quilt on the bed. It was the only thing anyone could notice and not just me. It had an ornate Celtic cross sewn down the middle, in rich, virtuous colours. 'Get rid of it,' I wailed in a fluster.

Tom whipped the quilt from the bed and stuffed it into the wardrobe. 'Why on earth would anyone put a cross on a bed quilt?' he muttered to himself, in astonishment. 'Even the Irish?'

'What do you mean "even the Irish"?' I quizzed him, wondering why we couldn't have gone to any of the minimalistic havens the city boasted with no crosses on the bed covers. 'The Irish saved western civilization,' I told him pointedly. I had just finished reading a book on it. Some bits I'd even gone to the trouble of learning off by heart but they still sounded like they had been learned off by heart so I couldn't use them yet. Spontaneity took a lot of practice.

'And look at *that*,' he urged me, pointing to the wall above the bed.

I stared at the spot he was pointing to. In a thick gold frame was a photograph of the Pope, the last time he had visited Ireland. It was years and years ago, in the late seventies. The time he had uttered the words, 'Young people of Ireland, I love you,' and the country had erupted into a frenzy that had lasted three days. The photo was of the Pope standing up in his Pope-mobile, waving to the enthusiastic crowds lining the street. Half the police force in Ireland seemed to be running behind the custom-made car, grown men who hadn't run in years, agony written across their distorted faces.

'We'll take that down,' I decided. I didn't fancy having the Pope frowning down on me while I lay on that bed getting up to no good. I locked His waving Holiness into a drawer.

'Now,' Tom murmured, 'now, that you've stripped the walls bare, let's get down to another kind of stripping.'

'Mmmmm.' I closed my eyes and the room spun. 'Whoa.' My hand grabbed the wall light beside me, the luxurious fringing tickled the palm of my hand. 'Come here and feel this,' I begged Tom, laughing. 'Nice feeling.' I was rubbing the tips of my fingers along the edge of the fringing, watching it sway lightly.

I turned to look at him and my throat tightened unexpectedly. He stood there motionless: his eyes had turned a deep ocean blue and were glazed with arousal. Did *I* do that? I wondered proudly. He began to open his shirt. 'Come here and feel *this*.'

Looking at his smooth velvet chest, I knew there wasn't a holy picture or a religious quilt in the world that could have stopped me from touching him. I crossed the room, laid my hand flat on his chest and slowly moved it down, lightly marking his skin with the warmth of my hand. 'Nice feeling,' I whispered.

He pulled me close, his fingers denting the small of my back. I could feel his heart pounding. He wanted me to feel it. My own matched his, thundering beat for beat. 'We're pounding the exact same,' I told him.

'Yes, we are,' he murmured and dropped his face until his forehead pressed against my forehead, and his nose softly touched mine, and I thought that I might faint if his lips didn't find mine there and then, if somehow they lost their way. But they didn't. They found them. As his mouth moved on mine, his lips seemed to whisper my name, 'Lola, Lola, Lola . . .'

It was a kiss that lasted until morning.

As we left the hotel in the morning, the same receptionist was on duty as the night before. 'Did you enjoy the room?' she asked.

I blushed and looked coyly at Tom. I hadn't really enjoyed the room but I had certainly enjoyed him.

He winked at me, a teasing flutter of his eyelid. 'It was splendid.'

'A real cardinal stayed in that room once,' she told us reverently, as if she was letting us share an age-old secret with her. 'We call it the Cardinal Ryan Room.' She patted her chest proudly. There was no doubt in my mind that the Cardinal Ryan Room had been her idea. 'We try to keep the holy theme going in the room. You might have noticed the picture of the Pope and the quilt.'

The aura of sin was glowing around us. I was sure she could sense it.

Tom took no notice of her as he scrawled his imposing, and highly illegible, signature across the bottom of the credit-card receipt. He thanked her and we left.

'He even blessed that room, you know,' she called after us.

'That's it. I'm going to hell for sure now,' I moaned.

'Can I come too?' Tom asked.

23. The Rest of the Week in Dublin

Tuesday, 31 March – Friday, 3 April 1998

'Elise phoned,' Perri greeted me, as I walked through the door the next morning, wearing yesterday's clothes and a self-satisfied smile. 'Aunt Potty died in her sleep last night.'

Perri, Concepta and Moira were staring at me imploringly, *begging* me with greedy, bulging eyes to ask about the money, not yet wondering where I'd been all night.

I ignored the three of them and instead shook my head sadly and said, 'That's terrible.'

Perri nodded. 'The funeral's on Saturday. We'll have to go down for it.'

'It'll be a sad day.' I sniffed.

Concepta exploded. 'Jesus, Mary and Joseph, don't you even *want* to know about the money?' Her massive chest was heaving incredulously.

'Of *course* I do,' I admitted, when I thought about it because I hadn't been thinking about Aunt Potty's money just then. My mind had been happily cavorting in room twenty-four. 'I just wanted to wait five minutes,' I told her. 'As a sign of, you know, respect.'

'Respect, my arse,' Concepta nearly choked. 'The graveyards are full of respected dead people.'

'Yeah, yeah,' Perri conceded miserably. 'You got it

all. Every penny.' Her eyes narrowed to slits as she tried to figure out what I had that she didn't, besides the money now, that was. 'Why *you*?' she wailed aloud. 'It must have been that last visit.' A reproachful glare. 'The one where you *sneaked off* to see her,' she said accusingly. 'Without me.'

'Hang on,' I said, suddenly feeling giddy, the giddy feeling you get when you discover a twenty-pound note hidden inside the lining of a coat pocket and you're broke, only much more giddy than that. 'I didn't *sneak off*. I was the only one who *would* go.'

Perri didn't give up. 'I don't know *what* you did to her,' she quipped, 'but that money will have to be shared out evenly between us all, you know.' She looked at me defiantly. 'Yes, it will.'

'That money's for my education, Perri,' I replied. 'And anyway, she might have only left me fifty pounds in an old envelope,' I added, praying that she hadn't.

'Well, she didn't,' Perri protested. 'Elise says there's at least ten thousand pounds sitting in the Bank of Ireland under the name of Bridget Flanagan.' Bridget Flanagan. So *that* was Aunt Potty's real name.

'Ten thousand pounds?' I shouted. It was an absolute fortune. 'Ten thousand *pounds*? *Ten* thousand pounds?'

'You'll need more than your ten fingers to count that,' Perri scoffed.

'Well, I won't be needing *your* ten fingers for sure,' I snarled back. When I left the comforting shelter of primary school to move into secondary school, Sister

Immaculate had handed me the classroom abacus and whispered, 'Child, use that when your ten fingers aren't enough.' I'd been bad at counting and maths. Then, in secondary school, I'd unwillingly been made to discover theorems and log books, and the abacus had been of no use whatsoever. I could put it to good use now.

'Ah, there's nothin' like money to get a family feudin',' Concepta observed drily, rocking on the back two legs of her chair, which groaned loudly.

Ten thousand pounds, I repeated to myself. Ten thousand pounds. I couldn't believe it. I swallowed hard. No need to worry about the college fees. Now, if only I could get Whiskers to agree to give me a part-time job – for a bit of extra pocket money and because I'd told JP and Tom that he had.

'By the way, where the hell were you all night?' Perri asked, suddenly noticing that I'd only just walked into the flat.

I smiled at her and said nothing.

That Friday evening I waited at the bus stop in Rane-lagh for my class of French students to arrive. They'd all behaved like saints during the week. Saints with very little mastery of the English language despite my best efforts. As I stood scraping away bits of a sticker that covered the bus timetable, my civic duty, I grinned to myself at the happenings of the last few days.

On Tuesday evening JP and Tom proudly announced the birth of Gallic Pleasures, their very own company importing luxury French goods into Ireland, now that the people there seemed to have the money to spend on such absolute necessities as *marrons glacés* and bottles of *eau de vie à la cerise*. The six of us celebrated with a crate of the best champagne that money, or more specifically Tom's money, could buy in their flat in Dalkey. JP and Tom had swollen with happiness as they showed us their still empty leather briefcases, soon to be filled with vast orders, and a stack of sharp-edged business cards. All evening Tom had plied me with secretive looks that held such undertones of promise that I'd had to excuse myself more than once and rush to the bathroom to splash my face with cold water. Of course, I'd done my best to return his lustful looks with a few suggestive ones of my own but stopped abruptly when Perri caught me and asked if I was suffering from indigestion. There was no hope for me, I decided on the spot, if my best endeavours at suggestive-glance-making could so easily be mistaken for stomach upset.

On impulse, before leaving, I invited Tom along for Friday evening's meal with my French class, and he readily accepted. I knew I'd spend the rest of the week worrying about how I could make sure that neither Laurent nor Clarisse made any allusion to our disastrous escapade in St Stephen's Green.

On Wednesday, Whiskers had generously agreed to let Free Birds practise in the cellar of the Tipsy Tinker and Concepta immediately moved in her drum-kit. Moira had stood *very* close to Whiskers when she'd put the question to him and, of course, he'd agreed. Seeing the ease of her success, and knowing I'd never have the same luck on my own, I hauled her back downstairs again with me and she easily made Whiskers agree to give me a part-time job once I started in college. He was a shapeless mound of putty in Moira's delicate hands and he happily agreed to fifteen hours' work a week, or however many I wanted. He'd claimed that he needed more time to go fishing. But it was because Moira had asked him. We all knew it and so did he.

Then, on Thursday, a letter slipped through the letter-box downstairs from Belle. She told us that she was going to ask Kevin to marry her and wanted to know what we all thought before she went any further. We grabbed the phone, breaking our own no-long-distance-calls rule. Perri advised her that she should do whatever she wanted and ignore everyone else. I thought I should give her better advice, so I told her to wait a while, which I thought sounded sensible. Moira fretted that Belle might be pregnant and I had to tell her that Belle was saving herself. Moira didn't believe me. Well, she *wouldn't*.

Fifteen denim-clad pairs of legs leaped off the number forty-six bus out from town shortly after six. Laughingly they insisted on the French way of greeting. Two kisses either side. My cheeks were rubbed raw. We meandered down the street towards the Big Mouthful where I'd arranged with Tom that he would meet us. They had the best pizza and mud pie this side of the Liffey, Perri had assured me. And, more importantly, it was cheap.

When we got there, Tom was waiting at the door. My heart did a jig. He said hello to everyone and lightly ruffled my hair, winking playfully at me as I walked past him. There was barely enough room for the seventeen of us to squeeze around three tables because the place was packed and I'd forgotten to book. But I made sure that Tom sat beside me.

We chatted easily and loudly, in French. It was my turn to be surprised when Tom joined in to discover that he spoke excellent French. His family owned a small vineyard near Bordeaux where he'd spent all his summer holidays growing up. There was so much about him that I had yet to learn. I almost wouldn't allow myself to hope that I would get the chance.

Despite several warning kicks under the table, Laurent ventured his version of the events of last Friday in St Stephen's Green to thunderous applause. The way he told it made the whole incident sound hilarious, and I don't know how but I came out of it with my dignity intact, for which I was very grateful. Tom stroked my leg under the table in between fits of laughter.

When the time came to say goodbye at half past nine, I hugged them tightly one by one and bundled them back on to the bus to make their way across Dublin to their host families. The best part of teaching was the farewells, I decided, for which I could summon more enthusiasm than any lesson during the past three weeks.

When they left Tom wrapped his arm around my waist and I huddled close to him. His lips found mine and he mumbled softly against my skin, 'I've been waiting to do that all night.'

'Me too.'

As we wandered down the street, my eyes locked on a small sign for a guest-house called the Rose Garden. I stopped in front of it as we passed and I raised my eyebrows questioningly, stroking his back with light persuasive touches.

He laughed knowingly. 'I don't need any persuasion, Lola,' he said, taking my hand and guiding me up the path.

'Are ye married?' the landlady wanted to know, as we tried to book ourselves a room for the night. I didn't dare say yes in case I said it too meaningfully. Ruefully, I figured that we'd stumbled on the only guest-house in the whole of Dublin that actually cared whether the guests who stayed there were married or not.

Tom didn't hesitate. 'Married three years last month,' he lied smoothly, and I nodded enthusiastically.

As we felt was expected of us, we duly, and with much ardour, behaved like a married couple for the rest of the night, and the very early morning too.

The first tentative rays of sun were sneaking into the room when I reluctantly tiptoed out of the room, leaving Tom sleeping soundly. Perri and I had to take the bus down to Ballyhilleen for Aunt Potty's funeral and I'd arranged to meet her at the bus station at seven o'clock. The journey would take about three and a half hours. And I could use all that time to dream.

24. Aunt Potty's Funeral

Saturday, 4 April 1998

Aunt Potty's burial took place after eleven o'clock mass. There was a good turn-out. As a measure of her popularity, the Aunt Potty of yesteryear would have been thrilled. But, sadly, the Aunt Potty in the battered armchair in the nursing-home wouldn't have remembered who anyone was. A few old men, deep lines crisscrossing worn faces, had their hats on as a sign of respect. They had known her when she was a girl.

There was no real sadness to the day. In my mind, the sadness had crept in years earlier when a strong woman had become vulnerable and confused, and forgotten who she was.

With the breeze tickling my face, I stood on my own by the side of the grave. I felt I had to stand there the longest. I had got the money. I owed it to Aunt Potty.

Father Rourke wandered down the gravel footpath with his loose gait, his prayer book tucked snugly under his arm. He was swallowed up by the church.

Neighbours and family friends clustered between the graves and headstones of the small, crowded cemetery. Slivers of conversation floated by me on the light air.

'I called over to the house to pay my respects last night. Didn't she look grand laid out in the front room?'

'She did. Very peaceful.' Then there was a pause. 'I don't know, Mary . . . but there was something almost . . . almost *saintly* about her. Maybe it was her complexion.'

A stunned gasp. 'That's *exactly* what I thought, Breda, may the Saints preserve us.' I could nearly hear the flustered sign of the cross she made.

Her *complexion* indeed. Elise had rubbed a circle of cream blusher on to Aunt Potty's waxen cheeks and stained her lips a healthy pink, a bit too pink for a dead person. My father had caught her doing it. I wasn't at all surprised. Elise firmly believed that there was *no* excuse, none whatsoever, not to look your best. Even *dead*.

Perri and I had only arrived home from Dublin that morning because we hadn't wanted to spend the night knowing that Aunt Potty was enjoying the sleep of the departed in the front room below us. JP had been too busy to come down with us. Business obligations, he'd claimed, as he rattled his empty briefcase. He still didn't know about the money or I felt sure he would've been there, propping me up by the elbow in what he figured would be my finest hour of grief, and delving into my pocket.

A melancholic sigh drifted my way. 'Sure, she had a great life . . . for most of it anyhow.'

'That she did, that she did. There's not many of us

left now, you know, Bridie.' The voice trembled with age but the words were clear.

There was a man staring at me darkly from across the other side of the grave. I didn't know his face. He was a stranger wearing a heavy mac.

My father waltzed from one tiny gathering to the next. 'Will you come back to the house for a cup of tea? Elise has enough food made to feed an army.'

'Of course we will, Seamus,' Martin Brady answered. Kevin was standing beside his father, his hands dug deep into his pockets. He didn't dare look at my father.

'We'd be delighted, Seamus,' said Mr O'Sullivan, Concepta's father, politely accepting for himself and Mrs O'Sullivan. Concepta was minding the pub for them. Mr O'Sullivan leaned towards my father and whispered, 'Do you want me to nip back to the pub and grab a few bottles of the lively stuff?' *Poitín*.

'Not at all, Eugene,' my father assured him, patting him on the back. 'You'll be well looked after.' And he winked.

'Ah, Jaysus, Seamus, I wasn't tryin' to say we wouldn't be.'

I wondered what they would talk about when they found out what their daughters were up to. Mr and Mrs O'Sullivan knew that Concepta had moved into the flat with Perri and myself. But that was it. They thought it was lovely for the girls to be sharing a flat in Dublin. Really grand.

Tom Reilly offered his condolences. 'It's a sad day

when it's one of your own, Seamus.' I had been in school with his son, Eddie. Eddie drowned during a family holiday in Donegal a year before doing his Leaving Cert. Tom Reilly knew all about loss. Ages ago Eddie Reilly had been the one to tell me about drinking Bulmer's through a straw. I'd never forgotten.

'Indeed it is, Tom,' my father agreed, and placed an understanding hand on Tom Reilly's limp arm. 'She's better off where she is . . . It's a better place . . . I know that doesn't much help the ones left behind.' He was speaking more for Tom Reilly than for himself.

'You couldn't be more right, Seamus.'

My father was much respected as the local garda. Of course, everyone would come to the house for a cup of tea. You wouldn't refuse a cup of tea and you wouldn't refuse Sergeant Flanagan.

My father strolled over to me. 'Come on now, Lola, I think you've been stood there for long enough.' He cast an arm around my shoulders.

'Yeah, you're right.' I turned to walk away. The stranger was still staring at me from the other side of the grave. 'That man over there is giving me an odd look,' I told my father, puzzled.

'Who?' His voice bristled in concern.

I pointed.

He squinted.

The stranger scuttled awkwardly towards the gate, his mac flapping behind him as he fled.

'What the hell is *he* doing here?' my father snapped.

'I warned him to keep well away from you, from all of us.'

'Well away from *me*?' I echoed faintly, and croaked, 'What's he got against *me*?'

'The bloody money,' my father cursed. 'The bloody money.'

I stared at him blankly. Then it dawned on me and my heart began to pound. The cavity of my chest felt too small to hold the fear in. *That* bloody money. The *gambling* money. JP had sworn to me that he'd paid back the money. The liar, I screamed silently. Now they were after me!

My father was coping really well, faced with the news that a member of the London underworld was here, in Ballyhilleen, looking for JP's money. I was full of admiration. It was like being five again. 'What are you going to do?' I wanted to know.

'Oh.' He breathed easily. 'Nothing at all.'

'*Nothing*?' I shook my head hard in disbelief. 'Nothing at all? But we're all in danger,' I whined pleadingly. 'You don't *know* these people.'

'Oh, I know Dr Miser all right,' he said flatly. 'Miser by name and by nature.' He laughed ruefully. 'Wouldn't even take the winter coat off him even on a fine spring day like today for fear that he'd lose a bit of body heat.'

I was thoroughly confused by now.

'He thought he was about to get his greedy hands on Aunt Potty's money and then she went and changed her will,' he explained, and slapped his hand hard

369

against his thigh and grinned. 'I *knew* her senses hadn't left her completely. She was just saving what was left of them for a rainy day.' He looked at the open grave endearingly. 'The wily old bird. She got the best care out of Dr Miser for years with that money dangling in front of him like a fat carrot.'

'You mean Aunt Potty was going to leave the money to *him*?' I asked incredulously. 'He was her *doctor*?'

He nodded. 'And he was furious when he found out that she'd changed the will a few days before she died.' He squeezed my shoulders reassuringly. 'As if it was all your fault.' He clicked his tongue disapprovingly. 'No penny-pinching quack is going to upset *my* little girl.'

'Thanks,' I muttered gratefully.

'That money's yours now,' he whispered, wary that someone might hear him discussing his business in the graveyard.

'Dad, why did she leave the money to me?'

'She told me that you reminded her of herself when she was a young girl.' He smiled indulgently at Aunt Potty's memories. 'You know, she had a great knack for remembering things from fifty years ago when she could barely remember last week,' he told me. 'You should put the money to good use. You should get yourself an education.' He'd been telling me to get myself an education for years. I hadn't listened then. But I was listening now. 'And don't let that brother of yours anywhere near it. He still has your confirmation money, if I'm not mistaken.'

I *know* he does, I thought, and I want it back.

It was true that my father had been pleading with me to go to college for years. He'd been unhappy when I left Ireland without a proper education and even more unhappy when over the years he'd realized that I showed no signs of returning. He saw education as something with which he could lure me back to Ireland, back to him. And, just as importantly, he wanted to be safe in the knowledge that I'd be able to take care of myself when the day came that he was no longer around. This meant getting myself an education. He reckoned I could go anywhere with an education, do just about anything. I was happy now to be able to give him something he'd always wanted. An education, even if it did mean buying one, would be my gift to him, my gift to me.

My father still had his arm around my shoulders and was guiding me towards the gate. 'I'm sure he'll give it all back to you, once this new business of his takes off,' he assured me about the confirmation money, brimming with confidence. 'It can't have been easy for him in London,' he told me. 'It's a hard place.' He'd never actually been. 'And then this nasty harassment thing . . . poor lad.'

He didn't see me roll my eyes. *Poor lad*, my arse.

'But he's bounced right back. Your brother will be the next Richard Branson, less the mercy of God,' he mused proudly, the unwavering affection clear in his voice.

The less mercy from God for JP the better,

I thought. He certainly did more than fine without it.

Back at the house, the funeral crowd swarmed, talk and laughter erupting from every corner. Elise moved from room to room carrying a tray laden with cups of tea. She did this with effortless ease, smiling graciously.

Belle was helping. She struggled with her tray of soup bowls. Every time the tray dipped she would glance anxiously at Kevin Brady, and he would smile encouragement and nod, letting her know that she was doing just fine. She never strayed too far from Kevin Brady, which meant that only the people standing in the kitchen were being fed.

Elise frowned slightly when she noticed this, just two tiny creases between groomed eyebrows. I took the tray from Belle and sighed. 'I'll do it.'

'Thanks a million,' she gushed, and slid over to Kevin, giving him a sweet, tantalizing smile.

Kevin blushed. He actually *blushed*.

My father, standing on the other side of the kitchen, watching closely, gulped his scalding tea anxiously.

I staggered out of the kitchen under the weight of a full tray of food and into the sitting room. Mary O'Keefe murmured sympathetically, 'Jaysus, poor Lola looks like an accident going to happen.'

My father followed me into the sitting room. 'Did you see *that*?' he hissed, thumb pointed accusingly towards the kitchen.

'I'm *trying* to concentrate on carrying the tray,' I

said, avoiding the subject. He wasn't to know that ever since I'd discovered Tom Hutherfield-Holmes I thought couples were great. Before, I could usually be relied upon to berate the mere suggestion.

'Right, right,' he mumbled. 'Sorry, sorry.'

Out of the corner of my eye, I spotted Perri and Mr O'Sullivan huddled in a corner. Perri's hands jerked tellingly as she spoke. Mr O'Sullivan's mouth hung open. His eyes were wide with incredulity or despair, or both.

'*Oh, God!*' I moaned, and with a heavy feeling of foreboding, I awkwardly threaded a path across the room, as quickly as I could, ominously thrusting the tray forward.

' . . . I just felt you had a right to know,' Perri was explaining. 'It *is* the nineties now, you know,' she said, a bit too bluntly and full of her usual self-righteousness.

I stood between Perri and Mr O'Sullivan with the tray, at a loss for what to say to ease the pain of what I was *sure* Perri had just told Mr O'Sullivan. 'This is a lovely soup,' I said, smacking my lips. 'Homemade.' I lifted the tray up.

'Seamus? Seamus?' Mr O'Sullivan's troubled eyes scanned the room, as he urgently sought my father. 'Seamus!'

My father hurried over. 'What's the matter, Eugene?' His gaze moved cautiously from Perri to Mr O'Sullivan and back again. The stern look should've told Perri she was in trouble whatever it was that she'd done to send Mr O'Sullivan spiralling into such a state.

Mr O'Sullivan's face was pale. 'Did you know about this?' he gasped.

My father looked at me. 'About what?' he asked carefully.

From out of nowhere, Elise and Mrs O'Sullivan were standing beside us.

'About *your* daughter and *my* daughter?' he demanded.

'Has this something to do with the flat in Dublin?' my father quizzed Perri. 'Have you fallen behind with the rent?'

Perri's face was a picture of self-righteousness.

Mr O'Sullivan answered, 'No, they have not!' The paleness of his face was replaced by an angry flush.

'Eugene, what is going on?' Mrs O'Sullivan asked anxiously.

'Perri Flanagan, here,' he jabbed an angry finger at Perri, 'has just taken it upon herself to tell me that *my* daughter is – is – well, she's a – '

'She's a lesbian, Mrs O'Sullivan,' Perri cut in curtly. 'A lesbian.'

My father pressed his hand to his forehead and feverishly kneaded his brow.

I gazed into the soup on the tray, feeling sorry for the O'Sullivans but mostly feeling that I didn't want to be there. Too many things had been happening since I moved back to Ireland. Some of the blame was bound to land on my shoulders. 'Oh, God,' I muttered, helplessly.

Perri continued, in a frank voice, 'And *we* are having a relationship.' She smiled and added clearly, 'Her and me, that is.' As if anyone would think it was her and *me*.

Elise clapped her hands in delight.

I dragged my eyes away from the soup and pledged, 'I have *nothing* to do with this.'

Mr O'Sullivan drew a few ragged breaths.

Mrs O'Sullivan seemed to stop breathing. Then, she gasped, 'She can't be.'

'Believe me, she *is*,' Perri purred.

The beginnings of an inappropriate smirk tugged at the corners of my mouth, as I suddenly remembered that Concepta had sat beside me during sex-education class with Sister Charles many years ago. Maybe that's where it all went wrong, I thought. Maybe Sister Charles should've explained it all a bit better and Concepta would've been saved.

25. Sex Education with Sister Charles

1984

'She's coming, she's coming,' Concepta sang, as she galloped back into the classroom. She'd been waiting outside in the hall to catch the first glimpse of Sister Charles. This was a big day for us all.

'Has she got anything with her?' a voice shouted from the back. 'Any blow-up dolls or equipment?' *Snigger. Snigger.*

'No,' Concepta answered, with a mischievous grin, and sat down on the chair next to mine. She was already a big girl at the age of fourteen. Even if her father hadn't owned the pub and the off-licence, she wouldn't have had any problem getting served drink. She'd easily have passed for over eighteen. I was really envious. 'This is going to be *brilliant*,' she puffed excitedly.

Sister Charles was the school's religion teacher. She was nearly six-foot tall with disciplined grey hair hidden under a stiff black veil and the posture of a ramrod. She carried a Bible with her everywhere as ammunition against the evil she might come across in the schoolyard.

Last Friday, at the beginning of class, Sister Charles

had revealed, in her stern voice, that next Wednesday's class would be different. This is what she said. 'As your moral instructors we have an obligation to make sure that each and every one of you leaves this school with an education that will carry you through adult life.' And she'd said it mightily, in one breath.

We were glued to every word, wondering what was coming next. We usually began the class with a prayer. Every class during the day began with a prayer. So, every forty-five minutes, at the start of each class, we prayed. But not this time.

'So,' she continued, sounding somehow less sure of herself now, 'Sister Paul has decided that you should also be *instructed* in, that is to say, be *made aware of* . . . the basics of . . . in . . . sex . . . education.' Sister Charles reddened as she hastily finished the sentence.

There was a loud cheer.

Sister Paul was the head nun and had spent years working on the missions in Africa. She wore sandals, with socks in the winter, and no veil. My father always said that she had a fierce liberal streak in her and he'd always said it in a slightly worried voice. Elise worshipped Sister Paul. So, this was *her* idea.

'Next Wednesday,' Sister Charles said, reluctantly. 'Boys in one room with Father Rourke. The girls will stay here with me.'

Some of the boys booed behind cupped hands.

'Why? What's the difference between the boys and girls, Sister?' Eddie Reilly wanted to know.

Sister Charles looked down on him from her

imposing height. 'Mr Reilly,' she said, very seriously, '*that* is what you will find out.' Her lips barely moved and she seemed to talk through her strained nostrils.

Concepta looked at me keenly and dug a round knee into my leg under the table we shared. 'On the ball,' she murmured approvingly.

'Don't get your hopes up,' I whispered back, glancing sideways. 'Sister Charles probably knows less about that stuff than the rest of us put together.'

'They should have got your mother in to do it,' Concepta sighed wishfully. 'She'd be brilliant ... I mean, she's *French*.'

'Let us pray,' Sister Charles ordered.

I dropped my head and thanked God that they hadn't got Elise in to do the sex-education bit. The whole school already knew who she was. And all JP's friends fancied her.

The big day arrived. When Concepta said that Sister Charles was on her way, the boys trudged off to a different classroom where Father Rourke was waiting.

Gerry Fields smirked at me as he passed by. Gerry Fields was the school hunk. He'd had muscles at thirteen. 'We'll compare notes in the yard after, Lola,' he said, with the certainty of a fifteen-year-old who'd never been defeated on the hurley field, or in the schoolyard. 'If you like,' he added, sounding very sure that I would like.

My mouth dropped open. Gerry Fields was talking to *me*. The two red patches on my cheeks spread like spilled ink devouring a sheet of white blotting-paper. I could feel them.

Concepta gasped and poked me hard in the ribs. 'Say something,' she urged. *'God.'*

'Maybe,' I spluttered, burying my head in a book.

Concepta sunk lower in her chair and groaned despairingly, *'Maybe?'*

Gerry Fields grinned. 'Playing hard to get, are ya? Well, if you're lucky, Lola Flanagan, we might even have to do some practical exercises.'

Concepta waited for a few seconds until he was gone out the door and then she exploded. 'Oh, *God*, practical exercises with Gerry Fields,' she thundered. 'I hope Sister Charles is going to tell us all the good positions.'

'Concepta O'Sullivan,' I blazed, 'you should be ashamed of yourself. I'm sure he wasn't even talking about *that* kind of exercise ... God ... No ... I couldn't.' The thought of it. 'I just like kissing,' I confessed.

'Kissing?' she scoffed, 'And just who have you kissed, Miss Flanagan?'

'No one yet,' I admitted gingerly. 'Why? Who have *you* kissed?' I demanded back.

Concepta started counting on her plump fingers. 'One, Eddie Reilly, two, Dermuid Henehan, three, Frankie What's-his-name.' She paused. 'That was only in a game of kiss and chase. Does it still count?'

'Yeah.' I nodded, impressed. 'I already knew about Dermuid Henehan. He told JP and JP told me.'

Concepta continued smoothly, 'Four, my cousin Michael from Galway.'

'Your cousin?' I choked. 'Isn't that against the law or something?'

'He's only my *second* cousin.'

'Oh.'

'Anyway, none of them were any good. They were like washing-machines,' she told me expertly, and started rolling her tongue against the inside of her cheek. The mound of flesh moved. Five circles to the left and five circles to the right, followed by noisy slurping. 'Lousy kissers the lot of them,' she declared.

I gazed at her admiringly and wondered what a lousy kisser could be like. I wondered would *I* be a lousy kisser?

'I bet Gerry Fields would be a good kisser, though,' Concepta pronounced.

'I bet he's had loads of practice.' I giggled.

'I bet his you-know-what,' she pointed purposefully under the desk, 'has already seen the light of day.'

Sister Charles slammed her Bible on to the table at the top of the classroom. 'That's enough talk,' she chided. She sat upright in the teacher's chair behind the table and opened a book.

I strained to read the name on the cover. I thought it said *Every Catholic Woman*. Well, if it did, it didn't sound very exciting. Concepta was looking at it too, and crinkled her nose in disgust.

With her head hidden behind the thick book, Sister Charles began to read. Her voice had none of its usual precision, as she mumbled, 'The sexual act is an expression of profound love that is used for the sole purpose of recreation within the unique boundaries of a loving marriage between a man and a woman . . .'

'It could hardly be a loving marriage between a woman and a woman,' Concepta sneered, in a low voice, while Sister Charles continued her embarrassed mumbling. 'The man waits for the *pen*is,' she pronounced it just like penance, 'to become erect and then inserts the *pen*is,' again, pronounced just like penance, 'into the woman's vagina where ejaculation takes place . . .' Sister Charles had a pained expression on her face. Penis . . . penance . . . penis . . . penance . . . penis . . . penance.

Concepta looked at me in exasperation. A look that told me she wasn't having any of this. 'Sister? Sister?' She raised her hand expectantly. 'What do they do while they're waiting, Sister?' She gave me a satisfied wink.

'Very good question, Concepta,' Sister Charles answered coldly. 'They hold hands and pray together.'

Sister Charles quickly dug her face into the book and began reading again. *Mumble, mumble.* 'It is every Catholic couple's duty to accept all the children that God sends them – '

Frances Mullrooney interrupted. 'What does a *pen*is look like, Sister?' she asked innocently.

There was a horde of stifled cackles.

Frances Mullrooney knew what a penis looked like. We *all* knew what a penis looked like. We studied the human body in Biology with Mr Moore. Mr Moore insisted that we call him by his first name, Finbar. Finbar *could* pronounce the word penis properly and, under Finbar's careful instruction, we'd all learned how to draw a perfect side view of the penis. Finbar even insisted that the drawings were to scale. His scale, I was sure. It just seemed *enormous*.

Concepta's shoulders were shaking beside me as she wriggled a crooked little finger under the desk. 'That's what it really looks like,' she told me in a whisper. 'I've seen.'

I believed her.

Sister Charles sniffed. 'What the *pen*is looks like does not concern you, Frances Mullrooney.' She sat up stiffly. 'And I pray that you will never be unfortunate enough to have to *look* at one.' She shut her eyes tightly, blocking out any picture that might assault her mind.

Sister Charles had no idea what went on in Finbar Moore's Biology class.

Frances Mullrooney stuck her hand up again. 'Sister?'

Sister Charles opened her eyes reluctantly. 'Yes?' she asked wearily.

'What about contraception, Sister?'

'Contraception?' Sister Charles growled low. 'There is only one form of contraception and that's abstinence.'

Concepta raised her hand purposefully. 'Sister Charles, I read in a magazine that women have

G-spots,' she said impudently. 'Sister, what *is* a G-spot?' She had to *force* her face to look confused.

I cringed in the seat beside her, not too sure of the answer but pretty sure Sister Charles wouldn't know either. Concepta had never told me anything about any G-spot. I'll kill her if this was something I should've known about. I'd bounce on her till she was flattened.

Frances Mullrooney wheezed admiringly. 'Ya brazen hussy, Concepta O'Sullivan.' Frances Mullrooney had been smoking since she was eleven.

Sister Charles was genuinely confused. She quickly flicked to the index at the back of her book. 'Noooo,' she said, after a moment. 'There's no mention of any G-spot here.' She hesitated. 'I wonder, girls, I think it might have something to do ... with ... with the point in every woman's life when she feels the presence of God for the first time. Yes, that could be a G-spot, couldn't it? A God-spot.' She nodded, the stiff veil barely moving. 'It must be a mod*ern* term,' she declared happily. 'The G-spot,' she mused. 'I wonder does Father Rourke know that term? He's a great man for the mod*ern* terms, you know, Father Rourke.'

We learned far less than we already knew during sex education with Sister Charles.

Gerry Fields cornered me in the yard at the break. 'Well, know everything there is to know now?' he quizzed.

Concepta, standing beside me with one knee bent and her foot resting against the wall, gave him a saucy look. 'We knew everything there was to know *before*,

Gerry Fields,' she teased. 'Only now we know the *real* meaning of the word penance, too.'

Gerry eyed her suspiciously while he wondered whether he'd bother getting her to explain or not. He decided not to bother. 'Coming down to the bike shed?' he asked me, nodding encouragingly towards the bare structure with the galvanized roof at the end of the yard.

My eyes flickered towards the shed. 'No, I can't,' I answered abruptly, scuffing the toe of my black patent college shoe as I kicked at the ground in front of me. *Damn, damn, damn.*

Gerry was tight-lipped. 'Why not?' No girl *ever* refused to go to the bike shed with him.

Concepta pounced. 'She's only joking, Gerry. *Of course* she'll go with you,' she coaxed, talking to him but *really* talking to me. Pleading, begging me to go and tell her all about it.

'No, I just can't,' I stuttered glumly.

Gerry squared his shoulders. 'Right, well, you needn't think I'll be asking again,' he promised sourly.

Concepta and I watched in a dismal silence as he walked purposefully over to Frances Mullrooney. 'Now there's someone who doesn't know how to say no in any language,' Concepta declared. 'It's your own fault anyway,' she decided. 'Why *didn't* you go?'

'Look,' I pointed a finger towards the bike shed. 'Who do you see?'

In the shadow of the bike shed, down on one knee, was Father Rourke pumping the wheel of his bike.

'But you could have gone *behind* the shed,' she insisted.

'But Father Rourke would *know*,' I gagged.

'"But Father Rourke would *know*,"' she mimicked.

'But he *would*.'

'Lola Flanagan,' she accused, shaking her chubby cheeks, 'it boils down to this. Between Father Rourke and Gerry Fields, you chose Father Rourke.'

I *had*, I realized sombrely. That's exactly what I'd done.

Gerry Fields and Frances Mullrooney headed behind the bike shed. Frances was smiling proudly at anyone who'd look at her. I was pretending not to.

Father Rourke gave them a friendly salute. 'What are you doing going back there, you two?'

Gerry answered guilelessly, 'Frances lost her mother's good necklace and I'm giving her a hand to look for it.'

'A quick prayer to St Anthony will do the job for you,' Father Rourke said encouragingly.

Concepta turned to me. '*You* could have lost *your* mother's good necklace, too,' she quipped.

'I couldn't lie barefaced to Father Rourke.' I gulped. How *could* Concepta think I could lie to Father Rourke? 'Anyway, what's this G-sport thing?'

'It's G-*spot*,' she corrected me. 'And if you go on like this, you won't ever need to know!'

26. After the Announcement

That Sunday afternoon, my father was giving us a lift from Ballyhilleen to the small town of Dungarvan about fifteen miles away. The Dublin bus left from the square there.

We picked Concepta up outside O'Sullivan's pub. She stood mournfully on the footpath by herself with a deflated rucksack planted at her feet. It was much colder than the day before. The weather seemed to have turned to match Concepta's mood.

My father tapped his fingers impatiently on the steering-wheel as she got in. He was eager to be away and praying hard that Eugene O'Sullivan wouldn't appear at the door. 'How am I going to face the man after yesterday? How am I going to face the man at all?' he muttered incessantly.

I didn't know the answer. I was just glad to be going back to Dublin and that I didn't have to face him. I was hoping to face Tom Hutherfield-Holmes.

An upstairs curtain twitched slightly.

Concepta looked up sadly. 'How do you think *I* feel?' She sighed, an answer to my father's question. Perri sat unmoving in the front seat and Concepta stared hard at the back of her head.

After the scene in our sitting room yesterday

morning, after the funeral that would give the neighbours something to talk about for months, Mr and Mrs O'Sullivan had rushed back to the pub. All they wanted Concepta to do was shake her round, shaved head and tell them that that Perri Flanagan had been lying through her teeth. But she hadn't done that. She'd bravely confessed.

And today, she'd left them sitting among the bottles and glasses of the pub worrying: worrying about what the neighbours would think, worrying about who would take over the pub now that Concepta said she wouldn't be getting herself a husband, worrying that they would never have any grandchildren. A bucketful of hopes had been emptied. Mr O'Sullivan had kept on asking Concepta if she was sure, wanting her to change her mind. But she'd assured them that she *was* sure. I hoped Perri was worth it.

My father shifted uneasily in his seat. He fiddled nervously with the gear-stick and played with the pedals, as he openly scrutinized Perri and Concepta. His eyes darted from one to the other and back again.

Perri's eyes were dull glass beads, as she returned his look with a blank stare, her head tilted to one side, unmoved. She didn't really care, her expression said, she was right to have said what she did.

Concepta spun her portly body away from him uncomfortably and stared out of the window. Her doleful sighs left their misty mark on the pane.

He was looking for a sign, it seemed to me. He squinted as he concentrated, as he usually did, his mouth hitched up to one side in a lopsided puzzled expression. He mustn't have found what he was looking for because he sighed deeply and flicked the key in the ignition. He was clearly puzzled that he couldn't *tell* from just looking at them. 'I just don't know,' he lamented. 'All this trouble and for what? What can I say to poor Eugene O'Sullivan now?'

With a lot of coaxing from Elise, he'd slowly, and a bit unwillingly, learned to cope with Perri's *sexualité*, as Elise called it, but that was a far cry from having to explain it all to Eugene O'Sullivan. Perri had told them when she was nineteen and, at first, my father had ranted for days, saying that she was only doing it to annoy himself and Elise. He thought he'd never be able to hold up his head in the village again. And him the village sergeant, and all. Then, he decided that she'd been led astray, that someone else was to blame. Now he'd learned to live with it, just about.

But he would have been a lot happier if she'd never discovered this *sexualité* of hers in the first place. He didn't even like the word. Too swank for him. He tried to avoid talking about it, unlike Elise who was peacock proud to talk about Perri's *sexualité*.

And now Concepta O'Sullivan was one of them, too. His little girl and the Enormous Conception. Together. He *liked* Concepta but this was asking a lot of him. I could read it in his face.

He eyed me in the rear-view mirror. 'That's Dublin for you,' he announced. 'I always knew they were loose-living up there.' He already thought that every gouger in the country hailed from Dublin. And now lesbians too, it seemed to him. 'Ah, Jaysus, girls,' he moaned.

We boarded the bus in silence. Concepta sat stubbornly beside me and left a sullen-faced Perri to sit beside the fella with the round glasses and egg sandwiches in the clear plastic Tupperware box, across the narrow aisle.

'You needn't think that you'll be moving into the box room with me,' I warned Concepta.

'Whose side are you on?' she demanded.

Perri strained brazenly to hear the answer. She used her left shoulder to push the fella sitting beside her back against the cushioned seat, as she leaned across him to get a better view.

'What do you mean?' I asked lightly, playing for time, not *wanting* to take sides because I would have to *agree* with Concepta but I had to *live* with Perri.

The bus hadn't even left the square in Dungarvan yet.

Concepta frowned. 'Are you thick? What do you think I mean?' she thundered. 'Do you think *she* should have told *them* or not?' Her voice was loud and agitated.

Perri leaned even further across her neighbour. He was now well and truly flattened against the seat, stuck to the worn velour covering, while she lay across him but he said nothing. 'Someone bloody well had to,' she snapped, from across the aisle.

The bus pulled out.

Concepta whipped around to face Perri. 'They're devastated now,' she bellowed about her parents. 'And it's all thanks to you.'

'If you'd had the balls to own up to being a *lesbian* in the first place,' Perri ranted, 'this never would have happened.' She flopped back in her seat. 'I can't believe you're blaming this on me,' she said indignantly.

Concepta puffed in disbelief. 'The cheek of *you*,' she shouted. 'Did I take it upon myself to tell your parents about your whoring and touring in Dublin?' she asked, in a mighty voice. I hadn't been back long enough to see Perri's whoring and touring, as Concepta put it, but I believed her. 'Not that that mother of yours would have minded.' She snorted. 'But I didn't. I could have. Yes, don't look at me like that with your beady snake eyes.' She tried to do an imitation of Perri's eyes. 'I *could* have told them. But did I? No, I didn't. And why? Why? Because I respect your right to tell your parents certain things yourself, that's why.' By the end of the sentence she was shouting again. And breathless.

I glanced around to see who else was listening. Unsurprisingly, the whole bus was agog. The driver was straining backwards in his seat trying to get an ear in on the conversation and had slowed to fifteen miles an hour, a more manageable speed for him. I was mortified to be associated with them.

Perri's placid neighbour, the fella with the round glasses and the egg sandwiches, coughed lightly. 'Why don't we swap seats?' he suggested quietly to Concepta who was hanging out of her seat, standing up before she could refuse. He came to sit beside me with a grateful look on his face. The heavy smell from the egg sandwiches came with him, too. I covered my nose with my hand and silently cursed him.

We were just a few miles out of Dungarvan with another three hours on the road to go and I knew that his name was Donal and he was in his first year in Dublin studying Computer Sciences. I knew that he didn't want to stay in Dublin once his course was finished because the streets were too busy, too many people, and the air wasn't good.

Donal's sandwiches were carefully packed in the Tupperware box with a neatly folded square of kitchen paper propped on top and held on with an elastic band. He had no hair on his face, the skin looked like it would be smooth for the rest of his life, and his side parting was perfect. He came home to Dungarvan every weekend, I found out too, because Donal missed his mammy.

It was hard to concentrate on what Donal was saying. The tone of his voice neither dipped nor rose. It just stayed the same. Mile after mile of constant droning. I did nothing to encourage him but still he talked.

Perri and Concepta were bickering furiously across the aisle. It looked like one of them might slap the other. Concepta's mighty left arm hovered threateningly but it would more likely be Perri who would do the hitting. She wasn't averse to giving the odd slap, as I'd found out over the last few weeks.

Donal said something to me.

I grunted. It was, to be honest, a bit of an indifferent grunt. I just wanted to sit on the bus and *not* have to speak to the person beside me. It gave me new sympathy for the meat-boner I'd harassed with question after question on the flight home from Brussels.

He said something else in his low, monotonous voice.

I nodded vaguely, not bothered to ask him to repeat what he'd said even though I hadn't heard. I didn't care. I just wanted to lose myself in my thoughts.

'You know, I used to have the same problem as you,' Donal announced, loud enough to haul my attention his way.

I raised an inquisitive eyebrow. I wondered which of my problems he had perceptively seized on through his wiry glasses: the criminal brother, the lesbian sister, the French mother, no future, no past, no education . . .

'No personality,' he droned eventually, managing to surprise me. The tip of his bony finger pushed his glasses high up his nose. There were two shiny dents where they'd sat. He peered down at me.

Donal, of the pleated egg sandwiches and well-licked side parting, had decided that I did not have a personality. 'Is that so?' I quipped icily.

He nodded. His glasses slipped down his nose. 'But then my mother gave me a brilliant book to read.'

'She's a great woman your mother,' I said sarcastically, wondering whether she dispensed advice while she was licking his side parting firmly into place.

Donal tapped his Tupperware box lovingly, not catching the sarcasm. Then, he smiled. His lips disappeared into his mouth. 'Do you need the name?'

'Your mother's?'

'No, *thicko*, the name of the book.'

'No,' I snapped. 'I don't.' Donal had called me a thicko, I realized bitterly slipping into an inward-looking sulk. Just because Donal had glasses he thought he was an intellectual, I tried to tell myself. But a cloud of depression hit me like a blacksmith striking his anvil. *Oh, God*, I worried, did I really look thick? Could you tell from looking at me that I didn't have a proper education? Did I need the name of that book, after all? Did I need the name of Donal's mother? Maybe I could swap Elise for her.

The bus came to an abrupt stop between Mullinavat and Ballyhale. It never stopped between Mullinavat and Ballyhale simply because it wasn't *supposed* to.

The driver hopped up from his seat, the cursing vivid and fluid, and his face flushed. The cursing was clearly a habit of long, I decided, from the apparent ease the man had in conjuring up the most imaginative and vile obscenities. From the yellow-stained fingertips on his right hand, I could tell he had a few other habits of long, too.

There was a blast of cold air, as the door snapped open and he climbed out angrily, rapidly disappearing around the back. Everyone on the bus turned in their seats to watch him. Except Perri and Concepta who were still arguing and didn't seem to have noticed that we had stopped at all. They were engrossed in a bitter row, not realizing that they were just saying the same things over and over to each other, and getting madder and louder every time they said it. It seemed pointless.

'What's the bus doing stopping here?' Donal asked, in his flat voice, the first words he'd spoken to me since he'd called me a thicko and I'd started to sulk making sure he wouldn't *know* I was sulking, which seemed pointless as well.

By now, there was no way I would allow myself to admit to him that I didn't actually know why the bus had stopped. 'I think the driver's just gone for a quick pee around the back,' I yodelled, injecting as much gusto into one sentence as I possibly could. There, I thought, that'll show him I have plenty of personality.

Beneath his glasses, Donal didn't look very convinced. 'There's a loo on the bus,' he argued. He pointed half-way towards the tiny cubicle.

'Give me a bush and a bunch of nettles any day,' I warbled, *full* of personality again, and hating him for making me feel that I needed to prove my abundance of personality to him, the mollycoddled weasel.

The driver reappeared, rubbing his dirty hands together. 'Right, everyone off,' he ordered brusquely. 'The fan-belt's gone.'

There was a lot of protesting and grumbling, and swapping of dirty looks. The driver gave as good as he got and I had the impression that he was used to this.

Donal cradled his Tupperware box and stepped into the flow of anoraks and coats that filled the aisle. I waited until he'd gone before I stood up. The strain of pretending to have a personality was really knackering and I was exhausted. I'd never had to worry about not having a personality before.

'I suppose *this* is somehow *my* fault too,' I heard Perri remark cattily to Concepta.

'I suppose somehow it *is*,' Concepta agreed, just as cattily.

The last one to leave the bus was me, on my own.

Forty-five minutes later an empty bus pulled up behind the first bus, forty-five minutes spent standing around in the cold, stamping my feet and trying to give myself warmth-inducing hugs by wrapping my arms around my shivering torso. It was the dampness in the cold that pushed its way beneath the layers of clothes I wore. The door slid open. We were all drawn simultaneously towards the warmth.

My toes were numb. Stray wisps of hair had found their unwelcome way into my mouth. 'Why couldn't we have waited on the bus?' I lisped at the driver, who'd spent most of the time fiddling aimlessly with the engine and artfully avoiding the icy stares of the other passengers. His hands were even dirtier now than before, and to no avail.

He just shrugged. 'Ah, I just thought we may as well all be mis'rable together outside,' he told me. 'No point in me bein' out here in the cold *on me own* tryin' to fix her up, was there?'

The withering look I gave him would've chased the snakes from Ireland if St Patrick hadn't already done such a good job.

Back in Dublin, Moira bounced on the three of us as soon as we stepped into the flat, her long limbs dancing wildly. 'I've got great news,' she crooned, her long weave of red hair bobbing excitedly. 'Really great news.'

'What?' I asked eagerly. I needed a bit of good news.

'We're going to play in front of a *live* audience,' she announced, wrapping her arms around Perri and Concepta. 'Free Birds are taking flight.' Then she stretched out her arms and buzzed lithely around the kitchen.

I was more than a bit surprised at the news that they might be playing in front of a live audience, thinking that they should probably practise on dead people first. And I was a bit disappointed that this good news didn't really include me – just when I really needed to be included.

Perri and Concepta quickly forgot their bickering of the last four hours and the hurtful jibes seemed to slip from memory like eels eager to escape the net. They hugged each other, Perri at once lost in the enveloping warmth of Concepta's generous arms. I looked on enviously.

'And *where* are you playing?' I asked Moira, once she'd finished circling the kitchen. Surely people weren't actually going to *pay* to listen to them.

Moira faltered for an instant and tried to hide a rueful grin. 'The Tipsy Tinker,' she admitted slowly.

The Tipsy Tinker. I sniggered quietly to myself, waiting for Perri to explode.

Predictably Perri's enthusiasm wilted. 'The Tipsy Tinker?' she repeated, disgusted. 'Downstairs? Downstairs with Whiskers and his bunch of boozing civil servants?'

Moira nodded encouragingly. 'Ah, come on, Perri,' she coaxed. 'It'll be practice for us. And I spent the whole of Saturday night sweet-talking Whiskers into letting us do it.' As she spoke the collar of her denim shirt slipped open. A chain of love bites trailed the length of Moira's delicate neck, a love map if ever I saw one.

'Moira, you didn't?' I shrieked, horrified that she would let Whiskers anywhere near her, even for the sake of her music.

'Didn't what?' she asked blankly. Her eyes followed my shocked gaze down to her neck. 'Oh, no,' she laughed. 'That wasn't Whiskers. For God's sake, give me *some* credit, would you?'

Perri stepped forward and expertly examined the marks. 'Yeah,' she concluded. 'Whiskers would never have taken *that* much persuasion.' Her finger, with its acrylic nail, traced the marks on Moira's neck with the precision of an artist examining a fine work of art.

'For all that lot,' she said knowledgeably, 'he would have signed you over the whole bloody pub, at the very least.'

'So, Moira,' I joked lightly, relieved, 'who was the artist?'

She paused. 'JP.'

That's why JP had decided he would be too busy to come to Aunt Potty's funeral. Moira's neck had been on the first page in his new agenda.

Perri pursed her lips in instant disapproval. 'Well, he certainly wanted to make sure he left his mark for us all to see,' she claimed, thinking, as I did, that JP had probably done this to make the point that he *could* have what he wanted contrary to what Perri had told him – not that he would have found it an unpleasant task. She closely examined the finger she'd used to touch Moira's neck and moaned, 'I'll have to disinfect the nail now. You never know where *he*'s been.'

'Thanks a lot,' Moira muttered.

'What JP Flanagan wants, JP Flanagan gets.' I sighed. He'd decided that he wanted Moira. Every time JP got what he wanted, it just reminded me that I rarely did. '*Plus ça change . . .*'

Perri smiled at me ruefully. *She* understood what I was trying to say.

Moira made a flimsy, dismissive gesture with her hand. 'Well, it suited me too,' she declared, reminding us that she'd been a willing victim just as we'd nearly had her pegged as a victim. 'Anyway, forget about that,' she urged us. 'Next Saturday night is our big night.' Her eyes met Perri's pleadingly. 'I know it's only the Tipsy Tinker but, Perri, it's a start.'

Perri sniffed scornfully at the idea of performing downstairs. 'I suppose we don't get paid either?' she griped.

'No, no money,' Moira confirmed flatly. 'But Whiskers did agree to free booze for the band members.'

'And their one-woman fan club too?' I added. Nobody was listening to me.

Perri's face still wore an expression of tedious indifference 'How *much* booze?' she tested.

Moira flushed and I could see that she was getting annoyed with Perri, who had always been hard to please. 'Look, Perri, why don't you go see the stingy fecker downstairs yourself?' she snapped irritably.

Concepta spoke up. 'Look at it like this, Perri, at least you won't have far to go to get home afterwards.' She pretended to climb a few stairs, arms swinging and legs pounding. 'As simple as that.'

Perri grinned. Concepta and Moira swapped winning smiles.

And I felt left out all over again. 'Moira, do you want to know what happened at *our* house this weekend?' Of course, Moira would want to know what had happened and I'd tell her, eager to paint myself into the picture again.

27. A College for me in Dublin and an Urgent Summons to Ballyhilleen

Monday, 6 April – Tuesday, 7 April 1998

I played with the application form from the college anxiously, twisting it, turning it, examining both sides. It was Monday morning and for the umpteenth time I read that the closing date for applications from *mature students* was 8 April. Still three days to go. And the form was *still* blank. I chewed my bottom lip. It felt swollen and tender. I had been chewing it for the last half-hour. The heaviness of ten redundant years weighed on my mind and I found myself wondering if I'd be able for college – even if I was paying.

'Just get on with it,' Concepta boomed into my thoughts. Her voice washed around the empty flat. We were on our own for the moment. Perri had suddenly decided that John Dooley still owed her some money and was gone to pay him a surprise visit, a nasty way for him to start the week off. Moira had sneaked off without saying a word to anyone. But she wasn't fooling me. She was gone to see JP, in Dalkey. The marks on her neck hadn't even begun to fade and she was off for more. The girl had no sense. Or maybe she did.

Concepta had volunteered to help me with the

college application. I hadn't filled out anything official for about ten years. Concepta, of course, claimed that *she* had. She didn't say what it was, though. 'OK,' I said determinedly, not for the first time that morning, and smoothed the black and white form lying on the table with the back of my hand, ironing out the creases of self-doubt. 'Certificate in Women's Studies and Social Development. Sound good?'

Concepta clapped her hands appreciatively and nodded.

The pen hovered promisingly above the sheet of paper. 'Name? What's my name?' I panicked. My mind had gone blank.

'Lola Flanagan,' Concepta answered quickly. 'That was an easy one.'

'Nationality?'

Her mouth twitched. 'Better put Irish down,' she advised me. 'They charge foreign students double. It says so right there.' She pointed to the prospectus. 'Better not go saying you're *French* or anything.'

'No, no, you're right,' I agreed. 'Anyway, I'm not *really* French.'

'Don't let Elise catch you saying that either,' Concepta advised me again. 'She still believes she reared a whole family of little French people in the fields of Ballyhilleen.' She tried to say this with a thick, rolling accent that was meant to sound like Elise's, except that it lacked all of the sophistication and seductiveness that made my mother's so appealing.

For the next few minutes, I tested Concepta with

questions from the form and she gave me all the right answers. Fourteen years spent in the same class in school meant she really did know nearly everything there was to know about me because things hadn't changed that much in the ten years I'd been away.

'It says here that as a *mature student*,' I coughed, 'I have to tell them *why* I want to take the course.'

Concepta looked at me thoughtfully and spoke in her more serious voice, the one I didn't hear a lot of. 'Well, you'd better not tell them the truth.'

Perturbed by this, I looked at her questioningly and almost at once wished I hadn't, as she took this as her cue to continue. 'That you feel inadequate compared to your older brother and untalented compared to your younger sister, and generally useless.' Her gaze was clear and frank.

She *knew*. I *did* feel useless. We didn't talk about it. We didn't need to. I agreed by not denying it. 'I can attach additional sheets for the answer, if I like. It says so here.' I waved the form for Concepta to see. 'I think I can fit it on the five lines, though,' I lamented.

Concepta shook her head and rolled her eyes. 'I don't know what all the fuss is about,' she said. 'It's only a year-long certificate course in fecking Women's Studies. You're not asking them for a qualification to build bloody nuclear weapons. And you're paying *them*.' She rolled her eyes again. 'Here, pass the form over to me. I'll do it.'

With a grateful smile, I handed it to her, wondering

why it was I thought that she could make a better job of it than me . . . and why she seemed to think so too.

She beckoned with her strong, chubby hand. 'And the pen.' She paused for an instant and puffed, as if gathering steam. Then, brow furrowed in concentration, she wrote. Her square handwriting quickly covered the five lines. She promptly slid the form back across the table to me. 'There you go.'

I read it. 'That's brilliant. Not a bit of it true, but it's brilliant.' I laughed. 'They'll have to let me in.' There was mention of motivation, self-improvement and a social conscience. I could never have come up with that.

'Are you sending it off to them today?' she wanted to know, making sure I wouldn't miss the deadline, either accidentally or accidentally on purpose.

'I'm going to drop it into the college myself this afternoon,' I told her. 'I want a look around . . . Did you know that they'll want to *interview* me, too?' Yeah, I nodded, incredulous, they will.

'Ah, for feck's sake,' she moaned. 'What next? A blood test?'

I looked at her gravely. 'You're not serious?'

I stopped outside a big town-house. The dark grey blocks stood solidly against a pale silver sky. The bronze plaque read St Peter's Private College for Further Development. The plaque glistened proudly. The only blemish was a smudge in the corner made by a passing hand that had strayed too near the bronze plaque. My fingers tingled with the urge to reach up and get rid of the smudge. This was going to be *my* college, I mused proudly to myself, no smudges.

Before I could do anything about the smudge, a young girl in a cheery red-fleece jacket burst through the door. Her face was set in serious thought, her eyes distant. I came to the envious conclusion that her thoughts were more than likely to be caught up in chapter twelve of some advanced economic and social-policy handbook. I hadn't spent any time with my head stuck in any kind of a book in a long time.

'Excuse me,' I said hesitatingly, hating to interrupt her concentration. 'Where would I go to drop off an application form?'

She gave me an absentminded smile, square train-track braces bared innocently. 'Sorry I was miles away,' she apologized, good-naturedly. 'The student union has organized a big party for tonight and I was just thinking about what to wear.' It was an easy, happy admission, followed by another smile. 'Anyway, you need to go to the Academic Affairs Office. Through the front door and second door on the right.'

'Thanks.'

There was a flurry of red as she skipped out of the front gate and rushed home to find that special bit of clothing that probably lay crumpled in the laundry basket. The one that never got washed because it was hand wash only. She would hang it up in the bathroom while she took a steaming hot shower then hose it down with deodorant. I knew all this because I did the same. I wanted to shout after her that it wouldn't change when she got older. For years, I had thought it would.

On the other side of the front door was a long, empty hall with dark carpets and fussy curtains. The name, St Peter's Private College for Further Development, had made me think of cool marble, air-conditioning and sleek vertical blinds, as had the feckin' fees. Not worn carpets and stark lighting. I only hoped that they used the money to obtain the best teaching skill. But having already seen their impressive prospectus I could more easily imagine that the funds were spent on glossy paper, the professional photos of students, who most definitely did not look like students, smiling confidently, and the beautifully worded text enticing the reader to part with the cash for the exceptional education experience offered by St Peter's Private College for Further Development.

I found the second door on the right, knocked softly and cautiously went in.

A middle-aged woman sat poised, facing a flickering computer screen. On the wide desk was a phone and a leatherbound agenda. Nothing else. Tiny earphones stuck out of her ears. The wire dangled loosely beneath her slackening chin. Her painted nails clicked sharply on the keyboard as she typed furiously. Her feet tapped a pedal under her desk. The name card on the desk read Philomena Doyle.

I coughed nervously.

'*Yas?*' Philomena Doyle whined, in a high-pitched voice. She didn't stop typing.

'My name is Lola Flanagan.' That's Lola *Estelle* Flanagan, Philomena,' I said, needing to make her think I might be different. 'I'd like to drop off an application form ... that is, an admissions form,' I hoped I was calling it by the right word, 'for next year – Well, it's for this year, really, but the next *academic* year.' Philomena Doyle and her frenzied clicking had clearly flustered me.

Reluctantly, the clicking stopped as she turned to look at me. 'Mature student?' she asked sneakily.

'Yes.' You only need be over twenty-three, *twenty-three*, to be a mature student, I fumed silently. Concepta had sworn to me before I left the flat that I didn't look like a mature student.

Anyway, Philomena Doyle was no spring chicken herself. And the third finger on her left hand was still conspicuously bare. I didn't point this out to her, of course, because *that* wouldn't have been wise. *That* would have been the kind of thing you might expect an *undereducated* person to say, not a person like myself, a person embarking on an education.

She pointed to a shelf. 'Put it in the red tray. No, *no, no*, that's the *purple* tray. I said the *red* one.'

They both looked the exact same colour to me.

Her eyebrows arched. 'I suppose your deposit is in there, too?'

'No,' I stuttered, suddenly wary that the decision to let me into St Peter's Private College for Further

Development might lie in Philomena Doyle's crêpe-paper hands, or worse again, that she might *think* it lay in her hands and somehow lose my form in a bout of selective efficiency. 'I didn't know you had to put a deposit in with the application form.' An apologetic grimace and a dire attempt to look sincere.

'This is St Peter's Private College for *Further* Development,' she stressed. 'We do expect you to be *somewhat* developed before you get here.' A cynical puckering of the lips.

I gaped at her. The *fecking* cow, I simpered to myself.

'Oh, yas,' she continued. 'It's all very clearly explained about the deposit in the prospectus.' She paused as she looked me up and down. 'You get it back if we don't accept you.'

I bit my lip. 'I'll come back with it tomorrow.'

'Yas, yas, that's all very well but I can't process your application without the deposit.'

'I'll bring it tomorrow without fail,' I promised her again.

She sighed in exasperation. 'You may as well take back your application form and bring it back with you tomorrow ... *with* your deposit.' Her head pointed towards the shelf: Take it back, take it back, it signalled of the form. 'Like that, there's no confusion,' she explained.

I snatched the brown envelope out of the *red* tray.

Philomena Doyle had started typing again before I was out of the door of the office. I fought the urge to slam it shut, to pull it so hard that it would bounce right off its hinges and the flying debris would puncture Philomena Doyle's puffed-up image of herself. She wouldn't have liked that at all. The *fecking* cow.

In my simmering rage, I barely noticed the door opposite, marked College Chaplain. But I *did* notice. And below that were the words, Father Des Murphy, in tiny gold stick-on letters.

My heart did a lazy somersault and the unholy rage I felt towards Philomena Doyle evaporated.

I only knew *one* Father Des Murphy. How many Father Des Murphys could there be roaming the streets of Dublin? Surely, it was him. Coincidence, fate, divine intervention? A little voice prompted me to find out, and before I could stop myself, or pretend that I was going to stop myself, I was knocking on the door, a dribble of persistent taps.

A strong voice called, 'Come in.'

The handle slid down and the door opened easily. Another good sign, I fooled myself. Sticking an eager head around the door, I announced, 'Father.' A solemn, fitting greeting.

Father Des Murphy, *the* Father Des Murphy, sat in a chair behind a cluttered desk at the end of the room. A flicker of recognition flashed in his eyes. He leaned back in his chair and folded his arms. 'What can I do for you?' he asked politely, but with a cold edge to his voice, like a sharp nip in the winter air.

That same old sensation came over me, that same old feeling that my chest was too small to hold my pounding heart and that I was bowing to a superior force. 'Confession,' I spluttered, saying the first thing that came to mind. Redemption.

His eyebrows shot up in surprise. 'I don't hear confession here,' he explained curtly. 'And I must say I don't get that many requests either.' A mirthful laugh. 'Not one of the more popular services.'

'Oh, that's OK,' I choked, slouching against the door with the relief. 'It was just a thought,' I told him. 'Just a silly little notion.' My father always warned me to think first. I could hear him tutting disapprovingly all the way from Ballyhilleen.

Father Des Murphy sat up suddenly and straightened his shoulders. 'No, you're right,' he said purposefully. 'If it's confession you're after, then you should be able to get it.' He rubbed his hands together. A bit too gleefully, I thought. 'Come in and sit down.'

'No, no, you don't have to,' I gagged. 'I don't want to put you out or anything.' I was glued to the door frame.

'Not at all,' he insisted. 'What's your name again?'

'Lola Flanagan,' I murmured, and prayed that he wouldn't bring up the St Stephen's Green episode. My humiliation would be complete.

'Pull up that chair there.' He pointed to an old armchair that looked like it had had the stuffing kicked out of it by many a non-repenting student.

Meekly I collapsed into it. 'OK.'

He blessed himself.

And I began. 'Bless me, Father, for I have sinned.'

The words came back to me easily. Even after all the years.

A slight nod of the head that seemed to say that he knew I'd sinned. 'How long has it been since your last confession?'

The red tongue of embarrassment licked my cheeks. 'Eleven years, Father,' I admitted. I should have lied. I know I should have lied. But the reluctance to lie to priests that I'd hauled around with me since I was a child got the better of me.

Father Murphy coughed and glanced nervously at his watch. 'I've got a student coming in twenty minutes,' he told me.

'I haven't sinned *that* much,' I spluttered.

'I'm sure you haven't,' he offered, in flimsy consolation.

I gave a sharp, indignant sniff. I must *look* like a sinner, I figured. *Feck*, what would he say if he saw Perri and Concepta? They *definitely* looked like sinners.

Father Murphy closed his eyes. His dark eyelashes looked like they had been steeped in soot.

I tried not to stare. I did try.

'I'm ready to hear your confession,' he murmured. 'What sins would you like to confess to God the Almighty?'

I spun off the list. 'I've lied to my parents, shouted at my sister and had bad thoughts.' I'd been confessing the same sins since my first confession when I was six. So I knew them off by heart.

Father Murphy bowed his head and began to pray, softly and quickly. A kind of priestly humming.

And while he was humming, I sneaked a look around his office, wanting to find out more about him, his life, any little secret that these walls would reveal to me. The scrawny shelves that filled the length of the wall were crammed with books, thick and thin, old and new. The odd trophy cup was squashed between the horizontal piles. I couldn't read the inscriptions. They didn't look like they were ever polished.

Behind Father Murphy was a framed photo of himself, two older people and a younger boy who looked like him but whose features didn't come together in the same handsome way. Strange the way that happens in families. It had happened in mine too. They were all smiling proudly in the photo. I smiled, too, just to see how I would fit in. Very well, I thought.

'Lola?' Father Murphy interrupted.

'Sorry, sorry,' I mumbled.

'For your penance now, you're to say two Our Fathers and three Hail Marys.'

'I will, I will. Thank you, Father.' I jumped up. 'I should be going now.'

Father Murphy stood up, too. He held out a hand. 'My door is always open to the students.' He blessed me with a beatific smile.

I didn't tell him that I wasn't a student there yet. But I swore to myself, there and then, that I *would* be.

'Come back any time you feel the need to,' he urged.

I smiled gratefully and shook his hand. It was warm and strong, and genuine.

It was a huge relief to find that the flat was empty when I got back because it rarely was these days. It seemed so much bigger too. There was a rushed note on the kitchen table. 'In the cellar!' it said, and was hastily signed by Perri. It read like an order to go down there. I shook my head ruefully. There was no way I would go down there to stand in Whiskers's cellar between the barrels of booze and the dust piles, listening to Perri, Concepta and Moira lambast each other in the name of band practice. I was heading back to bed. That's what you did in the afternoons if you didn't work, I decided. And that's what I was going to do.

The phone rang shrilly before I'd left the kitchen. It was hanging loosely on the wall and with each ring it shuddered.

'Hello?'

A man's voice sailed down the line. 'I'd like to speak to Lola Flanagan, please,' the voice demanded, in a no-nonsense kind of way.

I answered in the same tone. 'Speaking.'

'Lola, this is John Dooley here, from Vocab-U-Lary.'

'*Hello*, Mr Dooley,' I replied, hiding my lack of enthusiasm on hearing him. I hadn't recognized his voice.

'Lola, let me get straight to the point,' he said crisply.

Here we go, I thought.

'Your sister . . . a shame she won't be working for us any more.' He sounded relieved. 'She mentioned this morning that you weren't, ah, engaged at the moment and I was wondering whether you would be interested in a three-week contract starting next week.' A silence. A breath. 'No one else is available,' he explained quickly. It was as much an explanation as a plea.

Well, as my father always said, beggars can't be choosers. 'All right,' I agreed feebly. The last place I wanted to be was pinned to a blackboard struggling to explain the difference between the present and the present past.

'Excellent, excellent,' he replied, cheerily. He'd filled his blank space.

I shuddered. John Dooley had the knack of making even the cheery sound sinister.

'Now, then, your students will be a group of French businessmen being sent over by their company, which has just been bought by a *major* American player,' his voice resounded with an overblown sense of his own importance, 'and they need to brush up on the old language skills,' he tittered. 'Who better to come to than the renowned language school that is *Vocab-U-Lary*?' The greed in his voice dripped into my ear. 'Pop in during the week, Lola, and I'll give you the full low-down.' With that he hung up.

As soon as I set the receiver back on the cradle, the phone twitched again.

'There's more?' I quizzed coolly.

It wasn't John Dooley who answered. It was Elise. A confused Elise. '*Pardon?*' she quipped.

'Sorry,' I laughed. 'I thought it was John Dooley back on again.'

Elise sounded appalled. 'It is *not*,' she puffed indignantly. 'I remember what an ugly little man he was.'

'He hasn't changed,' I assured her.

John Dooley was quickly axed from the conversation. 'Ooh, *la*, things *have* been happening since you left yesterday,' she declared dramatically. Elise loved dramatics.

I waited.

And with a deep breath, she was off: 'Last night Eugene O'Sullivan came to the house and wanted to know if your father knew of a *cure* for Concepta. A *cure*.' She snatched a second to tut coolly. 'He has such a big problem with the *sexualité* of Concepta,' she said, in a level voice completely lacking in compassion because she didn't understand *what* the problem was. 'And you know what Mrs O'Sullivan wanted to know?' she continued incredulously. 'She wanted to know if Concepta could belong to a religious sect.' A cynical smack of lips. '*Eh, voilà*, I had to tell her that we all belonged to the only religious sect in Ireland. And then, your poor father. *Aïe! Aïe!* He is so bothered by this whole story – '

I tried to interrupt. 'Elise – '

But she continued, determinedly, 'The poor man said this could be the death of him. Those were your father's words – the-death-of-him. You know he detests problems with the neighbours. But still that doesn't tell me why these people don't want to understand. Can you tell me why, Lola? Can you?'

A quick answer. 'No, Elise, I *can't*.'

She mulled that over for an instant. 'No, I suppose you can't,' she agreed sadly. '*Aïe!' Aïe!* ' she shrieked. 'There's more.' The hand that wasn't holding the phone would be flapping madly, I just knew.

I yelped a mildly interested, 'Mmmm?'

'Hah, this also your father said would be the death of him.' She didn't sound convinced this time. 'This Kevin Brady boy, a nice boy, called this morning to bring Belle to work in his car. But your father saw Belle get into the car and he ran out of the house. He was so red. I, too, followed.' A breath. 'And there is your father standing at the car, shouting at this poor boy to keep away from his daughter. He called him, you know that word, that gouger word.' Elise couldn't pronounce gouger too well. It got stuck on her tongue. 'And then Belle starts to cry,' she choked emotionally. Elise could swing from emotion to emotion with the ease of a Russian trapeze artist. 'And all this and it is only eight o'clock in the morning,' she sobbed.

'So what happened then?' I prompted, as she expected.

'Well, then I only did what I thought would be good.' She pouted. 'I told Kevin to come to dinner tomorrow evening and we would all have something good to eat and talk like adults.'

'Well, I bet that went down like a ton of bricks.' I chuckled.

'Yes, yes, it did go down,' she said, in a serious voice. 'Kevin will come but your father has refused to be there. No, he will not be there, he says.'

'I don't suppose he'll be heading down to Eugene O'Sullivan's for a bit of pub grub either,' I joked.

'I need *you* to come down to Ballyhilleen.'

'No!'

'But he'll be there if he knows *you* will be there.'

'No!'

'I'll ask Father Rourke, too,' she pledged.

'That's not funny,' I fumed.

'But you need to come to sign the papers for Aunt Potty's money.'

'I can sign them whenever.'

'No, you can't. They have to be signed by a certain date,' she lied smoothly. A rustle of papers. 'Aha, they have to be signed by Wednesday.'

I knew she was lying. 'No, they don't,' I argued.

Elise became even more adamant. Another rustle of paper. 'Yes, I swear to you, they do. And if they are not signed by Wednesday, I must send them back unsigned,' she threatened.

My resolve withered. Giving in was the easiest thing to do. 'I can't come tomorrow morning. I've something to do.' I had to go and see Philomena Doyle with the deposit that I planned to ask JP to lend me while I waited for Aunt Potty's money to come through. 'I'll get the bus down in the afternoon,' I promised. I *hated* that bus. Why did there have to be any way of getting to Ballyhilleen at all?

'Good,' she claimed triumphantly. 'I *knew* I would be able to count on you.'

It wasn't as if I had had a choice.

Philomena Doyle's office was empty when I reached St Peter's Private College for Further Development the next morning. St Peter's *Private* College for Further Development. St Peter's Private College for *Further* Development. St Peter's Private College for Further *Development*. I couldn't decide which sounded better.

Hesitating between the red and the purple tray because I couldn't remember which one I was supposed to use, I decided to stick the brown envelope that I was clutching on Philomena Doyle's empty noticeboard. *Not* where it was meant to be. Now, that would *really* confuse her.

Across the corridor, I could hear Father Des Murphy talking. I listened but I couldn't make out what he was saying, only the rise and fall of his voice as he journeyed though his conversation. I hurried out of the door.

I had a good stretch outside the building, head tilted back, mouth pulled open, arms up and out, careful not to smudge the bronze plaque. I was very proud of that plaque. It glowed. And I was tired.

Perri, Concepta and Moira had stayed up practising down in the cellar until well after four o'clock in the morning. And at three when they'd decided they needed an audience, Perri had dragged me out of bed in my battered pyjamas to listen to their very own version of Bob Dylan's 'Tangled Up In Blue'. They were *good*, I'd had to admit. An electric lightbulb hung from the ceiling and made eerie arcs, and Whiskers was asleep in the corner on an iron barrel. His hairy chin lolled on his chest, and his belly jiggled as he snored. It was a very strange set-up. But I was the only one who seemed to think so.

The paperwork for the money Aunt Potty had left me did *not* need to be signed by any date whatsoever. This I discovered when I marched into the kitchen on Tuesday afternoon and pulled the envelope out of the drawer where the post was kept. I signed it there and then anyhow.

The dinner was a disaster. Elise fussed even more than usual. My father refused to eat anything. Belle tried bravely to pretend that everything was fine. Kevin Brady was so anxious that he kept on dropping his cutlery and apologizing. *Clink, clank*. Sorry, Mrs Flanagan. *Clink, clank*. Very sorry, Mrs Flanagan.

'I don't want any gouger stepping out with my daughter!' my father steamed at one point.

'That incident with the whiskey bottle was a long time ago, Mr Flanagan,' Kevin replied earnestly.

'Would anyone like more onion soup?' Elise held up a heavy ceramic dish, the hopeful expression on her face nearly hidden behind a blanket of steam.

Belle glared at my father. 'You can be *so* mean.' Her bottom lip trembled.

Here we go, I thought wearily. Waterworks.

My father took no notice. 'Once a gouger, always a gouger,' he muttered.

'There's more bread.' Elise waved a basket of rolls. The same hopeful expression.

Kevin took a deep breath. 'I can assure you, Mr Flanagan,' he began uncomfortably, 'I'm very serious about Belle.'

Belle's bottom lip trembled even more. Her eyes glistened. She rewarded Kevin with a grateful smile.

Elise waved a bottle. 'More wine?'

'Yes, please,' I begged.

'"Very serious about Belle",' my father repeated in a mocking voice. 'This, this . . . lark between the two of ye has been going on barely long enough to give me time to catch my breath.'

'I've known Belle since she was *five*,' Kevin protested.

'Yes, you surely remember the time that Kevin squashed the wasp that was going to sting me,' Belle pleaded emotionally. 'And he squashed it with his *bare hands*. It was when I was five.'

'Huh,' my father grunted begrudgingly. 'And it's taken you that long to decide, has it?'

Kevin looked at Belle and announced solemnly, 'No, it hasn't taken me that long to decide at all. I think I must've known right from the day when I saved Belle from the wasp.'

28. Belle and the Killer Wasp

I was standing in the playground pretending hard that the five-year-old screaming her head off a few yards away wasn't my sister. Eleven-year-olds had nothing to do with five-year-olds. Especially five-year-old screaming sisters. I sniffed the air disdainfully. Belle was a right cry-baby, I thought.

Perri drifted over, her wooden-handled skipping-rope trailing behind her like a tame snake. 'What's the matter with *her*?' she moaned.

Frances Mullrooney was sitting on a bench beside us, with a Jaw Breaker bulging out through her cheek. 'Perri Flanagan, is that your little sister over there screaming her head off like a banshee?' She sucked noisily. Frances Mullrooney ruled the playground because she could fight boys. She was as tough as nails. She'd just started smoking, too.

'Frances Mullrooney, how would you like the tooth fairy to bring you the jackpot?' Perri answered. I thought she was very brave. I *never* said anything like that to Frances Mullrooney. She'd already hit me once when she'd copied my maths homework and I'd got the answer wrong.

We both sneaked a look at Belle.

Perri glared at her from behind a long thick fringe

that fell in a smooth curtain in front of her squinting eyes.

And me, I stole a glance from under a heavy cap of crooked curls that always got in the way.

I longed for straight hair. Perri wanted curls. Neither of us had what we wanted. The other one did. Life wasn't fair even at eleven.

Belle was running around in small circles, swinging her plastic lunch-box with the tin clasps above her head, wailing, 'Get off me. Leave me alone.' Her long plaits leaped fearfully. 'The wasp's going to eat me. The wasp's going to eat me,' she lisped.

An audience of enthralled five-year-olds watched with their mouths hanging open.

I shook my head and sneered, 'All that commotion for a wasp.'

Perri couldn't have cared less. She yawned and pulled the skipping-rope into a tight coil.

Belle's screams got louder as the wasp drew closer.

Then, a determined voice called out, 'I'll save you, Belle. I'll save you.'

Frances Mullrooney stood up and planted her hands on her hips. She looked around her kingdom. Her eyes landed on the tiny figure flying across the schoolyard. She flopped back down on the bench with a callous grin tugging at the corners of her mouth. She rolled her eyes up to heaven, said, 'Gobshite,' and got back to sucking her Jaw Breaker.

Belle's saviour had been kicking a football on his own against the battered school wall. He often played with the school wall on his own. He was running towards Belle. The football shorts that were at least three sizes too big for him flapped around his spindly legs and bruised shins. A T-shirt with the neck stretched wide enough for all the world to see his bony shoulders hung loosely.

'That's Kevin Brady.' Perri laughed. 'He thinks he's Muhammad Ali, that fella.'

'Muhammad Ali's a *boxer*,' I told her. 'Not a foot-baller.'

'No way,' she argued. 'He's a footballer. I've *seen* him.'

Kevin Brady jumped and clutched at the air above Belle's head. Again. And again. And again. His tongue was clenched between his teeth.

The whole playground was watching now. Except Frances Mullrooney. She was wrestling noisily with her Jaw Breaker.

There was a triumphant roar. 'I've got it.' He waved his arm. 'I've got it in there.' With a grubby finger he pointed, satisfied, to his fist. The sudden pride in himself made him stand different and his clothes didn't look too big for him any more.

The congregation of five-year-olds looking on made amazed O shapes with their mouths.

'I'm going to squeeze it to death,' Kevin declared, through clenched teeth. 'That way it won't bite you at all, Belle, ever.' His face reddened as he squeezed.

Perri whispered to me, 'Won't it sting?'

Belle looked at him adoringly. 'You're really brave,

Kevin,' she gushed, the honest, grateful gushing of a five-year-old who was sure her life had just been saved.

Kevin opened his hand and Belle peered in. 'Is it dead?' she wanted to know anxiously.

Kevin nodded proudly. 'Yeah, it's *dead* dead.' He let the wasp drop to the ground and stamped on it.

Belle skipped happily over to Perri and myself. 'Kevin Brady saved my life,' she announced giddily, then added gravely, 'and I'm going to marry him.'

Perri quipped, 'He thinks he's Muhammad Ali.'

'I don't care,' she answered. 'I'm going to marry him.' She didn't know who Muhammad Ali was anyway.

I looked down at her, looking up at me. 'Oh, for God's sake, Belle.' I sniffed. 'You're *such* a child.'

Perri grinned at me. 'I remember *you* wanted to marry Father Rourke.'

'I did *not*.' My cheeks were burning. I still wanted to marry Father Rourke. But I hadn't found a way to do it yet.

Belle's face took on its confused expression, gaping mouth and wide eyes. If you didn't know her you'd think that it was simple she was. 'Why did you want to marry Father Rourke?' she finally asked, loudly.

Frances Mullrooney spun around to face us. 'Who wanted to marry Father Rourke?' she demanded, piercing me with one of her demonic looks. 'You,' she hooted, 'it was you.' She leaped up off the bench. 'Just wait till I tell everyone.' And in a flash she was half-way across the yard.

I groaned.

Belle's face crumbled. The deep cracks spread along her forehead and quickly slid down her face, splitting it into a hundred tiny pieces of misery. Then, she started to cry. Low, trembling sobs that grew into fierce howls of self-pity because she *knew* she was in big trouble after opening her mouth about Father Rourke.

School finished at three o'clock. The best time of the day for me, and no matter how tired I was after a day in the classroom, I always joined the stampede running out of the school gates. Little to big, everyone raced out like a pack of frenzied bulls in a Spanish street festival, screaming, *'Charge, charge.'*

I was going to kill Belle for telling Frances Mullrooney about Father Rourke. That's what I was going to do. I was going to *kill* her. Frances Mullrooney had told the whole class that Lola Flanagan's sister had told her that Lola Flanagan was going to marry Father Rourke. She'd forgotten to say that the sister was five years old and wouldn't live to see her sixth birthday. But we'd have to have the birthday cake anyhow. It wouldn't be fair otherwise because JP and Perri loved cake.

I joined the stampede out the school gates, school-bag strapped to my back. Perri had her skipping-rope wrapped around Deirdre Walsh's neck and was shouting, 'Giddy up, there.'

Deirdre Walsh played the donkey in the nativity

play two years ago when Perri was Mary and Gerry Fields was Joseph. Since then Perri had been the first fairy-light in the play, hanging on a tree where she couldn't cause any trouble.

Belle was nowhere to be seen.

When I got home Elise was standing in the kitchen, leaning over the counter in tight cream trousers, and a white top with no sleeves and a high neck. Her shiny black belt could have wrapped around her waist twice. The tiny bangles hanging from her wrists clinked. She was dressed like she was going to Dublin for the day. She dressed like that every day.

Perri and Deirdre trotted into the kitchen behind me.

Elise had her long fingers dipped into a bowl of narrow green beans. She fiddled delicately, tying the green strings into tiny parcels of goodness.

'Where's Belle?' I roared.

Elise smiled abstractedly, her mind on the beans, and hummed, 'Upstairs.'

I dropped my *maile scoile*, my school-bag, and taking the steps two at a time, attacked the stairs.

The door to the bathroom was open. My father was standing in front of the toilet, sighing impatiently. There was the sound of water hitting water coming from the bowl. His back was turned to Belle who was creeping up behind him. One long plait fell in perfect crosses down her back. A purple gogo with pink strawberries held the ends together. She was holding the second plait in her hand, nursing the loose strands. Another purple gogo with pink strawberries was in the other hand.

I stopped outside the bathroom and didn't go in. You didn't at eleven, but you could still at five.

Belle stood next to my father. 'I'll hold that for you,' she offered, 'if you put the gogo in my hair.' She held out the end of the plait and the gogo. 'Well, Daddy?' she insisted.

He looked around him flustered and tried to stuff whatever was hanging out quickly back into his trousers. He caught sight of me hanging around the door. 'Get your sister to do it,' he muttered. 'I'm busy, can't you see?'

My eyes met Belle's. 'If she comes near me, I'll cut them plaits off,' I threatened, from behind the door frame. 'I swear I'll do it.'

'For crying out loud,' my father wailed, and yanked on the toilet handle.

Belle had given up waiting for the gogo to be put back in her hair. By now, she'd emptied half the tube of toothpaste on to her toothbrush, even the giraffe handle was covered with the stuff, and she was scrubbing her teeth at the sink. The loose plait dangled into the bowl where she spat a mouthful of toothpaste on to it.

There was a moan from my father. 'Where's Elise? What's she doing?' he begged.

'She's tying beans into those parcels down in the

kitchen,' I told him, drawing lots of little mounds in the air with my fingers. 'And we're going to have to eat them.'

He rolled his eyes to heaven and mumbled under his breath. 'Couldn't we just eat beans, in tomato sauce, from a tin, like any other normal family?' he screeched. 'Not these flamin' fancy-notioned parcels made from streaks of misery.' On the odd day he had trouble coping with Elise, and the rest of us.

Belle turned to him. She had begun to comb her hair with her toothbrush. 'Daddy, will I go to hell if I say bad words?' There was a halo of blue-white toothpaste around her head.

'Yes,' he assured her, stamping his foot, 'yes, you will. Now, why do want to know?'

'Well, I keep saying fuck, fuck, fuck at the teacher in my head,' she confessed. 'I just can't make myself stop.'

That's when I decided *not* to kill Belle. If she carried on like this, we would have much better fun with her alive.

29. Finding Out About the Bet, and Gig Time in the Tipsy Tinker

Thursday, 9 April, and Saturday, 11 April 1998

My bus back from Ballyhilleen arrived in Dublin on Thursday evening a little after seven o'clock. I was happy to have escaped Ballyhilleen. After the disastrous dinner with Kevin Brady, a sulking, lip-trembling Belle had locked herself into her brightly painted Portakabin at the bottom of the garden and it had been one of those rare times when Elise was refusing to speak to my father. She was refusing to do any cooking as well. These last few days had been hell.

To make matters worse, during these times I was considered to be my father's daughter, the enemy, and the only one in the house who'd had a decent meal since Kevin Brady hurriedly left on Tuesday evening was the dog. It was just as well that Belle had imprisoned herself in her Portakabin and didn't appear armed with her usual load of dirty laundry because Elise wasn't doing the washing either, and for some reason, none of the rest of us dared cross into her territory and do it ourselves.

What's more, a perfectly folded brochure with details of ferry crossings from Ireland to France was propped up on the kitchen counter between two bags of lemons. It was meant as a bitter indication for all those in the house that she just might flee this adopted country and return to her homeland, which I knew very well she would never do. In fact, I'd nearly laughed aloud, my first laugh in days, when I'd spotted the brochure, except that my father had a very worried expression on his face and Elise was peering through the crack in the door, slyly checking his reaction, so I'd wisely decided to keep my mouth shut.

My father was taking this all very badly. A sure sign was that he had started talking to himself. Unintelligible mutterings that made no sense to anyone. And on the odd occasion, he even nodded in agreement with himself. But that didn't happen very often. He seemed to spend more time shaking his head sadly. He couldn't figure out where he'd gone wrong. He only wanted what was best for Belle. And it wasn't Kevin Brady. Nobody seemed to understand that.

With each passing hour Elise was growing in strength. The straight-backed armchair beside the fire in the sitting room had become her throne and she sniffed haughtily when either my father or I passed by and casually glanced in, pretending that we didn't notice her. I did this a lot better than my father. Every time he glanced in at the door, he looked like he wanted to run over to her and bury his head in her lap, except he was afraid that he might actually lose it completely if he did that. Elise's words could be as sharp as any guillotine.

Of course, there was no doubt in my mind who'd

win the war. The same person who had won every other time. The same person who was secretly enjoying every minute of her torturous campaign, nailed to her straight-backed armchair, sitting beside the unlit fire. Had the fire been alight, I'm not sure who would've glowed brighter, her or the flames. Her, I think, for righteousness was a great fuel.

I was crossing O'Connell Street bridge, wearily making my way to the bus stop to catch the bus back to Ranelagh, when I spotted JP and Tom walking towards me purposefully, though I doubted if I was the purpose. The weariness of the long-haul bus journey from Ballyhilleen immediately disappeared to be replaced by a twitching sense of elation. I hadn't seen Tom since we'd spent the night together after the meal with my French students. He'd been busy working with JP on Gallic Pleasures and I'd been busy organizing my education and embarking on a peace-keeping mission to Ballyhilleen, which hadn't ended in peace at all.

'Hi,' I sang loudly from a distance, unable to contain myself until I reached them.

'Lola,' Tom exclaimed. 'What a surprise. What are you doing here?'

I came to a halt in front of them and was about to describe my trying days in Ballyhilleen in pity-inspiring detail when JP interrupted brusquely, 'Can't stop, can't stop. On our way to see a man about a dog.' He tried to propel Tom forward by the elbow but Tom resisted, suggesting instead that we all go for a quick drink.

'We're busy,' JP snapped peevishly.

'Not *that* busy,' Tom contradicted him.

JP shot me a withering glance. Tom was *his* friend, not mine. Suddenly, he changed his mind. 'OK so. Just a quick one, though,' he reminded us.

We decided to go into the first pub we came across after the bridge and as we walked along I told them that Perri, Concepta and Moira were going to play their first gig in the Tipsy Tinker on Saturday night, hoping they might agree to come along . . . Well, hoping *one* of them might agree to come along, the one I wasn't related to.

Tom was thrilled, his brimming enthusiasm genuine, but JP just grunted in disbelief and it emerged that he and Moira had had a falling-out last time she'd been to see him in Dalkey. His lack of confidence was duly rewarded with a blistering look from me, loaded with a scalding dose of underlying scorn that only a brother would be able to decipher, repaying him not only for his mockery of the Free Birds – which didn't trouble me *that* much I had to admit, I'd been a bit surprised by the news of the gig as well – but also for nearly sabotaging my chance to spend a little time with Tom.

Tom left us sitting at a table while he went to order the drinks. I watched him lean against the bar and remembered how it felt to lie beside him, to reach out to touch him and know that he would be there. My heart told me that there would be more of those nights, a lot more, while my brain tried to warn me not to become too attached, I could get hurt. It was so much easier to listen to my heart.

Without warning JP leaned towards me and gloated in a whisper, 'You've done me out of fifty quid.'

I sneered back but couldn't resist asking, 'What are you going on about?'

He was really eager to say whatever it was he had started and the words came racing from his mouth, spilling down over his chin. 'I swore I wouldn't tell you this but Tom bet me fifty quid that he could get you into bed.' By now, he was rubbing his hands gleefully, his voice showing not a hint of regret or concern. 'I'm only telling you for your own good,' he supposedly justified himself. 'Anyway, I thought you were a safe bet . . . to stay *out* of the bed. I mean, he doesn't have a white collar and he definitely hasn't taken a vow of chastity.'

My heart did a row of worried somersaults. It couldn't be true. I didn't want it to be true. I *knew* Tom. Well, as well as anyone could after two nights together, one in the Cardinal Ryan Room. I decided not to believe him. 'You're an out-and-out liar,' I blazed. 'And a dab hand at it, too.'

'I'm not lying,' he boasted, confidently.

I wondered where this flow of confidence had sprung from. It was at the back of my mind to pretend suddenly that I knew it was a joke, to pretend that I'd agreed to share the fifty quid with Tom. But I needed to know the truth. Anyway, I comforted myself, JP had been known to tell the odd fib before now. It wouldn't be the first. I wouldn't believe him.

JP waited until Tom sat down beside us and leaned over to him. 'I was just telling Lola about our bet . . .'

'It was an easy bet to win,' Tom interrupted.

So it *was* true. I could hear my heart break, the sound of tiny cracks and then falling pieces. It was astonishing that neither of them heard it too. Holding my glass shakily between my trembling hands, I was torn between pretending I didn't care and letting him know that I did. I looked at him sadly. He didn't *look* any different to me than he did a few nights ago and I wondered how that could be knowing what I now knew.

He was shaking his head. 'There was no way it wasn't going to happen.'

'You had it all worked out?' I asked limply, hoping he would give me an excuse I could accept and, to be honest, I would've happily accepted the lamest of excuses. My breathing was even shaky now and there was too much emotion showing in my eyes, stinging, but I couldn't hide it.

JP interrupted quickly. 'The less said about that the better,' he joked with Tom, who seemed oblivious to what he had just confessed to. 'I'm a very bad loser,' JP explained.

I didn't *want* to think it but somehow I did. I thought, I'm the loser here. I'm the one who has lost.

The threads that were holding my self-control together were beginning to unravel steadily and the seams at the sides were quickly becoming undone. I especially didn't want to let the two of them see how much hurt they'd caused. I finished my drink as quickly as I could, making a feeble excuse about a forgotten rendezvous and left the pub. Neither of them seemed to think it odd.

Saturday evening arrived. There was great excitement in the pub and I tried to hide my unhappiness behind a façade of bustling, useless activity. The Free Birds' first gig was about to happen. The home-made posters had been up all week and Whiskers had even bought a new suit, though the person who'd sold it to him should've been locked up it was so awful, all flaps and buttons.

It was seven o'clock. A group of civil servants were clustered around a table in the Tipsy Tinker, sharing a pint of Guinness between them, while a few younger fellas, who had the carefree look of students, were at another table with two pints *each*. It made me wonder who had the money in this country.

Guitar, drum-kit, amplifier and other strange bits and pieces that I couldn't put names to, and borrowed from God knows where under the guise of God knows what, were stacked haphazardly down at the far end of the pub, ready to be put to use.

Concepta, Perri and Moira were skilfully working their way into a panic. They didn't know that I had been in my own panic, weathering an emotional storm, since Thursday. I hadn't been able to tell them about Tom. Putting it into words would just have made it all the more real, and it felt real enough already. I couldn't cope with any more realness.

Perri was convinced she was going hoarse. She *wasn't*. But all the coughing she was forcing herself to do to clear a throat that wasn't blocked was not helping. 'Did you hear that?' she choked, as she finished another round of manic coughing. 'I'm losing my voice.'

Moira had no spare guitar strings and she was convinced it was an omen, a very bad one. 'I can't play. I can*not* play,' she whimpered. Whiskers produced a reel of cat gut from under the counter and threw it at her, eager to help out. She smiled icily. *Cat gut*.

Concepta's drumsticks were missing. And Whiskers had a guilty look about him, as he slid behind the bar, head burrowed into his shoulders.

'Right, Whiskers, where are they?'

He shuffled around uncomfortably.

I tried again, louder to get him to take some notice of me. Talking louder to Whiskers was often the only way to get him to listen. 'WHERE ARE THEY, WHISKERS?'

He cowered away from me, but after a quick slug from the unlabelled bottle that he kept as a constant companion beneath the bar, he grew braver. 'I only wanted to play with them for a while, Lola,' he admitted, with a childlike innocence, and for the first time I realized that he knew my name. 'But I can't for the life of me remember where I left them.'

'That's because you live in the end of a bottle,' I said tersely. The terseness was really for Tom Hutherfield-Holmes. Whiskers was only a substitute.

Just as I was about to go looking for the missing drumsticks JP and Tom arrived. Tom smiled at me but I pretended not to notice, angry and upset that he seemed untouched by what had happened. Angry, upset and utterly downhearted. He walked over to me and bent down to kiss me on the mouth. My lips stayed rigid and cold. With a puzzled expression he asked if I was OK, if something was wrong. Still tight-lipped I swore that everything in the garden was rosy. But there were only thistles in my garden.

JP strode straight to the bar where he ordered two pints of Guinness from Whiskers. Reverting back to contrariness, Whiskers slapped two glasses of whiskey down on the bar. 'I said two *pints*, Whiskers,' JP pointed out.

'Well,' Whiskers shrugged indifferently, 'that's what you're getting.' He nodded at the two glasses. 'Take it or leave it. I don't feel like pulling a pint for you.'

The civil servants all nodded in approval at Whis-ker's surly behaviour. *He was some man, Whiskers,* they were thinking.

One of the students reared his head from his pint and shouted, 'G'wan, Whiskers, ya mangy shite. Give da man a pint.'

It was all new to Tom Hutherfield-Holmes and he had the wondrous look about him of a child who had climbed into a pop-up fairy book. 'The real thing,' he exclaimed loudly.

'Jaysus, who let in Prince Charles?' Whiskers sneered. 'Over to do a spot of colonizing, are ya?' he shouted over to Tom.

Tom beamed. 'Yes,' he answered jokingly. When he spoke, it was still as if he was hugging me, the words wrapping themselves around me. If I could even *pretend* that the bet hadn't happened, I think I might've been the happiest person in Dublin, swapping smiles with Tom. But it had happened. And I cared too much to pretend it hadn't.

Meanwhile, Perri and Moira were tucked away at a small table in the shadows. Perri was still coughing, between swigs of Lucozade, the Irishman's remedy for just about everything. Moira was hugging her guitar close to her. The reel of cat gut sat ominously on the table, as she glared at Whiskers and looked as if she'd like to strangle him with it.

Concepta stood beside me, her hands empty and useless without her drumsticks. 'Give me a hand looking for the drumsticks, will you?' I asked JP hopefully, feeling sorry for her.

'Nope,' he replied. 'I want to help settle Moira's nerves.' He was eyeing her with relish. 'I think I'll take the hands-on approach.'

Tom took a gallant step forward. 'I'll help you.'

I scowled at him and he looked confused so I scowled even more viciously.

Whiskers growled threateningly, 'Just look. Don't touch anything.'

Abruptly, trying my hardest not to let Tom see that I was breaking into little bits inside, while he seemed completely unaffected by what had happened, I barked out the orders: 'Concepta, you check the cellar. Tom, go upstairs. And I'll do around here.'

A few minutes later, Tom was back, grinning triumphantly. 'I found them.' He held the drumsticks proudly. 'They were beside the toilet.' His nose crinkled. Perri, Moira and I frowned at the sticks. What was Whiskers doing with the drumsticks in his loo? It didn't bear thinking about.

'That's it,' Whiskers roared, in a flash of lucidity. 'That's where I left them. In the bog. I remember now.' He filled himself a glass. 'I deserve a drink for that.' Any excuse would do, I figured.

'Don't tell Concepta you found them in Whiskers's loo,' I urged Tom, without looking at him, as I heard Concepta climb the wooden stairs up from the cellar, her biker's boots tattooing each dusty step.

Perri and Moira nodded furiously in agreement. 'God, she'd never touch them again,' Moira moaned. 'And I don't think she has a spare pair. She broke them last week during practice.'

'Ah, don't be cross at me, Moira,' Whiskers repented, as he waddled over to the table. He glanced over his shoulder as the door to the Tipsy Tinker opened. 'Cormac,' he called out in greeting.

We all turned to have a look at Cormac. A wiry little man with a mop of white hair. The corner of a folded newspaper peeped out of the pocket of his overcoat. His face was sullen.

'Cormac's in the music business,' Whiskers whispered, with a conspiratorial wink.

Cormac didn't *look* like he was in the music business. Cormac looked like he might be in the undertaking business.

Whiskers patted his belly smugly. 'I asked him to come over. Thought he might be able to give ye a few tips.' He was talking out of the side of his mouth because he was smiling at Cormac at the same time from beneath the bushy beard and beckoning him over. 'I look after my friends, I do.' His rough hand grabbed Moira's narrow shoulder and squeezed. He meant it as a show of tenderness but she winced in pain.

'Here I am,' Cormac announced.

'Welcome, Cormac, you're welcome. You'll have a pint of lemonade?'

'I will.'

Whiskers explained the pint of lemonade. 'Cormac's a retired alcoholic.' The pity in his voice was all too plain. He scuttled off to the bar.

Cormac didn't look too bothered that we all knew he was a retired alcoholic. His glum expression didn't change. It didn't get any more glum but it certainly didn't lighten up either. 'On dry land five years last month. The wife opened a bottle of Shloer to celebrate. We had a grand time. The bottle of Shloer and a leg of lamb.' Still the same expression.

Moira stroked the guitar she was clutching and ran a slender finger carefully along the taut strings. 'Whiskers tells us you're in the music business?' she said excitedly. Her head was tilted to one side, as she waited for an answer.

He nodded. 'Well, I used to be.' He looked like he wanted to be able to give another answer. 'Gave it up when I gave up the drink. Five years ago.' A regret-coloured hue descended on the gloomy expression. He squeezed his lips together.

Moira leaned forward enthusiastically. 'I bet you had a great time, though, when you were in the business. Did you travel around? Were you in a band?'

He shook his white head. 'No, girleen, I tuned pianos in Bray.'

Perri leaned back, perched impudently on the two hind legs of the chair and grumbled, 'Whiskers wouldn't know his arse from his elbow.'

Out of the corner of my eye, I spotted JP proudly showing his new business card to the civil servants, who were looking doubtful and suspicious. 'Is this one of those pyramid-selling things?' I heard one of them ask.

JP was outraged. 'It is *not*,' he fumed.

Tom gestured exuberantly as he talked to the student fellas at the table beside the civil servants. He called them chaps a lot. Very cute, I thought, despite myself and my resolve to find nothing appealing about him ever again. I was finding it very hard to make myself hate him – and my own reluctance was hard to deal with.

'Gaelic Pleasures, you said?' the one with the fluff on his chin quizzed.

Tom nodded. 'But that's *Gallic* not *Gaelic*,' he chided, in the nicest possible way – his way. Or, I quickly corrected myself, what I used to think was his way.

'Right, right you are.' Fluffy Chin raised his glass to his mouth and slurped loudly. 'And you're sure you don't do women?'

Tom's smile slipped a fraction of an inch. 'No, we specialize in luxury French goods.'

'But *no* women?'

'No women.' Tom sounded sure. He looked over at me. I tore my eyes away wondering why I was still looking at all and why he was still looking, feigning an interest in me. He didn't have to keep up the pretence, I thought bitterly. Even *his* impeccable manners, or what I'd thought were impeccable manners, couldn't possibly stretch that far.

Fluffy Chin was plainly confused. 'No women. Where's the luxury in that?' he wanted to know.

'But I will soon be able to offer you superior quality *foie gras*.' Tom beamed and I could swear that he winked at me. It was either that or an eyelash caught in his eye.

'Fwa wha'?'

JP appeared. 'That's meat paste to you,' he quipped condescendingly.

'I'll be having none of that, then. I'm a veg-e-tar-ian.' He exploded with laughter and the froth from his beer stuck to the fluff that decorated his chin. 'Me a veg-e-tar-ian. Fuck da. Loves me steak.'

JP steered Tom away, explaining, 'We need to aim for a higher clientele.' He looked back over his shoulder, the disdain etched in thick charcoal on his face. 'Jesus Christ,' he exploded. 'Billy Goat Gruff over there can't even grow a proper beard!'

Tom worriedly rubbed his own face.

'*You*'re not meant to have hair on your face,' JP consoled him, and I agreed silently from a distance, while JP's own stubble cast a subtle shadow on his chin. 'I *know* it would be nice at least to have the choice,' he continued, rubbing his own chin, 'but you've got your health, that's what my father always says, you've got your health.'

Tom didn't look convinced and was trying to steal a glance at his reflection in his glass.

JP persisted knowledgeably, 'Perri's the village lesbian and he thinks she's on a campaign to convert the rest of the village and humiliate the whole family, but at least she has her health. Belle lives in a Porta-kabin at the end of the garden and eats flowers but that's OK, too, because, yes, you've got it, she has her health.' He tilted his head towards me. 'Lola doesn't know whether she's coming or going and will probably be the downfall of the priesthood in Ireland but sure at least she's got her health.' He took a deep breath before delivering his final argument. 'The man himself is married to Ballyhilleen's answer to Brigitte Bardot *en brune*,' he stormed convincingly, 'and thanks be to God he has his health for that.' He bestowed upon Tom a lewd smile of the kind that would make milk curdle, the kind that I wasn't too sure should be put in the same sentence as mention of your mother, *even* Elise. 'You see *now* how your health comes in handy?'

Tom nodded, clearly thinking it wise to agree.

Cormac and Whiskers sat on bar stools mumbling softly. When Cormac would stare ahead of him blankly, it seemed to be Whiskers's cue to top up his pint of lemonade with the clear liquid that he poured from the bottle with no label, and it wasn't Shloer. Cormac *pretended* not to notice. He was out of retirement it seemed to me.

JP and Tom sat in the chairs beside me where Perri and Moira had been. They were getting ready to start the music. The three of us sat there and waited. I was trying desperately not to let the despair I felt show on my face.

One of the civil servants was whispering something in Perri's ear and she was smiling agreeably back at him, nodding enthusiastically. When he turned and left, she raced down to our table. 'Listen to this,' she drooled, 'his son works for a record company and if we're any good he's going to put a word in for us and bring him along to have a listen.' She turned around and raced back to the end of the pub again. There was a blast of excitement as Perri told Concepta and Moira about the civil servant's son.

Then she turned to the microphone and slapped the head sharply. 'Testing one, two, three,' she said. She'd waited twenty-five years to say those words in front of a live audience, and this was as live as she was going to get tonight. Except for the civil servants, I didn't really know if that lot were alive or not. 'Testing one, two, three,' she said again smugly.

JP rubbed his hands together gleefully. 'Now, this alone will be nearly worth the move back from London,' he scoffed, convinced they were going to make fools of themselves, and he was ready to enjoy it.

'Good evening,' Perri's voice belly-flopped into my pool of despair. 'Our very first number tonight goes out as a special dedication to JP Flanagan.'

JP lifted his hand to accept the exaggerated applause that Whiskers and the students sent his way. Tom was laughing good-naturedly at JP, lazily rubbing his stomach, a stomach that I'd also rubbed . . . in another life.

Ever since I'd found out about the bet, the sense of loss and humiliation had grown every time I thought of Tom. It was now like a tender bruise that didn't need much pressure brought to bear on it to bring all the pain flooding back. Having him sit beside me was enough. The throbbing started all over again.

Why did JP have to tell me? I silently sobbed. Couldn't they have had their fun and I need never have known? The bet had been cruel enough but telling me was the cruellest part of all.

'The request is from Moira here, on the guitar,' Perri continued intently. 'There's something she's been meaning to tell you, JP Flanagan. The Rolling Stones said it first and now I'll say it again.'

More roars of approval.

JP stood up and took a sweeping bow. I willed his knees to dislocate and his neck to snap, all very painfully. This was something I willed upon him so much for what he'd done to me that I was distraught, and disbelieving, when he stood up in perfect health. I couldn't even look at Tom, although I could feel him trying to catch my eye. I felt a boiling anger for JP, a revenge-bent rage. But for Tom, all I could feel was hurt and bewilderment, and a deep longing for him to jump up and tell me it wasn't true at all, that it had all been a joke.

Concepta hit the drums and, with a hard twist of her shoulders, Perri began to sing forcefully, 'You Can't Always Get What You Want'. Her conviction was intense.

The smug grin on JP's face disappeared and he muttered a few words that would've had him sent straight to Father Rourke in the confession box a few years earlier. He might've got what he wanted before but he wouldn't be getting it again. Moira was making that clear. JP wasn't used to such rejection, never mind such public rejection. He sat stony-faced, looking straight ahead. I felt no pity for him.

The music demanded your attention, somehow even capturing mine. With the husky singing, the pounding rhythm and the racy guitar playing, it grabbed your mind, charging inside your head. Despite the despair, hurt and anger, and although I thought I wouldn't have any room left for other feelings, I was suddenly proud, really proud, of Perri, Concepta and Moira. They weren't getting paid for singing, nobody except the usual crowd of civil servants and students had showed up, and one of Moira's guitar strings had just snapped, but I was proud.

Perri was taking chunks out of the microphone and Concepta's head was flung backwards, as she thrashed her dreams out on her drum-kit. Moira stood to the side, her head bowed forward and her fingers making the strings on her guitar perform a sensual dance for her.

The phone that Whiskers kept under the counter leaped to life as the song finished. Everyone clapped and, for a minute or two, the sound of the ringing was lost in the noise. When the clapping eventually stopped, it was still there. Whiskers made no move to answer it and it continued to ring.

'Answer the phone, Whiskers,' I called out impatiently.

He took no notice of me.

The ringing persisted.

Perri grabbed the microphone. 'Whiskers, the phone!' she ordered loudly.

Reluctantly, he heaved himself up off the stool and walked down the bar. He hovered next to the phone. 'Give us a few "come all yas'",' he ordered Perri. 'What?' he shouted into the phone. 'Who? Yeah, she's here. The whole flamin' family's here,' he said. He dropped the phone on the bar and pointed accusingly at me. 'It's for you.'

'Who would call you here?' JP wanted to know. He seemed to think if anyone was to get phone calls there, it should be him.

'I don't know.' I answered sulkily. 'No one.' I walked over to the bar and picked up the phone. 'Hello?'

'Lola? Is that you? This is your father,' a voice said, in a grave tone.

My blood ran cold.

'I've some bad news, a terrible business.'

The legs nearly went from under me. 'Tell me.'

'Kevin Brady has had an accident.'

My first thoughts were of Belle. 'Was it a car accident?' I stammered. 'Was Belle with him?' The music had started again. I stuffed a finger in my ear to block out the sound.

'No, no.' He sighed. 'It was an accident on the farm, the day before yesterday. He was leaning out to check the wheels of the tractor and lost his balance.'

'Is he . . . is he?' I couldn't make myself say the word dead, so I asked, 'Is he still alive?'

'Yes, pet, he's still alive . . . but he won't walk again.'

'Oh, my God. Oh, my God.' The Tipsy Tinker had disappeared and I was standing in the kitchen with my father, his arms wrapped around me. My troubles with Tom Hutherfield-Holmes shrank momentarily.

'At least he's not dead,' my father replied sadly.

'How's Belle?' I wanted to know. Poor Belle. Belle cried when my father put pellets down to kill the slugs in the garden. She would be taking this very badly.

'How's Belle? How's Belle?' he repeated slowly after me. 'She's *adamant*, that's how she is. *Adamant* that she's going to marry the lad.'

'What?' I exclaimed. It didn't seem like the right time to be talking about getting married, though I knew Belle wasn't one for right times.

'Oh, yes,' he assured me, in a tired voice, a voice that had tried all the arguments. 'You see, she tells me that she loves him. She tells me that it doesn't matter if he's in a wheelchair. He *needs* her now.'

'But Kevin must barely be conscious,' I argued. 'What does he think about all this?'

'For once, we see eye to eye.' A rueful laugh. 'Well, his eye is a lot lower than mine, but you know what I mean.'

'Yeah.'

'He doesn't want her to be shackled to a cripple. He's feeling a little bit sorry for himself,' he told me, then quickly added, 'So would I be, mind you.' There was a rustle down the line, as he shook his head sadly. 'They have him on all sorts of medication for the pain but I think the lad's head is clear.'

'You mean *drugs*?' I wondered how clear the lad's head could be.

'No, I mean *medication*.'

'What does Elise think of all this?' I asked. 'Whose side is *she* on?' Because we both knew that she would be on the winning side.

A miserable silence. 'Belle's side. She's on Belle's side.'

'I'll buy a hat so.'

30. The Big Day

There we were, waiting in the small church in Ballyhilleen. The church where I had been christened, done my first confession, received my first Holy Communion, been confirmed, and spent many hours lost in unholy thought innocently lusting after Father Rourke.

And now it was Belle's wedding day.

I had a hat.

Perri, Concepta and Moira were standing at the altar, brimming with confidence. The civil servant had stuck to his word months ago and brought his son along to their second gig at the Tipsy Tinker, and he'd liked what he heard. For the past five months they'd been busy working on an album of their own songs and charting their sure rise to fame.

Belle had insisted that they do the music for the wedding.

Eugene O'Sullivan and his wife had their place in the family pew beside Elise, JP and myself. With intensive coaching from Elise, the O'Sullivans had reconciled themselves to the fact that Concepta had fallen in love with Perri Flanagan – not their ideal choice of partner for their only child but at least she was a sergeant's daughter. And the village had stopped talking about it by now. They'd moved on to the new fully automated feeding system at the local chicken factory and the loss of jobs it would surely mean.

Kevin Brady sat proudly at the top of the church. His face was drenched in happiness. He greeted the guests he knew so well and affectionately clasped the hands that landed supportively on his shoulder.

He couldn't walk but he'd found something that people fervently whispered to him they would give their two legs for. His father stood beside his son and shook the hands that wished his son the very best. He was sure he had it in Belle Flanagan.

Father Rourke nodded to Perri.

She began to sing in her husky voice while Moira played the guitar softly and Concepta tapped her drums. It was a tender song they'd written together, the three of them, for Belle, called 'A Journey To Hope'. An emotional shiver ran through me.

Footsteps called lightly on the stone floor at the end of the church.

All heads turned.

My father and Belle were walking up the aisle, her hand lost in his.

Belle wore a column of ivory silk. Her hair hung loose. Her face glistened. The tears had started to flow at dawn and hadn't stopped since. They were tears of happiness.

'I always did say that your bladder was too near your eyes for your own good,' I heard my father murmur softly, as he wiped away a tear when they reached the top of the church where I was sitting.

She sobbed even more.

He took the hand he was holding and placed it in Kevin's. 'Take good care of her for me.'

'I will,' he promised. 'For always.'

I felt the strong fingers of emotion wring my own bruised heart.

Father Rourke gave a poignant sermon during the mass, the seeds of which, I realized only a few minutes into his well-aimed homily, had been skilfully sown by Moira in the refectory hours earlier. He began by telling us that he had prepared for this day and what he would say on this day many weeks ago. He had known Belle Flanagan and Kevin Brady since they were babies, and he realized that they needed no instruction in how to love, they were shining examples to us all. Then he said that he wanted to mention a story he'd heard only that morning.

Moira winked mischievously at me from the altar. I winked back at her, wondering why she was winking in the first place, but guessing it was just high spirits.

'I suppose,' Father Rourke continued firmly, 'that this is a lesson in how *not* to love. Now, now, I know what you're all thinking,' he raised his hands in a reconciliatory gesture, 'that this is a bit of a sad story for the day that's in it, and it is so I won't go into it. I just wanted to mention it.'

Perri, Moira and Concepta were trying their best

to conceal a set of smug smiles at the altar and I suddenly grew suspicious.

Father Rourke upped his tone. He loved a good story where he could take a firm moral stance and wasn't able to resist feeding his congregation a little more information. 'But I just want to say this. It's the story of a young girl who loved a boy very much and he led her to believe that that love was returned.'

The bells of familiarity started ringing in my head.

Father Rourke continued solemnly. 'And that love she felt grew to become the kind of Christian love that God fosters in all of us. But it turned out that this boy's affection was all a sham.' He slammed a fist into the pulpit. 'Yes, a mockery. He didn't love the girl. He led her on intentionally – I myself would say evilly – as part of a bet arranged by her own brother.' His gaze swept the guests. 'This is how *not* to love,' he declared purposefully.

Elise turned to me, disbelief etched on her face, wondering who could do such a terrible thing. 'Do you think we know them?' she whispered.

'Oh, I think so,' I answered her gravely.

'No!' She gulped.

I glanced at JP, who was squirming uncomfortably on the church pew. He glared at me. Then I sneaked a look at Tom Hutherfield-Holmes, sitting five rows behind me. I couldn't understand why he had the innocent, carefree look of someone who really hadn't a clue what was going on. Why didn't he understand that it was him Father Rourke was talking about?

I'd tried to persuade Belle not to invite him, said that it would be better for me if he wasn't there, but she was floating on a cloud of happiness and generosity, and that unfortunately included Tom Hutherfield-Holmes. 'Forgive,' she'd calmly advised me. When hell freezes over, I thought, and firmly locked up the little bit of me that was begging to be allowed to forgive him, the weak bit.

Suddenly Father Rourke's voice softened. 'And here before us today, we have a perfect example of love as it should be. In Belle and Kevin, we see a love that is all accepting, deep and considerate, a love that will stand the test of time, and any other test, too, of that I have no doubt. In Belle and Kevin, we see exactly how to love.'

With the exception of one or two chance late-night meetings in Temple Bar, icy occasions to say the least in the hive of Dublin's nightlife, I'd managed to steer clear of him since the evening of the gig in the Tipsy Tinker. For weeks after, he had tried calling me but there was nothing he could say that would change what had happened, so I decided not to talk to him at all, thinking it would be easier on me, thinking that I'd soon forget about him. I didn't.

Once they found out what had happened, at the point where I couldn't hide my misery any more, where it hung around me like a damp cloak, Perri, Concepta and Moira had immediately formed a protective screen around me that Tom Hutherfield-

Holmes had no chance of breaking through. And in a show of solidarity, but more probably to impress Moira than shield me, Whiskers had banned JP and Tom from the Tipsy Tinker. And now there he was, sitting only a few feet away.

The reception afterwards was held in O'Sullivan's pub. Mr O'Sullivan had insisted. It was his wedding present to Belle and Kevin, he'd said. After all, they were *almost* family now.

As I chatted to the guests, making sure that glasses were never empty, I could feel Tom's eyes follow me around as he waited for his moment, and as soon as I stepped into the only empty spot in the pub, he cornered me. 'Hello,' he said simply, as if that was all he needed to say.

Over his shoulder, still broad, still touchable, but still the shoulder of a betting bastard, I caught Concepta frown anxiously and Moira threw JP a disapproving look, as if this inevitable encounter was his fault. JP had been looking very sheepish since Father Rourke's weighty sermon. With a subtle nod, I let them know that I was OK, that I could fend for myself here. I was strong now.

'I don't understand what happened between us.' Tom sounded miserable, *genuinely* miserable. The talented lying bastard, I fumed.

'Let me see,' I mused, almost gleefully because I knew what was coming. I had prepared myself for this day, and Father Rourke's sermon, though not *entirely* accurate, had filled me with a wonderful sense of self-righteousness. 'I slept with you and in return you got fifty pounds,' I told him coolly and then paused purposefully, as if trying to work out some complicated mathematical sum, an overly perplexed expression on my face. 'You got money for sleeping with me . . . would that make you a – a male whore?' I tried to sound puzzled, as if I really didn't know, and was positively stumped. 'Money for services rendered and all that,' I explained.

To my great satisfaction, he nearly choked on his pint, I couldn't have asked for more, incredulity drowning all other expressions.

'You see,' I continued ruthlessly, 'ours was the story of a bet where the outsider came up trumps. Now, in equestrian terms, that makes me the horse and . . . well, staying with the animal theme, you'd have to be a pig,' I declared dramatically, delivering my well-rehearsed speech with all the spontaneity I'd practised so hard at. 'The first coupling of its kind, I'd say.' It gave me no great pleasure to compare myself to a horse, but it had been done before.

Tom faltered and took a dazed step backwards. Even now, as I confronted him with the plain truth, thickly clothed in insults as it well might be, he had the audacity to look like he couldn't *believe* what he was hearing. His face wore a horrified expression of pure and utter disbelief, changing every five or ten seconds to a different horrified expression of pure and utter disbelief. If I didn't know better, I would've thought that these were actually *honest* expressions.

Staggering, I thought, this ability of his to distort the truth and feed me back his own version.

JP noticed the commotion and quickly crossed the pub in a series of agitated strides. 'I have to talk to you,' he rasped urgently, and dragged me by the elbow to the corner of the pub. 'It wasn't true,' he rushed.

Irritably, I shook my arm loose of his grip. 'What wasn't true?' I demanded.

A sheepish grin shadowed his face. 'Ah, the whole bet thing,' he said limply.

'Yeah, *right*,' I agreed, just as limply. JP was obviously trying to save Tom Hutherfield-Holmes from further assault.

Suddenly Moira peered over JP's shoulder, her long hair falling on to the collar of his suit. 'What's going on?' she asked him sharply, and he winced as she poked him accusingly in the back with one of her long, narrow fingers. Perfect fingers for poking.

JP drew a deep breath. 'Look, there *was* a bet,' he acknowledged. 'That's what Tom was agreeing to when I asked him that time in the pub . . . but the bet wasn't on you.' He looked from Moira to myself imploringly, with more sincerity in his eyes than I'd seen there in a long time. 'I bet Tom fifty quid that the girls, the Free Birds here,' he sniffed, nodding towards Moira and unable to hide the irony in his voice now that they'd got a record deal, 'would not get a gig in the whole of Europe.' He winced again as Moira slapped the back of his head. 'Anyway, Tom had more faith than me and said they would. When he came back to the table, he thought I'd told you about *that* bet. He hadn't a clue what I'd said to you before.'

Moira was enraged while I stared at him coldly.

'I meant it as a joke,' he blurted beseechingly, 'but it got out of hand. Tom has been driving me mad all summer with his whining and none of you is talking to either of the two of us any more,' he whinged pathetically. 'It's been hell. And then bloody Father Rourke this afternoon to top it all off.' He looked at Moira almost admiringly . . . no, definitely admiringly. 'I guess I have you to thank for that.'

Moira smiled cunningly. 'You're welcome,' she said.

I didn't know what to say. No words would come at first but then, as the shock was replaced with anger, I struck JP with a furious torrent of questions. 'Does Tom know what you did? How could you do that? You're a bastard, JP Flanagan, do you know that?' *I* knew it. We all bloody knew it. 'Thought you'd get away with it, huh?' I grunted. 'Why didn't you tell me before now?' And what was I ever going to be able to say to Tom to undo the harm I'd done?

'It just got past the stage where I could say anything,' he admitted reluctantly. 'It became such a big *feckin'* deal.'

'That's because it *was* a big feckin' deal,' I snapped.

'Ah, Lola, you should've known that I'd never do something like that to you,' he tried to convince me.

'You told me you did yourself . . . and I believed you. So, what's the difference?'

'So why tell her today?' Moira wanted to know.

He eyed me warily and then looked at Tom. 'It looked like it was about to become an even bigger feckin' deal . . . if that's possible.'

Deep down I had that terrible sick feeling when you know you've done something wrong and you don't know how to put it right. I should've let Tom explain, I told myself. I should've listened. But, most of all, I should never have trusted JP's word. Somehow it had seemed easier to believe that Tom had wooed me for a bet than for myself.

Tom stood gloomily by the bar, smiling politely at one of my father's stories but it wasn't a smile that stretched to his eyes.

A strange force propelled me towards him. I didn't know what I was going to say to him once I got there, I just knew I had to try.

'Here she is now,' my father greeted me happily, 'the apple of my eye.' He put an arm around my shoulder. 'Well, one of them,' he corrected himself.

Tom avoided looking at me, examining the bottom of his glass instead. It was just an ordinary pint glass, nothing special, no need to examine it.

'Tom?' I said meekly, untangling myself from my father's arm.

My father immediately sensed that something was going on, and not being very comfortable around emotional scenes, he fled.

'Tom?' I tried again. 'I need to explain something to you.' He didn't look very interested, still examining the bottom of the glass. I persisted stubbornly: 'Would you put the glass down . . . please?' And I began.

'I'm sorry you had so little faith in me,' he said sadly, when I'd finished telling him what had happened, leaving nothing out. I expected him to say something else but he let an uncomfortable silence build between us.

I rushed to fill the tense gap. 'I know, I know,' I said, hearing how brittle, how vulnerable my own voice sounded. 'I'm sorry, too.' Suddenly I realized that I was getting all the blame while this was someone else's fault. I glanced over to the chair where JP had somehow managed to get Moira to sit on his knee and was stroking her thigh. 'I suppose *he*'s going to get off scot-free?' I mumbled, head-butting the air in JP's direction.

Tom smiled ruefully. 'JP was only being JP,' he told me flatly. 'Living up to expectations.' His eyes were brimming with disappointment as he looked at me dolefully.

'Don't be like that,' I implored him. 'Don't look at me like that.'

'I thought you were special, really special,' he said, and walked away.

I didn't feel special any more. I hadn't felt special in ages anyway. He was the only one who had the knack of making me feel special . . . and he hadn't been around in a long time.

I caught JP's eye across the pub and mouthed carefully, 'You bastard.'

He shrugged helplessly and Moira ruffled his hair playfully, any bad feelings between the two of them well and truly forgotten. He grabbed her hand and teasingly nibbled her fingers. She howled with laughter. JP has met his match in Moira, I thought begrudgingly, as I enviously watched him look at her with a blatant tenderness that he didn't even try to hide, as she spoke to him from her perch on his knee. The bastard had won again.

Later on, after several vain attempts to talk to Tom, I was sitting on a small stool idly chatting to Kevin when Belle joined us, to listen to me tell him about the college course I was starting the very next week, and Father Des Murphy, the college chaplain, and my part-time job with Whiskers in the Tipsy Tinker.

I'd already told him all about the new life I'd be starting, I'd already told everyone, but he seemed happy to listen to me again as I rattled on inanely about how I'd received the long book-list for my course and was able to buy most of the books second-hand, and the pre-term discussion with the course leader who was only a few years older than myself that had gone really well, and how I couldn't wait to become a third-level student in three days' time.

The only thing I wasn't talking about was the one thing that was really on my mind. Tom Hutherfield-Holmes. All the time that I sat there, I was wondering how it was possible to miss someone who hadn't really ever been part of your life because I was missing Tom Hutherfield-Holmes.

'Have you told her yet?' Belle interrupted my thoughts.

'No,' Kevin replied shyly. 'Not yet.'

'Go on,' she prompted him.

Kevin looked at her and seemed to draw strength. 'I'm going to write a book,' he proudly announced.

'That's brilliant,' I said excitedly. Belle had been trying hard to find something for Kevin to do, now that farm work was out of the question, something that he could call his own. To the surprise of nobody but herself, her first idea of silk painting hadn't worked out at all and that had been followed by half a dozen other disasters.

Belle smiled encouragingly. 'Tell her the rest.'

'Well, I've already done the first three chapters and sent them off to a publisher in Dublin . . .'

I gasped in admiration.

' . . . and they want to see more.'

My father leaned over the back of the wheelchair. 'It's a rural detective story,' he told me, happily adding, 'and I'm helping out. A man with my background and experience shouldn't go to waste, should he, son?'

'He should not,' Kevin agreed good-naturedly.

Once or twice during the conversation, I caught Tom's eye but I looked away again quickly before he could pierce me with his sadness. 'Forget him,' Concepta had advised me, as she hooked her arm through Perri's, and I thought that maybe I could try. But not today. Today I didn't want to forget him. I wanted to savour what might have been just for a little while. I wanted to be sad because I'd lost something.

It was well into the night when the cans tied on to Kevin's wheelchair rattled joyfully, as Belle sat on his lap and he wheeled her down the main street in Ballyhilleen, towards Mullrooney's guest-house to much applause. A ground-floor room for the honeymoon night, and the rest of their lives awaited them.

I felt a tingling presence behind me, as I watched them wistfully from the front door of the pub. Instinctively I knew who it was and my heart jumped, foolishly thinking it had been given another chance. But I didn't turn round, unable to bear the risk of more rejection.

'I'm sorry I was so hard on you.' His breath tickled the back of my neck and I could feel my sadness melt away under the pleasing heat. 'You couldn't have known,' he continued silkily, 'though you should have asked.'

'I should've asked,' I readily agreed. 'Am I forgiven?' I'd turned round to face him and was standing very close, so close that I would've been very embarrassed had he decided not to forgive me after all.

But Tom nodded and closed the tiny space that was left between us. 'I promise you, Lola Flanagan, that no one would ever have to pay me to be with you.'

God help me but I chuckled. I actually *chuckled*. I couldn't believe my luck.

He glanced hopefully at Mullrooney's. 'Do you

suppose they have any spare rooms in the guest-house?'

If we were destined to spend all our nights together in hotel rooms or guest houses that was fine by me. 'Absolutely,' I answered. *'Absolutely.'*

The rest of my life waited for me, too.